The
PUPPET
KING

TM KORNELSEN

IBSN: 979-8-9886514-0-6

Cover and interior book design by Victoria Wolf, wolfdesignandmarketing.com.

Edited by Kelly Lynne Schaub

First edition, 2023

For my best friend in the world whom I love very much.

ACKNOWLEDGMENTS

FIRST AND FOREMOST, I would like to thank God for giving me the heart of a storyteller and the strength and spirit to follow through on my dreams.

I would also like to extend my thanks and gratitude to my friends who watch me work and have been a constant presence of encouragement. I would especially like to thank Laura Dulski and Cory Hasik, both of whom filled the role of beta readers always answering the simple question, "Does this make sense?" And I especially would like to thank my friend of thirty years, Martin Zieren of Jena, Germany, who was instrumental in the research of this book.

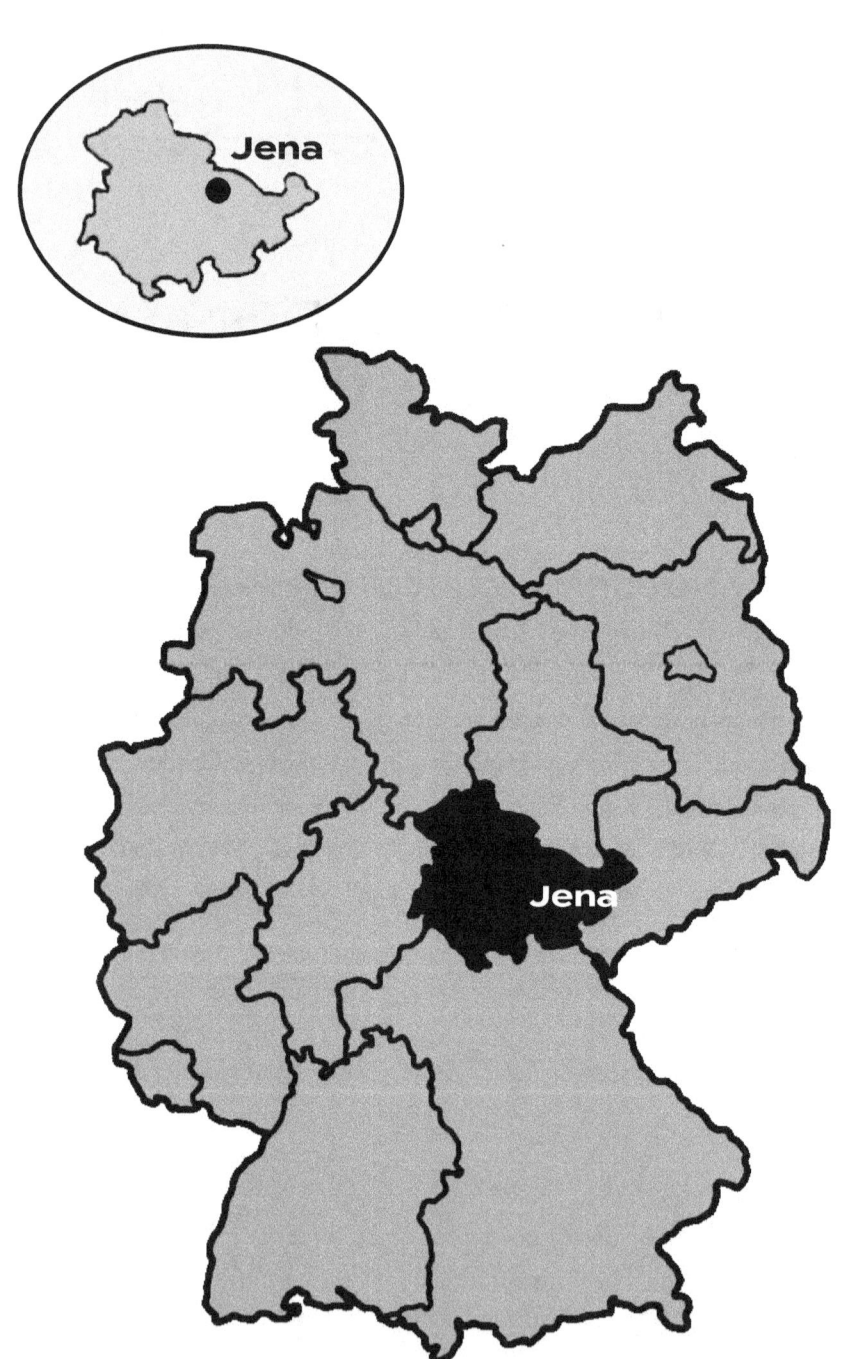

PROLOGUE

AS OF MIDNIGHT on November 9, 1989, East German citizens were free to leave for the first time in forty years.

East of the Berlin Wall, German Democratic Republic (GDR) citizens heard the unexpected news, and it became the catalyst for all Germans to freely move about without the fear of arrest or summary execution. But, before a new future could be formed, old walls had to come down. East Germans watched as their political system crumbled, and friends they'd never met descended onto both sides of the wall armed with sledgehammers and other tools to dismantle not just a wall, but an outdated ideology.

For years, the Berlin Wall stood as the greatest symbol of Soviet authority and Communism in the West. That concrete fence caged people and reminded Germans on both sides of Moscow's power, reach, and superiority. But no more. That superiority now lay in crumbles at their feet.

Loyal members of the GDR fled to the East, hoping for safety in Moscow. But not all of them. The last sitting General Secretary of the Socialist United Party retreated to his home in Jena, Germany, dragging his fiancée Margaret Stratton and their son Martin with him, where he would plan his comeback. Margaret's hopes for a better life were dashed; for Strauss, it was not over. It would never be over.

Isolated in Jena, Margaret watched her old black-and-white television set, one of many secretly riveted by the reports of possible reunification with the West. Something inside her spirit stirred, something within her came alive. She wanted to leave; she wanted freedom too, for herself and for her son.

She'd have to plan her escape quietly. She was still a prisoner, and so was her son, innocent no more. His father was a sadistic tyrant who poured all his prejudices into his young son, brainwashing poor Martin, grooming him to lead the next generation. Margaret could not deny the truth before her eyes. Martin became more like his father every day—mean, ruthless, and uncompromising.

Then it happened. The event Margaret had been waiting for: October 3, 1990, reunification day. There was no more East, no more West. Just Germany. Margaret could make a run for it. And run she did.

1

ERICH STRAUSS, the forcibly resigned leader of the German Democratic Republic, remained secluded in his fortress, a brick chateau built by his German forefathers within the mountainous landscape of Jena. The fortress was one of only a few possessions he was permitted to keep after the Western opposition parties ran him and the State Council from office over thirty years ago. He remained there alone and silent but with an active imagination. He permitted few visitors to his home high above the land occupied by common people. His guest list was tailored to a select few, those loyal during his reign who remained loyal after the West eclipsed his leadership.

Dressed in the military garb from his earlier days, the aging statesman paced, tending to each detail of his plan. His time was running out. With a thick Cuban cigar wedged between two fingers, he walked the stone floor of his study. He designed this room with all the modern conveniences solely for the purpose of thought. Here he could—for hours, without interruption—recollect the past and ponder the future of his Germany and beyond.

Strauss stood by an open window with only the sound of ruffling drapes from the wind, gazing down at the sleeping city with love and contempt. "How could they betray me?" he repeatedly muttered to himself. Ruling over his homeland was a victory enjoyed by few. But he no longer ruled. He, too, was the subject of the chancellor, the elected leader of a reunited Germany. He didn't completely blame the people of his country for his downfall, for they were brainwashed by the temptations of his opposition. Print and television carried the messages of those who defeated him, and he would not forget. How could he? The media was partly the reason he had been banished from office as General Secretary of the Socialist Unity Party and forced to live in an idle state, only to offer a reaction to the decisions made by the new chancellor. He was no longer the man of action—or so many thought.

I will regain my kingdom, he said to himself. Thirty years alone was enough to make any man mad or drive a mad man insane. During his time in the castle, Strauss carefully crafted the direction Germany would take once he regained his rightful position of power. Only this time, he would not be part of a committee, not "party leader" this and "party leader" that like the Soviets established. Not another Hitler, either, but more of a homage to the singular rule of the *Deutscher Kaiser. King Strauss*, he thought as he smiled down at the city with a wild beat to his heart. Throwing both hands above his head, he shouted, "King Strauss, King Strauss!" He placed his cigar in his mouth, still smiling from the wonderful sound.

Strauss walked to the window with his chest puffed out and shoulders firmly back. He prepared to address the crowd gathered beneath his balcony as they had so many times before. The reminiscence of thousands of grateful subjects beneath his bastion filled his mind as vividly as the actual event, more real now than when it took place long ago. Standing before the crowd, waving with both arms extended over his head, the king proudly looked down at each individual face in the front of the mass.

A knock on the door intruded.

"Excuse me, sir, are you in there?" called Schmidt from behind the door.

Strauss pulled himself into the present with the swiftness of light speed.

"*Ja*, enter," he called back to his old friend.

General Peter Schmidt was an elderly yet robust man dressed in the military's finest attire. He entered the study, closing the door quietly behind him. Medals and stripes hung from his chest to show he was of great importance. He walked to the large mahogany desk where Strauss often sat to think. The men embraced for a moment, kissing one another on the cheek, happy to share the visit. Schmidt took a chair on the opposite side of the desk so the business could begin.

"Did anyone see you coming? Were you followed?" Strauss asked his long-time loyal companion while extending a small humidor to offer a rare cigar.

"No, I don't believe so. Everything is fine. You wanted to see me? You said it was urgent."

"You have been my friend for many years, and you knew this day would come. The day I, we, reclaim East Germany and eventually the Western traitors, too. I will need your help and our old connections in doing so. Tell everyone who assists me in making this injustice right will be generously rewarded. Our friends around the world will never work again. That, I promise you."

"I have been waiting for this call for a long time." Schmidt smiled. "What is it you would like me to do?"

"You were my *Armeegeneral* for many years, and you managed to keep your position as defense minister even through Josef Jakob being elected chancellor. I need you to use your connections around the world to gain an upper hand and have Jakob discredited and removed from my office. I will then be able to regain my influence and rule over Germany once more, and then we can move beyond."

The military leader admitted the proposition was interesting, almost thrilling. "Anyone who stayed with their posts after you left has confided in me, they do not agree with the politics of the new leadership and the chancellor's passive ways. We have become a cowardly nation in the eyes of the world. We remain silent when tragedy strikes against Germans here and abroad, so afraid of asserting ourselves after what the Nazis did. We now assist other countries when our countrymen need help. Germany is in constant flux financially and economically, my friend. Yes, I will help you. I have friends who have remained true to you throughout the new regime, and that regime will hopefully soon end."

Strauss looked at his confidant with great happiness. "This will soon be our Germany again. A Germany we can be proud of, strong and without cowards in the government."

Strauss drew the curtains closed, making the room off-limits to everyone but his special guest. He walked deliberately to the Renoir painting hanging on the exposed brick wall across the room. Many artifacts displayed and some hidden in the castle were pieces seized during the last uprising. The prized possessions were now rightfully his, for he had killed for them. After gingerly removing the painting, Strauss revealed the facade of a wall safe. Covering the dial with one hand, he turned the combination. From the safe, he pulled a thick, sealed folder and handed it to Schmidt.

"What is in here?" Schmidt looked over the folder.

"In that envelope is the future of Germany. I have devised and perfected this plan for thirty years to take back what is rightfully ours. I want you to carefully read my instructions and intentions on each sheet of paper. After you have read and understood them, destroy them. This is not to get into the wrong hands."

"Yes, my leader. I will do just that."

"Now take them and go. Call your contacts, our friends, and carry out my every letter."

"When should I contact you?" Schmidt stood to exit.

"I will contact you, old friend."

"How will you know when the instructions have been completed?"

"I will know precisely when you are finished. Because my countrymen will be standing beneath my balcony crying out my name, and then I will know."

"Yes, my *Generalsekretär*." The military leader left hastily with his prize envelope in hand.

"Wait," Strauss cried out.

Schmidt turned and faced his *Generalsekretär*.

"How has that other matter been going? Did you find him?"

"No, sir. Not yet. But we are still looking. It appears his mother left the country. The hunt continues worldwide. If he is alive, we will find him," Schmidt reassured his old friend. "The process is long and sometimes tiresome. However, make no mistake, sir, we will find him."

"I have decided to tell Martin about the other boy and ask for his help in locating him. After I tell him, please inform him of your search strategies."

"I will. You are a very brave man, Mr. *Generalsekretär*."

"Thank you, and please keep me informed on that matter. I must find my lost sheep before I leave my earthly kingdom."

Before leaving the room, Schmidt watched his leader for a moment, no doubt surprised by his sudden decision to involve his son. Strauss turned as Schmidt closed the door after himself, opened the curtains, and glanced out over the balcony, sparing his countrymen another moment.

A sudden knock on another door drew him again back into reality. From a secret side door, a towering blond man, Strauss' son Martin, his firstborn, entered the room.

"Father, are you alright?" asked Martin, concern evident in his quivering voice.

"Yes, son, I'm fine. Thank you for coming so quickly. I want to ask a favor of you."

"Of course Father, anything. What can I do?"

"I need you to do something, to take over a job I assigned Schmidt, but before you do it, I must tell you something important. It may shock you."

Strauss waved his son to come in closer. Martin shut the side door behind him and sat down across the desk from his father.

Strauss did nothing more to prepare his son for the news.

"You have a brother. I am trying to find him."

Martin could not contain his feeling of betrayal.

Martin raised his voice in anger toward his father, something the young man had never done before. "What? How could you not tell me this sooner?" Martin shook his head, incredulous. "I have a brother? Where is he? Who is he?" Martin voiced all the usual questions a person might ask after being confronted with such surprising information.

"His mother left with the boy while still pregnant. I figure he should be a few years younger than you."

"How do you know it was a boy?"

"Your mother told me everything, always."

"And why would a woman leave you while she was pregnant?"

Strauss turned and looked out the window at the magnificent view and breathed a deep sigh. After a moment of contemplation, he took the burning cigar from his mouth and shook his head at his son.

"I don't know, really. I always wanted to be in politics. And when I was very young and eager to please, the Soviets backed me as *Generalsekretär* of the SED.

The elections were not secret, so anyone who struck a name from the national front list faced serious consequences. Then I became so busy with the affairs of this nation I was unable to devote any time to her. Then, one day, I woke, and she was gone. I looked for her at first, but as the years passed, she became impossible to find. I did stop looking for a time, but I never stopped dreaming I would find her and my son someday."

Strauss leaned over his desk and looked his son straight in the eye.

"I never stopped loving her. I want you to know that. Never!"

"Why haven't you told me this before, Father?"

"I didn't want to hurt you when you were young, and later what would it have accomplished? Nothing!" Strauss said shaking his head.

"What about my mother? Where is she?"

"Wait." Strauss threw his hand up, signaling Martin to stop speaking. "She is dead to you, I told you. She left you before you were old enough to remember her. I was never married to your mother, and that was not by choice."

At a loss for more words, he lowered his head in sorrow and sat behind his magisterial desk. He sloped back in his chair and gazed at his son, who still sat across from him, upright and clearly bothered. Strauss felt a tinge of guilt for telling his son half-truths. But he needed Martin's help to find his long-lost son, Martin's brother. His mother was of no consequence, having proven herself disloyal the day she left. At least, that's what Strauss kept telling himself. It would be better if Martin never knew that woman but idealized a woman who never existed.

"I must say this is the most incredible thing I have ever heard," his son said. "Why now? Why do you want to find him now?"

"Because it's time," Strauss raised his head and addressed his son using the voice of a leader. "I have plans for the future, and they include you and your brother. I want your help to find him and bring him here. I want all my children together while I'm still here and alive to enjoy them."

"Nothing is wrong with you, is there?" Martin asked, leaning forward in concern.

"You see, that's why I have faith in you—because you always cared for me and my health. I am fine, son, do not worry about your father. But please take responsibility from Schmidt and find your brother. He must know we're his family, a great and powerful family who lead and will someday reign over many nations."

"Where would I even start? What's his mother's name?" Martin asked.

"Here, I have written it down on this sheet of paper. Her whereabouts are completely unknown."

Strauss handed his son a scrap of folded paper with a name scribbled on it. Martin hesitantly opened the paper and read the name out loud: "Margaret Stratton."

Strauss uttered the name *Margaret* under his breath.

Martin placed the sheet of paper in his jacket lapel pocket. "Why me, though? Why do you want me to locate him?"

"Because you're one of the few people in this world I completely trust, my son. I know you will never do anything to hurt or disappoint your father. Schmidt is working on another matter for me. If you seek my old love, if you work on this matter, then this will free up Schmidt's time to concentrate on my other requests."

Martin stood across from his father for a moment. He slowly raised his head and looked deeply into his father's eyes, maybe for the first time in his life.

"Yes, I will do it," Martin said. "I will begin immediately."

"I knew I could count on you." Strauss smiled.

With the sheet of paper, Martin left his father's office. He quietly closed the hallway door behind him and stood for a moment. Schmidt came around the corner and saw Martin standing there with his golden head hanging down toward the floor, masked with a look of despair.

"Young Martin, it is good to see you again," Schmidt began.

"Yes, General Schmidt, it's a pleasure," Martin murmured.

"Your father gave you the surprising but good news, *ja?*" Schmidt asked.

"Yes, he did. I would describe it more as a shock than anything else." Martin snickered.

The two were uncomfortably silent for a minute, as the general did not know what to say to console the boy. He felt Martin's pain, as he helped his father hide the information for so long.

"Oh, I am to collect information from you regarding the search," Martin asked.

"I will bring it to you this evening. Is that satisfactory?" the general asked.

"I will be at my home. Please come by. I have much to digest and to think about."

"I understand, young Martin. I am sorry for you, but you should also be happy because you are no longer alone," Schmidt said, trying to be optimistic.

"Yes, happy. I will remember," Martin sneered.

Schmidt put his hand on the young man's shoulder and stepped in closer and lowered his voice. "Martin, I have searched for your brother for a long time, and I have had no success. If you are granted any luck, please call me. I will take great comfort in the fact that your efforts were fruitful."

"I appreciate all you've done for my father, and I will call you if I learn anything."

The two parted company and Martin left the castle the usual way.

WEEK
ONE

THE MASSIVE SHIP PULLED INTO New York Harbor after dusk, right on schedule. No horn sounded. The freighter's engines stopped, and the ship drifted effortlessly toward the dock. The only sound heard was the rippling of the flag at the rear of the ship. The black, red, and gold-striped colors of the flag glowed under the light of the moon, which contrasted the calm, dark water beneath the large boat.

Large, stocky men with dark knitted hats waited in the shadows to guide the ship and its few selected passengers to land. The bearded captain docked the freighter with ease, as he had so many times before. Within a moment, foot soldiers armed with Soviet AK-47s strapped over their shoulders appeared from the darkness to anchor and secure the vessel. The crew dropped ropes to tie the ship to the docking posts. Each man grabbed his line and pulled hard until their faces turned bluish just to get the transport to shore.

"*Beeilen Euch*," one man from the ship cried out in German, telling the crew to hurry.

While the ground men secured the ship, crew members exited. Men gingerly dropped a long, sturdy plank from the boat using ropes to guide it to a silent landing. Once the plank operators determined the area was not compromised, they signaled with a simple hand gesture that the harbor was safe.

Ten armed guards, all obviously military trained, exited the ship, escorting one undersized dark-haired man to meet his contact. The conspirator dressed not in the usual uniform of his homeland but as a chameleon, as an American. Guards took their natural positions and secured the grounds in orchestrated formation. They examined garbage cans and peered through the windows of other vessels docked nearby. No chances were to be taken tonight. The cargo was too important, too precious. While awaiting further orders, and with no verbal instruction, the guards continued to search the premises for anything suspicious, anything unusual. They moved in pairs about the dock in routine configuration. They conducted their surveillance without a sound or an utterance, speaking only with eye and hand gestures.

The smaller figure continued with one guard a hundred feet down the dock to a nearby abandoned boathouse, where his long-time informant and friend waited. The door was partially open as the man and his escort approached.

"Enter," an American man called out as the two drew closer.

The guard entered first and found one middle-aged man sitting in a chair. The man hid his identity behind a trench coat and a signature navy blue Fedora hat. The light was dim, the man barely recognizable. The stage had been set as usual. The guard found the boathouse safe and motioned to his employer to enter.

"Do you have my paperwork?" the scrawny man with the heavy accent asked.

Without saying a word, the gentleman in the chair stood and handed his contact two large envelopes. One envelope was sealed, the other open. The boss removed the contents from the smaller of the two packages and flipped through his purchase. He smiled and nodded, finding the items to be satisfactory.

"Give him the briefcase," the boss ordered his foot soldier in German.

The military man quietly handed the briefcase to the gentleman.

"Count it, if you wish," the boss insisted.

"I believe you. He's been so generous in the past," said the hidden man. "Our business is concluded?"

The boss looked at the papers and the contact, then gave a simple nod to acknowledge everything looked fine and he was free to leave.

The contact exited with his briefcase, but the guard stopped him. Without turning around, the German boss said, "Before you go, what is all this scandal I see on the television news about you accepting illegal campaign contributions? They are auditing you, *ja?*"

The gentleman slowly turned and said with his voice cracking, "There is nothing for you to worry yourself about. This is normal, everyday business in this country. Turn on the news next week, and it'll be someone else. It will never get back to you."

"I know it won't," the boss replied in a monotone voice.

The gentleman in the trench coat promptly left the boathouse and headed for his long, dark Mercedes parked safely off the harbor. The boss and his crony quickly returned to the ship.

"Shall we proceed?" one voice called out from the darkness to the boss.

The boss waved his envelope in the air and signaled the men to begin loading the ship. The soldiers armed with hand radios called more men, who were waiting a few minutes away from the harbor.

"Come now, we go," one man shouted in German then in English into his radio.

A moment passed. Headlights from freight trucks appeared in the distance. The boss spoke over the radio, bringing in each individual driver. Without discussing procedure, twenty men from the boat and ground crew unloaded sealed containers from the trucks by hand and with a crane, taking each container to the ship. Every transfer was made slowly and with great care. Their lives depended on it. The dark figures conducted what appeared to be routine business for six hours.

"*Schnell*," one man cried. "We must finish before dawn."

The men continued to load the merchandise, moving at a quicker pace. The workers were nearly ready to set sail east when an unknown figure approached from the distance. The soldiers covered him with their weapons, fingers on the triggers.

"Did you show paperwork to the last shift?" an overweight harbor security guard asked as he drew closer. The guard walked at his usual slow pace, suspecting nothing out of the ordinary. The foot soldiers remained silent but looked at the scrawny man as he calmly presented one of the two envelopes.

"We didn't see him when we arrived, but we were going to have these stamped before we left," he told the guard in a clear voice free of any accent.

From the envelope still in hand, the boss pulled papers authorizing him to take a shipment of coffee, tea, and other prepackaged beverages out of the United

States. The guard took the papers, and with the aid of a flashlight looked them over. The boss closely watched the guard's face and detected no signs of question.

"Okay, these look in order. I'll take them to get stamped. Be back in a minute."

"That would be helpful." With no visible expression, the boss observed the security guard as he left.

The men hoisted the last load onto the ship's deck. Dawn was on the horizon, and the ship needed to be gone before then. The ropes and anchors dropped earlier were untied and thrown onboard. Time was critical; the sun was about to show its evil face to the men of darkness. These were men with no faces, no identities—just mercenaries for hire. As the crew prepared the ship for departure, the boss continued to wait on the dock for the paperwork.

"I'll see you in two weeks," the boss told his cronies. "Travel with care. I have other business to take care of here, so I'll be flying back this time."

The shadowed men gave the boss one wave of acknowledgment before starting the engine. The boss knew his cargo was in safe hands. These men were the best the military had to offer.

The man under the fedora hat drove from the harbor with the briefcase secure on the passenger seat. After driving several hours south, he pulled to the side of the road and finally snapped open the attaché case. This was a long-awaited desire. Before his eyes were displayed stacks of United States currency, each tightly bound in paper, marking the batch of denominations. With one hand still on the wheel, he fondled the tiny slips of paper as if a beautiful woman lay beneath his fingertips. The man checked the rearview mirror looking for a tail or anything to cause alarm. Seeing none, he smiled and breathed a sigh of relief. Soon his millions would be deposited in a local bank and transferred to an account in a small European country; the account was set up when he began working in Washington, DC. European bankers would inflate the money with interest while cradling it in safety, awaiting his arrival.

Enough of the political racket, he thought. Proper upbringing and education achieved nothing but obtaining the job of a pawn, under constant scrutiny. Everybody seemed to be cashing out. Good intentions meant nothing in Washington, the man quickly learned from his brothers and sisters on the Hill.

Nothing. In textbooks, Washington was a place where elected officials made laws to combat crime and represent Americans. But as the man learned, Capitol Hill was home to more criminals than any inner city in the United States. Everything you said and did to improve the quality of American life was twisted under the media's microscope, while real criminals were offered interviews and roamed free.

The man put his payoff away and secured the briefcase. He pulled the car back onto the expressway and continued toward his Georgetown apartment, where many officials kept residences while politically active in Washington. The dark Mercedes passed through several tollbooths, each one photographing the license plate. Ironically, this was a new pilot program he actively petitioned for so the Department of Transportation could assist law enforcement officers in tracking criminals who fled from state to state. But that was the old him. He was a smarter man now. He drove at a moderate speed down the expressway. It was nearly noon, and the temperature had risen. The man finally removed his hat, retiring it to the back seat, and lowered the window.

Behind him, a four-door black Suburban pulled onto the highway and merged with traffic. The SUV accelerated. The two men in the SUV weaved in and out of traffic, speeding toward the German import.

"Is that the one?" the driver asked the passenger.

"*Ja.* License plate DIPLOMAT," the passenger replied with a German accent.

"*Das ist er,*" the driver agreed.

The Suburban paralleled the dark Mercedes on the left. The Suburban passenger had a clear view of the car's driver. The men agreed with a nod: the time was now. The driver kept equal speed and distance with the car. The Mercedes driver, still preoccupied with his new fortune, was unaware of the two professionals encroaching on his left. The truck's passenger rolled down the tinted window and threw a small, lit object into the car of the man with the fedora hat.

The bribed man, stunned, whipped his head to the left and locked eyes with the passenger of the Suburban. Before he could utter a sound, one silent shot fired from the truck ripped through the head and face of the Mercedes driver. The man collapsed forward with one foot pressing on the accelerator, and the German import picked up speed.

The Suburban dropped back, and the occupants watched as the Mercedes sped out of control down the highway. When the highway curved left, the speeding car vaulted off the road. The airborne vehicle flew two hundred feet before reaching the earth again. A massive explosion blew the car through the treetops into a fiery wreck. The car raged into flames. No person could survive such a blast. Green slips of paper dropped from the sky in its wake, falling up to a mile away.

Hundred-dollar bills showered the debris still engulfed in flames. Whoever got there first would have a lucky day. The assassins needed confirmation before spectators arrived. Onlookers gathered to watch the car burn and undoubtedly, collected the remaining bills that did not meet the fate of the man with the fedora hat.

The Suburban continued past the wreckage. The driver picked up a handheld radio and told the listener on the other end that the man with the fedora hat was dead.

"Ich verstehe." The commander told the driver he understood. "Return to headquarters," he ordered the men.

The driver made an evasive left turn and followed the route back.

Within minutes, state troopers were on the scene, securing the site of the tragic accident. Officers roped off the area to prevent people from getting hurt trying to get at the money. Firemen followed police to extinguish the trees and the remainder of the car that continued to burn in the aftermath. Several investigators milled around the wreckage like bees humming around honey.

"This is the worst car accident I've ever seen," one young officer remarked to an investigator.

"First thing, this was no accident, kid," the man responded. "How many people leap off the expressway with, let's say, about one million dollars in their car? Not many."

"Good point," the kid said, laughing.

"Plus, the burns don't add up with your typical car wreck. He looks like he had a little help."

One officer on the scene called for the experienced investigator to come closer and have a look at the smoking vehicle.

"Look, sir." Another officer pointed at the rear of the car.

"Oh shit," the old guy said. "Diplomatic license plates. This is just what I need. Everybody away from the car and regroup over there for instructions."

The officials backed away from the crime scene and the investigator jogged to his car to use the radio to call his superiors for help. It was a government vehicle, possibly a diplomat.

"We need special evidence technicians to scrutinize the scene for explosive devices before it becomes contaminated," he barked into his radio.

"Acknowledged," the dispatcher replied.

GWEN PATTERSON SETTLED into her first-class seat on the redeye flight back to the States as the jumbo jet readied to leave the gate.

"This flight is service from Brussels to New York, with one brief stopover in London," the flight attendant announced to the crowded cabin over the plane's loudspeaker, as though anyone might suddenly discover they were on the wrong flight. "Welcome aboard."

After the standard safety protocol talk during pushback and taxi, passengers were instructed in French, German, and English to fasten their seat belts and turn off their cellular telephones and all electronic equipment. Gwen smiled, understanding all three languages. During her decade of overseas assignments, she learned the languages quickly. How far and how fast she had come. She stowed her laptop and buckled her seat belt.

Gwen leaned her head back and gazed out the window as the plane waited for runway clearance. She stretched her legs forward and made herself comfortable. A slender brunette in her early thirties, standing five feet ten inches, she was a striking woman, and she knew it. Men often complimented her on her fair skin, citing an exquisite contrast to her dark brown hair.

"See you soon," she said to the beautiful city of Brussels as her plane picked up speed down the runway. The plane soon lifted her and the other passengers into the night. As the plane circled over the city, she wished she could still see the red-roofed houses that contrasted the lovely green setting. Europe held so much culture. She adored the architecture and the brick-laid streets. Gwen loved her frequent overseas visits, even though they took her far from her husband, Joshua

Patterson. *This is what I always wanted. Traveling to foreign lands and meeting people doing interesting and exciting things.* Gwen no longer feared being plagued with boredom. She loved Joshua. They'd been together since they met in college, but if she had to stay rooted in the same spot, going to the same building day in and day out, she'd go bonkers.

Gwen grew up in a small town in upstate New York with the Atlantic Ocean as her backyard. Her surroundings as a child were beautiful, she wouldn't deny; however, she always craved something more. She had been unsure what that was until she left for college. She had grown up so much since then. She was no longer that tall, lanky girl but a refined world traveler. She enjoyed visiting the beach and her old neighborhood, but her friends had long since fled. They had made their own way in the world, but doing what, Gwen had no idea. Gwen had suffered from tunnel vision throughout her young adulthood until she got to the network. Now the blinders were off, but everybody was gone. What little extra time she had around her travels and reporting, she gave to Joshua.

During college she discovered a knack for speaking with people and making them feel comfortable. People she spoke with would tell her anything. She suspected this talent after so many people told her about it, but she never thought it would lead to such an amazing career. Now a seasoned foreign correspondent for a major New York network, she had paid her dues during college internships at local television stations. She had loathed some of her experiences as an intern.

"I'm sorry, I was absent the day they taught us to get lunch," she told one employer. "What am I going to learn standing in a restaurant, picking up food?"

After graduation, she landed her first paid job as a reporter for a weekly show in a Pennsylvania suburb. During the wave of unrest comprising the Arab Spring, she got a taste of foreign conflict reporting and never looked back. Gwen changed jobs every year until landing at the top on NIN, her current network. People for whom she had fetched coffee now called her asking for favors. She enjoyed her status. She'd had interns of her own since then but treated them with respect. *Just because people aren't quite there yet doesn't mean they won't be,* she always thought. Network news was a small, incestuous business, and you never knew when you'd run into someone again and the position they'd hold.

She told one of her interns, "Everyone goes around in this business, and someday I may come to you for a job."

The student laughed, but Gwen knew he would always remember that, especially if it came true.

A loud, annoying beep Gwen was all too familiar with came from her bag. Once the flight attendant alerted them that they could use electronics again, she pulled her computer from underneath the seat in front of her and flipped it on, then entered her password. The network insisted on password-only access; management was always afraid if the competition got hold of the computer, the information on it would lose value. Gwen thought her bosses were paranoid, but she did as her supervisor Joe asked.

The computer flashed an urgent email message from her office. *Nothing like modern technology,* Gwen thought as she hit a series of buttons to get to the message. There was no need for phone outlets anymore with the use of satellites.

Gwen,
Your phone is not working. Come straight to the office. Need to talk.
Joe.

Simple yet direct. But that was Joe.

She opened her strike file to polish her notes. She was sent to Belgium to collect information about the looming automotive manufacturer's strike. Whether it happened or not, it was still a story. Belgium operated a major factory, and even a hint of strike would initiate a worldwide panic due to the resultant shortage of cars and car parts. She had her video clips handy from a Belgian television station that provided a cameraman. But she needed to complete a few last-minute details. She would need to gather the final information by telephone, since Joe had pulled her out before the workers were able to reach a deal with the government.

Workers were opposing the deal Belgian officials made with foreign auto manufacturers. The Belgian government agreed to import twenty percent more foreign cars, which would directly affect the price of their domestic sales. Workers feared layoffs and firings were in their near future. The question now was whether the government would reduce the number of imports or disregard worker's concerns, possibly causing a complete shutdown of all Belgian manufacturing plants.

Gwen wondered for a moment what could be so important that Joe would pull her off this assignment. The entire Belgian economy could be facing major disruption. Joseph Bess was Gwen's longtime friend, news director, and producer. Joe wore many hats: a one-time reporter, years ago, now turned management. Newcomers looked at him with skepticism because an idealistic reporter rarely turned out to be a company man in disguise. Some questioned his loyalty to preserving the truth or slicing expenses. But he had been in this business longer than Gwen had been alive. He discovered her, once a piece of coal but now a sparkling diamond. She had the utmost respect for him, and she never questioned his judgment.

After an hour on the ground at Heathrow, the plane took off again for the longer leg to LaGuardia. She tucked away her computer and slept across the Atlantic, waking when the plane began its descent from cruising altitude. Her body was attuned to catching rest on flights or in the back of trucks or wherever she was stationary when on the ground in a war zone. This facility annoyed Joshua, but it was a necessary adaptation.

Working in news meant she was required to keep up on what happened in her absence. Gwen searched for her headphones in the back compartment of the seat in front of her and tuned into the loop of yesterday's news. The evening report from New York started off showing a picture of Congressman Frank Solas, who had been under investigation for tax evasion. *So, what's new?* Gwen thought. She had beaten that story like a dead horse less than a month ago. She doubted his case would ever get to trial. Gwen put on the headphones and turned up the volume to hear the report.

A competing network reporter said, "The body of Illinois Democratic Congressman Frank Solas was identified through dental records after an accident just outside Washington DC. The crash triggered a fiery wreck that ..."

He was found dead? Gwen could not believe it.

The report went on, but Gwen removed her headphones and placed them on her lap. Stunned for a moment, she gazed out the window as the plane approached the shoreline of New York. The Statue of Liberty became visible from the window, lit up in the pre-dawn darkness.

I just interviewed him two weeks ago for the tax story, she thought. Gwen sat in a daze for a moment, reliving every word of the earlier interview. After the meeting, he was on the receiving end of many financial deals, but she couldn't nail them down. "Now I'll never know where all the unreported tax money was coming from," she murmured. She stared blankly out the window, her mind racing.

Why was he dead? He drove that route a million times before. Jail was an option for the congressman that Gwen could live with, but death? How could such a thing happen?

The plane reached the five-mile marker outside LaGuardia and began its final descent for the runway.

"Please bring all seats into their upright position and secure all carry-on items beneath the seat in front of you. Flight crew, prepare for landing," the flight attendant announced.

A BALDING JOE BESS sat in his midtown Manhattan office behind thick glass through which no sound could be heard, puffing out thick smoke from a cheap cigar. Joe pressed back his greased hair while weighing the validity of an anonymous caller's cry for help.

The muffled-sounding tipster telephoned Joe's unlisted number at home close to midnight the evening before. Wrestling with the idea and the purpose of the call placed by the masked dialer, Joe attempted to confirm the accusations made. The unidentified person warned of a civil uprising instigated by unhappy and unemployed people of Germany. After a day of phoning connections in Europe that proved fruitless, he was unable to confirm the statements made by the caller. Still, with such little information, Joe felt uneasy and unable to ignore the information. *This person went through a lot of trouble to reach me, specifically me,* he thought. *But why?* This was a question he asked himself every moment for the past twenty-four hours.

The word of an anonymous caller was hardly enough evidence to justify travel expenses for a team of people to fly overseas. Joe had a boss to whom he had to report. However, after a one-sided debate with himself, Joe could not ignore the possibility that an award-winning story may have fallen into his lap. One person, though, he could send without any authorization. *I do have some discretion,* he thought. His gut instinct told him to investigate it.

Gwen will go and investigate. She can speak with embassy officials and leaders of German organizations and get a feeling of the atmosphere. A civil war, he said to himself while shaking his head, *not another one.* Crewmembers could follow later if it was warranted, and if Gwen dug up unhappy citizens, even better.

Joe brought Gwen in from Brussels for a day and tomorrow he would send her out, but under a different name. No officials should expect her. With forty years in the news business, Joe had seen everything happen and every surprise there was to be had. Like other times, Joe's gut instinct told him something was starting, something big was happening right now. But what?

GWEN LEFT THE AIRPORT and hopped into the limousine provided by the network while the driver stowed her luggage in the trunk. She couldn't wait to get answers from Joe for pulling her off the Belgian assignment.

"Please go straight to the NIN building," Gwen instructed the driver as she slammed the door.

"Yes ma'am."

No other words were exchanged. Gwen picked up the cellular that hadn't worked on the plane and called the newsroom.

"Is Joe there?"

"One moment," the voice on the other end of the line replied.

Gwen didn't need to identify herself; everybody at the station knew her voice.

While Gwen was on hold, she asked the driver, "Where's the regular guy?"

"He took the morning off. He had something personal to do," the Asian driver said politely as he glanced in the rearview mirror.

What could he have to do at 5 a.m.? He's a college kid, Gwen thought.

"Yes?" Joe said when he came on the line.

"Joe, it's me. I'm almost there."

"How far away are you?"

"Leaving the airport now."

"I'll be in my office."

At 5 a.m., the trip from LaGuardia Airport into New York City's midtown took less than fifteen minutes. *At least I'm going to beat the morning rush,* Gwen thought. She was preoccupied with thoughts of everything from Belgium to

Frank Solas to her next big story. While recollecting thoughts of reports about Solas, she slammed into the back of the front seat. Something behind her *thump-thumped* against her kidneys. The day's rat race had already begun, and one of the rats stepped into the road, forcing the driver to jam on the brakes.

"You should wear your seatbelt," the driver said.

"What was that?"

"What was what, ma'am?"

"That thud against the back of my seat. Something heavy banged against the back of my seat when you hit the brakes."

"Probably your luggage, ma'am."

"That was no luggage."

"No worries, ma'am. I will look and take care of whatever is rolling around loose back there."

The driver pulled the car in the network's garage and Gwen exited the vehicle before the driver could open her door.

"Please bring the luggage upstairs to the thirtieth floor," she said to the driver already outside the car.

He nodded he would. However, he had other instructions. The elevator door shut, and Gwen was out of sight. Chen picked up the car's telephone and hit one preset number on speed dial. The phone rang once, and a man with an American accent answered.

"Yes?"

"She is in the building," Chen said.

"Going up to thirty?"

"Yes. What do you want me to do?"

"Nothing," the man said. "Just sit there for now, follow her if she leaves the building, and I will call you if I need you."

"Of course."

Chen hung up the phone and lit a cigarette, watching the elevator doors for a moment, waiting for any activity. Seeing none, he pulled the car around and backed into a dimly lit parking space but left the engine running. From behind his black uniform jacket, he pulled out a Luger handgun and popped open the trunk door as he exited the car. He walked around to the rear of the car and looked down on Lyle, the driver, bound with rope and gagged with silver duct tape. Lyle's face was covered in blood from a head wound he received during Chen's earlier evasive driving maneuver.

Chen first removed Gwen's luggage and placed it neatly in the back seat. With the trunk ajar, Lyle struggled. Chen quickly returned to his prisoner. With no remorse, he extended his arm and pointed his long barrel at the head of the innocent driver. One shot sufficed. In a split second, the act was over, ending all of young Lyle's hopes and dreams. Chen had mastered the art of execution—the reason he was so heavily sought after for his services. After finishing his business, he slammed the trunk shut then returned to the wheel of his vehicle, taking a long drag on his cigarette. The car must now be disposed of. It had served its purpose. The driver left the building undetected, heading on a direct route for the Hudson River. The river had always been a popular spot for unloading nasty packages.

THE HEAVYSET MAN on the phone upstairs leaned back in his black leather chair and locked a Cuban cigar between his teeth. He looked through his ivory tower window and thought for a moment. *How do you discourage a hotshot reporter?*

He picked up the phone and dialed.

"Hello?" his secretary answered.

"Get in here right away," the man demanded.

Without replying, the middle-aged woman hung up the phone and hurried to her supervisor's office. She moved down the hall quickly but remained calm, not wanting to arouse suspicion. Co-workers attempted to engage her in conversation as she walked by, but she smiled and kept going. She approached the high French doors of her boss' office. They were original cherrywood hand-carved double doors, and whoever sat behind them had great power. The door opened and she slipped through.

"What is she doing back?" the executive asked.

"Who?"

"Gwen Patterson." His face grew red, a sign of impending explosion.

"I have no idea, but I'll find out."

"I thought I told you I was supposed to be made aware of all her schedule changes. I was informed she was coming back, but not why. Where is she going?"

She lifted her chin to hide the hammering of her heart. "I was not even aware she was here, sir. Her schedule said she should be gone until Monday, at least."

"Find out why she's back early, where she's going, and who ordered it," he demanded.

The secretary ran from the office, slamming the door behind her. She had a great deal of work to do.

Sylvia, secretary to network president Charles Henderson, called downstairs to the newsroom. Writers of the thirty-second spots television viewers were familiar with sat in a collage of desks away from the noise and distractions that went with being in the hub of a communications network. Michelle was unknowingly Sylvia's best informant. She wrote local news coverage, but she always knew who was covering what and when—including Gwen Patterson.

"Newsroom," Michelle answered.

"Hi, it's Sylvia."

"To what do I owe this phone call from network management?"

"Nothing, really. Thought you might want to go for lunch later."

"Sure, meet me in the lobby at noon."

"See you then." Sylvia hung up the phone and right away called Henderson.

"Yes," Henderson said.

"I've made arrangements to have lunch with one of the news writers at noon. She and Gwen are friends, and she can fill me in."

"Very good. Find out what in the hell is going on around here. Don't let her know why you're asking. When it comes to the news business, this is a small town, and if anybody finds out what's going on, our FCC license could be up to the highest bidder. I have a lot invested in this company."

"Of course."

CLEAR ACROSS MANHATTAN on the Upper West Side stood an old warehouse that was once the home of immigrant factory workers but was later transformed into a series of sealed-off rooms. The six-story structure did not meet the fate of other area sweatshops. Instead, it took on a life of its own. Following a multimillion-dollar renovation to the building's interior, the building had become state of the art. Every door led to a sealed-off room and was completely soundproofed, as the designers wanted. Only the person who held the right combination along with a clearance card could enter using a keypad fixed on the outside of each door. One wrong number would trigger an alarm that would automatically lock down the building. No person could enter or, more importantly, be permitted to leave. Harsh questions were asked of those who attempted unauthorized access. Persons trusted with such combinations had to handle the numbers with great care. The exterior appeared to be a typical abandoned manufacturing building except for the coded door and window alarm that screamed to the ordinary citizen, "Go away." Barbed wire lining the roof completely cut off access to anyone who tried an alternative route.

Differing from the unchanged homely outer appearance, the inside was set up for something far more sophisticated, almost beyond comprehension. Each of the six levels served a separate purpose. Each floor monitored different types of people and situations, all for distinct reasons. Windows in the structure appeared normal with reflections from the outside, but on the inside, they were also sealed and soundproofed.

Nothing more than florescent lighting guided the silent men wearing expensive dark suits as they patrolled the hallways outside the sealed "offices." The guards roamed the hallways ensuring no unwelcome outsiders would accidentally discover the government's inner hub of communications, especially the government itself. Armed with the standard government-issued weaponry, the dark-suited men conducted spot-checks on all building's entrances and exits, demanding identification from all those who attempted access.

In a small backroom on the second floor, in a space no larger than a master bedroom, sat two men in business suits and headsets who were now also aware of the upcoming encounter between Sylvia and Michelle. Unable to bluntly ask the destination of the reporter, they too held a glass to the wall.

"We've got it," said the lanky Alex to his new partner beside him, Carter.

The team had been monitoring telephone calls for hours to learn and possibly curb events before they transpired.

"Henderson's secretary Sylvia is meeting with someone from the newsroom named Michelle," Alex said. "Apparently, she's going to find out about Gwen's assignment. For some reason, management is keeping plans hushed."

Carter looked curiously at Alex, his training officer and partner of only a few months. "This is a lot of trouble to find out what's on one reporter's agenda. What if Gwen's next assignment is bullshit? Why is the company assuming she's up to anything that could compromise the United States?"

"Look, kid, as you gain experience in this organization, you'll discover things that will make your hair stand on end. It made some of mine fall out." Alex grabbed a few strands above his ear. "Since the Cold War, the CIA has kept a close eye on all high-profile media organizations. Especially those with large bankrolls who can afford the expense of real, in-depth investigative work. We need to know what they're working on even before they do. Stories can't break until the company, our company, believes the American public, and the world, for that matter, is ready to hear about it. Truly free information would kill this country and send the world into chaos.

"You see, people want to live in a world where they believe the media is the fourth branch of government, watching over the other three to make sure no funny business is going on in Washington. But the general population can't handle a windfall of scandal. They don't want the whole story, just a scapegoat every now and then. So, in small increments the government leaks disreputable activity taking place in the ranks, the media reports it, and the public thinks everybody is doing their job. Everybody's satisfied. But the real dirty details that involve government covert operations at home and abroad, bringing drugs into the country and high-profile assassinations? Well, people just can't handle it. The population doesn't want to know how many people around the world are murdered in their sleep each night in the name of American freedom. Freedom was not a fight won with the signing of the Constitution. It's an ongoing fight every day by men and women of this country who supposedly don't exist. Make no mistake, the public and the media don't learn anything that isn't approved by the company well in advance. You're a part of a special section that watches the watchdogs. This section helps preserve American stability."

Young Carter sat with eyebrows cocked. "For years, my parents and I depended on the news media to find out what's going on in the country and in the world. Are you saying we censor television newsrooms and newspapers, the Internet, the entire media of the United States of America? By people who claim to uphold freedom and free speech? Censored by the people who the media is supposed to watch? That's insane."

"Insane maybe, but absolutely necessary. Could you imagine the public knowing everything we know? Everything the Directorate of Operations knows? Other governments around the world knowing what we know? Reporting where agents are investigating undercover and conducting covert operations? First our agents would die, then the public reaction and the panic would cause widespread hysteria. Following the public frenzy would be anarchy in this country. Anarchy would make us vulnerable to every nation around the world. Have you any idea how many countries could initiate an attack on us? All countries claim to love America, but that's because we send them financial aid. Wait until something destabilizes this nation—

countries will be lining up to take a poke at us. There's a lot at stake here."

"But the media must know something about this? About the censorship? How do journalists tolerate it? How is it that after forty years, the American public still doesn't know about it?"

"Listen, it has taken public and private officials years to set a complicated stage, if you will, for the American public. Only a select few working in mass media organizations know about it, only the few who need to know to make it happen. Some we call friendly agents were placed in their positions by us. During the last forty years, there has been a mass conspiracy among the military, corporations, and the extremely wealthy to consume and monopolize the media outlets. The major corporations, with the aid of influential leaders, have systematically bought up television stations, radio stations, and newspapers around the country. They've infiltrated the Internet, hushing influencers and making them march in line by dangling advertising deals. Once these groups buy the media, the information is easily controlled. Patriotic and military-friendly individuals run corporations. Sometimes public officials need to tighten the noose around some CEO's neck, but they usually respond favorably."

"This is all too amazing." Carter shook his head in disbelief. "What you're saying to me is, members of the military and influential people in Washington directly or indirectly own all the corporations that own the media outlets. The corporate owners then cast a dark cloud over any information a journalist might want to publish by intimidating the newspaper or television station's president or editor-in-chief. Is this what you're saying?"

"You catch on quick, kid. I see why the company recruited you."

Carter, holding his head, nodded in agreement. He would not divulge the new lesson in Conspiracy 101, even if his security clearance training hadn't emphasized silence and discretion and the punishment for disobeying. "Who would believe me anyway? It sounds outlandish."

Alex removed his headset and picked up the telephone, dialing a preset number on a secure line. A woman on the other end picked up the telephone and acknowledged the call.

"We have movement with two females at NIN in Manhattan and need surveillance."

"Understood," the woman replied.

Alex divulged the details of the scheduled encounter between Michelle and Sylvia while Carter listened and learned. The woman at headquarters in Langley,

Virginia, typed the information into the company's database. The two company associates planned to have the two NIN workers followed and recorded during their lunch meeting.

A red light appeared on their phone bank.

"Wait a minute, the light is on. Sylvia is making a call. Get your headphones, Carter."

The men replaced their headsets and listened to Sylvia's call.

THE ELEVATOR STOPPED on thirty at the NIN building. The doors opened and Gwen stormed out. By 5:30 a.m., most of the newsroom staff had arrived to set up for the morning show at 6:00. Gwen headed straight for Joe's office.

"What am I doing back here?" She crossed her arms, standing in his office doorway. "Can you tell me now?"

"Hi, kid. Come on in and sit down." Joe pointed to a chair across from his desk.

Joe had called her *kid* since she started there five years ago. But she didn't mind. He had a great deal of respect for her work, and from his perspective, in his sixties, she was a kid.

Gwen entered Joe's office and plopped down in one of the two oversized chairs across from his desk. In spite of sleeping on the plane, she was worn out from the trip.

Joe stood from behind his desk and walked casually over to close his office door. He sat on the edge of his cluttered desk across from Gwen and rubbed his forehead.

"How did you get here so fast?"

"The usual car." She slumped back in the chair, resting her head in her hand.

Joe frowned. "What do you mean, the usual car?"

"The usual short black limo, the one I always take. But the regular guy took the day off. I don't know who was driving."

He grimaced. "I should have told you on the phone, but I didn't think about it."

"What? Tell me what?" Gwen ceased all outside thoughts and gave Joe her undivided attention.

"That car was stolen yesterday from the garage. I have a police report around here somewhere." He turned toward his desk and shuffled stacks of papers.

"That's impossible. I rode in that car here just now. It's parked in the garage."

"Another thing. We haven't seen Lyle, either. He disappeared when the car turned up missing."

Her heart skidded a beat. "Missing? What do you mean, turned up missing?" Gwen stared at Joe, dumbfounded and in denial. Lyle wouldn't do anything criminal. He simply wasn't the type. "No, there's got to be something you're missing. That just doesn't sound right." She shook her head.

"I'll call the attendant. Maybe the car's still there."

The two continued to look puzzled at one another while Joe placed the call to Darryl, the daytime garage attendant.

The phone rang five times before Darryl answered.

"Yes?" He sounded exhausted.

"Darryl, it's Joe. Has the stolen limo been found yet?"

"Not that I know of."

"Where's the car that dropped Gwen off a few minutes ago?"

"She's back? I thought she wasn't coming in until Monday. Sorry, I wasn't down here when she arrived. There are no limos here, sir."

"Are you sure no limos at all?"

"I'll check the whole place and get back to you. Okay?"

"Yeah, okay you do that." Joe hung up the phone.

Gwen shook her head. "I don't know what to tell you, Joe. I rode in the same car. What happened to it, I can't say." She narrowed her eyes and snarled. "My luggage was still in the trunk."

"Something is going on here, damn it, and I'm going to find out who's screwing around." Joe slammed one fist on the desk.

Gwen remained silent for a moment then looked up. "Check the garage video surveillance tape."

Joe smiled ruefully.

Not able to do anything more about the car or her luggage, she pressed Joe about her sudden return trip and the next assignment.

"You're going to Germany."

"What?" she said in a high-pitched screech. "Germany? I just came from Belgium. Why did you have me come back here? I could have hopped right over. This is crazy."

Joe looked at Gwen as she sat there questioning his judgment, something she usually didn't do.

Gwen held her breath for a moment before asking the real question.

"Okay, what's going on in Germany?"

Joe placed a file folder from the top drawer of his locked desk in front of Gwen. "I got an anonymous tip the other night. A person called my house around midnight and told me what I'm about to tell you.

"The caller said student leaders are organizing in large numbers, orchestrating a movement against the government. It seems the socialists may be leaning Communist again. I thought most of those problems were solved after the wall came down, but we may not have heard the end of it. Unemployment is high and taxes are on the rise. I want you to talk to economic leaders and student protesters over there and see what all the fuss is about. Maybe there's a story, maybe there isn't, but we won't know until you get over there and talk to people. Don't worry about your strike story. Someone here will pick up the rest by phone. This is more important."

Gwen blinked at him. "Why didn't you tell me this on the phone in Belgium?"

"I want to scoop the other networks with this story, and you know how easily information can be taken from cellular phone conversations."

Gwen laughed. Joe was showing his age. He was more paranoid of modern technology than of protesters overthrowing a government. Keeping a competitive edge was paramount to Joe.

"Don't laugh at me, kid, it could happen." He smiled, looking sheepish. "Anyway, I'll give you the background here and you'll leave tomorrow, you got it?"

"Yes, I got it."

"I booked your tickets under your maiden name Stratton. I have a gut feeling, and I don't want anyone to know you're coming."

"Why?" Gwen tilted her head.

"I'm not sure. It's just a feeling. We don't know how big or small this thing is, and since you're going alone, I don't want to set off sirens of your arrival. Quietly see what or if there's a story and call me. If there's a story, I'll send someone to meet you out there."

Joe handed Gwen a thick file filled with clippings of newspaper articles spanning thirty years of public unrest along with more recent information about charges the people brought against their government.

"Most of the items in there I got from Frank Solas," he said sadly.

Gwen looked at Joe, understanding his grief. She leaned over and touched his hand.

"I've known Frank since college, but this isn't the time," Joe said, rubbing his face. "Anyway, Frank was on that earlier Washington committee to bring peace to East Germany and help bring them back into the Western fold. In there, you'll find the background on the former General Secretary of the SED and some of his sidekicks." He pointed to different enclosures.

"You'll fly directly into Berlin. In that file, you'll find names of individuals known to protest the government. Some are students and others are activists."

"What about their government are they protesting?" Gwen asked while flipping through the stack of papers.

"Since Frank was on that committee to help ease the unification process of the two Germanys, a lot of this I obtained from him the day before he died. The current chancellor of the country, Josef Jakob, was an adversary of Erich Strauss ever since he stepped down, shortly after the unification thirty years ago. But since Jacob took office, the whole country is on an economic downturn. It's as though someone is trying to sabotage his administration. Companies are closing, unable to afford the high taxes, so jobs are at a minimum. Overall, the cost of living has escalated considerably since the last elections. Citizens want answers about their tax dollars, which have sharply increased while government programs and the quality of their socialized healthcare have declined. So, who's to blame, the new guy? Problems with the economy fall deeper than one man. That's where you come in."

"Is any of this true? Can these protesters prove any of these accusations that the government is misappropriating tax money?"

"I don't know, but that's what you have to find out. If they can prove it and they go public with it, this government will fall faster than Rousseff of Brazil ever did. She'll look like a saint. We'll have a camera crew meet you there from a friendly television station. They won't have identification because the government censors their television stations. If asked, they'll deny offering American reporters any assistance. Get the interviews on tape and come back. It should take only a few days."

Joe crossed his arms and, with a look of concern on his face, gave her clear directions.

"Look, Gwen, I don't know where this story will go, but this is merely a cosmetic interview for right now. The way we got the tip bothers me, so don't reach too far just yet. These protests are the surface of something deeper, I can feel it. So, go in, get the interviews, and get out. Don't waste any time. I don't feel comfortable having you out there if we don't know what the underlying situation is."

"You don't have any idea?"

"No, but my gut doesn't lie. It never has. This story is so sensitive that management doesn't know you're going. Nobody does. Tell your husband, but that's it."

"Alright, seems easy enough." Gwen shrugged. "By the way, how much money are the protesters alleging the government stole?"

Joe put his head down and thought for a moment. He took a deep breath and looked at her. "We're talking about tens of billions in American dollars. That was the sum Frank said. I wish he hadn't died. There was so much more he could have told me."

"Well, if I was one of those citizens, I'd be pissed too."

"Here's your plane tickets, and if you need anything just call."

Gwen took the tickets and agreed to phone. She got up and headed out the door.

"Don't be a hero," Joe called out to her as she pushed the elevator button. "Just get the interviews and come home."

Gwen gave Joe a cheesy smile. He knew damn well what that meant.

Yes, but I have to find the right people first, and I'm not going to find them over Zoom. I have to get out into the field, Gwen thought to herself. *I love being out in the field.*

Gwen never just got interviews; she got the whole story. Joe gave Gwen one more nod as the elevator doors closed.

Joe went to his desk and leaned back in his chair. He rubbed his forehead and wondered what he had just done. He knew what he had done. He sent Gwen into a relative unknown, an unsafe situation. But was Germany in as much trouble as everyone thought? Was the situation that serious? Maybe he should have heeded Frank's warning.

THE ELEVATOR CAME TO REST on the ground floor. Gwen walked out. She moved deliberately, her bag with the folder tightly in hand as she headed out the revolving door. With her new assignment and the potential financial scandal it could reveal, she felt the thrill she craved as the only reporter who knew about it.

Standing on the sidewalk outside the NIN building, she threw her arm into the air to hail a taxi. A bright yellow cab pulled in front of her. Gwen opened the back door. She gave the driver her home address and reached out to close the door. Before she could grab the handle, an Asian man pushed himself into the backseat with her. He pulled a gun, held it low, and pointed it at the stunned reporter. He slammed the door.

"Get over and don't move," the man ordered Gwen. "Move! Drive!" he ordered the taxi driver, as he moved the .45 up to Gwen's head for a brief second for the driver to see.

The driver, believing it was a random robbery, complied and pulled away from the curb, merging into traffic. Clutching her bag, Gwen backed herself against the door behind the driver.

"What do you want, money?" she asked the Asian man.

"Money? You insult me. I am not a thief of money. What I want is far more valuable."

The driver continued the path initially instructed by Gwen. Gwen realized they were headed toward her home. She casually looked to the left, making eye contact with the driver in his rearview mirror. The two locked eyes, communicating almost telepathically. The driver began to turn aimlessly, taking the hint to not let the would-be robber know where she lived. As the cab continued in circles through midtown Manhattan, Gwen turned her attention to the armed man.

"More valuable? What's more valuable?" Gwen asked, petrified.

"You should know. You're the reporter."

"What?"

"Information! Do I have to spell it out for you? You're not so smart."

The man pushed the gun into Gwen's stomach and asked for her destination.

"Home, I was just going home. I swear."

"Not the destination of the cab, you bitch. You know damn well what I'm talking about. Don't you screw around with me, or I'll put a bullet in your stomach. I promise you I will."

Gwen stuttered at his threat, believing what the madman said, clutching her bag. "I don't. I don't know what you're asking. The destination of what?"

The cab driver broke in and told Gwen to give up whatever information the man wanted.

"Shut up and drive, or I'll put a bullet in the back of your head," the man snapped.

The driver looked straight ahead and pressed down on the gas petal as hard as he could. The cab accelerated as the two in the back seat continued disputing the answer to the man's question.

"Your next assignment? Where are you going? Tell me now!"

"My next assignment, what do you mean my next assignment?" Gwen's mind raced as she asked herself if he meant Germany. *That's curious,* she thought, as her attacker was Asian and he didn't sound German. *What interest does he have in Germany? What is he talking about? Is China involved?*

Gwen took a closer look at her assailant. The blood left her face as she remembered what Joe had told her only moments earlier about the stolen limo and Lyle, the missing chauffeur.

"Wait a minute," Gwen said to the man with the gun. "It's you. I recognize you now."

"Recognize what? Give me what I want, or I'll kill you."

"Did you kill Lyle? Did you hurt that poor kid? Tell me, damn it."

"Who the hell is Lyle? Do not change the subject on me."

"You were my limo driver this morning. You told me Lyle took the day off. You said he had something to do at five a.m. That car was stolen, and Lyle is missing. You monster! You killed him, didn't you?"

"Yes. I killed him," the man said with a sadistic grin. "He wouldn't give me the car so I could pick you up. He put up quite the struggle to save you. Are you satisfied? You're next if you don't give me what I want."

Gwen waited a moment to respond, swallowing the news that poor Lyle was dead. He only took the job to work his way through school, and because of her he was dead. Rage overtook her. She wanted to lash out and get even, but what could she do with a gun pushed into her stomach? As the cab approached Rockefeller Center, the vehicle suddenly shifted to the left. The driver jerked the wheel, reacting to a woman who had stepped out into traffic. Gwen and the man were thrown off balance, taken by surprise. Gwen seized the opportunity. She slammed the gunman in the chest with both feet, forcing his body to fall back against the door. She screamed to the driver to whip the car left again.

"Now, now hurry—turn left!"

The driver did as he was told. The man let off a bullet into the roof of the cab. With Gwen's added pressure against his body, he slammed against the door again. The man tried to regain balance and control of his weapon, one hand grabbing for Gwen's jacket and the other attempting to point the barrel of the gun in her direction. One more left turn was all it took. The door lock broke free, and the man tumbled backward head and shoulder first. Dropping his gun on the cab floor, he let out a horrible scream as his body hit the ground and continued to tumble through the crowded street.

Out the back window of the still-moving cab, Gwen saw her attacker roll down the busy rush-hour street. Other drivers were unable to avoid the man now lying in the road. Gwen gasped as a motorist with screeching tires rolled over his head, crushing his skull. Gwen threw her head down and pressed it into the cab seat, powerless to process the sight.

The cab driver hit the brakes with both feet, and the car swerved tail-first before it came to rest on a nearby sidewalk. Gwen flew forward from the impact and slammed into the front seat. The driver and Gwen looked at one another after the cab stopped. Both driver and occupant peered again through the rear window and viewed the gunman lying in the street with his head crushed, now unrecognizable. Gwen jumped out of the cab through the same door the man had fallen through a moment before and ran to her former attacker.

A crowd had formed around the dead man, and Gwen pushed her way through to the front lines. Gawking spectators tried to comfort the man driving the family car that struck the body.

"He came out of nowhere," the hysterical driver cried as he hovered over the dead man's body.

Men and women in the crowd put their arms around the crying man, repeating how they had seen the whole thing and it was not his fault.

"I think he fell from an open car door," one old woman said.

"No, he jumped into traffic. It was suicide," a younger man rebutted.

Police sirens wailed in the distance; witnesses had called the police. Gwen patted down the man and turned out his pockets. She wanted to know who he was and what he wanted. Passersby said nothing as she maneuvered from pocket to pocket. Finally, her search turned up a thumb drive taped to his stomach. Gwen ripped off the tape and placed the drive in her jacket pocket.

"That's her. Get her," two male voices shouted as she stood. Two other Asian men were forcing their way through the panicked crowd.

In a frenzy, Gwen threw her body into the pedestrians milling behind her and ran toward the cab. But the cab was gone, and so was her bag with the folder from Joe. The cabbie was nowhere to be found.

The men continued their pursuit. Gwen fled on foot toward Grand Central Station. Running past emergency vehicles responding to the accident, Gwen pushed her way through the crowds of people fleeing in the opposite direction. Gwen ran down several escalators and jumped the turnstile, hopping on the first train to stop at the station. The subway doors closed behind her before the men could reach her. She stood inside the car, facing her attackers through the unbreakable Plexiglas. The train pulled away from the platform while the men slammed fists on the windows, pleading for someone to let them on. This was New York City; once the train was in motion, it would continue.

Out of immediate danger, Gwen breathed a sigh of relief. She took a seat and leaned back, stretching her legs forward. Hands shaking, she attempted to make sense of the hijacking. She placed her hand inside her jacket pocket and pulled out the thumb drive. There were no identifying marks on it other than the digits 0822 engraved into one corner. Other than that, it was just a simple black rectangular thumb drive.

To Gwen's relief, the train was on its way to the Upper West Side. She remained on the subway until it reached a stop near her home. Keeping her head down and her coat collar up, she hoped to go unnoticed. Gwen left the stop and hurried toward her townhouse. With her heart pounding, she attempted to walk casually. Dodging cars and pedestrians, she hid behind each parked vehicle, ducking at the first sign of an Asian man, any Asian man, just in case.

After a few moments, Gwen approached the three-story brownstone townhouse she had renovated with her husband. Walking up the concrete stairs, she stopped as a wave of fear came over her. The luggage she left earlier in the back of the limo and had since forgotten about was waiting for her on the step.

She looked up and down the tree-lined street in a state of panic. Joe's words of a stolen limo came back, ringing loudly in her ears. She approached her bags with caution. She abruptly ripped open each bag. To her surprise, she found nothing extra enclosed and nothing disturbed. Everything was how she had packed it a day earlier. Her clothes and accessories were in perfect order. Removing the house key from her pocket, she entered her home, giving one last glance behind her. Seeing no one, she entered, dragged her bags inside, and locked the door, deadbolt too.

Gwen stood in the foyer of their home for a moment, collecting her thoughts. Sweat poured from her forehead. Finally, it hit her. *I was threatened by a man with a gun and chased home. What is going on?* She looked up the winding stairs of their home, listening for anything unusual, but detected nothing.

She and Joshua had remodeled the interior, and she completely redecorated it. They restored all the original woodwork and the hardwood floors to make their own personal sanctuary. The back of the house had large floor-to-ceiling windows that opened to a small, quaint backyard where Gwen had planted countless rose bushes. Even for their salaries, which were generous, the house was extravagant. Gwen never gave it much thought, since Joshua handled all their personal finances. She was never home long enough to open or pay a bill. She thought of their home as a haven where nobody could disturb her. It was the only such place in her life. Now she felt violated simply by a stranger leaving her luggage on the step. Somebody had been here, but whom? Just the dead Asian guy?

A faint noise in the kitchen caught her attention. Looking at her watch, she reminded herself Josh had not yet left for work. Trying to calm herself and steady her voice, Gwen called out, "Joshua, are you still home?" She hung up her jacket, kicked off her shoes, and headed for the kitchen.

"I'm in here," Joshua called back.

"Hi, honey." Gwen crossed the tile floor to her tall, handsome husband, who stood from the breakfast nook to greet her. She gave him a big kiss while they tightly embraced. He tasted like coffee.

"I'm glad you're still here." She leaned back to look into his pretty eyes, green behind his glasses. "By any chance did you see who delivered my luggage?"

"No, maybe it was dropped off while I was in the shower. I didn't hear anybody. By the way, what are you doing home so early? I thought you were out of town until Monday."

She narrowed her eyes and teased, "Sorry to disappoint you. Having the girlfriend over?"

Joshua laughed then stepped back from her, assessing her ragged condition. "What happened to your clothes? Your pants are torn, and you have dirt all over you."

Gwen looked down at her ruined suit. "I had a problem getting home, so I took the subway. I'll tell you about it after I take a shower and get some sleep. Joe called me back early. There was a sudden change in assignments, and I had to get back. But I'm leaving again tomorrow."

"What's going on?"

"Joe phoned me in Brussels and told me to come home right away and go straight to the newsroom. So I did."

"Called you back for what? Not that I'm complaining." He embraced her for another kiss.

"Guess where I'm going next?" She quirked her lips in a sarcastic smile.

"Where?"

"Germany."

Joshua loosened his grip around her waist and frowned. "Isn't that closer to Belgium than here? Why is he sending you back over?"

Exhausted, Gwen tried to bring her husband up to speed while her earlier incident took a back seat. "Some kind of student rallies against the current government."

Joshua always asked about her assignments but ten minutes later he couldn't remember a word of it; he seemed unusually attentive now. "There are problems within the German government, really? I haven't heard anything on the news."

"Well, Joe thinks we have the scoop on every other station, so he's sending me tomorrow."

"This sounds dangerous. Are you sure you want to go?"

"Oh, it's not dangerous. It's just some students organizing a protest. Kids do it here all the time, haven't you heard? At least tear gas doesn't kill." She said, making herself a cup of chamomile tea.

"Why are they protesting? What are they against?"

"They think the government is corrupt, hoarding tax money for themselves, and forcing people out of work. At least that's what I know from Joe. I'll find out more when I get there."

Gwen sat down at the kitchen table with her tea as the telephone rang. "Would you get it?"

Joshua answered the telephone and handed the receiver to Gwen.

"Hello?"

"Somebody saw you on the street with a dead guy after you left the office," Joe said. "What happened? Are you okay?"

"Yes, I'm fine. I was just going to call you." She glanced at her suspicious-looking mate. "The Asian guy who said he was replacing Lyle for the day, remember the guy I told you about who picked me up in the limo this morning at the airport?"

"Yes, I remember."

"Well, he hopped into the back of my cab when I was leaving the station."

"Oh shit. How do you know it was him?" Joe asked.

"I recognized him for the car ride this morning. I told him so—and, Joe, he said he killed Lyle. He said he killed Lyle to get the limo."

"I'll call the police right away. But you stay put. Do you understand?"

"Yes. But I'm fine."

"Why did he get into your cab?"

"He was demanding something."

"What?"

"I don't know exactly; it definitely wasn't money. He said he wanted to know about my next assignment. Then, before I knew it, he fell out and tumbled down the street and got run over by another driver."

"Maybe you shouldn't go tomorrow," Joe said.

"Why? What has any of this got to do with my story? I'm fine, just shaken up that's all. I lost the file you gave me with the background articles on the German protests. The cab I was in took off with my folder still in the back seat. But I'll go to the library and see if I can get some information. I'll talk to you tomorrow." Gwen abruptly hung up the telephone.

Joshua stood with both hands on his hips, staring at her. "Someone tried to mug you this morning for something other than money?" He shook his head at her cavalier description of the incident.

"It appears that way, but I have no idea what he wanted. He was so vague. He acted like I was supposed to know what in the hell he was talking about. I was more concerned about Lyle. I'll phone Joe later and hear what the police think. I'll tell you in more detail later tonight. I've got to get some rest, or I'm going to crack up." Gwen headed up the stairs with tea in hand.

Could this attack on Gwen be random? Joshua wondered. The chance encounter seemed too remote. The telephone rang again. Joshua answered it. He didn't recognize the voice of the man on the other end.

"Your wife should not go to Germany. The climate is very dangerous there this time of year."

"Yes, I know," Joshua said in a solemn voice. "But my hands may be tied."

"Just ask Frank Solas." The man hung up.

Joshua's fear blossomed full-force. *Not Gwen, not Germany, not now.* He wildly shook his head.

"I'm getting into the shower," Gwen shouted from upstairs, breaking Joshua's thought train.

He ran up the stairs to give his wife a kiss goodbye. "I'll see you tonight." He pressed his body to hers, aware of what he could lose and wanting to keep her safe.

"I'll look forward to it." She giggled and reached to fondle him.

"I've got to get to the office now." Joshua danced away, ran downstairs, grabbed his briefcase and hurried out the front door without his jacket.

SYLVIA OPENED HER DESK DRAWER and grabbed her purse to go to the lobby to meet Michelle for lunch. Before leaving, she made a stop in Henderson's office. She entered his office without knocking. Standing before his desk, she found her boss gazing out his picture window that provided the most beautiful view of Manhattan.

Without shifting his eyes from the view, he said, "Thanks, Sylvia, in case I forget to tell you later."

"No problem," Sylvia told her supervisor. She turned to leave but hesitated. She turned back and slowly closed the door behind her.

Mr. Henderson shifted his head and curiously looked at her, then quickly turned back to his view. "Yes?"

Sylvia had always been faithful to Henderson. She was a simple woman who did as she was asked. It was out of the ordinary for her to question instructions or ask for clarification or reasoning for anything. But she had to know why he entertained this subterfuge.

"Mr. Henderson, it's none of my business, sir, but you are the president of this network. Why don't you just call Joe yourself and ask what his plans are for Gwen? As the president, you have every right to know about anything going on in this building."

The whole request by Mr. Henderson and his reasoning was strange. She didn't know what he was getting her into, but with his recent late nights and secretive phone calls, something was going on. But what? What could this blunt, cut-the-crap kind of guy be hiding? She wanted an explanation so badly, even if it was simple or stupid. She just wanted something.

Again, without leaving his view, Henderson told his long-time assistant, "It's not that simple. I can't explain it now, but find out what you can from Michelle, please."

Sylvia nodded and left.

She frowned. Charles looked strange, almost frightened. She had never seen him that way before. His behavior over the last couple of days had become so mysterious she would call it peculiar. The way he stood gazing out the window was strangely calm, when normally he'd be irate. He had also been vague, when for as long as Sylvia had known him he had been direct. He never spared a feeling. Sylvia would do her part, however small, to help him out.

Sylvia and Michelle usually met on the ground floor in front of the elevator doors when they made lunch appointments. The elevator dropped Sylvia off first. She waited for five minutes with both eyes trained on the elevator while Michelle wrapped up business on thirty.

The descending elevator stopped on every floor. Five ... four ... three ... two ... then the doors opened and unleashed a crowd into the lobby. Michelle was the last to exit.

"Here I am," Michelle said as she approached, bright-eyed. "Have you been waiting long?"

"Not long, just a minute." Sylvia smiled.

Time was short, and they both needed to stay close to the office. Sylvia clutched her purse as they got onto the escalator heading down to the cafeteria in the basement of their office building. Sylvia had an odd feeling; however, she was unable to put her finger on it.

Sylvia and Michelle got in the employee's express line, which they considered one of the nicest features their company had to offer. They purchased coffee and a couple of sandwiches. Sylvia chose a table far off in the corner, away from noise and foot traffic.

To Sylvia's surprise, Michelle brought up the perfect topic.

"So how are things in the ivory tower?" Michelle asked.

Sylvia laughed, her mood becoming lighter. "Oh, fine. It's the same as usual. Never enough time in the day to do everything."

"How are the ratings?"

Sylvia's face lit up. "Really good. We owe that to Gwen. Her investigative news stories are terrific. It seems more than fifty percent of the population tune in for just her alone."

"She's good at what she does," Michelle agreed.

"What's she up to next?"

"Next?" Michelle said rhetorically. "She just got back from Belgium."

"She did?" Sylvia raised her eyebrows, surprised. "I thought she wasn't supposed to come back until Monday?"

"You sound puzzled. Her schedule changes suddenly all the time. Nothing strange."

"Why did she come back so soon?"

Gwen became the sole topic of conversation. Michelle explained to Sylvia the erratic change in Gwen's schedule. Without any suspicion, Michelle unloaded the information known on Gwen's brewing story in Germany. Sylvia listened to every word, taking mental notes.

ACROSS THE LOBBY, hidden behind an open *New York Times*, a man had also waited for Michelle to meet with Sylvia. Both women remained unaware of the CIA agent keeping a safe distance as he casually hopped on the escalator behind them. While the two women sat in the corner, talking, they remained completely unaware they were partaking in a three-party conversation, watched by casual eyes from across the room. With a special unidirectional microphone pointed at the women underneath his table, he picked up every word of what Michelle knew and didn't know. If the company couldn't get everything it needed now, then Gwen's telephone, her family, friends, coworkers and acquaintances would also be tapped until the company could pinpoint Gwen's whereabouts. Gwen would eventually notify somebody. While the women finished their lunch, the wide-eyed American also ate, watched, listened, and waited.

THE PHONE RANG upstairs in Henderson's office. Henderson eagerly answered, hoping to hear from Sylvia.

"Hello?" Henderson clutched the phone with a sweaty palm.

"So, what's her assignment?" a man asked on the other end.

Henderson knew immediately who it was. He and Congressman David A. Becker had spoken many times before.

"I'm working on it." Henderson swallowed. "I need time."

"How are you working on it?"

"That's not important. You'll have your information shortly," Henderson said in a less patient tone. "I don't have a bunch of bootlickers working for me like you do. These things take time."

On the other end of the line, Becker laughed. "No, no you don't. Call me when you get the agenda, okay?"

"As soon as I get it, you'll get it."

"Look, Charles, let me remind you, in case you'd forgotten how important this is. My ass depends on you. As crazy as it sounds, it does. I sit on the same committee as Congressman Frank Solas did. Do you think his death was an accident? Do you?"

"No sir, no I don't. But it has so little to do with me. I give you the information on Gwen, you renew the FCC license, and we never speak again. And I'll take care of that other matter, too."

"Never speak again? This situation isn't that easy. You should hope I don't threaten to kill you again."

HENDERSON WAS PLEASED with Sylvia's report. The story she described sounded routine, but Joe's secrecy and Gwen's travel plans didn't. The question continued to lurk in Henderson's mind that if Gwen was simply covering a story on the dwindling German economy, then why would Joe keep it under such tight wraps? That was a question he wanted answered, but Joe would never tell him. Henderson had people in Washington he needed to answer to. He may be president of the NIN network, but he was hardly in charge. To maintain his position, he needed to keep his "friends" informed.

As planned, Henderson called Congressman Becker, who was satisfied they received positive news. Details of the impending story were sketchy at best, but the involved government officials now had a crude outline of what was on the reporter's agenda. Henderson's money would be wired.

In an unscheduled midafternoon meeting, certain men each with specific interests came together in Washington D.C. in a closed-off room below ground located at the end of a long, dark corridor far from any prying eyes and ears. The walls were made of solid steel and concrete two feet thick. Rooms like this were built for meetings of secrecy such as this one. Only a select few in the capital knew rooms like this even existed.

The men flowed down the hallway into the private room single file. Wingtips followed combat boots as they took their usual positions around the circular conference table. A single, dim bulb hung from the low ceiling, swinging slightly as each man made his entrance. After the three guests sat, the master of ceremony rose from his seat and closed the steel door until the lock bolted with a distinctive *clink*. The lock activated the room's built-in alarm system that would begin a chain of events, should anyone try to enter. The lock further triggered the bulb to brighten and a humming noise that jammed any suspected recording devices. These devices were often brought in "accidentally."

"It's not as bad as I thought," Becker announced to the select few gathered around the circular table in the tiny conference room. Becker was comfortable with the information he obtained from Henderson, since he was all too familiar with the economic status of Germany. He helped bring the two sides together with the aid of Solas.

"Well? How bad is it then? What do you know definitely?" asked four-star General William Jones. Jones, a seasoned military leader, was known for his sharp strategy against enemies in the Middle East and here at home. He was the one man who could, but would never, intelligently answer questions about production of toxic gases and biological weapons. The aging general was closing in on retirement, and he knew better than anyone the future that awaited him as a retired United States veteran, so it was time to cash in or be left out. Jones had big plans.

"Not bad at all, from what I understand from Gwen's boss, Charles Henderson."

"Then what's the news? What in the hell is that girl up to now?" the impatient general asked the congressman.

"Henderson telephoned me a few minutes earlier and told me Gwen is in fact flying into Berlin tomorrow. She is working on a story about the country's economic crisis arising since Josef Jakob took office."

"Damn it." The general slammed his fist down on the table, forcing one water glass to tip onto its side. "If she finds out anything, we're all screwed. How did she get assigned this story, anyway?"

"We don't know, but let's wait a minute and think about this, okay?" said Victor Travis, the third member of the elite group, who was unusually calm. Travis, a seasoned weapons designer for the government, was helped into the underground sales department of arming nations by his old college friend Becker. "Let's hear the rest of what Becker has to say."

Becker told the men what he had learned from Henderson. "When she arrives, she'll be talking with economic leaders in the country who have experience dealing with financial problems, and she'll also be speaking with the student leaders heading the upcoming rally later this week. As far as we know now, nothing will compromise our plan. The economists will tell her what's already been all over the news. They know nothing about our group or our ultimate goal. Student leaders know even less. So don't worry."

"I'd feel better if we could control her and who she talks to," the general said.

"Sure, so would I, but she's not on the list of journalists who are compromised. She's a wild card," Becker said. "The only in we have with her is her immediate boss, Joseph Bess. He was a great friend of Frank Solas' and he respected him. Of course, he didn't know Frank was on the take, so we have that to our advantage. But if we can convince Joe to get Gwen off the story, we may be able to circumvent the entire situation."

"How do you plan on doing that?" asked Travis.

"Send someone to talk to him, one of our guys. I think it would need to be direct, in the form of a threat. Anything less would be transparent and dismissed by someone of his experience. Believe it or not, people like Joe are used to being threatened in that business," Becker said. "We could also talk to Henderson again, but even as network president, he doesn't have the tight hold over reporters you would think a president should have."

The general jabbed a stiff finger at the table. "But if she finds out why the country's economic finances are failing, we'll be exposed."

"No one in the country other than those involved know how the money is being diverted and where it's going," said Martin Strauss with his heavy German accent. "I don't suspect anybody in Germany could tell her anything that would lead to anyone in this room."

"How do you know? How can all of you be so sure?" asked the general. "Reporters have a way of digging and people have a way of slipping."

"No one in my homeland will slip. That I can promise you! If anyone does come close, they will join Solas."

"You did kill Solas then?" Becker asked. "It was your men? It was your doing?

Look, I want minimal body count here. You can't run around killing public officials without any warning and without a damn good reason. You had no idea any of that tax shit would get back to us. I've known that man for nearly twenty years."

"Casualty of war," the general broke in with a cold voice.

The four men looked at one another as the tension built in the room.

"Okay, gentlemen, this has gone far enough. Martin's men will not slip, and neither will yours, General. We've installed provisions here in the government to watch over the media. I believe our asses are well covered. So, relax," Becker told the group.

"One last option is you," the general said to Travis.

"Me? What do you mean? I just design your merchandise."

"Speaking of merchandise, where is my father's cargo?" Martin interjected.

"How in the hell should I know?" Travis snapped.

"I know where it is," Becker said. "Well, most of it anyway. The missiles and semi-automatic weapons are on their way by ship to a German port outside Lubeck. They will enter your country through the North Sea. They should be there in a couple of days, so alert Schmidt. Solas called me from his car while he was on his way back to Washington from the dock and told me the transaction was complete. However, the blueprints were given to Chen, who is now dead. He was killed when he fell out of a cab this morning in New York City."

"Dead? What do you mean dead? He had the only hard copy of the blueprints my father needs as soon as possible. Those were the blueprints designed by your man, Travis." Martin sounded more disgruntled with the way procedures were being handled. "You Americans, everything is always done half-ass!"

"Maybe not much longer," Jones said in an easy tone to Martin.

"So, you will run then?" Martin asked Jones.

The other three men looked at Jones with expectation.

"I have put together an exploratory committee. We'll see," Jones said. "But if I do run, I'll need money and lots of it."

Jones looked at Martin and heard what he expected.

"I will speak to my father," Martin said. "With you in the White House, that would make life easier for us all. But that is for later."

Martin turned his attention back to Becker. "Now what happened to Chen and the blueprints?"

"Apparently, he was trying to extract information from Gwen at gunpoint when he fell out of a moving vehicle and was hit by oncoming rush-hour traffic. This is why we can't always take the most direct route," Becker said. "Anyway, Chen had the blueprints in his possession at the time of his death, we believe. However, we can't be sure of that. Nothing was recovered from the scene of the accident."

"Oh shit. What about the blueprints? We need those for our own men. What now?" the German demanded.

"We'll get copies. Right, Travis?" Becker looked at Travis.

"Copies are not a problem. I'll get those tomorrow. I'll be in my New York office. Call me and we'll meet."

"I can meet you in New York in a couple of days. I have other business there," Martin said.

The two nodded in agreement they would meet when Martin called, at a location yet to be decided.

The general, eager to rectify the Gwen problem, jumped back into the conversation. "Good, we have that settled. But still, what do we do about Gwen? I think Travis should talk to her husband. Joshua is your employee and your friend, plus he's neck-deep in this shit. Tell him to get his wife off it, to use his influence and keep her home. How he does it I don't care, but to do it now."

"Look, Josh just designs the weapons you sell," Travis told the group. "He knows what he needs to know to get the job done, but that's it. If I start making demands on him that I can't back up with reason, he's going to start asking questions, too. I think it's best if we leave him out of this as much as possible because ultimately, without him our plans are moot. He's the only one I have on staff with the sophistication necessary to design these gadgets."

"You must have some hold over him. There must be some way you could convince him to help us," Becker said calmly.

"I don't know. Let me see what I can do. But don't count on it as a sure thing. I think we'll have better luck with Bess and Henderson."

"Fine. I don't care who the two of you try, but try somebody. I don't want to answer any more questions before congressional committees. I'm through with all that shit. Do all of you understand me?" the general shouted. He tugged his jacket straight then reverted to a civil tone. "If you need any military aid, call me."

"I'm glad you said that, because I do have one last idea, strictly as a precaution," Becker said.

The three men rose in their chairs and listened attentively to the congressman who held the key to their rising problem.

"General, I want you to use your friendships over at the CIA. Ask for a tail to be placed on Gwen wherever she goes, here in New York and over in Germany. Tell them to send someone from the private company who is already knowledgeable about the situation but won't ask too many questions. Instruct the agent that if Gwen at any time gets too close, they should remove her from the equation."

"Kill her? Are you crazy?" Travis stood. "That would bring more trouble and more questions. She is one of the most beloved reporters in this country. Nobody in the business would bury her one foot in the ground without a detailed inquiry into the circumstances surrounding her death. Nobody!"

"We may not have a choice. Let's wait and see. In the end, she determines her own fate. Let's hope for her sake this time she doesn't live up to her reputation," Becker said.

"How about you? Can you follow her over tomorrow?" Becker asked Martin.

"No. I'm on other business for my father. I'll be in the country for several days."

"Is it regarding that other matter? That search he asked me to help him with?" Becker asked.

"Ja. Schmidt has been searching records and looking for that woman for a long time. He has reason to believe she may have left Germany and moved to the United States shortly after she and my father split up more than thirty years ago. I have come personally to check it out so my father and Schmidt can concentrate on our mission. So I will stay and look here. I have places to check."

"Good. If you need help with that, let me know."

"Okay, are we in agreement on the plan? Do we all know what to do?" Becker asked the group.

A nervous Travis shook his head but agreed with his co-conspirators, for he had no choice.

"I'll see what I can do about getting a tail. Let me make a few calls, and I'll get back to you," the general said.

"Do it tonight, because she's leaving first thing in the morning. I want an agent in place before she leaves the airport."

With a simple nod, the four men made their unanimous decision.

10

"**WHAT DO WE WANT?**" the instigator of the crowd shouted through the bullhorn. "What do we want?"

"We want jobs!" the group of more than one thousand screamed back in unison.

The howling crowd of men and women was filled with youthful but distraught faces. Students nearing graduation and those already finished came to Berlin from their homes and universities throughout the country. They gathered as one on the steps of the reinstated capitol building, shouting slogans and singing songs to protest the country's dwindling economy. The crowd continued marching toward city hall, or *Rathaus*, in German. They marched up Martin Luther Strasse right to the front steps of Berlin's city hall. The tightly packed students continued to come, overflowing onto nearby Grunewald Strasse. Still the bodies grew in number. Students who wore T-shirts with abrasive language touted signs and banners calling for the resignation of Chancellor Josef Jakob.

"What do we want?" Heinrich Jakob, the son of the chancellor and the leader of the group, continued to shout repeatedly while standing on top of a fruit truck pulled onto steps of the capitol building by the angry mass.

"*Arbeit*," the crowd shouted in one voice. "We want jobs," was the only demand he received from the angry mob.

Business owners along the street closed their doors and secured their windows, in fear of looting. Cages rolled down from the store roofs created a barrier between themselves, their stores, and the growing crowd. Some business owners closed their shops to join the incensed group, equally dissatisfied with the government's strategy. Students jumped onto car hoods, following the lead of one. Trees lining the streets became ladders for those who wanted a better view into the windows of what had become the Parliament members' safehouse. Members of the mob climbed like chimps onto the windowsills of buildings as others beat garbage can lids together and blew horns and whistles to draw the attention of their leaders.

Business owners armed with rotting fruit from their stands chanted lyrics of their own, calling for tax breaks so they could hire employees and run their companies. Owners cried they had not seen a penny's worth of profit for ages. They too were hungry. Students grabbed and called for the baskets of fruit, which they quickly passed through the crowd. Apples, peaches, and oranges littered the street in a frenzy of color that stank. The building withstood the beating from the crowd, but the windows suffered when the fruit flew through the glass like rocks.

"Eat that—that's what we're eating!" one member of the crowd screamed as he stood in his ripped and haggard clothing. "We're rotting out here. You cannot ignore us any longer."

The fruit continued to fly, beating on the building's walls as well as raining on members of the crowd. The Parliament was in session, and the country's elders sat inside the building. With the backdrop of hysteria, they were unable to conduct a moment of business. The Parliament fled to an adjacent room to avoid the flying objects heaved through their windows. The elected officials could clearly hear the chanting through the broken windows, and they listened as the crowd grew in size and intensity minute by minute. Several officials became nervous and restless as the shrieking grew louder and the threat of beatings became apparent for anyone who dared to step outside.

"Come out here and face us! What are you doing with our money? Where are our jobs?" one voice shouted, audible above the rest.

A brick crashed through the window at the hand of one disgruntled graduate student unable to locate a job after securing two degrees from a major university. Students throughout the country from every school participated in the organized march. Determined participants traveling through the night to get there. One elder minister dressed in ancient garb dared to rise and pick up the brick lying on the floor near his seat in the room with the stunned government officials. From the brick, he removed a note that was secured with a rubber band.

The noted read, "Face us like men." The minister from the Bavarian region read the note out loud to the rest of the Parliament, who were now truly afraid.

"What do we tell them?" one minister asked the *Parlamentspräsident*, the President of the Parliament, Hans Gerfurt, who sat on a high podium before the group.

"I don't know myself," said the middle-aged Gerfurt, who sat shaking his head, unable to think of a rational explanation to satisfy the irate crowd. "Does anyone have an answer for them? Anyone?"

The ministers sat and turned to one another, looking for anyone who might be able to provide a reasonable answer. But no one stood.

"The tax money that was collected is being disseminated, but where?" Gerfurt asked. "This office has collected billions of dollars in tax money during the previous few years, and for some reason, we have nothing to show for it. The tax rate has soared since the arrival of the new Chancellor Josef Jakob. This is the highest I think it's ever been. Businesses are closing because the owners are unable to meet their tax bills. People are losing their jobs and social programs are in the toilet. There is not a nickel to be had."

"But it is us. We have approved these tax hikes," another Parliament member shouted. "It was at the request of our military leaders, remember? It was said we needed to strengthen and arm our country against possible aggressors. Those who were unhappy with the unification. It was also for the higher cost of government services. Doesn't anyone remember?"

A roar came over the room as the government representatives argued among themselves about who was to blame for this economic outrage.

"I say we contact Peter Schmidt and ask him what in the hell is going on here. We must also appeal to Chancellor Jakob. We will ask them both to come here and clarify the county's situation," Gerfurt said. "We need answers right away."

The representatives largely agreed with the *Parlamentspräsident*, all nodding to command the appearance of the chancellor and his military aides.

"But what do we do about that crowd?" a scared Parliament member asked. "I am not ashamed to say they frighten me. They sound crazed."

"I will address the crowd that has gathered outside," Gerfurt announced to his government. "I am the *Parlamentspräsident,* and it is my responsibility."

The other members were all too happy to let Gerfurt take the verbal whipping waiting outside. Gerfurt hesitantly rose from his seat high above the group and moved slowly toward the door. Screams of defiance came from outside as he moved through the doorway and toward the main floor.

"I am going to call the *Polizei,*" one member said after his leader left the room.

Gerfurt ordered the security guard to unlock and open the French doors of the Parliament's headquarters.

"Are you sure you would like to go out there, *Herr Präsident?*"

"*Ja.* I am certain. I must address and disseminate this crowd before someone gets hurt."

"*Ja, Herr Präsident.*"

The guard unlocked the doors and removed the reinforced steel chain he had placed earlier on the exit bars. The guard took the chain and moved back, holding one door open for the *Parlamentspräsident.* The crowd screamed at the *Parlamentspräsident* about money and work as he walked toward the edge of the steps. Few members of the mob moved back to clear a pathway for the Parliament leader.

"Please, please be silent. I have something to say to all of you."

After several minutes of insults and accusations, the volume of the crowd's roar lowered.

"I have something I want to tell all of you who will listen." Gerfurt extended his arms up and outward.

The man with the bullhorn called out to his fellow students to be silent and listen to what the *Parlamentspräsident* had to say. A hush fell over the crowd as all eyes trained on Gerfurt. The *Parlamentspräsident* became anxious as he looked into the eyes of the desperate students and business owners. Their stares were sadistic and scary.

"We have discussed the problems our *Deutschland* is facing. The Parliament feels your pain. However, we have no answers for you yet."

The crowd roared for the *Parlamentspräsident* to step down.

"Thief!" a member of the crowd shouted.

Gerfurt screamed back to the crowd, but his voice went unheard by the demonstrators. Gerfurt threw his arms back into the air, silently asking for consideration while he tried to address the crowd.

"We absolutely recognize the problem," Gerfurt shouted. "We do. We are commanding the presence of our superiors to answer for this turmoil. We do not understand it either. But we will try our very best to repair the damage. That I promise all of you."

The crowd became enraged at the lack of knowledge possessed by the newly elected *Parlamentspräsident*. Students pressed toward Gerfurt, shouting lewd and obscene comments about his lack of understanding of the country's economic crisis.

"So, what do you suppose we do? Stand here and starve?" one young man shouted at the *Parlamentspräsident*.

"I don't know what to tell you except to wait until we all hear from Chancellor Jakob."

Heinrich Jakob shouted through the bullhorn for calm among the group. Instead, rage grew among the students, who turned a deaf ear to young Jakob, whom they felt no longer represented their wishes.

The tall blond man with brown circular glasses moved toward the *Parlamentspräsident* in a defiant manner. "Your answers are not good enough. Do you know how long I spent in school and now I cannot find a job? I have nothing to speak of. It is your fault. Yours," the man said as he pointed his finger into the face of the *Parlamentspräsident*.

"It is not my fault, young man. You are responsible for your own destiny."

The mob rushed the steps of the *Rathaus*, crowding one another to reach the *Parlamentspräsident*. Every member of the group wanted to tell their tale of hardship endured since his government's arrival into office.

A man quickly cut through the crowd, pushing protesters to the right and left. Students fell to the ground as the man shoved each person to get near the *Parlamentspräsident*. With his right hand extended, he wedged through the air-tight cluster. He maneuvered his left hand into his back pocket for an unknown object. No one in the crowd saw him pull the blade from his back pocket before he drew it into the air and forced it into Gerfurt's throat. Gerfurt lost his balance and fell forward toward the young man with the knife.

"You are no *Parlamentspräsident*, sir, and you are no leader. You will lie no longer," the young man whispered into Gerfurt's ear before he pulled the knife hard across the man's throat and caused a large laceration. Blood showered members of the crowd from the gash. Gerfurt's blood streamed down his body, covering his clothes and forming a pool around their feet. Droplets showered the nearby members of the group as Gerfurt clutched his neck with both hands, forcing blood to flow upward toward his face. The *Parlamentspräsident*, who could no longer call for help, fell to his knees and then to his chest. Lying face-down in a pool of blood, the *Parlamentspräsident* was now unable to take a simple breath. The elder statesman fell unconscious as the madman looked down on the body of his elected official.

Police sirens howled in the distance as the man lay dying on the steps of the capitol. The crowd panicked at the murder they witnessed. As the sirens drew closer, alarmed students raced in every direction through the streets to avoid the police, who would soon take whatever prisoners were available to account for the murder of a high-ranking government official. Young people scaled the walls of nearby Tierpark Zoo to hide from the approaching officials. Members of the crowd were pushed and fell to the ground as their fellow students, fearing for their own safety, trampled their fallen comrades.

After moments of hysteria, police arrived on the scene, but no other person was present. Remaining Parliament officials were found unharmed, barricaded in their building. The only evidence of a violent protest was the bodies of youth lying trampled in the streets. Police lined the area with yellow tape and called supervisors.

Shortly, police discovered the corpse of Gerfurt, and the tone of the investigation changed.

11

AFTER COUNTLESS PHONE CALLS, General William Jones finally got the man he was looking for. The order came directly to the masked building in Manhattan.

"Looks like they've got plans for you," Alex said to his partner Carter.

"What do you mean?" Carter asked as he picked up his ringing telephone.

The agent listened as his superior in Langley said a few simple words, then Carter immediately picked up his jacket and headed out the door.

"What have they got you doing?" Alex asked.

"They told me top secret. But I'll call you for a beer when I get back in town."

"Will do. See you then," Alex delivered a formal salute to his coworker and friend.

Alex replaced his headset and continued monitoring telephone lines.

FOLLOWING A SHORT yet much-deserved and needed snooze, Gwen pieced her day together. *First things first,* she thought, beginning the necessary research for her upcoming story. After several phone calls to various taxi companies, the effort to retrieve her file of German clips proved fruitless.

"There's no driver here who even fits that description," one dispatcher told her. Gwen called the telephone directory information line and tried to locate the company's number that way. She gave the operator the name of the company she thought she recalled, "Go Taxi."

"We have no listing for that name," the operator told her. "We don't have a listing for anything close to that. Sorry."

Gwen sat in stupefaction, questioning what she had seen only hours earlier. *Go Taxi,* she thought. *I know what I saw.* Unable to shake the feeling something else was wrong, Gwen made a note of the company name in her planner to investigate it further after she returned from her next trip.

"I don't have time for this now. This is the day from hell," she said out loud.

With no other avenues open, Gwen headed off to the library to find and photocopy as much background information on German economics as was available.

Gwen kept the librarian busy seeking hard newspaper clips. The woman searched to the extreme, with articles filed away deep, on microfilm. While the librarian toiled to assist her favorite journalist the old-fashioned way, Gwen moved to more sophisticated technology. In moments, Gwen obtained the most recent reports of economic and financial news off the internet. And, while she continued to wait for the elderly woman, Gwen poked around the information superhighway, searching a broader topic.

What is generally brewing overseas? Gwen searched.

The first screen she pulled up on the computer hit her hard. With her mouth wide open, she read the article beneath the forty-eight-point headline, "Massacre on the Capitol Steps." The headline was clear, but the icon continued twirling as the computer pulled up more and more information. It took the age-old system a full minute to etch out the photograph taken of the Berlin capital steps with a mountain of bodies lying mangled and bloody. Aided by the photograph, Gwen got a detailed picture of the economic situation and the mood of the country. The article read:

Sixteen people were reported dead by police after a massive student uprising took center stage on the Parliament steps this afternoon. Parlamentspräsident Hans Gerfurt is confirmed dead, and police are handling his death as a homicide. He was found lying on the steps with his throat slit in a pool of blood. Police are seeking suspects in the investigation. According to sources, students overran the Parliament building, chanting slogans of protest against the dwindling economy and the downswing in the standard of living. Angry protesters called for the Parlamentspräsident to answer questions. Moments after he emerged from the building, an unknown assailant wielding a knife approached him and cut his throat. Sources report the offender whispered a message in the dead man's ear. However, nearby protesters were unable to hear the words or give significant identifying information about the suspect. Today's uprising is a backlash from years of financial browbeating taken by students and taxpayers ...

"Oh shit," Gwen said to herself. "What in the hell is this?"

As the icon continued to swirl, Gwen got a first peek at the front page. The journalist who wrote the story spared no detail in the article. The paper wove a tale of horror from the Parliament members' points of view. It quickly became apparent to Gwen that this protest, which she had missed, had everything to do with economic matters. Young people overseas were so enraged that one of them slit the throat of a high-ranking official in full view of other protesters.

The elderly, gray-haired librarian, slim spectacles hanging gently from the tip of her nose, returned with a triumphant smile and a high stack of newspaper clippings that needed the support of both of her arms. The tall stack fell back against her chest as she tried to manage the pile, then she leaned forward, and the mound collapsed on the table in front of Gwen.

Gwen finished reading the horrific story of murder and the vehemence of the German people while the librarian sorted the articles according to specific economic crises.

"Do you know which year the economic crisis happened that you're looking for?"

Receiving no response from Gwen, the woman leaned forward and placed her hand on Gwen's forearm. "Honey, are you okay?"

Gwen continued to sit stunned, but only for a moment. "Yes. Thank you. I'm fine." She tried to crack a smile.

"Did you find what you needed on the computer? Those things confuse me in the worst way."

"Exactly what I need, and more than I bargained to find," Gwen said in a soft voice.

"Is that good or bad, dear?"

"Good, I guess. I didn't realize times in Germany have turned so, so violent. My goodness, people are killing each other over jobs. It's incredible."

"No. It's not that incredible."

"What do you mean?"

The librarian sank into a seat facing Gwen. She leaned in close to the reporter, took a deep breath, and removed her glasses from her face, letting them hang loosely around her neck.

"Gwen, dear, you shouldn't be amazed by what people are willing to kill and die for. It's difficult for many Americans to understand the reasons. Young people today have never had to face the hard times that people all over the world face every day. We have everything in abundance here. There's plenty of food to go around and a pretty good supply of jobs for those who are interested. Okay, maybe everybody doesn't make the salary of a doctor, but people can get jobs that pay enough so they can eat. Others around the world don't even have that. Even minimum-wage jobs are hard to come by in some countries. If you make four dollars an hour in Russia, you're envied. You're living high on the hog. But I know it's easy for you and others like you to lose sight of that. Could you image spending four or six years in college and then going hungry because you couldn't find a job? I know it's hard to imagine, but it happens to decent hardworking people every day. I know it's hard to grasp. I moved here forty years ago from Russia because of it. And I have a degree in business. I weighed eighty pounds when I arrived in this county." The woman pointed her finger respectfully toward Gwen. "I had nothing when I came to this country. I spent my entire life working, preparing myself. And I still had nothing.

"For people to riot doesn't surprise me. Frankly, I don't blame them. Protests and death may not be the best means to an end, but it will get you there faster than talking, that I promise you. Many times, the government is to blame. Politicians are too often corrupt, and they're not doing what they're supposed to do on behalf of their constituents. When you go to Germany and talk to those people, you must remember how desperate they are. They have families to feed, too." She pressed her fist into her chest. "The world does not end at the American border. I love this country, yes. But I did not forget where I came from. The television news brings you many pictures from around the world. Every night we turn on the news and see about people fleeing here and there, starving, and being exterminated in Eastern Bloc nations. But how often do you consider the victims you see as real people with feelings? Everyone here is so immune to it. Television news is more like entertainment and less like actual news. When you go, be prepared to understand and empathize as well as listening and taking notes for your story. These are people's lives, they're not just a story."

Gwen absorbed every passionate word. Then she tilted her head. "I know what you're talking about. And yes, it is easy to lose sight of the people involved. But every day I cover something horrible. There's a bombing here and a war over there, and it's hard to wear feelings on your sleeve. If I did that, I would never get anything done." Gwen tried to rationalize her cavalier American attitude to the woman who was now so much more than a librarian. "But I do understand what you're trying to say, and I do appreciate it. Thanks."

The old woman smiled. "Here are the newspaper clippings you asked for. Go through them and leave what you don't need, and I'll put them away. Copy the ones you want, but just return the originals to the front desk before you leave the library. Okay?"

"Yes. That's great. I appreciate your help."

The old woman left Gwen alone with mounds of work to do. Gwen sorted through the painstakingly detailed stories and chose the ones that included credible and reliable sources. These were people she could contact in Germany after she arrived. She made copies, organized a thin folder, returned the originals, and packed her bag to head home.

ARRIVING HOME EARLY, Gwen decided to surprise Josh with a quiet dinner. She ordered takeout from their favorite Thai restaurant.

"Two orders of shrimp pad thai," she told the heavily accented clerk at the other end of the line. "Delivery, please."

After giving the woman her address, she hung up and moved into the kitchen to prepare two places at the table. From behind a mound of clutter in one of the lower cabinets, she pulled out an old bottle of vintage wine she had been saving for a special occasion. *I'm alive,* she thought. *What could be a better reason than that?*

Joshua called out to her from the living room. "Honey, I'm home."

You couldn't have come at a better time, Gwen thought. She turned to go greet him in the living room, but he met her at the kitchen door.

"You must have run the whole way." She stepped in close and looped her arms around his neck.

"I just wanted to see my favorite girl." He pressed his lips to hers.

Gwen closed her eyes and breathed in his familiar, comforting scent. A quiver of fear from her adventure tightened her stomach. Entwined as one, they moved back into the kitchen.

"I ordered dinner from that Thai place. It should be here any minute."

"That sounds great."

"I thought a romantic dinner before I leave again would be nice."

"Speaking of leaving, how long are you going for?"

"I don't know. I'm expecting it to be for only a few days, but it might be extended to as long as a week." She shrugged. "I'm not sure."

"I'm worried about you, and I don't think you should go."

Gwen stepped back and gave him a stern look. "What is wrong with everybody lately? I'll be fine. I've been all over the damn world. I've been through very hostile territories, and I lived to tell. I even went to the frontlines and reported live from Afghanistan. Why is everybody on my back lately? This seems simple compared to those stories."

"I'm sorry. I'm sorry." Josh rested his hands on her shoulders. "It's just that a guy I know from one of the German companies we do business with said there was a terrible protest in Berlin today and people were found trampled to death, and someone was murdered. I know that's the topic of your interview, these protests. You told me this morning."

"Oh, right. I saw that too on the internet this afternoon at the library. It was quite the bloodbath, I admit. However, I'm going to be talking to people one-on-one, mostly professional people. I'm not going to any protests or anything like that."

"I'd just feel better if you waited a while or if the network sent somebody else. It sounds strange over there. This situation seems unpredictable."

"Send somebody else?" Gwen put a hand to her chest, horrified. "No way. This is my story and I'm going. Plus who would dig deeper into the cause of all this better than me?"

"Then promise me you'll be careful. You're the only wife I have."

"I always am." Gwen rinsed their coffee cups and put them in the dishwasher.

"You've done your time overseas. What happened to being the next Connie Chung or Barbara Walters?"

"I like the assignments I get overseas."

"More than you love me?"

"Of course not." She turned to him.

They'd beaten this horse many times in their thirteen years together. But it was getting harder to ignore the way his shoulders hunched and the hurt look in his eyes whenever he brought it up. That he whipped it out now like some sort of trump card made her both suspicious and annoyed.

The doorbell chimed, interrupting the argument she might have launched. Josh headed to the door with two twenty-dollar bills in hand. "Keep the rest." Josh told the delivery boy.

"Hey thanks, man."

Josh closed the door and locked the deadbolt.

As they ate, Gwen watched Joshua's long-fingered hands. Her gaze flowed up his lean arms to his broad shoulders to his face and the light stubble on his chin. No words she could say would reassure him when he got into the "you don't love me, you're never here" corner. They met and fell in love before she discovered foreign correspondence and how it lit a fire within her that no domestic story could satisfy. That didn't mean she could travel so far afield without him here as her safe anchor, her haven. She hadn't been home in weeks, and she didn't blame him for missing her. The best way to reassure her man he was needed and loved was directly.

She bumped his leg with her foot, then slid her toes along his shin, staring at him until he looked up into her eyes. A seductive smile followed by tucking a bite between her teeth prompted that gleam she enjoyed evoking in his eyes. Challenge accepted.

The two ate quickly, staring at one another over the table through their entire meal. They polished off the bottle of wine, repeatedly toasting one another for reasons anyone other than them might find ridiculous.

Leaving the dishes on the table and the napkins on the floor, Gwen ran for the stairs, Joshua in hot pursuit, tickling her buttocks the whole flight up. With a soft giggle, Gwen fell as she reached the top step. Josh swept her up like a rag doll and carried her into their bedroom.

He tossed Gwen onto the bed then ripped off his shirt. Two buttons fell on the hardwood floor with a series of gentle taps. His toned chest and ab muscles flexed enticingly as he tore her clothes out of his way. He might be home alone most of the time, but Gwen appreciated how he never let himself go. She gripped his arms, thrilled at the taut spring of his muscle under hot skin. Her nerdy engineer was better looking now in his thirties than he'd been in college.

Throwing their clothes next to the bed, they shoved aside the covers, forcing the duvet off the mattress. Once under the sheets, they tightly embraced each other. Josh covered her with his body and grabbed her around her ribs while kissing her passionately. He moved his lips down her neck to her breasts, leaving a trail of hot marks from the strength of his suction.

Gwen threw her head back as his passion warmed her like a fever. She ran her fingers through his thick hair and he kissed his way lower and lower down her torso. He sampled every inch of her with his mouth, heading for her lower abdomen and hidden spaces. Gwen ran her hands down his shoulders and back, scratching his skin as his expert familiarity with her body brought her higher.

The pair rolled carelessly across the bed, moaning with delight. Gwen relinquished command of the activity to Josh. He needed the ego stroke as much as the physical one. He pinned her, shoving home roughly, and she delighted in the fierceness of his need. They rocked together, bodies swaying with every pelvic movement. They clung to one another, sliding in the sweat produced from their love. Gwen moaned in satisfaction, rolling her head back with her eyes sealed shut. Josh held her arms down with his brawny hands and buried his head in her neck. The force of his thrusts caused her pain as he neared climax, but he needed this festival of lust. And so did she.

GWEN ARRIVED at JFK International Airport at the crack of dawn with barely enough time remaining before her boarding time. Jumping out of the taxi with bags in hand, she ran for her gate. The security line wasn't too horrendous, but it still took time to weave back and forth in line, hand over her passport and boarding pass, take her shoes off, push her bags through the scanner, and then wait for them at the other end. The airline announcer started the boarding call for children, elderly, and those who needed special attention while the trays of items worked their way through. She reassembled her stuff, shoved her feet back into her shoes, grabbed her bags, and then ran to the check-in counter at the gate.

"You just made it," the perky airline attendant told her.

"Yes, I know. Can you take my bags here?"

"Of course, Mrs. Patterson. First class has already boarded, so you can get on and take your seat."

Gwen headed for her assigned window seat. She checked in all her luggage except one emergency overnight bag and her briefcase containing her laptop computer. This was routine in case the airline lost her luggage or if she found herself stranded, missing a connecting flight. Once seated, Gwen pulled out the file folder containing the most recent published information on Germany and its economic issues that she and the librarian compiled the day before. It took several hours, but she retrieved most of the information she had lost in the taxi.

Gwen's bag rang underneath the seat in front of her. She didn't need to look to know who it was. She pulled out her cell phone.

"Hi Joe," she said with a chuckle.

"Hey, kid, you were supposed to call me when you got to the airport."

"I just got here, literally. The plane was boarding when I got through security. I was going to call you in a minute."

"Yeah, yeah whatever. Why were you late? What happened?"

Gwen didn't feel like explaining the whole conversation of that morning to Joe, but he would never take no or nothing for an answer. Gwen leaned back in her seat and gazed out the window. Joe would have her on the line until the attendant demanded she hang up.

"Nothing happened. Josh went on and on about wanting me to stay home for some reason."

"Did he say why?"

"No, not exactly. He saw rallies on television last night and thought it was too dangerous for me to be there. I don't understand it. I went to Syria and Afghanistan, and he wasn't that excited. Men. I just don't understand you guys." Gwen laughed.

"Well, kid, I think this might be dangerous, too. So, keep your eyes and ears open. Any sign of trouble—come home," Joe belted out.

"What the hell is the matter with everyone today? There is no major risk." Gwen plucked lint off her slacks.

"With Frank Solas' sudden accident and you almost getting mugged for whatever reason yesterday, I would just feel better if you promised to stay on your toes. Okay?"

"Okay!" Gwen said with an exaggerated tone. "On my toes, ears open, looking over my shoulder, I got it."

"Hey, don't get gruff with me, little girl. I can turn that plane around and pull your ass back here." Joe was not joking.

"Okay. I'm sorry. Of course, I'll be careful. I don't want to die, but I'm sure everything will be fine," Gwen said in a reassuring tone.

A moment of silence stretched on the phone, both sorry for losing their tempers. Finally, Gwen released a soothing sigh and in a more relaxed tone, she told Joe again everything would be fine.

"I'll call you after I get there and set up my first interview. I retrieved articles from the library yesterday, so I have a place to start. Just call and make sure that American-friendly crew shows up."

"You got it. Talk to you later."

After one last male passenger boarded the plane, the door slammed shut and the crew prepared for takeoff. Carter took his seat in clear view of Gwen and relaxed. He had several hours to get shuteye. Gwen had no place to go other than the bathroom until they landed in Berlin.

13

JOE GREW MORE AND MORE concerned about Gwen's safety. He could not shake the feeling something bad was going to happen. Too much had already happened in the last forty-eight hours. He sat in his big comfortable chair, wondering if he was exaggerating the danger in his mind to create an excuse not to go. He entertained the procrastination for a while, putting off the inevitable—not a trait he valued in himself or others. He did not want to say goodbye to his old friend. But unfortunately, the funeral would go on with or without him.

Joe wiped his eyes of the few tears that slipped out and decided to do right by a good friend. He pushed himself back from the desk and stood. Grabbing his old, ragged tie, Joe walked to the mirror in the corner of his office and put it on. Looking only half bad, Joe headed out the door and into the newsroom, which was quietly bustling with activity. No one said a word to him, and everyone avoided eye contact. They all knew where he was going.

Joe reluctantly moved through the newsroom around desks and chairs. Every step was heavier than the last, as though he was pulling half the staff on a sled over a bed of rocks. His head hung low, and he shoved his hands deep in his pockets. He wore his dark jacket and topcoat and that old, ragged tie, which hadn't seen street action in months. He made his way to the elevators. One door was already open, appearing to deliberately wait for him. But in his grief, Joe did not care. He and his newly acquired companion headed to the parking garage.

When Joe arrived at the church, it was standing room only. Several seats up front were roped off for special guests, and Joe was considered among that crowd. He knew the room and they knew him, but most importantly, they all shared one friend: Solas. He was the common denominator among many: a good friend, a kind man, and a corrupt congressman. He padded the retirement purse like so many before and just as so many would after, not unusual for the Washington crowd. Except in his case, he didn't live long enough to spend it. *But it should be expected when you swim with the sharks, or at least when you do business with dangerous people.*

Joe sat up front with his head hanging down, looking at the floor, unable to even gaze at the closed coffin in front of him. An American flag draped over the casket so elegantly it gave Solas validation and standing in society. Dignitaries and visitors alike streamed past the casket, some reaching out to brush their fingers over the flag as though it was one more opportunity to touch their old friend and colleague. Joe took a seat and let out a great sigh. Joe could still see he was not alone in grief. Solas had touched a great many lives, and for that Joe was grateful to see so many people in attendance.

But there were some people in attendance Joe didn't recognize. They stood peppered among the crowd, stoic, unemotional, as though their minds were on something else. They wanted visual confirmation that Solas was dead, among other things. The coffin was closed, of course, due to the high impact of the blast. There wasn't much left of the body, or the vehicle Solas was traveling in. All in all, it was a finely placed bomb, but it did the job a little too well. No one saw him die, and that left some people concerned. That could be a problem.

One of those stoic guests sat right on Joe's six, breathing down his neck, perhaps waiting for the right opportunity to strike up a conversation or maybe just drop a little message. The tall man blended into the crowd beautifully. No one but Joe could have guessed he was a German spy sent to give Joe a cryptic, frightening message. A spy? But for whom? Which side was he on? Could he be working for the current prime minister, Josef Jakob, who wanted the truth to be told, or the duplicitous second-in-command military leader Peter Schmidt, who wanted Gwen away—far, far away from the truth, the prime minister, and Germany? Unknown. Joe could remain to pay his respects, but despite all his sadness, he knew the guy behind him wanted something, but what? Ask something, tell him something—all he could do was sit and wait. Joe was grateful to be sitting in a crowded room, which offered multiple witnesses and quite possibly a false sense of protection, but protection nonetheless.

After several of Solas' family and friends took turns at the casket, they took the first row to listen to the eulogy and awesome stories of their beloved brother, uncle, and friend. Behind the family streamed public figures, famous people, more distant relatives, friends, and in Solas' case, many strangers, perhaps supporters and constituents.

The man behind Joe was tall and blond with chiseled features, a man with a chiseled body to match. He did not look like someone to be trifled with. He sat there calmly, respectfully.

The eulogy began with Frank Solas' brother Benjamin Solas, an alderman from Chicago known around the windy city as "Benny the Penny" because there wasn't a time he couldn't make money. He arrived with his family, who were confused about the manner of Frank's death.

Joe listened to one sad story after another, with a few funny stories that were welcomed by the crowd. Emotions ran high, but Joe tried to keep himself in check; he was being watched, and he didn't want to appear weak. There would be time to cry later, and maybe the news crew would join him in a drink to honor his old mate.

The speeches wound down, and the room grew tired and hungry. What would a funeral be without a feast afterward? Only a select few would follow the hearse and lay the empty coffin to rest. The rest of the guests were to meet at Bourbon Steak in the Four Seasons, a Washington, DC favorite among those with money and influence. The entire restaurant was reserved that afternoon so the crowd could send Solas out in style. In style, it would be.

Guests walked behind the coffin, filing into the center aisle, but Joe stayed in place. So did the blond man behind him. At this point, waiting would be the best way to have their exchange. The pews emptied rapidly; the church had been packed, and the air was hot. Beads of sweat formed on Joe's forehead, though whether from the temperature or the anxiety building up over what this man wanted, he didn't know. The last of the stragglers left the sanctuary, leaving Joe and the blond man alone.

The blond man leaned forward, making the bench creak. His breath brushed Joe's ear, hot and smelling like acid. The man clearly had been on the move for a while without time to freshen up. Apparently, his work was never done.

"Your top girl is in trouble," the man said in a strong German accent.

Joe began to turn, shocked by those words, but the man told him to face the front.

"Don't look at me so you can live."

Joe took the warning seriously; he was at a funeral, and he didn't want the next one to be his. Who knew what kind of warning Solas had received but never heeded? Did Solas even get a warning?

Joe kept his eyes front and his ears open.

The man recited Gwen's flight number, destination, and location. "We can get to her anytime, anywhere, you remember that."

Joe didn't respond, not a word, not even a nod. He stared straight ahead at the cross on the wall, wondering the real dangers that lay ahead.

"What's the problem with Gwen?"

"If she gets too close over there, we may have to intercede. Reporting on riots is fine, but tell her to go no further. That is all. A surface scratch we can handle, but if she digs any deeper, she'll be digging her own grave."

Joe continued to listen, waiting for the man to continue, but nothing more was said. Joe took a quick glance behind him. The man was gone, leaving as swiftly as he came. The smell of acid cleared, as well as the musty smell of body odor that had taken over Joe's nasal passages. *How could someone smell so bad?* He was glad the blond man was gone.

Now alone, Joe took out his cell phone from his pocket. He'd recorded the entire exchange. Once a reporter, always a reporter. He was ready to record the second he realized he was being watched. Joe listened to the warning repeatedly, wondering what the riots were leading to. What would make a German spy intercede? The whole thing sounded nuts. Joe was going to keep this warning to himself for now, but only until he could think things through. There was no need to worry Gwen, not like she would even get worried or knew how to worry. Joe always did all the worrying for her, and that worked for her.

THE CELL IN Joshua's pocket rang. He dreaded this call, but he had to answer. This issue had to be dealt with. He slid his hand down into his pocket before the ringing stopped. With so much on the line, he didn't want to appear as though he were dodging calls. The caller ID confirmed it was Travis. *It would be my boss asking for those damn blueprints for the "side job."*

"Hello?"

"We need to meet. I need those plans." Travis sounded desperate.

"Hold on. I'm sorry, I can't give you those plans today. There's been a delay."

"What? Why?"

"I deleted the blueprint files off my hard drive as instructed, and that guy Chen insisted on taking the thumb drive that had the only copy. Now he's dead, and the drive is nowhere to be found." Joshua explained. "I have a friend of a friend who works at the morgue, and he went through the guy's stuff, but the drive wasn't among his things. I don't know where he put it. So, I need more time."

Travis let out a big anxious breath, then the phone went silent for a moment before he asked, "Can anyone read that file if they get the drive?"

"No." Joshua sighed. "It's encrypted. Without the password or specialty de-encryption software, they can't open it."

"You didn't back up the files at all?"

"Hell no. The guy who commissioned it was clear about what could happen to me if the files fell into the wrong hands, and I didn't want that stuff on my computer."

"But you must be able to reproduce the blueprints, or we have to find the thumb drive."

"It's possible to reproduce them, but it'll take time. That was an unusual and complicated project, as you know."

Josh was glad Travis moved on so quickly from locating the lost thumb drive. His gut told him Gwen had it. When Chen fell out of the moving taxi, witnesses said some woman they recognized from TV ran up to the body as it lay in the street and went through the dead man's pockets. Since Gwen said an Asian man tried to rob her in the backseat of a taxi, it wasn't hard to put two and two together.

Joshua rubbed his forehead. *Chen is dead, and my wife has the thumb drive that holds all of Strauss' plans for the East German takeover of the West. How did I ever get involved in such a mess? But at least Gwen doesn't know what she has, so that ignorance might keep her safe, for now at least. I need to get that drive, but how?* Josh's mind raced with ideas and answers, though none realistic or remotely possible. Gwen was a smart woman, and she would sniff him out right away if he started to inquire. For heaven's sake, he could not ask his wife for the thumb drive she had hidden away in her pocket.

Besides, the password wasn't anything she would figure out, and she was no computer whiz.

14

THOUGH THE NONSTOP FLIGHT from JFK was only eight hours, the time difference between Berlin and New York made local time almost midnight when they landed. Gwen was already dialing Joe's number while the plane taxied toward the gate. Hopefully, he had already found someone who knew the streets of Berlin and the players in the political game.

"Hi Joe, it's me." Gwen pinched the bridge of her nose. The time shifts were taking a toll, but at least she had an excuse to rest first before meeting all these politicians.

"Hi, kid. How was your flight?"

"Fine, nothing special. I spent it going through those articles and files trying to wrap my head and arms around the issues and identify questions."

The last few days had been unusually violent and deadly, giving them both an uneasy feeling. Waiting for the second shoe to drop wasn't a feeling either liked with Gwen so far from home.

"So, who's my contact? I'd like to do a meet-and-greet then go to the hotel to sleep before tackling the story in the morning."

"I did one better. He's going to pick you up at the airport and take you to your hotel. I sent you a picture of him. He's a cameraman we've used before but maybe not with you. His name is Rocco Wolf. He's thorough and good. He's from the States, but he's got a lot of contacts over there, so if he doesn't know how to reach someone, he knows someone who does. Got it?"

"Got it." Gwen waited for the photo to download. Mr. Wolf looked to be in his early to mid-thirties, ruggedly handsome and beefy with muscle, the kind of man to have earned his swagger. "I'll get back in touch with you after I sleep. Talk to you soon, Joe."

"All right, kid. Be careful, don't take chances."

As first-class passengers, both Carter and Gwen were able to deplane right away, but Carter had to get creative to make space between them. He didn't want to be noticed, for he had already been seen, just overlooked, and dismissed. Carter let Gwen exit first under the guise of being a gentleman instead of a spy following her. Carter exited the plane and stopped to tie his shoe and waste a minute or two. Both had to pass through immigration and passport checks, get their bags from the baggage claim downstairs, and then clear customs, which gave Carter plenty of time to blend in right behind her. Carter knew she might see him there, but he didn't want to give her the impression he was on her six. Now at a safer distance, Carter could begin walking at a normal pace as he kept his eye on her.

Carter kept his distance as Gwen moved through the line at immigration with file folder in hand. What Carter wouldn't do for a peek at those files, but they had already been stolen once. Twice would only confirm Gwen's suspicions about German activity. No, Carter would have to slip into her hotel room at some point and get a gander at what she collected, or at the least what information she found valuable. It might give him an idea of what direction she was taking or where she intended to start. But his curiosity would have to wait for now, at least until she separated herself from that folder and he located an associate with whom he could share the tail.

Gwen's bags came quick, quicker than Carter's, and he grew anxious. He didn't want to leave without his equipment, some of which he couldn't carry on the plane. As a government agent, he could probably get away with bringing extra onboard, but since he needed to blend in, he traveled today as a private citizen, which meant no extra luggage. Gwen, with bags in hand, headed for customs, where Carter could catch up. The two stood in different lines but headed in the same direction.

Carter was a few parties behind and in a different line, not moving as quickly. Of course, he didn't want to lose Gwen and screw up this assignment. He was being trusted to work on his own, travel to Europe, and follow one of the nation's most influential reporters. If he lost her, his boss would probably lose him. Carter wanted to stand out. He had big dreams for his career.

Finally, Carter got to his turn to see the agent. He opened his bags as instructed. His luggage set off more than one alarm. Rooting among his necessities, the agent inquired about all the recording equipment and various cameras in Carter's bag. Carter discreetly displayed identification that indicated he worked at the U.S. Embassy, and once that was viewed, no more questions were asked. Carter cleared customs and hustled to catch up to Gwen.

Thankfully, she was still waiting in the passenger pickup zone for her ride.

Carter found his ride, another agent from the Berlin office in a common black Mercedes. Carter got into the car and met his contact, another American with the gift of German linguistics who introduced himself only as Mike. Armed with a gun tucked neatly under his left thigh, Mike looked rough around the edges and untrusting. Carter didn't think too much about it. They waited at the curb for Gwen to be picked up.

GWEN'S FACE WAS well-known, so the passport agent waved her on through, stopping only for a quick stamp.

"Oh, you just left Belgium, I see," the immigration agent said passively.

"Yes, I know. It's been one of those weeks," Gwen said shaking her head.

"Well, try to have a nice day," the agent said.

"I will. You too."

Gwen picked up her bag and moved on through customs. She headed for the exit, keeping her eyes open for the man who matched the picture in her smartphone. The brisk night air revived her, though she buttoned her coat. She looked for a larger vehicle, a news van specifically, expecting Rocco to want to get right to work. But no van waited at the passenger-loading curb. No vans drove past at all. *Strange, even regular passengers are picked up by a shuttle van for hotels.* She shrugged it off as coincidence and waited patiently. She eyed the parade of BMW and Mercedes and Porsche, the bright lights of the loading zone gleaming off their curves; in Germany, these were as common as Dodge and Ford back home.

She stood curbside, peering into one car after another. At last, a dark sedan pulled up alongside her, lowering the window. Gwen looked in at the driver. He matched the photo from Joe, if scruffier around the jaw right now. "Rocco?"

"Yeah. You're Gwen?"

"Yes." She opened the door. Rocco jumped out of the car, startling her. He popped the trunk open and tossed her bags in the back, looking around constantly and moving quickly.

"Is everything okay?" Gwen watched him, puzzled.

"Get in! We can talk while we move." Rocco returned to the driver's seat.

Gwen knew what that tone meant. She sat and buckled in, then dropped the sun visor to use the vanity mirror as a rear-view mirror, scoping out anything odd. She observed several other European cars as they pulled away from the curb at about the same time, all heading for the same exit ramp to leave the airport. She continued to look as they peeled down the road and blended into traffic. Nothing suspicious stood out to Gwen, and Rocco had his eyes fixed on the road ahead. He picked up speed quickly and made a few odd lane changes, throwing Gwen off balance.

Rocco held the wheel like a racecar driver. They sped down the multilane highway toward Berlin's downtown. Gwen kept one eye in the vanity mirror but couldn't see anything unusual.

"Got your safety belt on?" he asked.

"Yes, why?"

"Hold on!" Rocco swerved the car onto the shoulder and then slammed on the brakes. Once the car came to a screeching halt, Rocco threw the car into reverse and sped backward toward the exit they had just passed. Gwen shoved both hands against the dashboard for support. She looked through the back window as Rocco backed up, keeping an eye out for other cars on the shoulder. Cars in the driving lanes flew past at alarming speeds.

Rocco shoved the stick into drive and merged onto the exit ramp into town, headed toward the Regent Hotel Berlin on Charlottenstrasse, less than one mile from the Rathaus.

"So, can you tell me now what's going on?" Gwen glared at him. "Why are we driving like the devil is chasing us?"

"Nicely put." Rocco smirked. "Probably because the devil might be following us." He explained while driving more carefully down the city's side streets. "The newspapers try to write about the financial instability, which is leading to social chaos, but the written word doesn't do the emotions justice. Something bad is going on, leaving even local officials wondering what. So, if the people at the city and state levels don't know, who does that leave?"

"The highest level of government, that's who."

"The highest level. Only the highest, and that should cause us all fear."

When they arrived at the hotel, Rocco helped Gwen with her bags. "I'll pick you up in the morning, early. I'll get a second person to help us with the technical work, someone I trust."

"Sounds good. I'll be here, but I'm using the name Stratton in case you need to ask for me. Joe insisted." Gwen rolled her eyes.

"Joe's smart." Rocco smiled. "I'll call you when I'm on my way."

"Okay, thanks." Gwen took her bags and headed into the hotel to check-in. "By the way, I wanted to start with Berger, Walter Berger, the chancellor's chief economist."

"I'll set it up," Rocco said as he walked back toward the car.

"ALL THAT WEAVING only attracts attention and rarely works," Mike said, plus he knew these tricks, having been trained by the best. As they left the airport, he took the middle lane and followed Gwen and her cameraman, matching their top speed. Mike kept his eyes on the road and Carter kept his eyes on Gwen, having already memorized the license plate.

When Gwen's car reversed direction on the highway, Mike and Carter shot right past them in the middle lane.

Carter pointed uselessly. "What the hell? That's them!"

Unable to do the same action, Mike drove past the exit.

"What the hell was that?"

"Did you see that coming? I didn't see that coming," Mike said in a nasty tone. "Who the hell could see that coming?"

"Damn it!" Carter smacked the dashboard. "Now what?"

"I know the streets. We'll back-pedal through the side streets." Mike guided their car to the exit lane.

"What's around that exit they took?"

"Mostly tourist stuff, shopping, and …"

"And, what?" Carter narrowed his eyes at Mike.

"Hotels."

"Hotels," Carter repeated, more confident. *How in the hell are we going to figure out which one? But at least we know the area where she is staying. Plus, she has a famous name, so she will be easy to find.*

"Let's get to the office, then we can call around and see which hotel she is in," Mike suggested.

"I agree." Driving around aimlessly would help no one. He was not here on a sightseeing trip.

The two continued to the next exit to regroup and to admire Rocco's driving skills.

15

THE NEXT MORNING came quickly. Too quickly. Gwen was still tired, but she had work to do. Rocco returned, clean-shaven and with his thick dark hair neatly combed. Standing, his physique matched the photo she'd seen, broad-shouldered and athletic, as opposite to Joshua's build as a man could be. To Gwen's surprise, he brought another cameraman she knew, Jacques Basile from Belgium.

"What are you doing here?" Gwen asked, happily giving her friend a hug.

"Rocco called me because he isn't sure who he can trust, and he heard we just worked together this week. So here I am." Jacques smiled back, arms wide open.

She and Jacques were confident in each other's abilities and their allegiance to the truth. If he and Joe trusted Rocco, by extension so could she. Now they could get to work, knowing they could do so candidly. The threesome hopped into the news truck and headed deeper into the city. Gwen had an early appointment with Walter Berger. She had developed a line of questioning that would hopefully lead to answers. The three pulled up to the Rathaus and waited. Gwen walked out front, noticing the blood stains still on the ground. The scrubbed spots showed signs of sun bleaching, but those marks were still unmistakably blood stains.

Gwen shuddered; how horrible that scene must have been. The video didn't do it justice. The intensity of the crowd must have been overwhelming. She stared at the stained stairs, trying to insert herself into the experience. It wasn't hard to do, as she had covered plenty of riots and war zones where emotions ran high and tempers flared. *Desperate people do desperate things*, she thought. But how desperate are they, and how desperate would they become? This was an unknown, a scary unknown, especially since one of the government's own was stabbed and killed so viciously. That act took desperation. Gwen looked up and around the buildings at access points, areas from where someone could have shot him so much more easily if he were the target. But that would have required premeditation, planning, and organization. The offender thought enough to have a knife with him, but he might always carry a knife with him. Since no one reported seeing the incident, the murderer got away. Answers of why Gerfurt would have to wait. It was hard to say if there was any premeditation at all or if Gerfurt was just a victim of rage and opportunity.

"We'll see, I guess," Gwen said to herself in a low tone.

Breaking Gwen's contemplation of things, Rocco called her name, pulling her back into the present. Gwen looked up at Rocco still sitting in the van. Without saying a word, Rocco motioned her to come closer.

She did. "What's up?"

"Berger wants to meet across the street at Neptune Fountain. He's afraid to be seen here with us, most likely, and he wants a more visible, casual setting, probably with more opportunities for a speedy exit, if necessary." Rocco raised his eyebrows.

Jacques was sitting in the back of the news truck scanning B-roll footage and ambient sound he had collected of the post-riot damage and the everyday traffic sounds.

The fountain was visible from where she was standing, so she told the guys she would meet them over there. A short walk would help her get the lay of the land. Jacques leaned over, and with a nod slammed the sliding door shut while Rocco pulled away. With a microphone in hand, Gwen flipped the on switch and casually told the guys to start rolling as soon as they stopped. As she approached the fountain, she noticed how open the pedestrian street was and the vast number of people who probably filled it just days ago. With a crowd like this, one instigator could start a stampede or fuel a stabbing. People were reported hanging from the trees and using them for a better view. The trees now looked tattered, and the flower beds had been completely trampled over. Gwen thought, *What a shame to see so much of the natural element suffer the consequences of destructive people.* She wasn't only thinking of the rioters.

Gwen refocused her attention on the fountain, a beautiful work of art with Neptune at the top, the Roman god of the sea. It would make a fine backdrop for the interview. As Gwen approached the fountain, she noticed an older man standing alone. He was wearing clear, understated glass frames and an expensive-looking gray suit. He had a handkerchief in his lapel, very old-school. *He looks like an economist*, Gwen thought. Berger had a slim frame and was noticeably tall with thinning white hair. He looked nervous, his head shifting his view from one side to another. As Gwen got closer, the weight of Berger's stare grew more intense. He looked skittish, as though debating whether to back out at the last second. People who talk to the press usually don't fare well among their peers once their people know they broke ranks and went public. Gwen was aware the media wasn't always kind to those desperate enough to seek help from journalists.

"Mr. Berger?" Gwen asked as she moved closer.

"Yes, Ms. Patterson. I am Walter Berger."

"Your English is very good," she noted.

"Harvard University, four years," he replied in a bragging tone.

Gwen took that education as admission he was fluent in English and knew the ways of the American economy probably as well as the German. "Wonderful. Thank you for meeting us. This is my cameraman, and I have technical support in the van."

Rocco nodded greetings as he placed the already-running television camera on his shoulder. Berger pursed his lips and asked to speak to Gwen off camera, telling her he would tell her everything he knew if she would keep his face off the television.

No reporter wanted the interviewee to appear dishonest by being unwilling to attach their face and their name to what they were saying. However, it was a highly useful technique if no other opportunities existed. Gwen would find another opportunity. After negotiating with Berger for a few minutes and assuring him of his safety, Gwen was able to turn the microphone back on.

"Before we begin, I'd like to ask where you were the other day during the riot."

"I was here, inside, hiding, I am ashamed to say," Berger admitted, only looking up at Gwen for a brief second. "My accounts for that day are secondhand, I'm afraid. I was in one of the offices consulting on financial matters that morning when the rioting broke out. First, it was just some protesters, but then the people multiplied and continued to do so until the streets were jam-packed. This type of unrest and violence is unusual for Germans." Berger looked down his nose at Gwen and Rocco. "We do things in an orderly fashion, without violence."

Gwen quirked her lips at his inference that such things were ordinary in the United States. "You mentioned financial matters. Let's talk about that. When Chancellor Josef Jakob took office, the country was in the black. Now the country is not just in the red but on the verge of going bankrupt, even unable to pay its debts. The country's credit rating is in jeopardy. So, let's get to the question everyone is asking. Where is all the money going?"

"It is difficult to say exactly, but what I do know is when this chancellor took over, there was a lot in reserve. Yes, that is true, but over time it dwindled. From what I can see, money is still going in, but it appears more and more is coming out for the exact same things we always paid for," Berger tried to explain. "It appears that shortly after Chancellor Jakob took office, the cost of everything went up considerably. But *why* is the question we should all be asking. Why such inflation? If we can identify why the cost of everything is so sharply on the rise, we may get answers."

Gwen nodded at Berger, appreciating the information. But she had a lot more to ask the economic advisor.

"Who organized the most recent protest, the one that ended in the murder of Hans Gerfurt?" Gwen placed her microphone squarely in front of Berger.

Berger looked up in the air as if searching for an answer, only to respond by saying he didn't know for certain.

"There had to be someone, at least one person in charge of this protest and this chaos?" Gwen asked, reframing the question.

"You are looking for one name," Berger said to Gwen with an air of authority. "You want to blame one person, but it's never just one person. It is possible in an attempt to do something great with the best intentions that other people with corrupt intentions insert themselves, ruining an opportunity for good." Berger asked her to look at the bigger picture and reconsider her narrow financial focus.

Gwen looked at Berger with great curiosity. *Of course, he knows more than he's saying.*

Berger continued. "All I can say for certain is there are several people posting online, organizing, but the one who gets the most attention is a young man by the name of Karl Reinhardt."

"Who is Karl Reinhardt?" Gwen wanted specifics.

"I do not know. Really, I have no idea. I have heard his name shared among young people and he has a following online, so much, in fact, members of the chambers know his name, which is impressive. But none of us know what he looks like. His online pages have no photos—

just meeting times, dates, and locations. But I have never heard of him advocating violence or asking participants to bring weapons."

"Since Reinhardt is contacting mostly young people, do you know where he intends to hold the next protest?" Gwen asked.

"No, I have no idea. I only know what I hear on the wind." Berger smiled, waving his hand in the air for dramatic effect. "I am not a follower of this young man. I only like to know what is happening so I can possibly avoid the massive crowds and potential chaos that sometimes follows. I am too old for flying fruit and scaling buildings." Berger chuckled.

Gwen smiled too, fully understanding Berger's unwillingness to insert himself into anything distasteful or undignified. She was glad to get a name, any name, at least someone she could follow up with about the incident. Now she had to hunt down Karl Reinhardt.

Berger continued to look nervous, scanning the streets and peering over his shoulder. Gwen was gearing up for a follow-up question when she heard a roaring car engine.

Cars were speeding past the *Rathaus*, and one abnormally loud engine roared in the distance. The sound became disruptive as the engine's thunder drew closer and closer. Suddenly, there was a loud, distinct blast as the car passed the three of them. Unable to dismiss the obvious source of the boom, the thunderous pop threw Rocco into action. He dropped his camera and threw his body over Gwen's to shield her from any bullets or shrapnel intended for Berger. Berger's beliefs may have been justified after all, Gwen worried, trying not to notice how good Rocco smelled or how tight his muscles felt pressed against her. Berger dropped to the ground in a panic, covering his head, evidently too scared to scream. The car with the bad engine and the backfire continued past the group.

Rocco pushed himself up off Gwen, apologizing, realizing no assassination attempt was made, but Berger's reaction made clear this was a country on edge. The backfiring engine ignited his fight-or-flight response, and now he was on the move. Berger took off, yelling back to Gwen that he would be in touch. Before Gwen could get up, Berger was in the wind, running down a side street without any traffic. Rocco helped Gwen to her feet.

"What was that?" Gwen asked.

"It sounded like a gunshot, but that car just backfired. Sorry for jumping on you like that, but I'm not taking any chances, especially around here—plus Joe would kick me into next week if anything happened to you."

Gwen dusted off her pants and looked around for Berger, but he was long gone.

"He said he would be in touch, whatever that means." Rocco shrugged.

"Actually, that's okay. He gave me good ideas about national expenditures. We should identify companies that sell to the government and find out about cost, pricing, and why the price of everything is so dramatically on the rise." Gwen stared off into the direction Berger ran.

She turned her attention back to Rocco. "First, we need to find this Karl Reinhardt guy. I have a feeling he's someone we should be talking to. Anyone who can gather crowds like this must know something."

"Agreed." Rocco nodded.

"I'll need more official contacts in the Parliament, too. People love hearing the official version of what's going on," Gwen said. "I'll call Joe. Can you call who you know?"

"I sure can. Let's hit the road for now." Rocco looked up and down the four corners of the road.

Later that day, Rocco dropped Gwen off at the hotel so she could freshen up before dinner and go through her notes. Gwen wanted a shower after lying on the ground and a nice glass of wine while she worked.

Dressed in her bathrobe, Gwen leaned back, relaxing in her chair, when she noticed an envelope lying on the floor just inside her hotel room door. Someone must have slipped it there while she was in the shower. Not thinking much about it, she picked it up to see who the message was from.

Berger did get in touch with her, and in quite a hurry. Inside the envelope was a name, Ansel Decker, the former economic advisor to the East German socialist party leader, Erich Strauss. Decker was a loyalist to Strauss, but he was creative enough to keep himself relevant in the current administration.

But what could Decker tell me? Gwen wondered. This would take research, starting with a call to Joe. Joe could get background on this guy and find out what his involvement could be. Gwen reached for the phone and dialed.

16

VICTOR BRACED HIMSELF for an unpleasant conversation with Martin Strauss; the redrawn plans were not yet ready to hand over. The two met up in a public place. Travis would have it no other way; Martin was a dangerous man. Outside a coffee shop on the Upper West Side, the two men met and went inside to sit like civilized people. The two men passed several open tables until they found the right one. They sat side by side, unwilling to put their backs to the door. Sharing one corner of the small square table, the two men turned their coffee cups over and thanked the waitress as she filled the cups with a smile.

"If you gentlemen need anything else, please just wave me down," the young woman said, angling for a good tip even though this would be a small check. Travis thanked the waitress and told her they would just be having coffee for now. The young girl said if they changed their minds, she would be around.

Now the two men were alone and isolated from the usual cafe crowd. Without looking at Travis, Martin got right down to business.

"Where are my plans?" Martin asked.

"I don't have them. There's the problem." Travis was upfront, trying to appear honest and on board with the program.

"I don't like problems," Martin said with a stern look on his face.

"Joshua designed the device your father requested, and everything was fine. As requested, the files with the blueprints were kept secure; the only copy was on a USB thumb drive. Chen insisted, even threatened Joshua to hold the thumb drive for safety, so Joshua let him have it. He felt he had no choice." Travis' voice got louder for a second, but looking around, he reined in his volume.

In a hushed voice, he continued to explain so no one else could overhear. He reminded Martin what had happened to Chen when he tried to steal Gwen's files and the fate he met.

"It's unknown what he did with the key drive, and now we're trying to work our way through the dilemma."

"I see. That is unfortunate." Martin folded his hands neatly on the table. Martin was eerily calm, and Travis was concerned with what the German was thinking.

Without taking a sip of his coffee, Martin got up from his seat. "You better figure it out, and quick. We're running out of time. Most of our comrades are getting into place. So, figure it out, fast!"

His words and tone did not make Travis feel good. He dialed Joshua's number as he left the café. Joshua didn't pick up, so Travis headed to the office. When Gwen was out of town, Travis could usually find Josh at the office.

Joshua was sitting at his computer developing blueprints for a legitimate buyer when Travis came through the door. Josh looked up, and the two men made eye contact. Josh knew something was wrong, but he didn't want to know what. He got himself involved in this mess, and he would stay involved until he could work his way out. When Travis walked by his desk, Joshua got up and followed like a minion. What choice did he have? He followed Travis into his office but didn't bother to sit.

Travis, still taking off his coat, told Joshua about his unpleasant meeting with a very unpleasant man, and that the two of them needed to figure out something about those plans for "the client," as he was known around the office. Allowing other office personnel to hear about an illegal project wasn't good for business, so Travis and Joshua dubbed Strauss "the client" when discussing relevant issues in-house.

"I can redraw them, but I can't do that instantly. I told you that." Joshua huffed, crossing his arms. "He's going to have to be patient."

"Work as fast as you can, please."

"I have my notes, don't you worry." Joshua pointed to his temple. "They're all up here."

17

NOT LONG AFTER the disappointing meeting with Travis, Martin hit the road, heading southbound for two hours, seeking the home of his father's one-time mistress and mother of his brother. An old address was Martin's only place to begin. He firmly gripped the steering wheel with both hands as he barreled down the Garden State Parkway toward a small town on the Jersey Shore, as it was called by locals. Forked River was nothing fancy, populated mostly by the everyday worker-bee types happy to make ends meet and have enough for a weekend kegger. Few enjoyed living along the actual shoreline with houses on the sandy beaches. They needed real cash to afford waterfront homes, so those residents made the long, daily commute north into New York City.

Martin continued to close the gap between himself and his assignment. He became more driven as he got closer to the only address he had. Martin counted down the exit numbers with impatience. His mind functioned in kilometers, so the measurement of miles confused him. This was just one more thing for Martin to hate about this rival country.

Martin drew close to Margaret's house, or so he thought. Having driven up and down Lacey Road multiple times and not seeing a house, he pulled into the address, which was now a business. Across the street from a big empty lot, a carnival company was packing up their trucks from a week of springtime fun. Martin snarled. The address was wrong or old, but either way, the owners inside might be able to answer this question. He took a moment and a breath before entering. He did not want to raise suspicions, he just wanted answers.

Martin entered the front door of the shop, and a nice older lady greeted him immediately.

"Can I help you, young man?"

Martin listened to her voice but heard no hint of an accent and moved closer to her. She did not appear to look anything like the woman in his father's photographs.

Martin responded with a smile and, leaning into his accent, he explained to her how he had come so far seeking his long-lost aunt named Margaret Stratton, and this was her last known address to her friends and family in Germany.

"Can you be of any help?" Martin asked showing her the slip of paper with the address clearly written.

"Well, let's see. I don't know her, but we can look it up." The old woman clicked on her computer behind the desk. Martin leaned forward to watch her, not because it was in his nature, but to expedite the gathering of the information he sought. Martin allowed the woman to take the lead, since he did not know how to search American websites for this information. Standing right behind her, he looked over her shoulder at the screen, thinking what a nice woman she was and wondering if Margaret would be the same way. Martin brought all his anger and disdain to his search for a woman he knew little to nothing about, but he needed his brother, and she must tell him where he is.

The woman continued with her frail, bony finger, scrolling up and down the pages filled with dozens of women named Margaret Stratton, several in New Jersey alone. Apparently, in America the name Stratton was common, and now Martin had more work to do, more roads to learn, and more people to talk to.

"Would you like me to print this page for you?"

"That would be helpful, thank you."

"That's fine, young man. I see you're anxious. Your aunt must be important to you."

"She is. The family very much wants to find her." Martin smiled to keep the old woman comfortable.

The woman explained to him directions to the locations. With this short list, Martin returned to his car and plugged the addresses into the rental GPS.

One after the other, he found and dismissed the women on the list until only two remained. He was hot, tired, hungry, and frustrated. He worried she might have left New Jersey, too. How would he ever find her?

Now he was off to a neighboring town called Lanoka Harbor. Martin was relieved to learn this address was a short drive, and he could get down to business. A simple left and another right brought him to the house. A real dump.

Who would leave my father and a castle for this garbage? Martin shook his head. *She probably didn't know and was too ashamed to come back.*

What else could he think that would make any sense? But at least this address was still a house and not a tool shop or some other nonsense. Martin parked out front along the road and got out of the car, taking in the entire block in both directions. It was a common neighborhood, a place no one would look for anybody. Martin walked up the driveway, keeping one hand in his pocket. Going up the front concrete stairs, Martin knocked on the front door. A young man answered.

"Can I help you?"

"Yes, I am looking for my aunt, Margaret Stratton, and I was given this address." Martin tried to look over the young man's shoulder into the house.

"Oh, you just missed her," the young man said with a big smile.

"I just missed her?" Martin asked. "What time will she be back?"

"You misunderstand. She isn't coming back. She sold us this house a while back. She moved out of town."

Martin nearly fell over when he heard the news. But somehow Martin already knew his nightmare in this country was far from over.

"Do you know where she moved?" Martin asked. "My relatives in Germany have been looking for her for a long time, and they have sent me all this way to find her. Can you help me?"

"I'm not sure. I thought at one point I heard her say she was moving to Whiting. It's a small area west of here, famous for retirement communities."

"Retirement communities?" Martin repeated dumbly.

"It's a place where people go to die." He smiled.

"Die?"

"I'm joking. It's just when people move there, it's usually their last move. It's an adult-only community with price-controlled housing and community-run activities. Older people seem to like it. It's an easy environment."

"I will go there and look. Thank you." Martin gave a pleasant smile, holding back his disbelief about this woman's absence from this address.

Martin didn't want to throw up any red flags of suspicion. He had a job to do, an unpleasant job, but the less people knew about him or his trip the better. Martin got back in his car and hit the wheel with closed fists, screaming in German about his displeasure of missing this woman again. After taking a deep breath, he again looked at the printout of addresses. There was one address for a Margaret Stratton in Whiting. Could this be it? Could it be her? Surely it couldn't be that easy, Martin asked himself. Schmidt had looked for decades. At last, he would find this woman and make her pay for all her bullshit. Martin put the address into his GPS and headed back the way he came. He stayed on the woodsy Lacey Road for miles and miles, seeing nothing more than pine trees and the occasional car.

As Martin got closer to the retirement communities in Whiting, the rate of speed took a serious dip. Cars moved slower than the posted speed limit, causing delays and forcing Martin to miss green lights. These delays only enraged Martin further, as he was desperate to find this woman so he could learn the location of his brother.

The GPS read a few more blocks before the next turn. Then Martin would see the woman his father loved so much. The woman who broke his heart and left him for a foreign land. Sitting at the red light, Martin took the opportunity to look around at the humble yet quaint surroundings that provided security and shade to those who hadn't achieved much but deserved more than to spend their last days sleeping in the streets. When the light turned green, he impatiently began the last leg of his journey, which felt longer with every turn of the wheel, never reaching the road's speed limit. One elderly driver after another pulled out in front of him, and each drove slower than the last.

Angry and annoyed, Martin found the address on Constitution Boulevard and pulled over to the curb. He looked down at Margaret's photo. It was taken years ago, but the overall facial structure should be the same. Martin stared at every detail of the woman's face, especially her eyes. There was always truth in the eyes, Martin learned from his father at a young age.

"The eyes don't lie, even when the mouth does," Strauss once told his son.

Having replaced the photo in his pocket, Martin checked the rearview mirrors and took a slow gaze at the neighboring homes. No one was out, and the coast looked clear. He got out of the car and headed up the driveway. He would show her the evidence if she tried to lie to him. Martin opened the outside screen door and knocked loudly on the inside door, once, twice, three times, but no one responded. He peered through the living room window, the only window not covered by shades or curtains. To his surprise, he could see straight through the house and the back window into the backyard, where a woman was working in the garden.

Martin took another look around and saw no one, so he headed around the garage and into the backyard. Martin walked up to the woman kneeling in the dirt. She didn't hear him approach. She squinted over her shoulder at him with the sun in her eyes, clearly startled.

Got you! Martin smiled to himself, matching her features to the image he'd memorized. *Finally, got you!*

"Can I help you?" Her voice quaked. Margaret's heart pounded at having been caught off guard by this man in her backyard. The privacy she created behind the house was no longer her friend.

"You know who I am. I have come on behalf of my father," he said sternly, with both arms at his sides.

"No, I have no idea who you are, young man." She stood and shook the dirt from her gardening gloves, removing them slowly. Old memories rushed to the front of her mind as she looked more closely at him. The curve of his jaw, the shade of his eyes. That hairline, the way he stood. He looked just like … *Oh no. Could this really be my Martin?*

Margaret tried to remain calm. She suspected he was indeed her son, yet she wasn't entirely sure. The last time she'd seen him, he was a small child. "I think you have the wrong person."

As soon as she said those words, she wondered why she said them. A small pushback such as that would do nothing to deter a man who had clearly traveled a distance to find her. Margaret looked at his shoes, nice European leather, not the average American tie-up sneakers. His footwear matched his accent all right, German, one hundred percent.

"I do not have the wrong person," he replied. "You are Margaret Stratton, former lover of Erich Strauss, my father." He practically dared her to lie to him.

Margaret sighed. He grew up as she suspected he might; his father's son, full of hate and anger, problematic, just like him. Margaret blamed herself for not taking Martin with her, but even at the age of three, he was on his father's path, a path of corruption and lies, developing an innate sense of superiority and heightened morality. But at least her daughter had not inherited that.

Margaret could not deny the name he had called her, for she was Margaret Stratton, and he found her using that name. All she could do now was deny or minimize her role in his father's life.

"I'm not that woman. You have the wrong person." Her gaze flicked to the back door.

Martin must have anticipated she was going to try to make a break for it. He grabbed her by the wrists and yelled at her to stop lying. "When you left Germany, you were with child. Where is my brother?"

"You don't know what you're asking. There is no child, no child!"

Martin continued to hold Margaret by her wrists and pulled her inside. She screamed. "Let me go, damn you, let me go!" She didn't fear rape, but was he capable of killing her? She had no idea the instructions that maniac sent him with, nor did she know if he knew she was his mother, too.

Martin was hearing none of it, easily pulling her across the yard. Trying to pull back and resist him, Margaret kicked and screamed for help. This was likely why Martin wanted her indoors rather than out in the open, screaming so loud even the hearing-impaired might realize someone was in trouble. Practically lifting her off the ground, Martin forced her through the door and into her home. Once inside, Martin took a quick look around and pushed her into the living room and forced her back until she fell onto the couch. He pulled his phone from his jacket pocket and snapped a picture of her, his temper growing more foul. "I know who you are. My father is positive you were carrying his son when you left, and my father doesn't make these kinds of mistakes. Now, where is he, woman?"

"I have no son," Margaret had divorced herself from ever having had a little boy and pressed the pain of that abandonment into the darkest corner of her mind—she'd had to leave him to save herself and Gwen. Yet here he was, standing in front of her, as large and scary as his father.

Martin combed through her photos on the furniture and hanging from the wall, dropping them on the floor after looking at each one. "Who are these people?"

"They're nobody: friends, distant relatives, no one Erich knows."

Margaret blanched, realizing she had confirmed Martin's suspicion, cementing his mistrust of her.

"You were with my father then, were you not?"

Mother and son looked at each other for the longest moment of Margaret's life. She hadn't given anything that much thought in the last thirty years since she considered leaving Germany. Now here stood her grown son, lost to her for all that time, left by her to be reared by a maniac, a supremacist, a war instigator, trapped and fueled by his own delusions. Had she taken a greater risk and brought Martin to the States with her, he might have had a chance at a better, quieter life, not listening to hate-filled rants until he was filled with it himself. *How can I ever forgive myself*, Margaret thought, *how?*

Martin charged through Margaret's house, damaging photos and heirlooms with careless abandon. The mess Martin made as he moved through her home appeared to be more of a bullying scare tactic to wear her down and get her talking. As frames and trinkets fell to the floor and shattered, Margaret looked for an opportunity to run. But to where this time?

"There is no other son. Stop this right now!" Margaret stomped along behind him. "Leave immediately!"

Martin stopped as one photograph caught his eye. Margaret frowned in his path of destruction, not believing for a moment he listened to her words. Grabbing a picture from the wall, Martin shoved it in Margaret's face. Within an inch, Martin pointed to the young woman. "Is this your daughter?"

"Leave her out of this. She has nothing to do with anything that has to do with you or that monster!"

Martin slapped Margaret across the face hard. "My father is not a monster! He has sacrificed for me and his country. He is a man who will save his people, his country, and eventually the world from mediocrity. The people who remain will one day thank him, bowing at his feet, and you will too!" Martin pointed in Margaret's face. "You will be sorry you abandoned such a visionary, a strong man!"

Martin ripped the picture of her and Gwen from the frame and stuffed it in his pocket.

"What are you doing with that? Give me that!" Margaret put out her hand uselessly.

"She is important to you. I can tell this. I'll keep this photo just in case, as you Americans like to say. Just in case."

Not seeing a single photo of a familiar face or a brother, Martin left Margaret's house confused but somewhat satisfied she might be telling the truth. But he did not let her know that. Why would his father believe there was a brother? He had too much to think about right now. *I will return to Germany in a few days with this photo, and I will email him the one I took off the wall to be sure she is my father's former lover.*

18

ROCCO, JACQUES, AND GWEN traveled through the city to the University of Berlin, located in the former East Germany side, where teaching had been heavily influenced by Communism, leading to discontent among the students, especially those who remembered the smell of democracy. At this institution, politicians could meet with professors and students to identify areas of interest and goals for the future. The Free University of Berlin was an important location in the fight for one Germany, and it now upheld the fight to prevent any future annexations.

Rocco put Gwen in touch with student leaders who could describe the bloodshed they witnessed at the rally that turned into a violent riot the other day. Several student leaders met with Gwen in a university office, all sitting casually on the floor and in office chairs. Gwen looked around at their faces, noticing how young they were. They reminded of her own college days. They wanted their faces shown, and their real names used while they talked about what they wanted, stood for and expected from their government. They were all young, idealistic, and naïve. But it made for good television, and she needed B-roll and, truthfully, they might know something that could help her with the story.

With Rocco behind the rolling camera and Jacques gathering audio, the trio was on their way to learning what they could about the financial crisis gripping Germany, at least from the perspective of college students. Gwen wanted to know what they did and didn't know without all the drama of a street riot.

The spokesman for the group said, "It started several years ago, but it was considered at that time insignificant because everyone recognizes there are economic highs and economic lows. Even the simplest person knows everything goes up and down.

But as prices went up and access to certain goods became more difficult, salaries remained stagnant. People questioned how long this would last. Citizens demanded information from the government about why Germany was struggling when their friends in different countries saw none of it. Then, as a society, we were rebuffed by our own government that mentioned how things could be much, much worse. We could be unemployed, they responded. We all agreed that would be much worse."

The students nodded, looking around at each other. Then one of the female students continued, "Our elders kept their mouths shut and continued to work for the same money year after year, even though the work grew harder and harder. We watched our parents make cuts to the household budgets every time costs increased. We were patient, we waited and waited, trusting those thieves in Berlin."

"We are fools," one young man shouted. "Damn fools!"

"How could we know and see this downturn turn into a recession?" another student said.

"Well, if someone doesn't figure something out soon, this recession will become a damn depression! I graduated with a degree in engineering, and I can't find a job! Are you serious? Me? I can't even get an interview!"

The young man shook, pale from stress and exhaustion. The ongoing marches and campaigns had taken their toll on these students, who only sought answers. They were above violence right now, at least.

Gwen was not dealing with ordinary rioters looking to make trouble, but well-reared, educated young individuals at a complete loss about why times were so tough. Gwen looked at Rocco, then at Jacques, who was sitting among the students holding the microphone.

Without a word, they all agreed this was bigger than mismanaged money, something disturbing was happening. But what?

A noise in the hall preceded the door swinging open and startling everyone, more so Gwen and Rocco than the students.

"What is going on here?" one of the two young men at the door asked.

The students breathed a sigh of relief, clearly recognizing the pair, but Gwen and the crew did not recognize either of the newcomers.

Gwen stood to appear unafraid, her height an asset. "Who are you?"

Jacques, with microphone in hand, moved toward the door to grab sound. Rocco took a cautious stance next to Gwen, ready to react if necessary.

"I'm Karl Reinhardt," one man said.

The other said, "I'm Heinrich." He did not give his last name.

"You're Karl Reinhardt?" Gwen asked.

"Yes. Who are you?" Karl asked.

"I'm Gwen Patterson, an American journalist from New York City."

"I know you." Heinrich smiled. "Yes, we know who you are now."

Gwen told Karl how she received his name the day before from Walter Berger, who suggested he could shed light on the riots and other issues.

"We will see. Let's meet tomorrow at a safer location," Karl said.

Heinrich and Rocco agreed. Rocco gave them his cell number, and they arranged a secure place to meet where they could have a conversation about what they thought was going on.

"Let's make it tomorrow, early," Rocco said. "We'll wait for your call."

The group disbanded and everyone returned to the safety of their homes that night.

Gwen called Jacques and Rocco over to share her thoughts about taking these questions right up the stairs of the capitol.

"After talking to the guys tomorrow, I think Parliament is our next stop," Gwen said. "It's the only way to push this story forward."

"I know a few people," Rocco said. "Let me make a call, and we'll see who's available to speak."

AS THE DAY gave way to evening, Germany settled down for dinner, but it was still early in New York and business was booming. Neck-deep in story tips and leads proposed by a newsroom full of Gwen wannabes, Joe was actively keeping the news machine moving, looking for that next big story. As he read one half-bad idea after another, the phone rang, and, assuming it was another story idea, Joe answered it more gruffly than normal.

"What?" Joe belted. "I'm busy in here!"

It was the receptionist. "Mr. Bess, the police are on the line for you."

"The police? What in hell for?"

"They wouldn't say. They want to talk to you."

"Put them through," he said, exasperated.

Now what? Joe thought.

The phone rang again, and Joe answered with a slightly more polite tone.

"This is Detective Sean O'Malley of the NYPD, Mr. Bess. I'm afraid I have unfortunate news for you."

Joe's heart dropped, imagining the worst, and he was usually right. He settled back in his chair, removing his cigar from his teeth and holding it squarely in his free hand. "What is it?"

Detective O'Malley had Joe's full attention, though it might not have sounded that way. Three days ago, Joe had reported Gwen's usual limo and its driver Lyle missing. But after Gwen insisted that she rode in that very limo after her return from Belgium, there remained one question: where was Lyle?

"We found your missing limo abandoned under a viaduct not too far from the Red Hook Waterfront in Brooklyn. I'm sorry to tell you, but your driver Lyle was found in the trunk, deceased."

"I was afraid of that." Joe rubbed his face. "Gwen Patterson took that limo from the airport to our building two days ago. Some Asian guy was driving, said Lyle had the day off."

"What time was that?"

"Let's see … she got to my office at 5:30 … she called me from the airport after she was picked up, just after five a.m. Later that day, that same guy hijacked a cab she was getting into and waved a gun at her, demanding information. She recognized him and he bragged about killing poor Lyle."

"Did you or she report any of this to NYPD, Mr. Bess?"

"She managed to kick him out of the cab into traffic. He was struck and killed. It may have slipped her mind to involve the police. Maybe you have an Asian John Doe clogging the morgue."

Detective O'Malley made a barking noise in his throat. "Maybe. I don't suppose he identified himself to Ms. Patterson?"

"No. Can you tell me how Lyle died?"

"Shot, close range, in the back of the head after he was bound at the ankles and wrists with heavy-duty tape. It looks like he was shot inside the trunk," O'Malley said, not sparing any of the dirty details. "We thought that was kind of odd, since they had him neutralized with the tape and the trunk. What was the point of killing him unless he could identify his attacker? We're also wondering if it's a possibility that Lyle was shot in the trunk to keep the car clean so whoever did it could use the car to pick up your reporter. Is she working on something dangerous?"

Joe could not answer that question or any of the others. "I don't know, but I will tell Gwen to be extra careful. I'll have the family's information sent to you. If you learn anything else, please call me directly." Joe wanted to wrap up the gruesome conversation so he could track down Gwen, tell her what happened and warn her of the potential danger.

"Thanks, Mr. Bess. If I need anything, I will call. And, again, sorry for your loss."

"Thanks," Joe replied as he hung up.

Joe sat straight up at his desk, rubbing his face and running his hand through his hair. The news was too much. Lyle was murdered just to get close to Gwen, but why? Who was behind this?

AS GWEN CAME through her hotel room door, her phone was already ringing. Falling onto the side of the bed, Gwen reached for the phone, guessing it was Joe; the time was about right.

"Hi Joe."

"Hey, kid, we need to talk." Joe sounded down.

"What is it?"

"It's Lyle. They found him."

"I don't suppose they found him alive?" Gwen asked.

"Actually, kid, are you sitting down?"

"I'm lying down, why?"

"Well, the news is not good. They found him bound and shot dead in the trunk of the limo you took here. The police said he was rolling around in the trunk for more than a day. He was probably back there while you were in the car. Damn it, Gwen, Lyle's murderer drove you here! Who was that guy?"

"And who hired him?"

Lyle had been murdered so someone could get close to her, and he did get very close to her, but that person only died by accident. If the Asian man hadn't died, would he have carried out his orders, and if so, what were they?

"Whoever sent him could send someone else, kid, so keep your wits about you."

"I will. I am."

This incident reinforced her concern about the seriousness of this story and her concern about her situation.

19

GWEN WAS INTO THE THIRD DAY of her economic story, but she didn't feel like she was getting any closer to the facts. She spoke to one witness after another, one who saw this but didn't know that. All the information she collected so far was circular. She needed to break out and learn something new. *This is hardly an exposé of my caliber*, she thought.

But Rocco did receive a text from Karl containing a Berlin address where the five should meet privately and, most importantly, they could meet safely. Rocco didn't immediately recognize the address, only that Weinbergsweg ran alongside an open-air park, which could be a good thing or a bad thing, depending on how they looked at it. It could be a good thing because the group could see anyone suspicious coming from a distance, but it could also be a bad thing because of the tall, wide trees that could provide cover if someone already knew Gwen was coming. They would have to take the chance.

Rocco told Gwen to saddle up and Jacques, too. They were on the move to an abandoned garment manufacturing building in the lesser-traveled side of Berlin. The building descended several floors beneath the street level, specifically designed to hide the sweatshop workers who once filled them for Germany's finest designers. They climbed into the unmarked news van and began the slow journey to the old factory set centrally in the vintage clothing neighborhood. *Interesting spot,* Gwen thought. She wondered about the location and the advantage to meeting there. But Gwen told the boys she would go alone if she had to, so off they went.

"I want you to stick with me," Rocco said.

"What? Why?" Gwen frowned. *I'm not a child.*

"Because this isn't the greatest part of town, and they aren't exactly asking us to meet in a café. There must be a reason for such a seedy location. I don't trust anyone, not right now. So, you stay on my six. Got it? We aren't going to have any heroes today," Rocco glared at her in the rearview mirror.

Jacques said, turning his head slightly in Gwen's direction, "Stay within arm's length of one of us."

"Fine." Gwen realized this wasn't an argument she was going to win.

She wasn't sure if things were any more dangerous than the day before, but things certainly felt weirder. Tension hovered in the air. Rocco drove the van while Jacques prepped the camera and tested the satellite equipment. Gwen gazed out the window as the neighborhood changed from beautiful streets with touristy hotels and fancy shops to a darker and more dangerous environment. Gwen opened her reporter's notebook and wrote down questions and thoughts she wanted to speak about with Karl and Heinrich.

It would be easier to frame these questions if I knew more specifically who or what was behind the missing money, Gwen thought. *Then we could get to the why.* Gwen was trying to be creative in her questioning to elicit answers that would lead to new story angles and hopefully identify new sources for follow-up questions.

Gwen, Rocco, and Jacques arrived at the building's address, but it was nothing the three of them expected. All the factories and stores on the block looked abandoned, like a ghost town. The address marked a vacant storefront from the street, but the back of the building yielded much more to see.

Karl and Heinrich waited in the shadows until all three got out of the van. The two college men said they wanted to make sure Gwen and her crew came alone. Rocco shot B-roll material while Jacques unloaded the audio equipment. All three looked around, confused, absorbing the blighted environment while wondering why the guys would choose to meet in such a dilapidated area.

They walked into a wasteland of discarded raw materials once used to make Germany's finest clothes, name-brand fashions one would see in the fanciest shops on the finest streets of any city. Old rolls of cloth were stacked in the corner alongside headless manikins with old measuring tape hanging around their necks. Old sewing machines and other obsolete, abandoned equipment scattered the floor and throughout the facility, covered in dust and cobwebs. Old ordering sheets written in different languages littered the floor and blew around with the wind as it freely came through windows that no longer held any glass. That too lay on the floor, shattered, a safety hazard if any neighborhood children came to explore.

It was hard to believe a facility in this condition ever produced anything of great monetary value. This building and the whole block were evidence and another reminder of all the German people had lost, another indication of the far-reaching financial crisis.

As they cleared their path, kicking debris to the side, they made their way to the back of the building, unsure where Karl and Heinrich would lead them. They all passed through the showroom and stood waiting for a functional elevator to take them to the bottom floor.

"What's on the bottom floor?" Rocco asked.

"Privacy," Karl replied. "Privacy."

After the elevator reached the bottom floor, the door opened. To Gwen's surprise, the room looked somewhat functional, but for meetings and gatherings, no longer for its initial intended purpose.

"You guys meet with other organizers here?" Gwen asked, impressed.

"Yes, I know this building well," Karl said. "My mother once worked in this clothing factory when times grew tight. My mother was a wonderful woman, and she didn't want her children going without, so when things changed, and my father's work was no longer enough, she came here and got a job. She was a marvelous seamstress. She could make anything," Karl said proudly with a smile. "Then whatever happened, happened, and the money dried up. No more orders came, and workers were laid off. This was a fully operational clothing house until a couple of years ago. I would come here after school and do my homework and wait for my mother right over there." Karl pointed to an old desk and chair still sitting in the corner.

"Come on, let's begin," Gwen said abruptly shifting the conversation back to business.

Without even opening her notebook, she asked a barrage of questions. The guys answered what they could and what they knew, but their information was limited. Rocco shot the guys tightly to avoid giving away their location. They intended to continue using this facility as a meet-up point for future rallies and other issues.

"I appreciate all your input and the risks you're taking, but if I'm going to make serious headway on this story and get any meaningful answers, then I need to reach someone at the top," Gwen said.

"Well, I think I can help you with that." Heinrich grinned. "I am Heinrich Jakob."

Gwen stood straighter and took a long look at the young man who she believed just revealed himself as the current chancellor's son.

"I want you to know who I am, because it is not just anyone who could introduce you to someone so important," Heinrich said.

"Someone so important?" Gwen repeated.

"Yes."

"You're Heinrich Jakob, son of Chancellor Jakob?" Gwen confirmed for the camera.

"Yes, I am." He gave Gwen the affirmative she wanted.

Gwen looked back over her shoulder at Rocco, who seemed unfazed by this revelation.

"So, you have someone important we should meet? Who?" Gwen asked, clearly wanting to get this story to the next level.

Karl motioned to Heinrich. Heinrich gazed into the darkness of the next room, and in a raised but respectful tone said, "It's safe. You may come out now."

Hearing those words, Rocco took a protective stance next to Gwen. Jacques also turned with curiosity. But to everyone's surprise, this simple old woman stepped out of the shadows and stood before them in a beautifully tailored suit and short heels. She wore eyeglasses typical for a woman her age, with a matching chain around her neck so she wouldn't lose another pair. She stood only five feet tall, but her presence was impressive; she clearly was not someone to be trifled with. She introduced herself. Rosa Dyke was one of the German Parliament's oldest representatives and was considered one of the more stable and knowledgeable members.

Frau Dyck told the crew she believed members of Jakob's own staff were funneling the money to buy weapons at the direction of former General Secretary of the SED, Erich Strauss. While she and Strauss remained good friends, she never agreed with his politics or his vision for the world, a world dominated by him, his supporters, and their ideas of superiority. She warned that while a lot of money was missing from the nation's budget, she didn't believe he was using all of it to buy weapons.

"Where could he hide billions in weapons? No." She shook her head. "I and others in Parliament believe Strauss is using some of the money to buy weapons, but also some of it he is using for something more sinister, more dangerous than we can probably imagine." Raising her index finger at the group, she warned them, "Do not underestimate him."

She told how Strauss' personality had changed, devolved since they were young, and ideas he once easily floated as possibilities were no longer accepted in a decent German society. Strauss' ideas marginalized different groups and infringed on too many individual rights.

"As a person like me grew, I evolved, and I realized like so many others that inclusion and compromise are key to a healthy and peaceful society—not one group dictating to all the others what is acceptable and what isn't without as much as a say or even a vote."

Gwen picked up on the one key piece of information she had been yearning for since she was assigned this story. "Excuse me, but you said he may be using the country's money for another project. What project?"

Rocco zoomed in on Frau Dyck's face to capture the emotion as well as the words.

"I don't know. He bought acres and acres of property years ago, sites that contain old bunkers from WWII. These bunkers go deep underground, and they contain sleeping quarters, cafeterias, office space, and laboratory space. He could be doing anything down there, anything," she repeated in a soft tone. "He has gone mad, you know."

The group stood firm, their minds racing with the possibilities of what Strauss could do with all that land.

Gwen asked, "He has to be buying those weapons from someone, so who's getting all the money?"

Frau Dyck smiled and nodded. "That's correct, young lady. Follow the money."

Everyone looked at each other. Finally, they had a new lead.

"I will see if I can find a name or two and send it to you through Heinrich. I speak to this young man all the time, no one would suspect anything," Frau Dyck said.

"That would be truly helpful," Gwen said. "If you can get me names, I can take it from there. I just need to know where to start and who is willing to talk."

"Done," Frau Dyck said. "Give me a few days."

"Heinrich, after I get those names and I have more information to go on, I think that would be time to talk to your father." Gwen hoped Heinrich would provide assistance with that introduction as well.

"Yes, let's see where Frau Dyck's information takes you, and after that I can help you with my father. He is a good man. He will want to help," Heinrich said.

ON THE OTHER SIDE OF GERMANY, soldiers-for-hire were preparing for the ship's arrival. They were told to expect a large ship carrying Strauss' precious cargo that left New York Harbor a few days earlier. Crossing the sea with the engines running at full capacity, crew members took turns at the wheel, giving their skipper a much-needed break. Captain Minh and the crew didn't want to waste any time. They had a deadline. Tonight would be the safest night, as identified months earlier. The crew happily worked overtime, proceeding full-speed ahead, destination the Port of Hamburg, Gateway to the World.

Waiting on dry land, Schmidt's men gathered in a nearby warehouse, not too far from the docks where the crew was expected to disembark. Schmidt's men came in groups to get their orders, change clothes, and prepare for the long night ahead. Marc, one of Schmidt's right-hand men, oversaw the ground troops. He emerged from the crowd, giving instructions and assignments to the two-dozen men, all of whom subscribed to Strauss' way of thinking. Each man was given a specific job, an area to cover, and all were ordered to carefully surveil the area for anyone who didn't belong. A few men changed into port authority police uniforms to redirect any unexpected vehicles or foot traffic. The men were ordered not to shoot unless fired upon or if it became necessary. One bullet could trigger a firefight and draw the attention of the real police. Quiet was key. The goal was to move the merchandise from the ship to land vehicles without drawing attention to their presence.

However, they were armed with weaponry and tactical gear; each man carried a MP5 or an Uzi submachine gun. The Uzi was a favorite among many paramilitary groups for being cheap, attainable, and fully automatic.

Marc wanted to rally the troops, to reassure them they were on the right side of history. He hopped up and stood on a crate to see over the crowd and be seen by them as well. With an MP5 submachine gun in one hand and two sidearms strapped securely to his waist and his thigh, he waved his free hand to indicate he was ready to speak. The middle-aged man welcomed the room of Strauss supporters and told them they were trailblazers in the fight for their survival. It caused an uproar among the soldiers, all of whom served Germany well at one time or another. But now they took their training to the shipping docks to begin what they were told was a fight for German survival.

"Your mission is true. You are on the right path. The path to victory," he shouted, holding his gun high above his head. Thunderous applause broke out among the men, all of whom would follow Marc into hellfire and go out in a blaze of glory.

Quelling the rally and lowering his voice, Marc told the soldiers stealth was vital. "You must be invisible," he said. "I need you to break into two teams. Team one, you will take the high ground and watch your brothers' backs. Team two, you will wait on the ground and be responsible for unloading the ship. Team one, you will provide them cover."

The men had donned matching black-knitted caps for camouflage and bullet-proof vests on their chests. Their arms were entwined around their rifles in a resting position while they gave their attention to their commander.

"Keep your eyes open and on one another." His fingers drifted in the air from one man to the next. "The ship is expected before midnight. That will give you enough time to get the cargo unloaded and transferred to the rails, where it will head to storage."

Parked inside the warehouse were several medium-sized tactical vehicles, Austrian designed, all gassed up and ready to go. On Marc's orders, the solders took formation according to their team assignment and climbed on their military rides sitting side by side, guns aimed at the sky secured between their knees. The overhead doors opened, exposing them to crisp night air. The men pulled down their black caps until ski masks covered their faces. They all looked the same. The engines roared and the men quietly focused on their mission as they headed outdoors and closer to the docks. The rumble of the trucks' engines would make too much noise and draw attention, so the drivers held back. They would stop short of the destination, leaving the crew to move on foot with stealth-like wonder, bringing all their years of training to bear.

The sun had set, the moon was a crescent, and the night grew dark, providing the perfect backdrop for a covert shipment. The soldiers' black attire blended with the night sky. Schmidt's men, ordered by Strauss, converged on the dock like clockwork. They took their positions throughout the port, taking strategically high points for surveillance while others took cover on the ground, wearing their crowns and camouflage made of Marram grass, a local beach grass.

They also wanted the best view up the Elbe River, waiting for the ship's captain to signal. The monstrous vessel, reflagged and with the transponder off, would come tonight to the waiting berth and moor while Schmidt's footmen did Strauss' bidding.

Captain Minh took great care driving the ship; any mistakes would be costly. Without transponders and the computer system off, Minh had to navigate the shipping channel by only hand and sight, a dangerous proposition at night. Even for a skilled captain such as Minh, it was a challenging task.

The captain radioed from the bridge that the cargo was beyond the North Sea and at the mouth of the river, beginning its final sixty-eight-mile journey to the pre-purchased slot. It didn't take much convincing, just a briefcase of Euros, to have the local port authority's top guy look the other way. With all their ducks in a row, Strauss' men were ready to proceed. They would get their cargo and use the railway system to move their merchandise out of Hamburg to a safer, more secure location. The Port of Hamburg annually received more than fifty million tons of cargo, so who would possibly notice a small shipment of weapons and other arms?

"We have just passed through the gateway," one of the ship's crew said over the radio, keeping a watchful eye from the ship's flybridge. He was referring to the entry point of Germany's largest seaport.

This was to alert the crew to be on their guard as they made their way up the river, smoothly, of course. The men were all set, dressed for the occasion, weapons at the ready. The crewman knew what was at stake and was mindful of all those who had already died for this fight. They had to succeed, or their fellows had died in vain. They, too, believed they were acting on the winning side of history.

A few men sat on the ship's flybridge wearing the customary work gear to appear casual and provide the typical image when a cargo ship moved past, so as not to raise any red flags or cause any suspicion. The ship with its Canadian flag flying high would not cause any concern for the men or the cargo. Canadians were typically considered benign people.

CIA AGENT ALEX, at the behest of his boss, called a counterpart in the German government, telling him about potential gunrunners using the Hamburg docks tonight as an arrival point. The G-man alerted Hamburg police, who dispatched their special weapons and tactical officers to handle such jobs. Alex made one more phone call to ensure Carter knew about everything happening on his watch, telling him all about the expected gun shipment in Hamburg. Carter was still in Berlin, watching Gwen from a distance.

Acting on this phone tip from a familiar source, local officers from Hamburg headed for the same docks. Members of the German police who were on the side of law and order were given the go-ahead by *Küstenwache des Bundes*, the German Federal Coast Guard, and the port authority to arrest any crew members on the ship allegedly carrying illegal weapons. The corrupt port authority agent who gave police the go-ahead knew exactly what those officers would be walking into, and he didn't say a word. How could he without revealing his bribery? What could he say? "Hey, I took a bunch of Euros so some gunrunners could move their merchandise." No, there wasn't a thing he could say except give the go-ahead and allow officers to act on the tip if they felt it was legitimate. Not wanting to see the outcome of his handiwork, the shady agent left his post early that night, going home sick. With his neatly filled briefcase in hand, the agent checked out and left for the night.

The SWAT team was on their way to investigate or intervene, if necessary. The whole point of a SWAT team was to de-escalate or prevent harm to others.

Normally, when a SWAT team came, people perked up and took notice; these were the best of the best of local police, well able to handle fluid situations and difficult interactions, especially when emotions were hot and tempers were running high. But now their skills would be put to the ultimate test. Twenty Hamburg SWAT team members were dispatched to the docks.

Since this wasn't a hostage negotiation, the SWAT leader Lt. Stephen Lang didn't call for any snipers to provide overwatch. Each team member took one of the normal positions to cover the docks and each other. Entry officers would be the most crucial because once the team had the mariners in custody, they would have to clear the ship.

The SWAT team, wanting to surprise the ship's occupants, came by water, assuming they would look to the land for police cruisers. Using two amphibious five-ton cargo transport vehicles, the SWAT team moved up the Elbe River with their lights off and their engines on low. This was not a transport Schmidt's men would have chosen: an American import with an aluminum hull.

Lang told the men to begin their approach and signed off ten-David. At various points, men quietly jumped off the boats to take positions under area docks. Some wearing waders and others wearing scuba gear, these officers approached the targeted area from the southeast, so they had a clear view up the Elbe River as it flowed northwest into the North Sea. Based on the tip, this was the location.

Schmidt's men took their positions and assumed radio silence until the ship was close enough to signal. Waiting for the ship's arrival, the soldiers were patient and thoughtful in all their movements and careful even with their breath in the night air.

One guerrilla on watch trained his eyes on the river, watching for the ripples to move faster and become larger, indicating the ship was drawing near. Gaps appeared in the ripples; something was interrupting the water flow that wasn't there earlier. He adjusted his perch and took an alert posture, removing the safety from his Blaser R93 and peering through the scope. In ideal conditions, he could accurately fire more than 790 meters and not miss his target. The river here was only half that wide.

A soldier high on his perch broke radio silence, telling his comrades they were no longer alone. "*Wir haben Gesellschaft.*" These simple words began a cascade effect, putting every soldier on heightened alert, waiting to hear the slightest snap. As the moments lapsed, the soldiers heard in the distance the low engine of the transport boat as it idled up the river. The soldiers waited calmly to see if the boat was there for them or just passing by. The disruption in the ripples continued as the river flow picked up speed and developed small whitecaps on the top. The wind blew colder and faster in the night air.

Another soldier, hearing that low engine, swung his Barrette M95 in the direction of the sound and set up his bipod. The large-caliber rifle was classified as anti-material—to be used only on military-grade vehicles because shooting at people with it was against the Geneva convention. One well-placed shot would kill the engine or sink the craft.

"Ich habe das," the soldier said, indicating if there was to be a shot, it was his. The men calmly waited for the ship and their uninvited guests.

Marc radioed Minh and told him to take his time; they had an issue to handle closer to the dock. "I will call you when the coast is clear." Then he told his crew, "It looks like we're going to turn the lights on tonight and show our unwanted guests out."

That was all they needed to hear. Everyone cocked their weapons.

"I thought we weren't going to have any fun tonight," one soldier said with a chuckle.

All eyes were on the water. The SWAT team was made. They too were dressed in dark clothes and not easily seen, but their footprints gave them away. As their boats drifted upriver, they randomly kicked up their engines, giving away their location. The sniper with his Barrett intended to sink the boats, giving the men an opportunity to swim away. Another soldier with his smaller caliber rifle moved in closer to clean up any stragglers who didn't get the message. They were under strict orders for a zero-body count, if possible. Schmidt didn't want any needless death investigations that could impede Strauss' timeline. But "if possible" were the keywords. These men had killed before, and for the right cause, they would kill again. Through their scopes, they scanned the riverbank, looking for anything out of place. Schmidt's men were at a relaxed, heightened state of alert. Only a well-trained soldier could be calm under such circumstances. But they had the upper hand, so they remained unseen.

The owner of the Barrett M95 manually released the thumb-lever safety while calmly but clearly saying, *"Ich habe ihn. Feuer?"* asking Marc for a go-ahead to shoot.

"Sink them, but without the fireworks." Marc meant to not hit the gas tank or anything that would cause an explosion or fire.

"Verstanden," the soldier said, indicating he fully understood.

Squeezing the trigger, the gunman let go one round, hitting the hull of the cheap boat that immediately took on water. Stunned by the sound, the officers took cover only to realize they were on their way down. The police leaped from the boat one after another. As they swam toward the shore, a masked individual on the shoreline aimed his MAC-10 at them. The soldier let a few rounds go into the water, falling short of the men who swam for their lives, struggling from being weighed down by their gear. Officers got the message fast that they were not alone. Following the leader, they submerged, swimming with the current and creating the greatest distance between them and the men with the guns. With the opposition having a weapon sufficient to take out a boat, the police were outgunned, outnumbered, and ambushed. A masked gunman like this was rarely alone. The current betrayed the officers not once to reveal their location but twice as it swept them downstream. One by one, they disappeared into the darkness of the Elbe River.

Marc radioed Minh and told him to get the ship moving again; time was of the essence. Minh kicked the engines into gear and continued the slow pace to the docks. The crew headed below deck to prepare to unload the numerous crates all containing the same product. They had many pallets to unload; the job would take much of the night. On land, several soldiers mobilized forklifts and others moving equipment to help expedite the transfer. Putting recent events in the rearview mirror, and with no other signs of interruption, the soldiers were back on schedule, moving at a fast clip. While several men kept watch and gave cover, still on their perches, the rest of the team replaced the safeties on their weaponry and securely hung their guns across their chests, keeping them close just in case.

Once the ship was in range, Minh flashed the Aldis Lamp using Morse Code: dash, dash, dash, pause, dash, dash, pause, dot, pause, dash, dash, dot, pause, dot, dash. This spelled out Omega, Omega, the name of the operation.

Marc, looking through his binoculars, read the flashing lights and told his men the ship was approaching. As the ship slid up alongside the dock, a crewmember dropped a long, heavy nylon rope, the first of several. The soldiers grabbed up the ropes and tied them to the moor, securing the ship tightly.

As a precaution, Minh told two of his crewmembers to grab rifles and take a defensive position on each side of the forecastle in case any unwelcome guests remained. Minh climbed down to the dock using a rope ladder hanging from the pilot door. Minh wanted to meet with Marc and get his money before the crew opened the gangway.

"So, what was the delay?" Minh asked Marc.

"Police. Someone squealed, but we sent them on their way," Marc said laughing. "Didn't you see them swim by you?"

Minh laughed too. "Nope, I didn't see any drowning police. You got the money?"

"Here it is. Everything for you and your crew. You can count it."

"I don't think that will be necessary." Minh lifted the bag of money by the handle. "If you cheat me, you can call someone else next time."

Marc smiled. "I wouldn't call anyone else."

As Minh took the cash, he could tell by the weight it was all there; he had been doing business like this for a long time. Minh waved his free hand, signaling his crew that the deal was done and to drop the gangway so Marc's men could embark.

Two soldiers, both of whom were weapons experts, embarked first to perform an inspection. It wasn't that Marc didn't trust Minh, but it was always better to verify. The soldiers embarked and quickly went into the hull of the ship, where Minh's men would hide Strauss' cargo among other legitimate containers. The two men randomly picked a couple of crates neatly stacked on wooden pallets and began their inspection.

One of the crates was opened and checked for content. The men were pleased to see nicely packed Uzi submachine guns. Another random crate pried open with a crowbar held a beautiful lot of MAC-10 submachine guns, a cheaply manufactured favorite among terrorists.

Both crews worked in sync, as though they had done this many times before. One pallet after another was removed from the ship and taken the short distance to the railway, where another crew waited to place Strauss' weapons in storage until needed.

IN BERLIN THE PHONE RANG once, twice, and on the third ring the general picked up. "Schmidt, *hier.*"

"This is Martin. I'm still in New York, and we have a problem."

Schmidt sat down in his chair and took a deep breath. The one thing Schmidt did not like was problems. He didn't want to have to tell Martin's father; Strauss didn't like problems, either.

"Minh's friend is dead. He was in New York and got killed. He had the thumb drive with the only copy of Travis' plans, but he was killed in a traffic accident several days ago, and his body has already been disposed of, so there is no way to find out where he was staying or go through his things to find the thumb drive. This is a big mess over here, just like this country."

"Be calm, young Martin," Schmidt said, being the voice of reason. "There has to be another way. There is always another way."

Schmidt, holding his head in his hand, thought deeply for a moment. *We need this blueprint. We must find a way.* "Do you know who developed the blueprint?"

"A man who works for Travis, his name is Joshua. Travis assured me two days ago he can recreate the blueprints, but I am still waiting."

"Find this Joshua yourself, if he is the only one who knows how, and make him get it done. This design is critical to your father's plan," Schmidt said firmly. "Do not take no for an answer."

Martin hesitated on the other end, then said, "*Ja,* that is what we will do, what we must do. You tell my father I will bring him his blueprint."

"You are a good son," Schmidt said taking a softer tone. "Martin, you are a good son."

AFTER FOUR DAYS and several unreturned phone calls, Gwen finally got Decker on the line. Gwen was not happy with the delay in response, and barely disguised her irritation.

"We need to talk, we need to meet," Gwen said most sternly. "I have got to put our story in chronological order and give context to what I'm finding. The facts individually don't mean anything, but if I can put them in a meaningful timeline, we may have something." Gwen deliberately used "our story" and "we" to impress upon him a sense of responsibility for helping her identify the truth. It was a cheap reporter's tactic, but it worked; some people felt so guilty.

Decker gave Gwen an address and told her to meet him there in an hour: *Unter den Linden 8*, just south of the zoo. She scribbled it down.

"Come in through the side door. It's a discreet entrance, and I will make sure it is open for you," Decker said.

"Okay." Gwen let her annoyance show in her tone. "We'll be there in one hour."

Gwen gave the slip of paper with the address to Rocco, who said, "I think this is a library, but let me double-check."

It was indeed a library. Gwen told Rocco about the side door suggestion.

"That's weird." He shrugged. "But we'll follow his instructions and see where it takes us. Don't worry, I've got your back."

"I know you do, and I appreciate it." Gwen smiled at him.

The address did lead them to a library, a grand, old library with a history spanning more than four hundred years. The Berlin State Library was now the property of the Prussian Cultural Heritage Foundation, and it remained one of the biggest libraries in all of Europe, a crown jewel for Germany. Under the foundation's protection, the library's contents were no longer at risk from those who wished to change the nation's history but preserved for those who wished to learn from it. A true scholar could lose themselves for days in this facility. This would be an excellent site for them to have a quiet conversation among books of history while they tried to unravel and make sense out of the present. Someday, Gwen imagined her findings might be housed in a building such as this among the world's greatest stories.

Rocco drove around the side of the library, closer to the river, to look for a place to park. Jacques had the audio equipment packed and Gwen had her notebook in hand. Rocco found an isolated spot under a lime tree, and after taking a quick look around, he said he wanted to first go and check the door to make sure they were all in the right place. Gwen gave him a nod. A library was an odd place to meet, but at this point the location was the least of her worries. She needed to call Joe with something, anything, but it had to be substantial.

Rocco checked the door. Gwen saw in the passenger mirror it was open, just as Decker said it would be. Rocco headed back to the van to grab the camera and other pieces of equipment while Jacques and Gwen hopped out with their gear in hand. They walked toward the door until it suddenly opened. The three stopped, surprised, not expecting to see anyone. After a brief pause, Decker poked his head from inside the door and told the group to hurry up, come in, and follow him downstairs. They glanced at one another and hurried toward the door. Rocco held open the door while Gwen and Jacques ducked inside.

Rocco gave one more look around the parking lot and saw the only person he expected to see parked off in the distance, Agent Carter. Rocco gave Carter a quick nod. Carter responded with a quick slip of his glasses, signaling everybody was fine.

Once inside, the reporters stood on the dark landing, the light out above their heads.

"Why is it so dark in here?" Gwen needed more light for her interview.

"I unscrewed the light bulb," Decker said. "I did not want to be seen."

Rocco looked at Decker and nodded.

"Follow me." Decker moved down the dimly lighted staircase. Holding onto the railing, they proceeded down the stairs after Decker, who clearly knew this facility well.

This should be good, following a world-renowned economist into a moldy base-ment without masks. We're probably breathing in mold spores, disgusting, Gwen thought.

With minimal light and keeping their voices down, they quietly shuffled by the stacks of papers and piles of books lining the hallway that had yet to be cataloged and introduced to the library's main floors. The hallway was crowded with stacks of independent thoughts, both handwritten and typed, and others catalogued through photographs, each author wanting to contribute to the global database of world knowledge. *Everyone has something that makes them special,* Gwen thought as she looked at all the documents waiting for a reader and recog-nition. The world was full of untapped potential, and it was refreshing to see it all in the raw, available for consumption and not taken to the grave. Joe once told her the graveyards of the world were the richest places on earth, so much untapped potential lay beneath the ground, never having been shared with the world. So sad, so unfortunate for the world as much as the artist.

Decker led the crew into what appeared to be a research room used by advanced students who wanted to peruse outdated, handwritten material from times long past. It was a place to contemplate, to lose oneself in the thoughts of philosophers and poets. A microfiche machine sat dusty in the corner as a testimony to a different time that abruptly gave way to its younger cousin the computer. The room was filled with this type of equipment, and Gwen anthro-pomorphized that it willfully stepped aside in the name of progress while still refusing to disappear in the event it would be needed should the wireless age betray them. It was a war room, ready for recall.

Gwen asked Decker, "Why meet here?"

"I came here as a youth, and I know it is quiet and no one ever comes down here." Decker sounded calmer. "We will talk here. I have things to share."

"Good," Gwen said. "I'm ready to listen." Gwen looked for a place to put her stuff down because she was ready for business.

"But first, I want your word no one will know it is I who told you." Decker held out his hands, concerned and seeking assurances. "I want to help, but I don't want to be dead, you know?"

Rocco set up the tripod, keeping one ear on the economist while Jacques hooked up wireless lavalier microphones for Gwen and Decker.

"During the past couple of days, I have accessed some documents. Apparently, I have not lost all access to everything. In fact, I have been included on a few documents thanks to Schmidt, but I am not sure why." Decker shrugged. "I am willing to talk to you, but you have to camouflage me, yes?"

"You mean disguise you?" Gwen tried not to roll her eyes. "Yes, we can disguise you, and we will." Gwen tapped her shoe, revealing her annoyance. *Too many people have died already, but he has hardly told me anything worth killing him over.* Gwen's patience grew thin, and her agitation with men who insisted on the cloak and dagger but didn't have the goods to back up the costume became harder to hide.

Rocco set up a bright light in the background to give heavy shade to the front of Decker's face, creating a dark silhouette. Jacques explained briefly how they would change Decker's voice in post-production. With the foreground lighting off and the background lighting up, Rocco set up one more light only for Gwen, who need not be disguised. Her dark hair gleamed with auburn highlights where it fell forward off her shoulders in the bright light, something hidden in her genes she'd always wondered about. She knew nothing about her father or his side of the family.

As Gwen held up the thumb drive, Rocco zoomed in to color-balance the camera.

"Done," Rocco said.

"Alright, let's begin," Gwen announced.

Gwen, not identifying Decker, introduced him as a "government official" on the side of the German people and law and order.

Decker talked to Gwen about emails citing specific terms, but those terms remained undefined. Gwen asked Decker to elaborate on what kind of terms he found so disturbing.

"This email talked about the underground empire where they are 'developing the formula for the new realm.' I don't know what kind of formula they could be talking about or what the underground empire is, but it's another clue to the disappearing cash and the unknown allocation of money." Decker read from the email he had printed out.

"The underground empire?" Gwen smiled to encourage him. "What is that?"

"I don't know. But the email goes on to say they are on schedule, everything is falling into place, and they are soon looking to release the formula. They are on schedule, it says." Decker sounded worried. "Now you know as much as I do, which is not enough."

"How is the money situation with Germany?" Gwen wanted an update on losses.

"The same, if not worse. With the economy in disrepair, people are unable to pay their taxes, so the funds coming into the government are less. Fewer funds to account for does make it more difficult to divert money, as it would now more likely be noticed," Decker said. "I do not know, is that positive? It does not sound so to me."

"Basically, you're saying there's nothing left to steal?" Gwen asked.

"*Ja*, there is no more to steal. Someone has it all or close to it." Decker dipped his head sadly.

"May I keep this email?" Gwen reached for the paper.

"*Ja*, keep it, use it, if it helps you." Decker handed it to her. "I will send you anything else I receive."

Gwen glanced at the header. The sender email address was a department name rather than a person, sent to a group name and bcc'd to Decker. "You don't know who sent this email?" Gwen watched Decker carefully.

"No, I don't know. I have heard nothing for months, a year, maybe, and now I am on some high official's group email? It makes no sense to me."

"Well, Herr Decker, it doesn't really work like that," Gwen explained.

"What do you mean?" Decker asked.

"You were bcc'd outside the group it was meant for. Someone sent this to the official group email, but for some reason this person wants you to know what is going on. Now if you're not part of the corruption, then maybe we all have a friend on the inside." Gwen raised her eyebrows and cracked a half smile.

Decker looked surprised. Gwen looked over her should at Rocco and Jacques, seeking their responses to this revelation.

"We may not be alone here," Gwen said. "We need to find the inside man."

WEEK
TWO

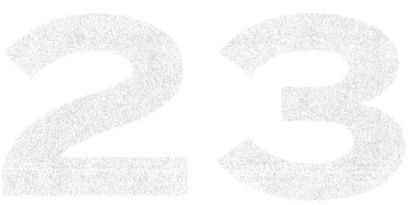

FULFILLING HIS FATHER'S ORDER, Martin went looking for Joshua to convince him to create a new set of plans on the spot if he too was unable to supply the originals. Martin and Joshua were on the same side, or at least they were supposed to be, Martin thought. Stopping at a chop shop where a mutual friend did business, Martin picked up a homemade battering ram fabricated from large-diameter steel tubing, just in case Joshua's door was locked. The rear plate featured a removable three-pound weight for balance and adjustability so Martin could be comfortable when he did his dirty work. Walking down the street with his new friend in a canvas bag, Martin counted down the street numbers as he closed in on the Patterson home.

TRAVIS GAVE JOSHUA a proper warning about the seriousness of the situation. He did his part in the past few days. He redrew the design of the drone to Strauss' specifications, making specific adjustments to increase its payload. He ensured its stealth and silence, and he made the modifications to hang weapons, if necessary. He also drafted a second version of the same drone meeting a different specification Strauss requested, though as to the purpose of that design, even Joshua was in the dark. At this point, with everything that had happened, he wasn't sure he wanted to know anymore.

Joshua spent his day off at home. He wanted his Gwen there too, safe and sound. He planned to do things around the house to surprise her when she returned from Germany. He puttered around, performing endless tasks to straighten up and turn their messy house back into a cozy home. He was empty-ing the dryer in the laundry room at the back of the house when he heard a knock at the front door. The sound was heavy and loud, not the soft, gentle tap made by the mail lady. Maybe solicitors. Joshua left the clothes on the top of the dryer and lightly walked toward the front door. He wasn't expecting anyone.

A tall, shadowy figure outside the door stood on the stoop, leaning in with both hands straddled on either side of the doorway. His body language read impatience capable of rashness. The privacy glass was two-way; only light came through clearly and easily. Joshua continued to move in closer, trying to identify the tall silhouette standing only feet away. The stocky figure knocked again and then rang the bell.

The man pounded on the door, shouting, "Let me in, or I will let myself in."

Joshua took a step back.

"Have it your way," the man said. "Americans are such cowards." He lifted something long and heavy-looking from a bag. "This is your final warning."

Joshua, realizing the gravity of the situation, shouted, "Okay, okay, wait a minute, wait a minute, I'm coming, I'm coming."

Sweat broke out as he realized Travis' dealmaker was on his doorstep. The German accent made that obvious. He could not avoid being in business with the rough and tumble. No more designing from a distance.

He glanced around the room, looking for anything he could use as a weapon. The nearby lamp would not be effective. However, a letter opener on the desk on the other side of the room would make a decent dagger. It was a gift from his mother; he hated to ruin it. He struggled to think clearly as the stress of the situation overwhelmed him. This man was coming in one way or another.

Joshua inched toward the door and opened it to length of the chain. Truly, the chain was useless. With the door ajar, Joshua glanced from the iron pipe to the man's face. "Who are you? What do you want?"

"That is a conversation that would be best had inside." The man pushed the door open, forcing Joshua to take several steps back. The chain broke like a toy under the strength of his arm.

"Who are you?" Joshua said with a stronger tone.

"You know." The imposing blond man nodded while taking slow, deliberate steps toward him. "I am in business with your boss, and now it appears I am in business with you." The man pushed his index finger squarely on Joshua's chest.

"Business? What kind of business? What the hell are you talking about?" Joshua stood straighter, confident this man was not here to kill him.

"You are the weapons designer assigned to the project, and I need my father's designs now." He looked straight into Joshua's eyes using a soft, easy tone.

Travis had told him about Martin Strauss. It wasn't what Martin said that disturbed Joshua, but how he said it. Clearly, he wasn't leaving empty-handed. Joshua couldn't give this man a unique copy. He ordinarily kept archived files of his work in case the client needed instructions or information after the originals were delivered. The first time he designed these drones, the client had demanded no trace be left, so he'd had to waste most of his week re-drawing them when Chen lost the thumb drive. Screw making that mistake again. He had a copy on his computer at the office. Seeking a delaying tactic, he forewent mentioning he had the design on his home computer.

"I've been re-drawing them this week. You probably know Chen lost the only copy in existence."

"Yes."

Martin's threatening posture indicated Joshua had made a sizeable mistake in taking this assignment, but this was a bell he could not un-ring. He needed to fix this somehow without angering Martin or Martin's crazy father. He needed to disentangle himself from the plot and rid himself of his new friend. In a flash of insight and inspiration, he decided to provide a flawed plan, something to hold them up until he could talk to Gwen, ask for her help and beg her forgiveness. Travis would be no help. Gwen was going to be mad, so mad. Josh's heart squeezed and his breath grew shallow. This whole situation could backfire, and she could leave him.

"The work is done, but it's on my office computer. I'll need to go there to get the file for you."

Martin looked at him with great skepticism and suspicion. He picked up a framed wedding photograph from a shelf in the living room, a five-by-seven in a polished silver Tiffany frame. Martin studied the photo and then threw the picture on the table. The glass cracked. Joshua flinched. He didn't want to ask why Martin did that, hoping he didn't recognize Gwen.

Martin eyed Joshua again. "You better not be bullshitting me, as you people like to say, because I will kill you."

"No bullshit, man."

Through pursed lips, Martin said, "This better not be a trick. You were paid for these plans and paid handsomely."

"I know, I know. I'll get you your plans, but they're at my office. It's closed for the night. Can we meet tomorrow?"

Martin did not take the bait. This son of a dictator was not going to be fooled. "Get your coat. We are going together right now." Martin grabbed Joshua's coat for him and shoved it in his chest. "You drive."

Martin picked up his canvas bag and, holding Joshua under the arm, the two left through the front door for Joshua's office. It was not a long drive, but it gave Joshua enough time to think about what he was going to do.

Understanding the weightiness of the situation and the importance of his designs, Joshua wondered not for the first time how his mobile flying killing machine would be used. He planned to make an alteration, change something subtle to ensure the machine's ineffectiveness. This weapon was special, a drone capable of carrying a thousand pounds of equipment. It had a silent propulsion system with an enhanced navigational system, making it possible to send it to a specific address, kill the occupants in the structure without any warning, and disappear into the clouds. In the most critical cases, once it completed its orders, the drone would self-destruct so no one could identify it or swear to what happened. It permitted the operator or owner complete deniability. This design was extraordinary, meeting every assassin's need. A killing machine for all occasions, Joshua once thought with conceit.

Even though he had changed his mind about a few things, he still could not help loving the complexity of his design, the intricate nature of the engineering, and the fact it was his creation. The design's development was more painful than birthing a child. This was not a design Joshua would be so careless with, so irresponsible as Chen had been. The Germans already had killer drones, but Joshua's drone would change the game. With its quiet design and self-destruct feature, a killing could occur and leave no trace, no evidence of who sent it. This would be handier for Strauss; better than his current drones he would be forced to use with the delay of these plans.

What were the chances Gwen would get this story or that it would be a story at all? He had run these questions through his mind ever since Gwen returned from Belgium and announced she was on a return flight to Berlin and why. His participation, however insignificant it seemed in the beginning, would soon come to light. He had a lot of explaining to do. Gwen wasn't the most forgiving when it came to corruption and helping those with malintent.

At the Midtown Engineering building, Joshua opened the door and the two headed to his office. As his computer booted up, he pictured the slight alteration he would make to sabotage the design, and on the way here he composed the email he needed to write.

"Get to work," Martin yelled, making him jump. "Move it. I am not playing games here."

"I'm looking for the file." Joshua clicked through random files. "Don't stand there staring at me. I need to concentrate."

"Don't try to leave," Martin said.

"We're on the top floor. Where am I going to go?" Joshua snapped, gesturing around at all the windows.

"I will sit right here." Martin stomped out of the office, pulled up a chair and planted himself right outside Joshua's office door. Martin sat upright, uptight, holding his canvas bag on his lap as he kept watch.

This was what Joshua needed—alone time with his computer and his email. He brought up the original plans and made a copy to keep an unaltered original for one more person.

Using the copy, Joshua made slight adjustments to the current schematics, making the weapon impossible to work in this form. He dug an empty thumb drive from the office supply stash in his desk and saved the altered plans to give to Martin. By the time another engineer figured it out, Joshua would have worked everything out with Gwen.

She would forgive him; she had to. He did it all for her. *Isn't that what all guilty men say?* Joshua thought. *I did it for you, for us.*

He'd been unable to sleep and eating poorly as the decision to take on this project weighed on his conscience. When Travis dangled the cash under the table, Josh saw it as a means to an end. Gwen's foreign correspondence took her to the ends of the earth, often for weeks at a time, and often to dangerous places. He'd compromised and sacrificed so much he wanted for their marriage over the past decade, telling himself her assignments overseas were a temporary aspect to her job. She was well-paid for the work but would make more working in-studio as one of the anchors. He'd thought when she launched her career back in college that was her ultimate goal. If they had enough money, she could stay home, focus on getting that top desk spot, and be with him. They could be together all the time like they used to be. Desperate to hold her attention, he compromised his patriotism and ethics.

Finished with the design and its new flaw, Joshua opened his email and typed quickly. This letter proved harder than anticipated but he needed to explain. He would send it to his wife with a seven-day delivery delay. This way if he could find a way to get out of this mess, he could rescind the email and Gwen would never have to know anything. If not, if this entanglement continued to deteriorate, then Gwen would know everything, absolutely everything.

AS THE CREW LEFT THE LIBRARY after their meeting with Decker, Rocco's portable phone rang. He answered in a cautious tone as they walked through the side door and back toward the van.

He listened for a moment, then grabbed the back of Gwen's jacket and pulled her backward a few steps.

"What's wrong?" She stumbled and shot him a confused look.

"Something doesn't look right. Stay here. I want to check the van before we get in."

Gwen saw Rocco was not in the mood for a discussion. He handed the camera equipment to Jacques, telling him to stay close to the building with Gwen while he took a closer look at something.

Rocco could still see Carter parked off in the distance, thankfully a good spy doing a good job. He moved in closer to the van and looked through the windows, at least those that were not tinted. He didn't see anything unusual, just extra video equipment and their personal items as they had left them. He slowly bent down, getting on his hands and knees and then on his elbows, lying on the ground to get the best look at the undercarriage. While uncomfortably looking around, Rocco pulled his phone from his front pocket and returned the call.

"What do you see?" Carter asked.

"A small black box with visible wires." Someone wanted Gwen dead, and this person didn't care who he took with her.

"Well, if the colors are blue over red, you're as good as dead," Carter said. "Why don't you get away from the van, man? We still need you. I can arrange alternative transportation."

"I can't leave this van here like this. Someone could get hurt." Rocco was now in an even more uncomfortable position.

"What do you suggest?"

"I can't disarm it without giving myself away, so I'll let the bomb do what bombs do, I guess." Rocco raised his eyebrows and cracked a half smile.

"No, no—that'll attract too much attention!"

"No, it won't. If anyone is watching from a distance, they might think they got our girl. It'll give her more time to quietly move around, ask questions. Just have the station drop off another van around the corner, by the intersection."

DOWN THE STREET on a roof lay a woman with a special skill set that, combined with unpleasant friends, made her a catch for Strauss. With her long blonde hair tucked neatly up in a knitted cap, she lay on her stomach low to the roof, binoculars held firmly in her hands. She watched Rocco checking under the van and wondered how he could have known.

"Damn it, something's wrong," she mumbled. Someone was either watching her or watching them. Whichever, this bomb was too obvious, and it wasn't going to do the job.

ROCCO CRAWLED BACK from the van and stood, dusting off his hands. He walked back to Jacques and Gwen and told them someone wanted to put an end to the story, permanently.

"What?" Gwen wrinkled her brow in concern. "What are you talking about? Is that a bomb under the car? Who were you talking to?" Gwen barraged him with questions. This story was sensitive, but was her investigation so threatening someone would want to see her dead and the whole news crew, too?

"I called a friend to ask what I was looking at because I wasn't sure. When we left the building, I spotted that black piece hanging below the driver's seat. It looked strange. I may not know bombs, but I know my van."

"I can see it, too, now that you point it out," Jacques said, adding to

Rocco's story. "Thank God you saw that. But why would someone do that?"

"Someone wants this story to go untold, that's for sure," Rocco said to Jacques while looking down at Gwen. "If we proceed, we need to be more careful."

"If we proceed?" Gwen snapped. "We are proceeding! This is proof positive we're onto something huge and we're getting closer."

Rocco's phone rang one more time. "Yes?" He frowned. "Yes, by all means, please hold a moment." Rocco handed the phone over to Gwen. "It's Rosa Dyck."

Gwen perked up and grabbed the phone. "Hello, Frau Dyck. Thank you so much for getting back to me." Gwen held the phone against one ear while plugging the other ear to hear better.

Rocco grabbed a loose brick from the street and circled the tree next to the van, looking up at the branches. Gwen glanced over her shoulder at Jacques, who looked concerned with Rocco's plan. She wasn't sure what Rocco's plan was either, but the look on his face as he climbed into the tree reminded her of a twelve-year-old boy bent on mischief.

"I have names for you of American involvement. Maybe you would have more luck on your end identifying the relationships and finding out if they participated in the financial scandal," Dyck suggested.

"We'll certainly find out," Gwen said. "Let's hear them." She pulled a pen and paper from her pocket and crouched to use the camera case as a desk.

Dyck asked, "Would you rather meet in person? These names may shock you."

"We can talk more later, if necessary, but I would like to hear those names now if you don't mind," Gwen pressed, not wanting to miss this opportunity.

"All right, *liebchen*, if you are ready, here we go."

"Oh, I'm ready."

"Okay, got your pen?"

"Yes, thank you, go ahead." Gwen toned down her excitement, responding to Frau Dyck's kind consideration.

"First, I heard the name of Congressman David Becker. I believe he also sits on your Federal Communication Commission. I believe Becker is acquainted with Erich Strauss. The two of them may have gotten together and played a game or two of golf in recent years. Now, I don't know if the FCC part has anything to do with it, but I thought it might be worth mentioning since it is such an important role in America, especially in regard to the First Amendment; you are well-acquainted with that, I am sure. I don't know how much or even if Becker and Strauss' relationship matters, but there it is."

"Yes, that is surprising. But I'm going to assume nothing."

"Now the other name I picked up on is another congressman. Does the name Frank Solas mean anything?"

"Ah, yes, it rings a very loud bell."

"What is that, *liebchen*?"

"He's dead, ma'am. He died in a car accident, nearly a week ago. He was presumably going home, but he had a pile of money in his car that no one seemed to know anything about." Gwen jotted down the name. "But this explains part of it, or at least gives me ideas."

"Oh, I see," said Dyck. "We heard about it, but truthfully, we didn't believe it. It sounded impossible. Didn't he sit on the Central Intelligence Committee?"

Gwen's face dropped, reminded of the access Solas had to people and information. "Oh my God. This is so unbelievable. He was a good friend to my boss. Joe will be heartbroken."

"I'm sure," Dyck said. "But, you know, my mother always told me equals form company. Just to give you something to think about when you're considering whom you can trust."

"I understand. As we say in America, birds of a feather flock together, but please go on." Gwen frowned at the leaves shaking in the tree as Rocco kept climbing.

"The third person is not such a big surprise, General William Jones. He is a friend of Strauss, and they have been seen together in Jena when the general is in town on other matters."

"Other matters? What other matters could a United States general have in the former East Germany?"

"Well, *liebchen*, if you didn't know, the general's mother is from here."

Gwen's heartbeat loud in her ear. "I didn't know that." She rarely admitted not knowing a fact. "So, the general and Strauss may have the strongest connection of them all. The general may be the man with the answers, but if he's helping Strauss, that may be a crime, and he's unlikely to confess anything. I'll need time to think about him." The breadth and depth of the collusion spread before her. America, or some of its so-called citizens, might be helping liberate German finances. *This is incredible.*

"Yes, his loyalties may not be unilateral, but bilateral, yes?"

"Interesting thought, yes." Gwen clucked her tongue. "Let's stay in touch."

Gwen wondered for a moment at the possibilities of an American involved in such dubious German affairs: hard to believe, unconscionable if true, and what an enormous embarrassment to the current administration. Her head spun with names, committees, friends of friends—too much to handle. While Gwen pressed on, she kept one eye on Rocco, whose plan looked more like a suicide mission.

Rocco looked down from the top of the tree and signaled to Jacques to keep Gwen and himself back against the library wall. Gwen, on the phone, looked annoyed at being herded but moved back against the wall.

Rocco lined up the brick and, hanging onto the tree with one hand, steadied his hand over the van. *DZ is a go.* Feeling lucky, Rocco dropped the brick. As planned, it crashed down through the sunroof. Glass shattered everywhere, creating a thunderous sound. The brick hit the driver's seat and bounced to the floor. As he predicted, the shift in weight ignited a vast explosion that rocked the parking lot with flames reaching as high as Rocco up in the tree. Flames erupted as a second, smaller explosion rocked the van. A whooshing sound followed the vacuum left by the vibration of the explosion. Metal *clanked* on the ground as van parts rained down in a radius of several hundred feet. The odor of C-4 was distinct, hard to miss, and smelly as hell.

That was a lot of explosives to kill one woman, Rocco thought, appreciating the true heinousness of the guilty party responsible for all this. *These people most definitely don't want to be exposed. I just hope we all live long enough to see this through.*

Dark, black smoke billowed toward the sky and blackened the breeze that swept through the city. People would soon notice the rush of ash and the smell of metal in the air. It was time to go.

Dyck, still on the line, shouted, "What was that? What's going on over there?"

Gwen, her head buried in Jacques' chest where they huddled against the library's wall with their backs toward the fire, shouted, "Hold on. Hold on a minute."

Gwen shouted at Rocco, scrambling down the tree, "Be careful." She shoved Jacques toward the tree trunk. "Go help him."

Jacques ran to the skeletal remains of the van, trying to figure out how to help Rocco get down. Police sirens in the distance prompted all three to look at each other. They had no reason to run, but Gwen did not want to be tied up for any length of time now that they had the names of American involvement and their next lead. They needed to keep moving to keep the story going while the iron was hot, and it was hot—in flames, literally. Rocco continued his descent and Jacques stood by waiting to lend a hand.

Gwen turned her attention back to Dyck. "Are you there?"

"*Ja*, I am here. What happened? What was that?"

"Someone put a bomb under our news van. This is getting serious."

"*Liebchen*, things have been serious for some time. Someone knows you're here and what you're doing. You had better be very, very careful. I will contact you when or if I get more information, but for right now, I think we should all lie low."

Gwen was mad. She had no intention of lying low, and especially not now that someone had tried to kill her. *Game on*, Gwen thought. *Game on.*

Rocco hit the ground running and the three grabbed what they could, then took off toward the intersection.

"Follow me," Rocco shouted.

"Where are we going?" Gwen asked.

"I have a ride. Follow me."

The three ran close to the buildings until they got to the parking lot at the corner. Another news van from the same company sat there with doors open. Jacques and Gwen followed Rocco into the vehicle. Gwen felt doubly lucky; they were missing a few items, but they had their footage and their lives. She was sweating as Rocco started the van and let out a big sigh of relief when the engine turned over. A delay now would be inconvenient.

They were on the move once more, tearing ahead to their base of operations, the hotel. Gwen looking over her shoulder through the back window at smoke billowing in the distance, appearing smaller and smaller. Police cars were heading toward the scene, passing them along the way. The sirens and sounds died down and the awful smell dissipated as the distance grew larger and larger. Gwen looked at Jacques with relief, then turned to Rocco and thanked him for saving all their lives.

"I don't know how you noticed that bomb, but thank you, just thank you." Gwen struggling for breath, her limbs weak and shaky. The close call finally caught up with her, and all she could think to do in this moment was call her husband and Joe. *A sudden brush with death will make you reassess your priorities*, she thought.

"I want to get to the hotel. I have a few calls to make," Gwen said to Rocco.

"Yes, I think we could all use a break for a moment." Rocco stared at the road with his hands at ten and two, driving the speed limit to not attract attention.

CARTER SENT A few agents dressed as Berlin police to the scene to collect evidence from the explosion. Quite possibly, the company might be able to assist in identifying who placed the bomb or at least who made it. Bombers were creatures of habit; they found a material they liked and a trigger that worked, and it was like signing their name to every explosion. Carter and his people would do what they could and then bring Rocco up to speed.

ROCCO PULLED INTO the hotel garage and parked the van. Gwen grabbed her notes and Rocco grabbed her arm.

"What's wrong?" Gwen asked.

"We all walk in slowly. We all walk in together," he said firmly. "I go first."

Gwen understood more danger could lie ahead, and after what they just experienced, now was not the time to pull rank. She needed to be a team player.

The three moved cautiously and looked carefully at everyone they passed. Rocco was looking for an assassin, and Gwen was looking at Rocco. She was becoming suspicious of his super stealth powers but didn't voice her curiosity, weighing the benefits of his abilities. Jacques covered Gwen's back as usual. The three got to Gwen's room, unlocked the door, and retreated inside. With a sigh of relief, Gwen took her notes from her bag. She needed to call Joe, but she wanted to do a few things first. As they sat to discuss their next move, Gwen looked sternly at Rocco.

"Get Heinrich on the phone. Get him on the phone now. I want to talk to him."

"Okay, why?" Rocco dialed the number he had been given earlier.

"I think it's about time Heinrich arranged an introduction, don't you?" Gwen said through pursed lips.

"An introduction to whom?"

Jacques turned in an ear with interest.

"His father, the chancellor," Gwen snapped.

The two men looked at Gwen. She set her jaw, more determined than ever. *Time's up.*

WHILE ROCCO CALLED HEINRICH, Gwen called Joe. It was about time everyone was brought up to speed. The circle of trust was growing smaller, and despite what Rosa Dyke implied, Joe was inside her inner circle whether Solas was a crook or not. Joe would not have stood for it, had he known about it.

"Joe, it's Gwen."

"Where have you been? I expect a call from you daily!" He barked.

"I know, I'm sorry, a lot has happened in the last several days. But we're making progress," she said, trying to sound encouraging.

"Every day you call, every day. Understood?"

"Okay, I'll make an effort to call every day."

Joe let out a sigh of acceptance. "So, what have you got, kid?"

"A lot, and you're not going to believe it. But I do need your help with a few things I can't do from here and, frankly, I don't have the time to piece it all together. I've spoken to members of the German government, and they have shared disturbing, scary news."

"I feel a migraine coming on."

"Your feelings were right. I need you to check out the finances of people in our government, some very important people. You're not going to like the names you hear."

"I never like the names I hear," Joe said. "But, strangely, it's never a surprise once the truth shakes out."

They said together, "And the truth always shakes out."

Gwen had a brief chuckle at their one-mindedness.

"Alright, let's hear them," Joe said.

"First, Congressman David A. Becker. He sits on the FCC."

"Oh man," Joe said under his breath.

"What's wrong?"

"I heard through the grapevine he's been calling here nonstop for Henderson, and Henderson has been trying to pull this story harder than a rotten tooth. That might explain a few things, though."

"What things?"

"Damn, we have a wolf in the hen house, and I didn't even know it. He must have the network president over a barrel, but that's for another time." Joe sounded disappointed. "I'll need to keep him out of the loop until we nail down the facts."

"The person who gave me this information seems to think Becker and Strauss know each other personally. That's another angle to investigate once you look into Becker's finances."

Joe agreed.

"The next name is General William Jones. According to my source, he has been seen in Jena, Germany, in the company of former East German General Secretary Erich Strauss. I had no idea, but my source tells me Jones has familial ties to Eastern Germany. Apparently, his mother is from the area and quite possibly that's how he knows Strauss."

"Maybe the two are related?"

The phone fell silent for a moment as they shared a moment of enlightenment.

"What if they are related?" Gwen asked. "What's his mother's maiden name?"

"I don't know, but that's another angle to look at, otherwise why would Strauss and Jones be chatting it up on the streets of Jena? They must know each other from somewhere. Good girl. I'll look into Jones' finances as well."

"That's one interesting angle, Joe. I've got to hand it to you," Gwen said. He was her mentor, and she was proud of that.

"Who else? Anyone else?"

"Well, yes, but ..."

"But what?"

"The third name I was given was Frank Solas."

"What?" Joe bellowed. "Solas? That's bullshit!"

"No, Joe. I was given his name, and didn't you say when his car exploded cash flew everywhere?" Gwen tried to bring Joe back into reality. "Joe, I know he was a good friend, and that won't change, but wasn't it you who taught me it's virtually impossible to fully know another person?"

Joe sat speechless for a few seconds, but the silence was deafening for Gwen.

"Are you okay?"

"Yeah, I'm okay. It just doesn't add up," Joe said. "I've known that man for a million years, and it just doesn't add up."

"You know me, so believe me when I tell you it does add up. You don't like what it adds up to."

Joe chuckled, then asked Gwen, "Who is mentoring whom?"

Gwen shared in that momentary giggle. "I know it's difficult, especially now after his death, but you need to look into his finances as well. Can you talk to his family in Chicago?"

"Yeah, I'll give his wife a call and see what I can find out. I don't expect Solas would tell his wife if he was up to something, though."

"I know, but it's worth a shot. I would call, but I don't know her, and you can probably get more through friendly conversation. So, you have what I have. Let's see where it takes us."

"What's your next move, kid?"

"Rocco's calling the chancellor's son to arrange an interview."

"You think you have enough to have a go at him?"

"Well, I can't properly check on the general and the congressmen from here. I've met with student leaders, checked out rallies, and even met with a couple of government officials, none of whom seem to know where the money is going, just that it's gone. If Chancellor Jakob doesn't know where the money is going, then at least we can nail down that point on camera, preventing him from doing an about face later."

"Good. Keep me informed. Every day, Gwen. Every day."

"I will. Talk to you soon. But call me if you learn anything."

"Will do." Joe hung up.

Gwen turned her attention back to Rocco, who was still on his phone, doing her bidding. Rocco finally got Heinrich on the line, and he didn't seem at all surprised by the call.

Rocco pressed speaker. "Gwen is ready to sit down with your father."

"If she is ready, my father is too," Heinrich replied. "I will speak to him and suggest tomorrow. I will call you back."

"Good. I think Gwen wants to move quickly, too. No pressure, but time is a consideration, especially after today. We need to move up the clock." Rocco looked at Gwen for a nod of confirmation.

"Yes, I heard about the explosion on the news. I recognized what was left of the van. I wasn't certain, of course, but I knew your group was poking the snake. Looks like it snapped at you."

"Snapped. That's one way to put it. If your father agrees, identify a safe space, because I don't want to cut it that close again."

"I understand. My father as chancellor wouldn't be allowed anywhere without proper safety precautions anyway."

"Yes, I know," Rocco said in a hushed voice, giving Gwen a cryptic look.

THE NEXT MORNING, Rocco prepared for his secret meeting secure in the knowledge that Gwen would be completely safe today. What could be safer for Gwen than being with the chancellor and interviewing him with his entire security detail in tow? She couldn't be in better hands. Rocco handed Jacques the address of where the interview was to take place with basic directions to the area, just in case. Then he reluctantly excused himself for a few hours, leaving Jacques and Gwen on their own, but he needed to check in with his superiors.

To Gwen's surprise, Jacques showed up at her hotel room door alone. "Where's Rocco?"

"He got a phone call early this morning and said he had a meeting back at the station." Jacques shrugged. "Don't worry, I can hook up both of you with lavaliers and work the camera myself. Plus, with the chancellor's heightened security, less is more, I would think."

"Odd time for a meeting, but you're probably right, less is more. If you have everything you need, let's go." Gwen grabbed her jacket.

The two left Gwen's room and headed down the hall for the elevator. Pressing the down button, they both waited in silence, Gwen missing Rocco's presence and protection. She took comfort in Rocco's company, knowing he was more than he claimed to be but unsure of what exactly. Rocco said he needed to do something and that was that—they were on their own.

Jacques and Gwen left the hotel and strolled toward the parking lot. She didn't want to admit she was worried without Rocco's keen eye for detail. Who knew what could happen? Out in the fresh air, the sun was shining, and for a moment Gwen felt more optimistic, but that feeling fizzled as they got closer to the news van.

As the two approached their ride, in unison they briefly paused and looked at each other, both taking deep breaths. Jacques, moving first, unlocked the doors, and with that minor success, they both climbed in on either side.

"In for a penny, in for a pound, as my mother always told me." Gwen cracked a smile as they took their seats.

"What does that mean?"

"It means if you're in, you're in, and if you're not, you're out. Basically." She shrugged. "And we're both in until the end."

"That we are, my friend, until the end."

At this point, they were both gambling, but with whom they had no idea. The two looked at one another as Jacques put the key in the ignition. It was hard not to recall the events from the day before. They both held their breath as Jacques turned the key and the engine rumbled to life. They each let out a sigh of relief, hoping yesterday was a one-time experience. That incident made them both edgy and suspicious. But they were both smarter than that; someone was out to stop their story. Jacques was only a newsman. Camera and audio were the name of the game, not bombs and tree stunts. That was Rocco's bag—clearly.

Gwen's wheels spun as they made the short drive to the Reichstag Building near the Platz der Republik in Berlin. The building was constructed in 1894. By American standards, it was an old, rehabbed structure. This contrasted with the European mindset, which considered a building such as this to be like-new. They made their way over the bridge that crossed the narrow Spree River bisecting the city until they reached the wide-open grassy area across the street from the Parliament building. Gwen took in the sights as Jacques navigated the last few blocks and looked for the appropriate place for guests to park. The park was lush and beautiful, normally an area where residents and tourists came to relax, grab a bratwurst from the local street vendor, and be lazy for the afternoon, but not today.

Today the grounds hosted a kite convention for flying enthusiasts from all over the world who brought their colorful wind-driven and motorized kites of varying sizes and shapes to fill the sky. Each had an individual meaning to the one controlling the strings and motors. When Gwen and her mother would drive down from upstate New York to vacation along the Jersey Shore, Gwen had been known to fly a few kites. She had enjoyed flying them on the beach, especially when she was a child. Gwen loved the colorful nature of the gear and the collage it created over the park. *People are so creative,* she thought.

Gwen pulled her phone from her pocket, wanting to grab a few pictures to show Joshua when she got home. Gwen snapped several wide shots of the area with the beautiful Parliament building as a backdrop. She zoomed in on a few of the unique motorized kites as they hovered over the grassy knoll. Joshua would appreciate being thought of in the middle of her workday.

Jacques pulled into the Parliament's public parking area and found a spot in clear view of every direction. Gwen hoped this would provide some sense of security, unlike yesterday. Right in front of the entrance door, Jacques brought the van to a stop. Gwen looked around, having previously taken Rocco's keen eye for granted. While they remained in the van, having arrived early, they prepared their equipment.

EARLIER THAT MORNING, Security Chief Soren received a summons to go at once to the chancellor's office.

"I have heard from my son, and I will be meeting this morning with Gwen Patterson of New York City," Chancellor Jakob said most firmly from behind his austere desk of dark wood under antique lighting.

"I have no interview on your schedule, sir," Soren said, knowing full well about the interview scheduled last evening, having already been told by his other superiors the night before. But Soren wanted to retain his cover and hide his real allegiance, so he responded to the chancellor with a most curious look on his face.

"I set this up myself with my son. Ms. Patterson will be here soon, and I want the conference room reorganized with the kites in the background out the window. I think that would look nice." Jakob held his hands up, pantomiming the view. "I want it to look pleasant. I don't want the pictures overwhelmed with the gaudy, materialistic things displayed in this building."

"Yes sir, I will have it done, sir." Soren excused himself to leave the room so he could carry out his boss' orders.

Soren reached for the phone to call his security staff, but he abruptly stopped as a thought swept over him. The chancellor never handled his own press. Something must be wrong; it was too soon for Strauss to have been discovered. But if that was not it, then something still was most definitely not right. The idea of the interview gave Soren pause. *Yes*, he thought. *Maybe this is it, maybe this is our opportunity, the opportunity we have been waiting for.* Soren's pulse increased at the wonderful idea his imagination had just offered. But this was not a decision he could make on his own; a ruling like this must come from the king.

Soren sought private refuge several floors below and pulled out a special phone carried by each highly trusted member of an exclusive group. He dialed one of the pre-programmed numbers, and the line on the other end rang.

STRAUSS WAS SITTING behind his desk in his castle fortress in Jena when his phone rang.

"*Ja,*" he answered.

"My king, this is Soren. I must talk to you right away."

"Yes, of course, my son. I always have time for my young people. What do you need of me?"

"You wanted to know if Gwen Patterson was getting too close. She is to interview Mr. Jakob later this morning in the Parliament building. I have no idea what Jakob will say. He went around the press office and scheduled the interview on his own, or through his son, I think he said."

That woman moves faster than my Martin, Strauss thought. *She is closing in, but I am faster. I must prevail.*

"I have an idea, sir, but I didn't want to do anything without your permission," Soren said, breathing heavily.

"What do you think, my son?" Strauss was a master manipulator. Calling misguided young men and women 'son' and 'daughter' and using endearing terms like 'brother' and 'sister' always reeled in those who sought inclusion and belonging, regardless of the nasty end it brought them. Strauss could recruit the unrecruitable.

"I just realized we have a window of opportunity, my king, but we must act quickly."

"What is the opportunity?" Strauss asked.

"Jakob will be seated in the main conference room. There are huge windows and a kite festival in the park. The festival can provide great camouflage."

"Camouflage, my son? What do you mean?"

"The motorized kites can act as cover if we add some color or a floral pattern to one of your new prototypes. Then we can fly that test drone right up to the window and stop Jakob for good. And, with the confusion of the kite festival and the noise from the motors and the crowd, by the time anyone realizes what has happened, the operator will have flown your drone right out of there."

"You are brilliant, Soren! Brilliant! You will have a great future with the new monarchy," Strauss said. Strauss offered some helpful ideas to Soren's suggestion. The devil was in the details, as Strauss always said.

"You are the one who is brilliant, my king! Brilliant!"

"I must hang up and make an important call. I know exactly who will be perfect for this job," Strauss said.

"Excellent, my king, excellent."

Strauss disconnected the call with a sinister smile. *What luck*, he thought, *what luck*. Strauss made his important call, the catalyst to set his greatest dreams and most dreadful plans in motion.

SOREN CAREFULLY STROKED his chin as he thought how Strauss would feel about organizing an assassination on such short notice, but he would do anything to impress his king.

He returned to his floor and reconfigured the room as the chancellor had asked. Jakob would sit by the window for his interview with Gwen, right in the middle in plain view as he had requested. Oddly, the layout suited the purposes of both men, and Soren was just following orders. A front shot would kill two birds with one stone. Shoot Chancellor Jakob from the front and have Gwen take the fall. Strauss' idea was perfect.

AS GWEN AND Jacques approached security, the guards stood per protocol. The guards knew Gwen on sight but needed to follow procedure and examine her belongings, or at least give the appearance thereof. As Gwen walked up, she and Jacques placed their equipment and bags on the table and then individually walked through the building's metal detectors. When both breezed through security, the guards barely gave their belongings a glance; the whole world knew Gwen Patterson. In spite of being a tall woman, she was hardly a physical threat. She was only a threat to corrupt politicians, but that wasn't the guards' problem. Everyone smiled at one another, business as usual.

She and Jacques picked up their bags and equipment and continued to the elevators. On the top floor, another member of the security team greeted them. With a big smile, the receptionist showed them to the conference room and said the chancellor would be joining them shortly.

"The chancellor asked if you would be able to set up in this corner?" the receptionist asked, showing them the seating area by the windows.

"Yes, sure, but why?" Gwen asked.

"The chancellor thought the kite festival would make a nice background for the interview," she said with a pleasant smile.

Gwen smiled and nodded. "Of course, nice choice."

Gwen laughed as the receptionist left the room.

Jacques asked Gwen what was so funny.

"The background suggestion. Everyone wants to be in TV." She shook her head. "It's fine."

"Oh." Jacques smiled and laughed, understanding the joke.

As they finished setting up their camera and equipment, the chancellor came over to introduce himself to his special guests, whom he said he hoped would leave as friends.

"Ah, Ms. Patterson, may I call you Gwen?" the chancellor asked.

"Of course, Chancellor. This is Jacques from Belgium. He will be working with us today on camera and sound." Gwen turned to properly introduce Jacques. Proper etiquette was important in her job, especially when she met high-level officials or dignitaries.

Jacques stepped over and extended his hand, which was quickly grabbed up by the friendly chancellor.

"Very nice to make your acquaintance, Jacques. I hope you found the building without too much trouble."

"Yes, no trouble. What a beautiful building."

Gwen beamed; everyone was using their best manners today.

"Let's sit down and get better acquainted. Would either of you like anything to drink?" the chancellor asked.

"No, thank you, we're fine," Gwen answered for them both. "Let's sit and see if you can get me up to speed."

She and the chancellor took their assigned seats, then Jacques placed a lavalier on the chancellor's lapel. Gwen was already wearing hers. As the two got more comfortable in their seats and with each other, Jacques took the opportunity to zoom in, focus, and get his white balance correct before the real action started. Jacques continued to work behind the scenes, and once the lighting appeared suitable, Jacques recorded B-roll and cutaways before taking his position behind Gwen. He had told her in the van he planned to frame the chancellor in an over-the-shoulder shot behind her to be able to zoom in for a close-up and zoom out again for dramatic effect. While she and the chancellor exchanged small talk, Jacques asked for a quick audio test to ensure he got every word.

"Testing, testing, one, two three, testing," Gwen said. The chancellor laughed and repeated the same words, also in English, and Jacques gave a thumbs-up.

"Got it. We are good to go," Jacques said. He hit the record button and the red light came on. "In three, two ..."

On the heels of the silent "one," Gwen hit the chancellor with questions like swinging a sledgehammer at a nail.

"Sir, I would like to apologize in advance for my forthrightness and the lack of continued pleasantries, but you have a serious problem in your country, and I am going to get to the bottom of it, one way or another."

The slightly stunned chancellor dipped his chin.

"Now you can help me, and if you do, you may be able to help yourself politically. But if you don't, you may look as guilty as the people who are behind all of this. In America, the word is 'collusion,' and that's not a very nice word." Gwen didn't want there to be any confusion; she meant business and she wanted him to know.

"No, Gwen, collusion is not a nice word, and no, I am not conspiring with anyone." Jakob shook his head. "These issues began before I was elected, and now, I am the one to suffer the consequences. That is hardly fair without giving me the proper opportunity to fully investigate these matters."

"Some would argue your people are suffering the consequences, Chancellor."

"Yes, I understand. What I meant to say is we are all suffering one way or another, but I am not responsible for their pain, and I need time to prove it."

"Right now, I believe you're an innocent bystander in all this, I do." Gwen extended her hand. "I believe you're just as confused as the rest of us. But you as chancellor have a great deal more access to information, and it's time you use that access. Don't you think?"

"Yes, we have been taking steps to investigate these financial matters. My office has begun an official inquiry into the cash flow issues of Germany.

"But first, I want to apologize to the German people for any stress this may have caused them. I want all to please know we are doing everything in our power to review our finances and trace back the funds. We will get to the bottom of this, you have my word."

"That sounds reassuring." Gwen empathized with the chancellor, as he did present like an innocent man. "So, what are you doing, exactly?"

"My office has sent inquiries to many governmental departments and agencies, each of which has reported financial losses totaling in the tens of millions. We are seeking itemization of department losses and where the money was sent. And, if they are unable to identify where it was sent, they certainly will be able to identify who signed the checks and who cashed them. There is always a trail when it comes to money." Jakob said this with a slight smile.

"When did you make these inquiries?" Gwen scribbled notes as he spoke.

"Recently, over the last couple of weeks, as the losses became more and more evident," the chancellor said. "There came a boiling point, as you say, where the losses and the debt became clear and undeniable, so whatever financial shell game the people behind this are playing, well, let's just say they can hide it no longer."

As the two continued to talk, Jacques kept his focus on the chancellor, holding his shot steady. But a buzzing sound coming from behind him, outside the window, grew louder and louder, overtaking the sound of the kites. Taking his eye off the camera, Jacques looked out the window as the buzzing sound turned more into a small engine roar.

What is that? Jacques thought. *Damn, it's going to ruin the audio.*

Jacques turned back to the camera as the interview continued. Without Rocco there, Jacques wasn't sure what to do about the noise. Jacques kept quiet and did his job until the noise became loud enough for Gwen to look around, clearly hearing it, too.

It only took seconds for the noise to overtake the conversation. Gwen interrupted the chancellor as he spoke, pausing the interview for a moment so she could turn to Jacques to ask about the noise. "What is that? There's a noise out there that doesn't sound like the rest."

"I know, I hear it, too. But I didn't want to interrupt the chancellor while he was speaking," Jacques said.

The chancellor graciously smiled at Jacques for his good manners, and Jacques returned a respectful nod.

Suddenly the noise became so loud the sound filled the room. Jakob uncrossed his legs and looked attentively at the window, joining Gwen and Jacques.

"Do you see anything, Jacques?" Gwen asked.

Jacques looked out the window. "I only see these kites. It must be one of their motors. But the motor sounds too big for the body weight."

"Body weight?" Gwen asked, confused.

"Yes, like a race car, big engine, but with a small, lightweight body."

"Okay, now I'm with you," Gwen said, slightly embarrassed.

Her slight smile wiped from her face as a large blast came through the window behind Jacques. The shockwave forced Gwen's eyes closed as she reacted involuntarily to the glass particles blowing across all three of them in the corner. Popping sounds continued and tatted across the floor as Gwen threw herself down, using her arms to cover her head. The sound was loud and unmistakable, yet in the moment still unbelievable. Millions of small shards of glass showered the room and covered Gwen, Jacques, and the chancellor. Gwen, on the floor, was too surprised to scream. She looked over and saw Jacques lying face down on the floor. Unfortunately, he didn't hit the ground fast enough. By the time the gunfire stopped, Jacques lay bleeding on the floor. A bullet had entered through his back, knocking him face down.

Gwen, keeping her head low, crawled over to Jacques, who was still alive, his eyes open looking at her with the love of a brother.

"Jacques! Jacques!" Gwen shouted. "Jacques!" Gwen continued to shake his body as he lay face down on the floor, blood draining from underneath him, pooling around his head and neck. It was gruesome and hard to watch, but Gwen could not look away from the hole in his back. Not knowing if Jacques would survive, she checked the condition of the chancellor. Jakob's luck was far worse than she feared. Still in his chair, he was tipped backward on the floor with a large, unmistakable hole in the center of his chest. There was no wondering about his fate now; the chancellor was dead.

"Oh my God!" Gwen shouted as she continued to look over the chancellor, trying to find a pulse. "Help! Help!" Gwen, on her knees, screamed for help as armed guards smashed open the door.

They appeared almost immediately, to Gwen, but there was a momentary delay. Several guards rushed over to the chancellor, knocking Gwen out the way as though she was nobody in this scene. Falling on her side, Gwen was not used to such rough indifference, but she reminded herself she was in the room with a chancellor. One of the guards leaned down and checked for a pulse, probing several places. He shook his head at the others.

"What happened here?" one guard yelled at Gwen.

"I don't know! I'm not sure," she shouted back while still lying on the floor.

"The window—someone fired through the window." Gwen pointed at the broken glass, frazzled, which was unlike her.

Another guard checked Jacques for a pulse.

"Is he alive?" one guard yelled.

"Ja! Just barely," he said. "I have a faint pulse."

Jacques was no longer responding. Seeing all the blood, Gwen was not hopeful. Using his radio, the guard called for backup and for the ambulance already on the scene to immediately come up to the top floor. The ambulance was on constant standby for the chancellor in the event of an emergency, but this time it would carry Jacques. Jacques needed to go and go now; he had only minutes left. However, the chancellor was out of time.

In less than two minutes, the paramedics arrived and rushed over to the chancellor. On their hands and knees, they repositioned his body, lying him on his back, if only to verify his death and look at his wounds. They confirmed for the security detail that Jakob was dead, doing so with only nods and grim faces. Another paramedic rendering aid to Jacques held pressure on the wound while a third man wheeled in a stretcher. They quickly scooped up the cameraman and placed him on the cart, wheeling him off while radioing the hospital as they moved out the door. This left the dead chancellor, Gwen, and a handful of unfriendly security guards.

"What happened?" another security guard screamed at Gwen. "And don't tell me someone was hanging from the top-story window, damn you!"

Gwen suddenly realized things were taking a worrisome turn. She tried to get up from the floor and use her position to assert herself. But that plan was quickly thwarted with a hard shove back to the floor by one of the men on the detail.

"Don't you move! Don't even try to get up!" the man said pointing his submachine gun at her face.

Gwen put her hands up, "Don't shoot, I'm Gwen Patterson." Gwen spoke to the men as though her name should mean something.

Evidently, it did mean something; it meant to some of them paydirt. The chancellor was dead, and she was to be blamed.

"I do not give one shit who you say you are, woman! Do not even breathe!" screamed the security agent holding the MP5K submachine gun.

Gwen stared down the short nose of a nasty weapon. That specific gun was known as a "room broom" because of it would literally sweep the room and kill everyone in sight in a second. It was a favorite among German security agents. With its minimal weight and compact design, it offered a decisive advantage for carrying concealed on the agents without limiting their movements.

It appeared Gwen encountered the one agent who didn't seem to care who she was, nor did he want to hear her side of the story. Unfortunately for Gwen, shifting the cloud of suspicion to her all but absolved the real shooter and his drone kite, now no doubt gone from the window and the grounds.

"Someone get the vice chancellor, get George Nikolaus, now!" a guard yelled.

"No, we must keep him away from this scene until it is fully secure," another guard shouted back.

"He is the chancellor now!" the guard holding the submachine gun on Gwen said. "Thanks to her, Vice Chancellor George Nikolaus is now the chancellor of Germany."

In all the chaos and confusion, Gwen wanted to withdraw from the commotion. She pulled herself backward on the floor, looking around for somewhere to retreat.

The guard with the submachine gun kicked her in the foot. "Give me one reason, I beg of you, just one reason and I should not cut you in two?" He was holding the right hardware to do just that, cut her in half.

Gwen stopped moving and waited for a signal from the guard, any signal. Everything was out of control. Her heart raced and she perspired heavily from fear and nerves.

SEVERAL FLOORS BELOW, the vice chancellor was sitting in his office on a private phone call waiting for the characters in Strauss' play to carry out their lines. He could hear the hurried footsteps of several men rushing toward his door, and without knocking, the chancellor's security detail charged into his office addressing him as "Herr Chancellor."

Without so much as a flinch or a wince, Nicolaus said to the person on the other end of the line, "They are here. It's time for me to begin." Nicolaus hung up the phone before he even looked up at the guards. Secretly unsurprised by this day's events, Nicolaus calmly asked the guards, "What did you call me?"

"Chancellor Jakob has been shot. He is dead! You are now the chancellor. We must go to the safe room now until we remove the assailant!" The guard grabbed the chancellor under the arm and raced him down the hall to a secure elevator that descended many floors below the surface.

"Who shot the chancellor? He was my friend," Nicolaus said this with a smirk buried deep in his lips; Jakob was no friend of his.

"We believe it was that TV woman, Gwen Patterson from America," the guard said in a normal tone, calmer now on the descending elevator. "She has a stupid story of a gun-shooting kite, which makes no sense!"

"The window was broken," one agent said, offering the possibility of her story.

"She could have broken it herself! There is no proof of any flying gun! This is all nonsense!" said the agent lacking in murderous imagination but certain of Gwen's involvement.

"Was she searched on the way in?" Nikolaus asked.

"We will be asking those questions of the men at the front door, and we will get to the bottom of this! I promise you, sir. We will get to bottom of this!"

The chancellor smiled ever so slightly, unnoticed by his company. He said simply, "Arrest her!"

WHEN SHE WAS UNABLE to get her feet under her, the men grabbed her under each arm, lifting her from the floor like a ragdoll. At the direction of Chancellor Nikolaus, Gwen was placed under arrest before she was dragged from the conference room by two oversized, angry guards who had already called their headquarters for backup. Running up the stairs to meet them were several buff men from the *Bundeskriminalamt*, the BKA. They said they were taking primary jurisdiction of her case, and the federal prosecutors would have to wait. Gwen had heard of the BKA; from what she understood, they were the German version of the FBI blended with the Secret Service.

This elite agency worked in cooperation with the federal government and state police. The BKA investigated international organized crime, acts of terrorism, counterterrorism, and other matters as they related to national security. They provided the chancellor with protection, much like the United States Secret Service guarding the president. And much like the United States Secret Service, they didn't respond well when their protectives were murdered on their watch. The BKA provided protection for a dozen members of the government, from the chancellor to other high-level officials identified as being at risk. They also offered protection to federal witnesses, but Gwen was not considered a federal witness—she was a suspect.

Typically, if requested, the BKA would take responsibility for specific large-scale investigations, especially if they involved national security or special public interest. This was of public interest: a dead chancellor and a reporter at the center of the crime, and her co-conspirator unable to speak, having been injured in the attack.

"Where are you taking me?" Gwen asked, panicked. "Where are we going? I haven't done anything wrong! Let me go!" Gwen pleaded with the agents as they swept her from the room, down the hall, into the elevator, and out the back door to a waiting Mercedes Sprinter van, conveniently designed without windows.

Without saying a word, the agents placed Gwen in the back of the transport van, handcuffing her wrists to a pole in between the seats. Gwen continued to voice her innocence, but the agents were having none of it.

Gwen looked around, and the sight worried her. The van's cargo section was dark and spartan, fit for a criminal, fit for a murderer. The lack of windows disturbed her most of all; she would not know where they were taking her. But at the same time, the windowless van provided a false sense of security. When they pulled away from the Parliament building, no one would know she was in the back. Gwen believed the killer would come back after learning she was still alive. She couldn't rule out the possibility she wasn't the intended target, especially considering the car bomb from the day before. Too much murder had taken place around this case, and too many attempts to murder. *Yes*, Gwen thought, *this story is going to be huge.* She was dealing with motivated people.

Once Gwen was secured in her seat, cuffed, unable to move, and certainly unable to escape, one of the agents sat across from her, securing his weapon's safety lock. The other agent hopped out of the rear and locked both Gwen and her guard in the back. He reappeared in the front driver's seat.

"I didn't do anything," Gwen told the guard in the back with her. He would not even look at her. "I'm a victim here. I could've been shot as well!"

The agent turned his head and looked directly into her eyes. His eyes were piercing blue, more scary than beautiful, like the eyes of a wolf.

"But you weren't shot, were you?" the agent asked though pressed lips. "Were you?" he asked again, louder. "How is that?" The guard held a long, lingering glare at Gwen, more evidence of his skepticism of anything she might have to say.

"As soon as I heard the first popping sound, I hit the floor. It was a reflex. I was a war correspondent in Afghanistan and other war zones, you can check. Bombs were going off all the time, there was always gunfire. After a while, you hear that sound, and you drop without even thinking. It becomes a natural reflex." Gwen leaned forward, gripping the pole, trying to convince her jailer of her innocence. "Plus, just yesterday someone tried to kill me."

The guard looked at her in disbelief.

"It's true. I was with my crew, Jacques, who was shot today, and my cameraman Rocco. We were all there. We were interviewing someone at the library yesterday. Someone put a bomb under our news van, and it blew up." She hoped he had heard of the explosion or had seen the shell of the van left in the parking lot. She also conveniently left out the fact that Rocco set off the explosive, unwilling to leave the bomb intact where someone innocent could be hurt. Gwen was in enough trouble.

The guard looked skeptical. "Who did you meet there?"

"Who? What difference does that make?"

"It makes a difference," the BKA agent said sternly.

Gwen shook her head and sat back. "Well, I'm sorry, I can't tell you who we met. I promised my source I would keep their confidence."

"Their confidence? They will never know you told me. Now who is it?"

"But I'll know. This person is a high-level official, and I must keep their confidence. I'm sorry, I want you to believe me, I do, but I can't sell someone out just to save myself. Don't get me wrong, I do want out of this mess, but some things are more important. My word is my currency. Without it, without that trust, I sell out who I am as a person and everyone I ever promised to protect. I won't do it." Gwen defiantly turned her head away from the guard.

Gwen would not throw Decker under the bus. He went out on a limb for his country, for her, and he believed her promise of anonymity. She would guard his name with her life.

The BKA man stopped harassing her, sitting back against the wall with his eyes closed.

Gwen didn't know whether she had made any progress; he didn't share his thoughts.

In the driver's haste, the van hit a pothole with the back tire, giving the agent and Gwen a jolt. The slight bounce propelled Gwen forward, straining her wrists handcuffed to the pole. Reacting quickly, the agent caught her by the shoulders, pushing her safely back into her seat.

"Are you okay?" he asked.

He still held Gwen's shoulders. Their gazes locked. Gwen noticed something different about him and the way he looked at her. The anger so evident minutes earlier was now absent, replaced by a mix of curiosity and doubt. Those wolfish blue eyes held definite appeal, showing every emotion.

"Yes, thank you," Gwen said softly. "I'm fine."

"Are your wrists injured?" He touched her hands gently and used a much softer tone.

"No, I'll be fine, nothing's broken." She looked away from his concerned and handsome face, heat rising to her cheeks at his solicitousness.

The van drove around the building and pulled up to the rear of the detention center set way beyond the locked gates and barbed wire. They backed up to the door for the offender's safety as well as for security reasons. The driver put the van in park and walked around to unlock the back door. Gwen looked up at the agent, waiting for him to unlock her handcuffs. But he surprised her. Instead, in that moment of shared privacy, the agent said, "My name is Johann."

"What?" She raised her eyebrows.

"My name is Johann."

Gwen sat speechless, observing Johann, wondering about his sudden change in posture. Did he believe her? That was a personal step she had not expected.

The rear doors opened and, with a stern voice, inconsistent with his recent demonstration of civility, Johann told her they had reached the end of the road.

"Let's go." Johann pulled his keys from his pocket and unlocked the handcuffs, reconnecting them in front of her without the pole between. A new politeness showed in his manner despite his verbal curtness.

He helped her down from the van. A second agent joined him on the opposite side of Gwen, and they escorted her into the detention facility for processing.

"What's going to happen?" Gwen asked Johann.

"The prosecutor can put you in detention without a judge's order for up to twenty-four hours, that is the maximum. If he is to keep you there longer, he needs to file paperwork. Foreigners are treated the same as Germans, but tell the prosecutor you need a translator, and he will request a certified interpreter."

The other agent looked at Johann quizzically.

Johann and the other agent brought Gwen through another set of locked doors, where she was met by female officers who would take her the rest of the way.

"This is as far as we go," Johann said to Gwen.

Frightened, Gwen nodded, indicating she understood.

Johann and the other agent turned to leave. Suddenly, Gwen remembered something.

"Johann."

"Yes?"

"Who will call Heinrich to tell him about his father?"

She liked Heinrich, and she knew despite how bad things looked right now, he would come to know the truth eventually.

Johann turned. Tilting his head, he took a step closer to Gwen. "You know Heinrich Jakob?"

"Yes, I do. Please tell him I'm sorry about his father. I know you can't tell him I didn't do it, but please at least tell him I'm sorry for his loss."

Johann gave a simple nod. The female officers took Gwen inside and closed the door behind her.

HEINRICH ANSWERED A KNOCK on his door by looking through the peep hole. *"Ja?"*

"This is Soren with Chancellor Jakob's security detail. I must speak with you."

Heinrich opened the door and stood aside, allowing Soren and his associates to enter his home.

"What is it?" Heinrich asked. "Is my father alright?"

"Please sit, Heinrich, we have distressing news," Soren said.

Heinrich sat at his dining room table and Soren sat across from him. Soren's associates stood behind him wearing expressions of sympathy.

"I have bad news, my friend. Your father was shot today. It happened during his interview with Gwen Patterson at Parliament."

"Shot? That can't be right!" Heinrich jumped up but felt light-headed and immediately sat back down. "Where was his security? Where were you, Soren?"

"He wanted to be alone with her. He told me he had private things to discuss with this American journalist. As he is, was, the chancellor, we did as he wished."

Heinrich knew what his father wanted to discuss with Gwen. He had arranged the interview.

"Where is he?" Heinrich swallowed, confused by the news and feeling ill. "Is he going to be alright?"

Soren leaned back in his chair and let out a sigh. "No, I'm sorry, he isn't going to be alright. Security has already taken him away. He didn't make it."

"Take me to him, I want to see my father!" Heinrich stood, agitated. "This is incredible. How is Gwen? She was there interviewing him, yes?"

"That's right." Soren smirked. "You set up your father's interview with Gwen Patterson for this morning, no?"

"Yes, I did! How is she?"

"She's fine. She was taken into custody and taken to detention."

"What? Why? Why would you detain her?"

"She is being accused of your father's murder."

Heinrich stood there, unable to speak, unable to move; the state of shock had taken him like a large wave in the ocean. Heinrich felt dizzy, confused, unable to verbalize anything, any thought. It was as though he could not remember his native tongue. The other two members of the team helped Heinrich to his sofa, a soft surface should he collapse. The two other agents demonstrated more sympathy than Soren.

"Are you going to be alright?" the second agent asked. The agent knelt on one knee, making eye contact with Heinrich, holding him on the shoulder.

"*Ja,*" Heinrich said.

"Is there anyone you want us to call for you?"

Heinrich shook his head, refusing any further intervention by his father's former security team.

"Call us if you need anything," the agent said. "You still have friends in the BKA."

"I understand. Thank you," Heinrich said.

The agent stood and the team looked at Heinrich carefully.

"Don't worry, I'll be okay," Heinrich said.

Heinrich bent over with his head in his hands, face to the floor, unable to get one clear thought. Soren and the agents left. An hour passed before Heinrich looked at the clock. The shock of the news must have been wearing off and the loss of his father, whom he loved so much, gripped his heart, squeezing hard like the devil wanted him dead. Heinrich needed to think. He needed a minute more to think. Whom could he call? Whom could he trust?

Karl. I will call Karl, he thought. Grabbing the phone, Heinrich dialed his loyal friend, hoping he would be home.

"Hey buddy, what's up?" Karl asked.

"My father was killed. Can you come over? I need to talk to you."

"I will be right over."

Heinrich and Karl sat side by side on the sofa, Karl being silent and supportive. Heinrich told Karl everything Soren had said about his father's murder, but neither could believe Gwen would participate in something like this. It just didn't make sense.

"Go ask her," Karl suggested.

"Ask her? Ask her what? 'Did you murder my father?'" Heinrich was upset, his eyes still filled with tears.

"Yes! You should go to the detention center and ask her precisely that." Karl looked plainly at Heinrich. "What other choice do you have?"

Heinrich stood silent.

"Who else would tell you the truth?" Karl asked. "If it was her, and I don't believe for a minute that it was, but if it was her, how did she get any weapon in there?"

Heinrich could not deny Karl asked many good questions. And, now thinking more clearly, these were questions he should have asked Soren.

"We should go now. I will take you there," Karl said.

With Chancellor Jakob's body barely cold, Heinrich still had some clout in the country. The son of a murdered chancellor ought to be given deference to any request, however unreasonable. Heinrich called the detention center and told officials he would be coming over shortly to speak with Gwen Patterson. No one was to tell her, just in case. Heinrich did not want Gwen getting her story straight; he wanted spontaneous answers.

After a short drive, Karl pulled up to the center, parking in the first available spot. Heinrich jabbed at the buckle to undo his seatbelt, in a hurry.

"Be calm, Heinrich. Be calm. Talk to her, but most importantly, listen to her," Karl said. "I simply can't imagine she has any part of this. It doesn't make any sense. What could she possibly have to gain by murdering your father? Remember what we're up against here, what we've all been fighting for."

Heinrich stilled his hands, remembering who the true enemy was. As of this morning, it wasn't Gwen.

"And, also, I think she might be the only person who can tell you what really happened to your father. We don't know how Jacques will fare in surgery, or if he'll ever be able to tell us anything."

Heinrich listened to his friend, who spoke reasonably. Heinrich got out of the car and told Karl to wait for him. "I don't know how long I'll be."

"It doesn't matter. I will be here waiting, my friend." Karl smiled.

Heinrich was greeted politely; officials and staff wanted to extend their condolences. Heinrich graciously accepted their sympathies and thanked each person. Chancellor Jakob clearly was a liked man. Heinrich hoped his father would have been proud of him for demonstrating himself so stoically.

After the crowd of guards and administrators dissipated, one female guard showed Heinrich back to Gwen's cell. Heinrich walked up to the door slowly, watching Gwen most curiously, waiting for her to turn him away. But she did not. Instead, she jumped up and greeted him.

"Heinrich." Her face was a mask of sympathy, tears brimming in her eyes. "I'm so sorry, how are you?"

"Open the door," he said to the guard.

"But that is against protocol, sir. This is for your safety," she told Heinrich.

"Don't worry about me, just open the door. I will call you when it's time to come back."

She eyed Gwen with suspicion. Surely, she too knew of the reporter's fame and shared the feeling that Gwen was not a threat, but the accusations were so mindboggling it was hard for anyone to imagine, especially those who knew or had ever met Gwen.

Heinrich slipped through the slightly opened door, the female guard immediately shutting it behind him. She took one last look at Heinrich for nonverbal confirmation he wanted to be left unattended with the prisoner. Heinrich nodded at the guard and told her he would call out when he was ready to leave. She locked the cell door with both inside and walked away.

Gwen looked at Heinrich, waiting for him to say something, anything. But he didn't speak.

After a minute, she explained in a low voice, "I know what you've probably been told, but none of it is true. I didn't hurt your father. I was lucky not to get shot myself. Jacques is in surgery. I don't know if he's going to make it, and no one believes me when I tell them what happened." She gripped her hands together, knuckles white. "I don't know who to trust. Something is very wrong here. I think someone is out to get me."

Those words turned Heinrich's face red. "My father is dead in the morgue, and you think someone is out to get you? How dare you? What about my father?"

"I'm sorry, I'm sorry." Gwen put her palms up, hoping to calm him. "I'm very sorry, Heinrich, I know this is disturbing, I know that." Gwen chose a more confident tone and spoke forcefully. "I know your father is dead, and for that I am truly sorry, but that doesn't change the facts."

"The facts?" Heinrich repeated.

"Yes, the facts."

Heinrich took a more relaxed posture as Gwen's confidence grew, filling the cell with her self-assuredness. She might be locked in a jail cell for the moment, but she was persistent in declaring her innocence and unwavering in the details of her story.

"I was sitting across from your father. Behind me, Jacque heard a buzzing sound or something like a loud motor coming from outside the window behind him. He was having difficulty hearing me and your father through his headset, and as the sound grew louder and louder, he turned to look out the window. At that point, the noise distracted me, too, so I paused the interview, and we were all looking out the window trying to figure out if it was one of the motorized kites. We didn't know. It sounded like a lawn mower."

Heinrich sat down, hands folded in his lap, obviously taken by what Gwen described. Gwen grew animated, standing over an attentive Heinrich describing the day's events but withholding the more gruesome details to spare Heinrich the awful description of his father's bloody body.

"It was sudden, Heinrich. It was very sudden. I heard a popping sound, and instinctively I dropped to the floor and covered my head. It was reflex, an involuntary reaction. If I hadn't, I would be just as dead as your father. I promise you; I had no idea what was going on until it was all over. The attack was very loud and very fast. And, when it was over, your father was gone, and Jacques was barely breathing. I don't even know if he's alive or dead—they won't tell me." Gwen teared up. "Jacques is such a good friend. I can't believe this happened to him."

"He is alive. I called the hospital before I came. He is critical, but he's alive," Heinrich said in a calm, even voice.

"I'm glad. That makes me feel a lot better. Thank you. I thought help had arrived too late, but apparently not. I'm thankful for that."

"Why would you think help would come too late? The agents should have been there instantaneously." Heinrich frowned.

"That's what's odd. They weren't instantaneous, not at all. It felt like two or three minutes passed before anyone came through the door. My timing could be wrong, but I don't think so." Gwen sat next to Heinrich on the bench. "I had time to check your father and hold pressure on Jacques' wound before anyone came through the door. I swear there was nothing instantaneous about it at all."

"They should have been in the room during the interview, no matter what he wanted. Protecting the chancellor is their one job, as you Americans say."

Gwen and Heinrich took a long moment looking at one another trying to consider the possibilities of what Gwen had just described and process its meaning, if they were both correct.

"Someone on the security detail? Is that what we're thinking?" Gwen asked carefully.

Heinrich jumped up, appearing offended. "Betrayed by one of his security agents? That's ridiculous."

Gwen stood, not wanting to lose what little ground she had gained with Heinrich. Grabbing both of his hands she said, "They took my phone. If you can get it, I took several pictures of the kite festival on our way to the interview. I wanted photos to show Joshua when I got home. If you can, go to your father's conference room down the hall from his office, you'll see the broken window, the blood on the floor, the position of our setup. You'll see everything I've described."

Gwen begged Heinrich to check her story, believing it would vindicate her. If she could win Heinrich's confidence, despite his father's death, he would make for a powerful ally in Germany and in their courts.

"I will go to his office. I will look. But if you're lying to me …"

"I'm not lying. I have no reason to lie. Your father's death is a part of this story, the reason I'm here. It must be, nothing else makes sense. Think about it. Why else would someone kill him and get me out of the way at the same time?"

Heinrich looked thoughtful and nodded. "I will be back after I check a few things out." He turned to the door. "Guard."

The guard opened the door.

As Heinrich walked out, he turned to Gwen. "I fear you may be right about the security. But I equally fear if you're wrong, which leaves you in here. Neither presents a good outcome. Does it?"

Gwen stood in her cell, holding the bars, watching Heinrich walk off to the waiting car outside.

"Guard," Gwen shouted. "I'd like to call the American Embassy now."

HEINRICH AND KARL arrived at the Parliament building only to be met with more hollow sympathy. Heinrich continued to demonstrate stoicism, but his manners were becoming stretched; he wanted the truth. He asked security to take him and Karl to the room where the incident occurred. After a brief phone call to the BKA seeking permission to access the room, the guard escorted the men upstairs. Pulling the victim card, Heinrich asked for time alone in the room to come to terms with his father's death. Karl put his arm around Heinrich's shoulders in a show of support. The guard politely excused himself and told the men to take their time. The guard backed out, shutting the oversized French doors as he left, leaving the two in peace.

As soon as the coast was clear, they examined the room for evidence based on Gwen's description. Heinrich closed his eyes for a moment, feeling for his father's spirit, but the room remained static, cold, and impersonal.

"Now based on what Gwen told you, your father should have been sitting right over here." Karl gestured to the chairs in the windowed corner overlooking the park.

The two crossed the room to the corner Gwen described. The blood was cleaned, but a discoloration, evidence of his father's presence, remained. Heinrich stood at the site where his father died, looking down at what was left. A brown, dried blood smear stained the floor, his father's blood, his blood. Heinrich wept. Emotionally, it was too soon, but he couldn't wait. The evidence would not remain for long, and his access would certainly dwindle with time.

"What window did Gwen say was broken?" Karl asked, looking around the room.

"I knew it," Heinrich said. "She lied to me."

Heinrich looked around the room and saw no broken windows. He frowned. "I knew it. She lied to me."

"Don't jump to conclusions. Let's take a closer look around. Maybe the window didn't break, maybe it was open." Karl was grasping at straws, clearly refusing to believe Gwen's guilt.

Heinrich went up to the window where Jacques' blood still stained the wall and carpet. "Neither window is broken, Karl. None of them are broken. She did not say the window was open, she said it was shot out."

"It looks like they cleaned up a bit," Karl said. "Would cleaning include fixing a broken window? This quickly?"

Heinrich saw what he came to see. The layout was correct, but the facts in Gwen's story didn't check out. As the men turned to leave, Karl, walking alongside him, took three steps before the specific crackle of breaking glass came from beneath his shoe. He looked down at the floor, swiveling his foot to the side to reveal particles of broken glass.

The two men glanced at one another and let out sighs, relieving the pent-up anxiety of having to leave without knowing the truth. They now had the truth; they found the broken window. Heinrich considered this small fragment of glass a victory for Germany. It proved the security detail lied.

It was confirmation of a story that moments ago he did not believe, but his faith in Gwen was completely restored. The men took photos of the room and picked up every piece of glass they could find, putting the pieces securely in their pockets.

Heinrich left the building smiling at everyone, business as usual, but it was a façade. They were onto something, and now that something had killed his father. Who would be next?

They had to get Gwen out of jail.

A LITTLE OVER A YEAR AGO, Magda Katz worked in the Washington D.C. offices of the U.S. State Department. She was a divorcée in her thirties without financial means except for her modest government salary as a State Department courier. Yet she enjoyed the finer things in life, as most Washington women did. So, newly divorced, and nearly broke, Magda needed a side hustle. She was not the typical government hire. The government normally detected and weeded out people like her, people with vices and extremely over-extended credit. They did that for the most obvious of reasons: folks in that bind were too easily bought. People like Magda were a liability, but she fell through the cracks, and that would prove to be a costly mistake, though not for her.

Being divorced in Washington could be an expensive proposition. She needed to become a modern woman who pulled her own weight and earned her own way, and she didn't like that one bit. She had little to show for her forty-hour work week, as evidenced by her biweekly bank deposits. But she must cling to her job as an errand woman until something more lucrative presented itself. She had one thing going for her: her looks. Sexy women in Washington always attracted men of means, but holding onto them and taming their wandering eye was another matter. She learned a few things from her failed marriage, and she planned to put that education to good use. If she found another successful man who was in the black when it came to the green, she would catch him, marry him, and keep her mouth shut this time, especially when it came to his extramarital indiscretions. Anything was better than working as a gopher for a living.

Magda had been in the Capitol Building on errands many times before, familiarizing herself with members of the House and Senate. Crossing paths with these influential characters excited her, but she wasn't looking for an affair with someone already married—she wanted the whole checkbook. Magda was on one of her everyday errands when she crossed paths with the man who would improve her circumstances and change her life.

Like many astute men, Becker sensed her desperation, her fear, and her need for financial supplements. She was dressed like a diplomat but carrying a messenger's pouch. She had a great eye for clothes and no wedding ring. Putting two and two together, he thought she might be open to earning an extra buck. But first he needed to learn more about her. Could she help, would she help, did she even have the ability to help? All questions the congressman needed to answer but he couldn't ask. He needed a ruse.

When the opportunity presented itself, he swooped in to talk to Magda.

Magda was in a hurry, moving swiftly through the congressional halls, when she bumped into someone. She dropped her pouch and folders, spilling her papers on to the floor. In typical Washington fashion, the other person was much too important to help and hurried onward. This gave Becker his opportunity, his in. Thinking quickly, the congressman removed his wedding ring, placing it in his coat pocket to enhance his appeal to a single woman. Becker stepped in fast before he missed the opportunity to introduce himself to this State Department employee and assess her usefulness.

"Here, let me help you," Becker said, making his tone most cheerful.

"Oh, thank you, but that's okay. I'll get it."

"I insist. I'm Congressman David Becker," he said hoping his title would get her attention. He reached for her papers with his left hand, flashing the empty finger.

Magda watched this action then looked up and smiled. "I'm Magda Katz. I work for the State Department."

Becker smiled and nodded, taking her hand and helping her to her feet. He already knew a lot about her. "You seem to be having a tough day."

"It's just been one of those days, you know?" She shrugged.

"I'm in Congress, of course I know." He laughed. "May I call you Magda?"

Magda laughed and nodded in the affirmative while smiling politely. The moment turned awkward when she said nothing further. Becker took his chance.

"Hey, would you like to get a drink after work? You can tell me all about the sexy life at the State Department."

"Sexy? Hardly, but sure, I would love that," she said casually.

"Meet me at the Capitol Lounge on Pennsylvania Avenue at seven p.m."

"I love that place. See you then." She smiled.

Magda had her papers in hand again, all in a mess, but she didn't care—she had a date. Her heart jumped for joy. A man with position, power, and money—this was one date Magda wouldn't miss.

Magda arrived right on time. So did Becker. They met at the bar where Becker began with a round of drinks and stories about the stress of his office. Without asking Magda, he ordered her drink after drink to relax her mind and loosen her lips while he stayed sober. He listened to her talk about her ex-husband, the women, the money, all the while nodding in agreement about how wronged she was. She would certainly take the money, but he needed to be sure she was right for the job. She needed to be able to hold his confidence.

"You know, Magda, money is power," he said. "If you had your own resources, you wouldn't have to put up with any man's garbage again."

"I know, but my skills are limited." She shook her head, the loose movement showing she was sufficiently relaxed. Picking up her drink, she added, "The only reason the State Department hired me at all was because I speak Spanish and German. I translate from time to time, but when I am not doing that, I'm running around the capitol, as you know. It's going to stink when summer hits."

Becker's heart skipped a beat. After "I speak German" she was still talking, but Becker wasn't listening. That was a bonus he didn't see coming. *German*, he thought, *yes*.

Magda threw her head back, polishing off another drink. Before her empty glass hit the table, Becker raised two fingers to signal to the bartender for one more round. The bartender, knowing Becker well, replenished the lady's glass without delay.

"Oh, you speak Spanish and German?"

"Yeah. I have a German mother and a Spanish-speaking father. Odd combination, I know." She tossed him a sloppy smile, throwing back the new drink.

What a rare skill set for an American, he thought, *completely conversant and fluent in German. A useful asset.*

He needed to reel her in, which would be easy. *Who doesn't like easy money?* Then he would use his connections to reposition her overseas. That would be more challenging, but nothing he couldn't handle, despite her lacking other qualifications.

With only a few calls to cash in a few favors, it took less than a week for Becker to move Magda out from behind an unimportant desk at the State Department in Washington D.C. and put her behind an important desk at the U.S. Embassy in Berlin, Germany. Important to Becker, at least before she outlived her usefulness. She had access throughout the country and could be a point of contact for Becker carrying out Strauss' orders. In return, she could not only enjoy her former lifestyle but exceed it.

Magda's position of power gave her the control over her life she most craved. Berlin's famous Brandenburg Gate was a phenomenal backdrop for the American Embassy on the Pariser Platz, another pricey area for German real estate. Magda lived well now, and she wasn't going to let anyone ruin it, especially Gwen Patterson, who already had so much.

As Minister-Counselor for Economic Affairs, it was Magda's job, by definition, to promote American commercial trade interests within Germany and generate support for America's economic policy priorities, not the other way around. An ex-courier was hardly qualified for the job of lead economic diplomat, but this wasn't her true job. Becker sent her with an exquisite, hand-picked staff who knew what to do and all the right people who could help. Magda was thankful her team members were far more educated and experienced on German-American economic strategies than she. They handled the American business promotion, leaving Magda to manage other matters above and beyond her staff's knowledge. They only needed her signature, which she gladly gave without reading a word.

Truthfully, the best part about Magda's job, that in her view held the greatest promise for her future, was all the parties. Entertaining foreign dignitaries and government officials visiting from home was essential. She loved mingling with powerful men who were grateful for the work she put into their American-German business arrangements, though she personally hadn't done a thing.

"No problem," she always said with a warm smile and a roving eye. "No problem at all."

And it was no problem, at least not for her. She had other responsibilities.

She was sitting behind her desk in the American Embassy when her private phone rang. She was in a meeting but interrupted the conversation to pick up the line. The news was of the chancellor's shooting, and even better, Gwen's detention. The caller sounded delighted to share the news, as happy as Magda was to hear it, though she was surprised. Magda thanked the caller for the information and gently replaced the phone in its cradle.

Magda smiled at Rocco Wolf, her meeting that morning. Believing she retained Rocco's loyalties as a double agent, sent by the Americans but newly loyal to Strauss, she shared the good news that Gwen was being detained, accused of shooting Chancellor Jakob while under the guise of an interview.

"I guess your story is now over," Magda said snidely.

Rocco nodded, not giving any outward reaction to the news. "Yes, I guess it is. I will continue as though I know nothing until I hear from someone through official channels."

"Good idea." She smiled at Rocco. "I don't want anyone to know we're talking, even though I love our talks."

Rocco didn't respond.

"I hope you didn't like her too much," Magda said, trying to gauge Rocco's availability and interest.

"I'll be in touch." Rocco got up to leave the room.

As he walked out the door, Magda picked up the private phone, eager to give Becker the great news. Today, Magda would earn her money.

30

ROCCO WAS WORRIED.

He reported to the embassy as requested this morning to update his contacts back home about Gwen's progress. Fortunately for Gwen, there wasn't much for him to tell except they were taking the story day by day, interview by interview. He was careful not to share too much; friends didn't wear signs, and neither did enemies or spies. He didn't wear a sign either.

That the chancellor was assassinated in Gwen's presence while he was not with her felt too coincidental. Magda knew he was a spy, as did her superiors. What did she know about the shooting—and its timing, to have him in her office when it happened?

Gwen would not get the support from home she needed, and no one in the embassy could be trusted, or so it appeared. He had to recruit help. He would not leave Gwen sitting in jail. Immediately after leaving the embassy, Rocco called Carter and asked to meet at a local coffee shop, Café Einstein Stammhaus near the Tiergarten.

The two men took a cushioned corner on the upper deck in a private, quiet area of the chichi coffee shop where the waiters wore black and white suits. They compared notes and discussed their plans. Keeping their voices down, they tried to identify a strategy, a sure thing.

"Gwen is in big trouble, but she's innocent," Rocco said.

"How can I help?"

To Rocco's surprise, he didn't need to do any recruitment. Carter was willing to step out of his official CIA role to help an innocent woman. "We need to get her out of jail, find her a lawyer."

"I don't think so," Carter said with his nose in his coffee.

"What do you mean?"

"I don't think a lawyer will get there fast enough." Looking at Rocco, Carter said in a hushed voice, "She'll never see the inside of a courtroom, at least that's what my sources are telling me. They need a scapegoat, and she's it." He took another look around. "Or maybe not."

"What do you mean? What have you heard?"

"We have ears on Heinrich Jakob, as we would on any leader and their family, and we heard something very interesting an hour ago. Heinrich was speaking with Karl, and they intend to break Gwen out of jail tonight." Licking his stirrer, Carter looked at Rocco, clearly waiting to see how he would take this piece of intel.

"Break her out of a German detention center? That's crazy."

"Listen to me, listen carefully." Carter pointed his swizzle stick at Rocco. "This story she's working on, do you think it was an accident the chancellor was murdered while in her company? Do you think she'll get a fair trial in Germany, a foreigner accused of killing their beloved chancellor? Do you think she'd live long enough to get to a trial? Do you think our embassy will help her based on what and who you know there? Whose side is our embassy on, anyway?"

Rocco felt the answers ought to be a no-brainer. But the scariest part about asking these questions was they needed to think before they answered them.

We're Americans, we're supposed to protect our own, he thought.

He sat silent for a moment, in awe. Someone else had noticed the cards quickly stacking up against Gwen, and soon they would stack up against anyone who questioned the impending financial collapse. Rocco remembered the creepy smile on Magda's face after learning of Gwen's arrest. There was nothing to smile about. Magda thought Rocco was playing for both teams. Rocco kept up the charade to keep the lines of communication open, to learn what he could about the adversary, but he remained loyal to his home team. Anyone who tried to redirect his loyalties was certainly the adversary, or at least was on their payroll. Carter was right; Gwen could trust no one, so that meant neither could they. If

Gwen was to get help, it would be from them.

"No, I don't believe in coincidences," Rocco said with conviction. "I think Gwen is a patsy, and we need to help her."

"We will. Let's follow Heinrich and Karl tonight and see where they lead us. Heinrich still has a lot of access, so let's see how he uses it. I don't want to reveal what we're up to until we must. It's best we lay low and just observe until we need to intervene. In the meantime, I need to prepare documents to get Gwen out of the country, should it come to that. I'll make some calls later tonight."

All the men in Gwen's life were lining up to help her. Rocco briefly wondered if the gorgeous reporter was aware she had that effect on men. Anyone who spoke to her longer than five minutes would know she wasn't a damsel-in-distress type, but those big doe eyes of hers and the long, dark hair falling around her beautiful face, that svelte figure … Carter spoke with such loyalty and integrity, a man of action searching for the truth. Rocco understood the feeling.

They both wanted Gwen out of jail, and fortunately so did Karl and Heinrich, who had the most reason to want the truth to come out. Rocco and Carter decided they didn't need to figure out how to extricate Gwen from the jail cell; Heinrich and Karl would figure that out. They just needed to see what those two guys were going to do. Carter had ears on Heinrich, now Rocco wanted eyes on him, too.

Later that evening, Rocco and Carter stripped the lettering off one of the news vans and parked way in the back of the detention center's parking lot. They didn't want to be seen or caught, as everyone was running on minimal sleep. They sat in the dark, under the overhanging trees, watching but unable to get a clear view. Rocco pulled from his bag his German-made tactical night-vision binoculars, giving him a clear view. The two sat waiting for something, anything to happen.

Carter looked over his shoulder at Rocco with his elaborate gear. "You got cool toys, man."

THE FULL MOON filled the night sky with light, which was not helpful for the rescue crew, who needed to stay hidden. Breaking someone out of jail was no small offense, and even more so when that person was accused of killing the chancellor.

Heinrich and Karl waited in their car, parked down the street a short distance away from the jail, in the dark but with a great view. The shift change would give them a fifteen-minute window while the second shift was distracted, getting ready to leave, and the oncoming night shift wasn't yet at their assigned posts. The mid-shift personnel would want to run out of there while the night-shift staff unenthusiastically punched in for duty. Plus, there was always the cross-shift chatter and gossip when no one was paying attention. The jail staff behaved no differently than any other group of people who worked closely together, sometimes too closely. They waited and watched for the next shift to pull into the detention center parking lot.

The two friends planned to slip through the *klappfenster*, a top-hinged window opening at the bottom wide enough so a skinny guy could slip through. It wasn't the brightest design for a detention center, but the designers probably never envisioned a chancellor's son breaking into a jail to break out a detainee accused of murdering his father. This would be a first for Berlin. But once they got in, they remained unsure of how they would get Gwen out.

GWEN WAS LYING with her back to the wall on a hard, metal bunk. She'd been inside a prison cell before, interviewing inmates, and the one thing they always said to her was that for safety they lay on top of the blanket and stayed awake, vigilant. Gwen planned to use this to her advantage in case they tried to introduce another person into the cell who was a real criminal.

She sighed. She couldn't sleep anyway. Every time she closed her eyes, she saw Jacques' and Jakob's blood and heard that awful sound of bullets tracing across the floor around her.

She was lying on her bunk fearing the worst when she heard a familiar voice.

"Get up and put your wrists through the bars. You're being moved," Johann said.

Gwen shot straight up, heart pounding. This was it—she would disappear from here. She turned toward the door to look at the BKA agent with his bright blue eyes, still not sure if he was a friendly face.

He looked sternly at her and she did as she was told. She placed her hands through the bars and was shackled around the wrists. He opened the cell door.

"We're leaving," Johann said as he shackled her wrists to her waist. "Keep walking, no matter what. Keep your eyes straight and your mouth shut." He stood straight and looked her in the eyes. "Can you handle that?"

Gwen nodded. As earlier, Johann's eyes were windows to his thoughts; he looked earnest. If her gut was right, she was not going to disappear into a kidnapper's abyss.

Johann handed one guard a stack of papers and they waited for the woman to sign. Johann kept his eye on the guard, toe-tapping, and Gwen kept her eyes on the floor.

"Keep an eye on this one," the female guard said.

"Oh, I will," Johann said most convincingly. "I need all the evidence, too. The feds changed their minds, and they are going to handle this one. They took one on the chin, and I guess they're looking to get even."

The female guard, without question, handed Johann a bag of signed and sealed personal items including Gwen's clothing, shoes, purse, her passport, and her cell phone. All her evidence was in there; she hoped it hadn't been wiped somehow.

"Good luck, sir," the guard said.

With one hand under her arm, Johann escorted Gwen from the building.

"Keep it moving," Johann said harshly, still in hearing range of the guards.

Johann walked Gwen outside and toward another black Sprinter van. Johann placed Gwen in the back, but this time he didn't chain her to the pole. Instead, he unlocked her cuffs and unchained her waist.

"Wait until we pull away, then leave the chains here and climb up to the front seat," he said low enough for only her to hear.

Gwen nodded again.

As Johann pulled away from the detention center, he pulled up next to another car. Gwen could see nothing from the windowless back. Johann told her it was Heinrich Jakob and Karl Reinhardt and said for her to come forward now. She smiled, eagerly clambering into the front seat.

The two men looked surprised to see a freed Gwen sitting next to Johann of the BKA. Apparently, many people were convinced of Gwen's innocence and were all ready to put their careers and lives on the line.

Johann motioned for Heinrich to lower his window, and he did.

"Follow me so we can talk," Johann said to the guys.

Heinrich, still looking surprised, nodded and started the engine.

Johann led the way, and Heinrich pulled out behind him. "There is another car behind them, do you see it?"

Gwen checked the passenger rearview mirror. A second set of headlights followed them. "Is that a problem?"

"It is Wolf and Carter."

Her heart leapt, glad to hear Rocco was so nearby. She felt safer. "Who's Carter?"

"A CIA agent. I want to get everyone to the same place at the same time, so everyone can lay their cards on the table. I am not one usually to take such risks. I am a government man, you see, but I know in my heart something isn't right. I didn't sign up to incarcerate or railroad anyone, and I feel that is the case here. Some people in my unit were happy to learn of your arrest but not sad of their chancellor's murder. Their happiness didn't match what was happening, they were acting strange, so it too became undeniable to me, something was very wrong, and I didn't want to be a pawn in it or a part of it. So, today, I took a chance on an American reporter, two American spies, a chancellor's son, and a student activist." He groaned comically. "Oh my God, what have I done?"

Gwen blinked at him in the dark, trying to absorb all he'd just said. "Thank you?"

After the group traveled a safe distance from the detention center, and no calls came for them on the police radio, Johann pulled over in a vacant parking lot outside the city limits. Johann got out first quickly, followed by Gwen, who was all too happy to breathe the fresh air of freedom.

"Let's wait for everyone and figure out what to do. We can't stay here too long," Johann said.

Heinrich, Karl, Rocco, and the CIA man all pulled in and parked next to and behind Johann. Gwen ran to greet Rocco, who gave her a quick hug. She did a double take at the man with him, who seemed familiar but, in the moonlight, she wasn't sure.

Heinrich was anxious and eager for information. "What is going on?" he asked. "We were coming for you, Gwen."

Johann laughed.

"What?" Heinrich said, throwing his arms out.

"And how were you going to get Gwen out, exactly?" Johann asked, still smiling.

"Well, we intended to go in the window, but we weren't sure yet. Gwen, I swear we were coming for you." Heinrich looked at her, his face sincere. "I know the keys were in the drawer."

"Great. You break her out, then the police, or even worse, the BKA, are looking for three fugitives instead of one. Great plan," Johann said.

"Well, at least we were going to do something, not just leave her there," Karl said. "And how were we to know you wanted to help?"

"True. I'll give you that," Johann said.

"Okay, enough," Gwen said. "You all helped, and I thank all of you for it. All of you, you're risking a lot, and I appreciate it. Thank you. But where to from here? We can't make plans here on the side of the road. Where are we?"

Johann said, "We're safely out of the city, but we do need a place to hide for the night and a place to talk. That's why I let your two spies join along."

Gwen halfheartedly smiled and looked over at Rocco and his friend, but neither smiled back.

"Spies plural?" Gwen raised her eyebrows. "Rocco?"

"I'll explain what I can later. Right now, we need to get off this road," Rocco said. "Carter, this is your expertise, where to?"

Carter pulled out his map and looked for a safe house. After a quick scan, he directed all three drivers to a CIA hideaway in Rathenow. "It's less than an hour west of here, about seventy-five kilometers. We have a house there on Havelweg, it backs up to the Stadlkanal." He traced the route with his finger. "It'll give us quiet and privacy. There are several rooms there, so we each can get some rest. There aren't too many places open at night, low traffic, which is good. But there are places nearby where we can pick up food and supplies to hole up for a couple of days."

"Lead the way," Johann said. "Gwen will ride with me for safety. I can listen to the radio, and if anything changes, I will blink my lights twice and turn off. Gwen and I will go another route, and we'll just meet you there. I don't want all of us getting caught together."

The others nodded in agreement. Keeping Gwen out of jail was paramount until they had a plan in place to identify all the players and expose what was happening.

Rocco and Carter arrived first, parking around back, out of sight from curious eyes. They directed the other two vehicles to do the same. Telling the others to remain outside, the two American men searched the house room by room but found it empty. Heinrich, Karl, Johann, and Gwen were let in through the back. They combed the kitchen for supplies. It had been a long day.

Rocco and Carter pulled all the curtains shut and turned on a low light. Gwen disappeared into the bathroom to change out of the prison wear into her normal clothes. She dug in her purse for her makeup bag. The contents of her purse had all been removed at the prison and everything was jumbled. After using her remover, she splashed water into her eyes then brushed her hair. Her hands shook, but she wasn't sure whether that was from adrenaline or low blood sugar. She hadn't been able to eat the prison food they offered, too wound up after the horrific events of this morning.

Refreshed, she joined the men at the table to munch down the simple meal of meat, cheese, crackers, fruit, and other snacks Heinrich and Karl had stopped to get.

Gwen set down her bottled water. "Carter, you look familiar. Why is that?"

"I followed you here."

"Yes, I know you did." She narrowed her eyes at him.

"No, I literally followed you here. We were on the same plane from New York. I was sitting a few rows behind you. But I lost you on the highway with Rocco's evasive maneuver on the way to your hotel."

"That was you?" Rocco laughed. "I thought you were following us, but I wasn't sure, so I did a quick one-two and gone you were."

"Yeah, that was me. But I caught up with you two later." He turned back to Gwen. "I've been on your six since you got here. My job is to keep tabs on you and your investigation. I was ordered to report any progress to my superiors."

"If that's Carter's story, then what about yours?" Gwen glared at Rocco.

"What do you mean my story?" He tried to look innocent.

"None of us are buying it. Who are you, really?" Heinrich asked.

"You're government, but which one?" Karl said.

Rocco looked over at Johann for help, or at least support.

"Don't look at me. I have no idea where you work." Johann smiled, tipping back in his chair. "For all I know, you could be a German."

"At this point, we're all breaking the law, okay?" Heinrich said. "That includes me. My murdered father's name will only carry me so far and for so long, but that name will not absolve me of helping an accused murderer break out of jail. So, I am risking everything here, and I am willing to do it for the truth. I am leaving nothing on the table. So, I think it's only fair that I know, that we all know, who are you? Exactly?" Heinrich leaned toward Rocco. "If you can't trust this group, who can you trust? There is no one else."

That resonated with the entire table. Gwen needed to know who was on her team and who wasn't. She was desperate to finish this investigation. If they were going to do it together, then they had to be completely honest with one another.

Rocco took a long look around the room. "First, I'd like to say if I could choose a team, I'd choose the five of you. You're among the bravest people I've ever had the pleasure of serving with. I want you all to know that. Gwen, you've got guts, woman, I'll give you that. Most reporters would have left town after the first threat, but not you."

Gwen was moved by his words but remained mute, curious what would be revealed next.

"Carter, are you coming out with me?" Rocco asked.

The other four turned and looked at Carter's wide eyes.

Gwen looked between the two American men. "What in the world? Who are you people?"

"We're both spies for the CIA," Carter confessed. "But we don't always work for the CIA. Our employment is fluid and flexible."

"But why were you following me?" Gwen asked. "Why would they want you to report on my progress? Why would the CIA care what a news reporter does overseas?"

"Those are questions I'd love to ask my bosses. But truthfully—Rocco, correct me if I'm wrong here—I think I was sent to get in Gwen's way, not to just keep tabs. What do you think?"

"I agree." Rocco looked grim. "When I was in the embassy this morning, the woman I was meeting with seemed happy Gwen got locked up. I think someone is trying to scapegoat you, either the Germans or the Americans. But one way or another, you're being thrown under the bus, sweetie."

"So, you're a spy too?" Gwen asked. "Spy-slash-cameraman? Excuse me?"

"More than that, I'm a friend of Joe Bess'. He asked me to be your cameraman. I have experience, and he wanted you protected. It seems he was right when he said he smelled something wrong with this story lead coming from a foreign and an anonymous caller. But doubly useful, because I'm a triple spy." He grinned.

"A triple spy? What in the hell does that mean?" Heinrich asked.

Gwen crossed her arms. "It means he's a spy for the Americans, but the Germans or someone on the German side thinks they've turned him, but all the while he's remained loyal to America, making a one, two, three, triple spy."

Rocco smiled at Gwen. "Yeah. See? She's got it. So, spies in the embassy who think I'm helping them don't know I'm really helping Gwen. It confuses them. But as long as I'm not confused, we're all good."

"I'm confused," Karl said. "This is too crazy. Someone or some people have gone through a lot of work to interfere with this story. Why? Who cares so much about some trampled Germans at a protest or missing money, even billions, that they send spies and murder the chancellor, assuming it's all connected?"

Gwen looked around at her team. "That's the question the six of us will answer if you're all up for it. Who wants to finish this story once and for all?"

One by one they each pledged allegiance to the group, swearing they were on the right side of history, and they would finish this story together.

Gwen turned to Karl. "It's all connected. I can feel it in my gut."

Rocco rubbed his face. "We need to sleep. Tomorrow, we need to contact Joe. He's probably worried about you. I told him you were arrested."

"He knows?" Gwen barked.

"Yep."

Gwen turned to Heinrich. "What can you tell us about your father's vice chancellor, the new Chancellor George Nikolaus? Is he friend or foe?"

31

AS THE SUN ROSE the next morning, Gwen awoke from a much needed and welcomed rest. The safe house did its job. The quiet and security wrapped around her like a blanket. It didn't shut out the horrors of the day before—the bullets, the breaking glass, the blood, and death, being handcuffed and incarcerated. But she did sleep. The scent of coffee wafted through the house, waking her.

As of this morning, Gwen's time in Germany was over, at least for now. She was a fugitive, and there would be no more interviews on this side of the Atlantic. She needed to get home and talk to Joe. But how would she get out? Soon the authorities would know she had escaped with the help of a BKA member.

She put on her face, then joined Rocco and the other men in the kitchen, though Carter was absent. Heinrich looked hollow-eyed but resolute. Gwen reached across the table to squeeze his hand. He smiled at her briefly, then looked down at the table.

Johann said once the authorities put two and two together, he would be out of a job, but he still had his BKA connections, which were invaluable. Only four of them could freely move about, and the six of them had to come up with a plan, fast. Two things everyone immediately agreed upon: Gwen needed to leave Germany, and the new Chancellor George Nikolaus was not to be trusted until more could be learned about him and his loyalties.

"He seemed too eager to have Gwen arrested," Johann said. "I was there, and Nikolaus made that decision with little to no evidence. I could see holding your passport, but the arrest was too swift. We do not perform summary judgments here in Germany. We are a country of laws."

"Where is Carter?" Karl asked.

"If I know him by now, he didn't sleep and he went out for supplies," Rocco said.

"What supplies?" Karl asked.

"We'll find out in a minute, that's him pulling up the driveway," Johann said at the window. "In the meantime, let's have something to eat."

Over coffee and breakfast, the team continued to discuss their options, what to do next, and shared their opinions about differing theories behind the financial crisis. Everyone spoke openly and freely. A new sense of trust filled the room. But everyone had a different view, each reaching a different conclusion.

"Gwen, I was thinking ahead, so I obtained travel documents for you," Carter said. "It was a little hard not to see this coming."

Rocco rolled his eyes and extended his arms to his sides. "Who could see this scenario coming?"

"Well, clearly I did." Carter fanned his smug face with Gwen's travel papers.

"Okay, children," Gwen said. "So how will I get to New York?"

"Well, for the interim I changed your name to Laura Dee." Carter handed her the papers.

"How did you come up with an alias like Laura Dee?" Gwen asked.

"Let's just say it was available." Carter shrugged. "It doesn't matter anyway, because the second you land in America, everyone will know who you are. Just keep your real passport hidden at the bottom of your luggage until you land, and then switch them out."

"Do I have my luggage?" She looked at Rocco.

"No. I couldn't risk going back to the hotel after what happened at Parliament. The place was probably being watched."

"It's a good thing I keep the important stuff on me. Has anyone heard how Jacques did after surgery?" Gwen leaned forward.

"He came through it fine. He's downgraded from critical this morning. I checked. But he's still in their ICU."

Gwen sighed in relief. "Okay. Laura Dee I am. Whatever works here. Thanks, Carter." Gwen accepted her new name.

"But how will she get out of here?" Rocco asked.

"I think she should take a train to Paris or Madrid and fly home from there," Carter suggested. "Police should have the local airports covered by now."

"No, police will have the train stations covered too, at least locally," Johann said.

"I have a good friend who can get you out by private plane to Andorra," Heinrich suggested. "From there you can take a bus to Barcelona. It's about three hours, but that will be the closest international airport to Andorra. I think it's a little farther than the mandatory police checkpoints. Plus, no one ever looks at Andorra."

Gwen frowned. "Forgive my lack of knowledge in geography, but where exactly is that? Apparently, I have never thought of it either. Andorra doesn't even sound like a real place."

"That's because you're an honest person," Johann said laughing. "It's located between France and Spain. Good location too, very isolated."

"Yes. I am an honest person. Thank you for recognizing that. But what does that have to do with anything?"

"Andorra is the tiniest country," Johann said smiling and squeezing his thumb and forefinger together. "It has less than eighty thousand people, but it is one of the richest countries in the world."

"How so?" Gwen asked.

"Tax shelters," Karl said. "I'll bet tax shelters. Even Europeans barely know about that country. Luxembourg is a more common tax shelter, but I guess if you really want to stay off the radar, Andorra is it."

"It's a tax haven for those who like to make their money disappear," Johann explained. "But they got caught a few years ago. In 2015, The U.S. Treasury Department accused Banca Privada d'Andorra of money laundering. They like to keep their customers' secrets, what can you say?" Johann shrugged. "Then they signed an agreement with the United States, Europe, and other countries called the Common Reporting Standard. It reads that Andorran banks will be more open with who is hiding money in their country. But I guess you are only guilty if you get caught, right? This is all so new, so we shall see. They still offer only numbered accounts not linked to any names, a favorite among tax evaders, money launderers, and dictators."

Johann clapped his mouth closed as soon as he said it. The six of them fell silent. What did they just stumble upon?

"A favorite among dictators? Yes, I think I need to go through Andorra." Gwen smiled, scheming. "They're probably excellent at laundering dirty money and hiding stolen money."

"No," Carter said, cutting into Gwen's ideas. "No. No. No. You need to get home. You need to get to New York City. Forget it, Gwen. Forget it."

Rocco agreed. "You'll be of no use to us or the story if you're recaptured. You have to leave. But Andorra is a place we could investigate."

Rocco looked around the room at the other possible contenders. "Come to think of it, this isn't the first time I've heard that name among my peers. I never gave it much thought until now. But if someone is hiding German money in Andorra, then maybe my new girlfriend Magda might know a little something about that. I should give her a call."

"Your new girlfriend, really?" Gwen rolled her eyes.

"Yeah. Magda is an unqualified economic affairs advisor who wears other hats as well. Anyway, I was meeting with her at the embassy when she got the call you were arrested and she was just a little too happy about it, which now leads me to believe she's probably involved in something unpleasant. I know she's fond of me. Maybe I can use that, I don't know. I do know she's made several recent trips to Andorra, but I can't imagine it would be for herself. At the time of her travels, I never thought anything of it."

Looking around the room, Rocco asked, "Where's the phone? Let's do this right now."

Johann handed him the landline and placed it squarely on the table. The group gathered around the table to hear what Magda would say.

"Put it on speaker," Johann said.

Rocco smiled and hit the speaker button. The team was on the same page.

Rocco called Magda's direct line. Gwen hoped she had already arrived at work; it was still early, especially for a lady who wanted a life of leisure.

"Hello?" a woman answered in a hushed tone.

"Hey, Magda, it's Rocco." He made his voice upbeat.

"Hi Rocco. What's up?" she asked. "Did we have something scheduled today?"

The team remained silent, all carefully listening for a lead to the next part of their story.

"Since I regularly check in with you, I wanted you to know I'm taking a few days off for a little side trip. I've got business to handle."

"Oh, that's nice. Where are you going?" Magda asked carelessly.

"Well, I have some personal business to take care of, so the main office won't know that I'll out of town for a bit, away from Berlin."

"That sounds mysterious," Magda said, sounding curious.

"Well, it is. I have to make a banking trip, you know, an Andorra run," Rocco said. "But keep that under your hat."

The six of them waited, breaths held. Would she bite? Would she offer any leads?

"Oh, you bank there, too?"

"Well, not yet, but I'm going to check out some banks and possibly open an account, preferably at one with no names and all numbers you know?" He chuckled, sounding like a man on the take.

Johann quietly put up his hand to ease Rocco not to lay it on too thick. Rocco nodded.

"If you don't have a bank, maybe I could recommend one?" Magda said.

The group held their collective breath and looked at one another, hopeful in the offer Magda just made.

"Sure, that would be great. If there's one you're familiar with that is ultra-private, then yes, a recommendation would be excellent. It would certainly save me some time."

"I know some people who use Banc Sabadell d'Andorra. It's very reputable and very, very private," Magda said. "I'll text you with the address."

"That's great. Thanks for your help. I'm sure if your friends are satisfied, I will be, too."

Gwen hoped she would mention a friend or two.

"Oh yes, they are," Magda said. "I may open an account there myself. Hopefully, sooner rather than later."

"Well, if you're going to open an account, then your friends must really like their services," Rocco said, still fishing.

"Yes, I do a good job," Magda said.

No such luck. She might be a bought woman, but no one could say she wasn't loyal to her buyers.

"Alright, dear, I'll get in touch when I return," Rocco said.

Johann threw his hands up again, signaling Rocco to rein it in, tone it down or something. Gwen pressed her lips together, struggling not to laugh.

"Call me when you get back, we'll have coffee," Magda said, sounding delighted.

The call disconnected, but Rocco hit the line one more time to make sure. When a dial tone sounded, Rocco hung up again.

Johann shook his head. "You can't do that. You can't put the moves on a woman so strong like that, especially when you act as you can barely tolerate her in meetings."

"How would you know? Anyway, I did my best. Hey, at least I got a bank name." Rocco sat straighter; his pride not really shared by the group. "And it does give us confirmation that Andorra is the place, or at least one of them."

"This is true. At least Andorra will not be a wasted trip, we hope," Johann said.

"But you still need practice with women," Heinrich said with a smirk and a nod.

"No, he doesn't." Gwen raised an eyebrow at Rocco. "Stay away from her, she's trouble."

Heinrich said, "My friend will be able to fly you and Gwen to Andorra, where you can personally put her on a bus for the Barcelona airport. ALSA buses run daily."

Gwen gave Heinrich a stern look, as though the men in her life were trying to get rid of her.

"You should take Karl in case you need help. I need to stay in Germany and attend my father's funeral. It is being held the day after tomorrow in Saarland."

"Yes, I know. I'm sorry I'll have to miss it," Gwen said.

"I know," Heinrich said.

"Are you flying there?" Carter asked.

"Yes. I was invited to fly with some dignitaries who plan to attend. Why do you ask?" Heinrich asked.

"I think you should drive," Carter said.

"Why? It's seven hours by car," Heinrich said.

"Whoever took your father out may see you as a threat. Your name still means something in this country. You're the son of an assassinated chancellor. You can mobilize crowds. People will listen to you. You really should drive and stay off the main roads."

"He may be right," Rocco agreed.

"Yes," Johann said. "It is a temporary inconvenience, but it isn't worth the risk."

"You should drive alone. I'll follow you to your father's funeral," Carter said. "Then I'll find a perch and make a nest. From there I can keep an eye on you and watch the crowd, looking for anyone who doesn't belong."

"That just leaves you, Johann," Gwen said. "What's your plan?"

"I have a friend who used to work for the East German Stasi. His name is Herman Gottlieb. I will contact him. I have a feeling he may know something. Just because the Stasi were disbanded doesn't mean they aren't still in communication. This all feels so East German-like, so ruthless, nasty. You know what I mean?"

"I do know what you mean," Rocco said. "Too many people are being killed and the reasons come too easily. Plus, the car bomb at the library? That was very professional."

"Only people in high places with a great deal to lose hire professionals who are willing to murder for money," Johann said.

The team agreed. They were looking for criminals inside the German government, well-positioned people or pawns who could easily move about and move money for their real leader, whoever that was.

Rocco's phone chirped and he looked down. "That was fast." Magda sent the address for the bank, so now he and Karl had a destination: Avinguda del Fener,

7, AD500 Andorra la Vella, Andorra. Rocco showed Karl the address. "I think we can find that."

Karl nodded, "We'll find it."

"So, Heinrich, who's your friend with the plane?" Gwen asked.

"Marcel is a friend from school. I've known him for years. His father is super rich, and he is, or he was a supporter of my father's. I already called him. He said he will help."

"Good. Where does he keep his plane?"

"Northwest of here, at Tegel. It is close, and we can pull right up to the plane, quietly get Gwen on board without drawing any attention, and off you three go," Heinrich said. "And, since you're staying within Europe, no questions, no passports."

"Let me see my new ID," Gwen reached for it.

Carter handed her the paperwork. It seemed in order. Rocco took it from Gwen and checked it over. Running his finger over the seal and the photo, he said, "Not bad, not bad at all. This should get Gwen into America. We'll have to let Joe know you're coming to ensure you get through customs, just in case the Germans have called ahead."

"I don't think Joe has that kind of pull." Gwen shook her head.

"I assure you, he does." Rocco handed back the fake papers.

Gwen looked curiously at Rocco, but she didn't question him. She had just learned Joe was good friends with a spy, and she didn't see that coming. What else didn't she know about her good friend Joe?

"But how will we stay in touch?" Gwen asked. "I may need to contact you guys."

"Here you go," Carter said pulling out a brown bag. "That was my other stop this morning. I picked up six disposable phones. They're all clean, but, Gwen, I'm not sure yours will work in the U.S. Take one anyway, just in case. They're all preprogrammed with the other five numbers, and all the numbers are identical except for the last digit. We can talk and text anytime."

"Are you going to get matching T-shirts too?" Rocco asked with a smirk.

"It's a good idea, Carter, even if Rocco's jealous," Johann said, trying not to laugh. "Hey, he's a good spy, always has a contingency plan."

Each member of the team reached in and took a phone, closely looking it over.

"Keep the ringers low, buzzers on, and check them frequently," Carter said. "You too, Heinrich and Karl. We don't know if someone may be coming for you or your friend. The way things are going, these people are willing to kill anybody."

The group nodded in agreement. They would stay in close contact, reporting anything they learned to Gwen. She was the engine; she kept the story going. They were all resolute in this fact.

The team packed up and began their journeys.

Johann had sensitive calls to make. Reaching out to a former member of the Stasi was no small quest. With his present legal status unknown, he planned to wait at the safe house until he could reach out to his network.

Heinrich headed home to pack for the funeral, and Carter followed.

Gwen, Rocco, and Karl left for Tegel Airport in Berlin to meet Heinrich's friend. Gwen hated to leave her things in the hotel, but she couldn't return. The police were guaranteed to be watching the hotel now, and they would probably pick up anyone for questioning if they tried to fetch her stuff. The hotel and her belongings were abandoned.

32

CARTER STAYED BEHIND in Germany for two reasons. He couldn't leave Germany without Gwen, and, since technically she didn't leave, Laura Dee did, Carter would continue his "surveillance." Right now, the less the CIA knew about Gwen's escape and her return trip, the better. Carter didn't know whose side his bosses were on. He didn't know whose side anyone was on anymore except for their team of six. They seemed to be the only six people in Germany interested in the truth. Everyone else looked to have a personal agenda and selfish goals, even at the cost of a man's life, the dead chancellor, whose only crime was trying to unify a country and ensure its financial stability. Unsuccessfully, of course.

Heinrich packed his best suit. He had a long drive to meet relatives in Saarland, where his family originated. Several of Jakob's supporters chartered a private jet the day of the funeral, but Heinrich declined. He agreed the drive would be a safer choice, and it might do him good to have alone time to think about his father. He felt better with Carter on his six to keep him company for those seven hours. Maybe it was all for the best. Heinrich hadn't been back to Saarland since his father became chancellor. It would be nice to see his siblings and extended family again. His mother spent most of her time here, at the family home, despite her husband having to work in the capitol. Returning to Saarland would be a welcome change. Fewer people, open land, and clean air. Saarland was a good place for someone to clear their head.

Heinrich and Carter mapped out Heinrich's route so Carter could tail him but remain out of sight and at a safe distance so as not to raise any flags or draw any attention from the wrong people. Everything and everyone needed to look normal, as though no one suspected or knew anything. Heinrich was helpful in providing Carter with a detailed description of his hometown so Carter could pick the optimal location for his surveillance of the funeral attendees. Carter didn't know what he'd find or if he'd find anything at all. But much like an arsonist who was always in the crowd, the team was hoping for the same possibility. Maybe the chancellor's killer would be among the mourners. The funeral was to be held at Heinrich's childhood church. They were of Protestant faith, and the openness of their religion would make all the attendees feel welcome, even the chancellor's murderer.

GWEN WAS EN route to Andorra in the company of Karl and under Rocco's watchful eye. He would protect her, ensure her safe passage up to a point, then Gwen was on her own. The scariest part for Rocco and Joe was, what if someone was following her? What if someone was following them now? They used all the evasive maneuvers he knew, but someone would always be smarter. The threesome arrived at Tegel Airport in a nondescript vehicle. It looked like they were alone. But to their surprise, Marcel was waiting for them at the entrance, happy to help Heinrich's friends.

Rocco provided airport security with the appropriate paperwork before the three were permitted onto the tarmac. Marcel needed no paperwork; he was known to security, as were his brother and father.

"Well, I wish you three the best of luck," Marcel said. "Do you need anything else?"

"No, I don't think so," Rocco said. "Which plane is it?"

"It's the Gulfstream 650 at the end. The door is open, the stairs are down, and the pilots are waiting," Marcel said. "You wanted the minimal amount of crew, right?"

"Yes," Rocco said.

"How far can this type of plane fly?" Gwen asked.

"Oh, do not worry, Ms. Patterson, my dad's plane can fly on a single tank for about fourteen hours or so. Andorra is nothing, trust me. Andorra is just around the corner."

Rocco had the plane's tail number, and the three drove slowly past many fancy private jets held in the shared hangars. It was a sneak peek at how the rich and famous lived with their luxury aircraft and the convenience of flying at a moment's notice. *I'm well-paid, but damn*, Gwen thought. Tegel Airport held serious money in aircraft and cars that were parked while their owners flew across Europe.

Gwen, Rocco, and Karl boarded the Gulfstream 650 for the roughly six-hour flight to Andorra's nearest airport. Once onboard, the threesome took their seats. If their plan was to work, they needed to hurry. None of them wanted Gwen recognized until she was out of the country.

AS THE PLANE taxied down the airport runway, Marcel waited until he was out of view, and then he pulled out his cell phone and dialed.

"*Ja*," said the voice on the other end.

"She is on her way home, take rest, take rest." Marcel hung up.

ON THE PLANE, Rocco gave Gwen one more number.

"Don't write it down, and don't put it in your phone. You need to memorize this number right now and never forget it. This number is secure, and you can leave me a message if anything goes wrong."

Gwen studied Rocco as the wheels went up, repeating the number inside her head until she was sure she had it. From the sober look on his face, this man she had grown to trust as much as Joe was serious, and he suspected the worst.

Once in the air, the threesome brainstormed ideas and theories, none too outrageous, Gwen told them. She wanted to hear it all, even the most outlandish. The discussion went from the innocent to the mild and included the downright absurd. Gwen told the men of her taxi incident the previous week, but Rocco interrupted and confessed something.

"I think Joe had a clue about the seriousness of this situation before you ever got on the plane. Why else would he have arranged my involvement as your cameraman?" Rocco said. "He knew, and he sent you anyway."

"He sent me because I'm the best at what I do." Gwen said. "I knew it was dangerous the second he said the word anonymous in the same sentence with phone call. That's never a good sign, but I don't scare easily."

"We know," Rocco and Karl said simultaneously. They looked at each other and laughed.

"You know the man who tried to rob me in the taxi?" Gwen raised her eyebrow. "It didn't end well for him, did it?"

"The reason you're here is because someone from this country made an anonymous call to Joe, someone we don't know but who doesn't want whatever is happening to succeed," Rocco said. "That's the only good sign we have."

But Karl, the youngest, the least experienced, not a spy, not a reporter, just a student who wanted to do the right thing by his fellow German citizens, made the most poignant observation.

"What if it's all connected?"

"What if what's all connected?" Rocco asked.

"Everything. Everything that has happened to her and to us in the last week or so," Karl said. "Could the story, the reach of the involvement, be that big? The phone call, the Asian man, someone wanting Carter from the CIA to follow you, Joe asking Rocco to protect you, just all of it?"

"All of it connected?" Gwen said rhetorically. "Maybe you're onto something here."

"What are you thinking, Gwen?" Rocco asked. "You made a connection, didn't you?"

Gwen fell silent and stared off deep in thought. What if the dots did connect? Where would it take the story?

Gwen began to frantically feel her chest up and down, her outside jacket pockets and then her inside pockets. She remembered something. She was looking for something. Recalling where she had placed it, she unzipped an upper outside breast pocket and inserted her hand.

"Oh wow! Here it is, I forgot all about it. Here it is!"

Her fingers found the thumb drive.

"Here what is?" Rocco asked.

Karl looked even more curious.

From her pocket, Gwen pulled out a rectangular thumb drive and showed it to Rocco and Karl.

"What's on that?" Karl asked.

"I don't know," Gwen said. "I just don't know."

"Where did you get it?" Karl asked.

"This is the drive I took off of the man who assaulted me in the back of the cab last week."

"The guy who fell out of the cab and got run over? The dead guy?"

"Yes, that guy. I searched him, but he had little on him, just this drive and no identification to speak of. This was the only thing he had, so I took it."

Rocco took Gwen's thumb drive to get a closer look. "Only one way to find out."

He pulled open a small laptop computer from one of several compact black bags he'd brought with them. Once it was booted, he plugged in the thumb drive.

They waited, huddled around the tiny screen. A window popped up asking for a password.

Rocco tried a few different ways to access the data. "It's encrypted. No dice."

Gwen scrunched her lips in disappointment. "Is there any way to break the encryption?"

Karl said, "There could be, but you would need a specialist. A hacker."

Rocco snapped his fingers. "I know a guy in New York City. As long as you're going there." He opened a messaging program and typed a series of numbers and letters.

"What's that?"

"It's a contact ping for my guy. You can't telephone him and expect an answer. I send a message, he calls. Up here it's not likely to get to him, but as soon as we land, the message will go out. I'll call you on the burner and give you the address where to find him." He closed the laptop and removed the drive, handing it back to Gwen.

THE SMALL PLANE safely landed and Rocco, Karl, and Laura Dee all deplaned. Rocco personally brought the woman formally known as Gwen to the bus station to ensure she was on her way. With her new identification in hand, she boarded the bus for the three-hour drive to Barcelona Airport, where she would catch a nonstop flight to JFK in New York City. The real challenge would come at the airport in Barcelona. Would the new identification work? Was the passport professional enough? Gwen would find out sooner rather than later. Carter was a real spy working for the real CIA, so hopefully, the passport was up to standard. She trusted her friend to get her home.

After putting Gwen safely on the bus, Rocco checked the laptop to see if his message sent, and then he and Karl headed for the bank. Magda had given Rocco a great tip. He never imagined the Banc Sabadell d'Andorra would clean up dirty German cash.

Rocco and Karl headed up a mountain road looking for the bank's address.

"Considering the country's small size, this should not take too long to find," Rocco said.

Rocco was driving while Karl handled the navigation. The road had curves, so care was in order. They needed to get there alive. Fortunately, the signs were posted in French and Spanish; neither Rocco nor Karl spoke Catalan, the country's native language. They could only hope the staff of the bank was as linguistically gifted. After a few moments of checking the building numbers, the two finally arrived at Banc Sabadell d'Andorra. It was a small, simple building with a bright yellow sign. Not something so fancy one would believe they were cleaning millions, if not billions, of Euros. They must use their fee for something else, because they were certainly not spending it on this location.

They pulled off the narrow road and stopped out front, to the left of a steep hill. Rocco and Karl took a good, hard look out the passenger-side window and observed the bank's occupants for a minute, checking for security guards, routines, and any ordinary-looking females who may be of use. Rocco was a stud, and he knew it, but right now he needed information.

A plain woman worked alone behind a desk in the back. She clearly was an account manager who would be able to answer all types of questions. Rocco needed to go in alone, sweet talk her, and see what information she could offer.

"Maybe you should go in as a customer instead of acting like an investigator?" Karl suggested.

"Yeah." Rocco resisted the urge to patronize the kid. His innocence was sweet. "But first I need to confirm this bank will even open an account under such sketchy circumstances."

"You don't know the circumstances were sketchy."

"What do you mean?"

"Well, according to what Gwen said she has learned so far, and according to what Berger and Decker said, whoever is doing all this could just blatantly be moving the money over. Some people are really that bold. They don't care who knows."

Rocco looked at Karl for a long moment, realizing how right he was.

"What is it? What's wrong?" Karl leaned away from Rocco's intense stare.

"Nothing. Nothing's wrong." Rocco smiled at him. "You're right, very right."

"What do you mean? About what?"

"The simplest answer is usually the correct one. I had forgotten that for a minute. Thank you." Rocco shook his head.

"Spies make everything so complicated." Karl rolled his eyes.

Rocco laughed.

Both men look out their window and into the bank window. *What are the chances something could be this simple?* Rocco thought.

"I'll bet you anything whoever is behind all this blatantly opened an account here and is freely moving more and more money over, so many Euros at a time," Rocco said. "I'll bet there's no big secrecy about it. Whoever is doing it probably feels entitled to it. They probably feel justified because the amount is so astronomical."

"Anything is possible, you know?" Karl said. "Why don't we check?"

"Let me go in alone, just in case." Rocco flexed his shoulders. "I can work the ladies better alone."

"Please." Karl laughed.

"Leave your phone on," Rocco said as he opened the door. "If anything goes sideways, like you hear sirens, just leave, don't wait for me. I can get myself out of here, but I might not be able to explain you."

"Got it." Karl moved over to the driver's seat.

Rocco slammed the door and walked into the bank, mustering his swagger. Women were naturally drawn to confident men.

The door shut silently behind Rocco. Several bank employees looked up at him, none helping. Rocco quickly swept the room with his gaze, looking for anything he might have missed from outside, anything out of the ordinary. Not seeing anything or anyone suspicious, Rocco made a beeline for the desk of the woman in the back. The nameplate on her desk read "Maria."

Maria carried the expected chip on her shoulder of a woman often ignored and overlooked by handsome men, so she didn't give Rocco the flashy smile he ordinarily received from the ladies.

"Excuse me, are you the lady I can speak with about opening an account?" Rocco asked softly in German.

"Yes, I can help you," Maria said, using the same language. "Please sit down. Will you be a single account holder, or will this be a joint account?"

"I'm very single." Rocco rolled his eyes. "Sometimes I feel like I'm going to be single forever."

Maria gave a slight smile, "Don't worry, I'm sure you'll meet somebody. So, are you a citizen or permanent resident of Andorra?"

"No, I'm a German citizen, but much like my associates back home, I am looking to move some cash into your country." Rocco looked directly into Maria's eyes, hoping she understood his meaning.

"So, what type of account are you looking to open?"

"Well, that depends."

"On what?"

"I will need your complete discretion, Maria. May I call you Maria?"

"Yes, of course. We are all discreet here."

"Well." Rocco moved in closer, narrowing the gap between them. "I'm part of the financial dealings in Germany, you know, with the government?" Rocco looked briefly behind him. "Do you know what I speak of?"

Maria took a hard, long look at her new customer. Her brief pause told Rocco a great deal. First, he was in the right place. Second, she knew something.

"Well, that depends on what dealings you're talking about." Maria dipped her gaze to paperwork on her desk.

"I may need to move money for my boss, but I want an account of my own to put a little away for myself and any future wife I may have." Rocco gave her a clever smile.

"Oh, so then you work for Schmidt too?"

"Yes, yes I do." Rocco reinforced his affirmation with a slight nod, though he nearly fell out of his chair. *Did she really give me a name?* Rocco thought. *Schmidt. Who is Schmidt? And where is Schmidt? And who does he work for?* Too many questions for now, but that would be the next mission.

Rocco was excited on the inside, but his training kicked in, keeping his expression unfazed. Maria looked at him like she was not fully convinced. Rocco could tell she needed more evidence of his relationship with Schmidt, something to gain her full trust.

"I work for his boss. You know of whom I speak, don't you, Maria?" Rocco gave a casual shrug.

He took a risk, believing the top guys never do the tedious, menial work like opening accounts. *It's always someone the top guy trusts, especially when it comes to money. There must be trust.*

"Yes, I do." Maria smiled. "But for him, there are several of us opening numerous accounts. With his people, it's an all-day affair. I trust this is not the situation today?" She sounded irritated.

"No, no, my lady, not today. Today, I am here for a personal account." Rocco flashed his innocent smile and turned on his bountiful charm.

"Good, you I'm happy to help." She smiled again, visibly relaxing. "So, let's open an account for you and your future wife." She pulled out forms from the drawer.

"That would be ideal. I knew you were a woman I could trust, Maria."

Flattery got Rocco everywhere. He showed her his fake identification from the same supplier Carter used.

33

MARTIN HAD AN UNSUCCESSFUL meeting with a weapons expert, who looked at Martin as though he were a fool. A wave of shame overcame him; he was not a weapons expert, so he had not looked at the drawings Joshua gave him. He wouldn't have known the design was flawed. But was it flawed in its original form or had Joshua grown a conscience and backed out of their deal without saying so? It would not have mattered anyway. Martin would have killed him if he tried to back out. Perhaps Joshua did what he could to disentangle himself from the underground empire. Well, unfortunately for Joshua, he was not schooled in commitment—out equals dead. Martin needed to do what he needed to do, but first, he would call his father to obtain permission. Pulling out his cell phone, he dialed his father.

The phone rang only a few times. Strauss was often in his office, looking out over his future empire, daydreaming of his new reign and his family's monarchy. Martin quickly explained to his father that he discovered the drawings were flawed and that he wanted permission to wrap up Joshua like the loose end he was. Strauss was disappointed to hear that Travis' man was not dependable, for his underground movement depended on loyalty and support. This was a movement of magnitude, not a game one could quit when one felt one had played enough. So, yes, Joshua would die today.

"You have my permission, son. Take care of this traitor before he makes a bigger fool out of you or jeopardizes my plans for the new German empire," Strauss said with the conviction of a man who would be king.

Martin was a man of violence and intimidation. He had learned from the best. He went alone; witnesses required more killing, and he wanted to leave this hellhole as soon as possible. He liked to do his own wet work. He picked up his battering ram before he circled back to take care of a liar not worthy of life. Most likely, Joshua wouldn't let him in a second time. Even an American wasn't that stupid.

GWEN'S PLANE LANDED at JFK airport just after 3 p.m. local time, but the real challenge was to get through customs and security hoping the Germans hadn't alerted Homeland Security. Gwen did as Carter instructed and hid Laura Dee's passport in her purse and held her real one in her hands. As a public figure, people recognized her on sight, especially at JFK. A phony passport would attract more attention than deflect it, plus as far as she knew, she wasn't wanted for capital murder in America. Gwen breezed through security, waving to the TSA agent, who waved and smiled back. Leaving the regular way, Gwen hailed a cab as soon as she got through the exit.

"Take me home," she said to the driver, giving him the address.

"Yes ma'am," the driver said.

Heading from one end of the city to the other, Gwen looked through the window with relief, glad to be home after sixteen grueling hours of travel. As the cab got closer to her house, Gwen grew more and more anxious. She hadn't seen Joshua in more than a week, and what a week it had been. She had so much to tell him, to get his perspective on.

The cab pulled up and she paid the driver, eagerly getting out. The cab drove off as she ran up the townhouse steps.

The moment Gwen stepped through the front door, her skin crawled, and her senses went on high alert. Someone had tossed the furniture, dumped drawers and papers on the floor, pulled all her books off the shelves. If the perp was still here, he could have knocked her to the floor like a wave in the ocean. Gwen remained by the front door, surveying the mess for the home she left behind and listening as hard as she could to determine whether she was alone. Heart hammering, she took stock of easily fenced valuables still present—their stereo and television, a crystal vase she kept on the bookshelf, her journalism award made of gold still hanging on the wall; this was no simple burglary.

After a minute, Gwen reluctantly stepped forward, the only sound the cracking of broken glass beneath her feet. Careful not to touch anything, she continued to listen in case the burglars were still here.

A sick feeling of dread dropped into her stomach.

"Joshua?" she called out. No response. Then louder, to reach upstairs, she called, "Josh?"

But still she heard nothing. He must not be home. Thieves usually watched a residence and struck when no one was home, didn't they? More confident, Gwen stepped over and walked past the broken décor, the smashed pictures, everything she owned. These were her belongings, things she earned and valued before she left. Her priorities and her values had changed in the past week. Family and freedom were now at the top of her list, not trinkets.

She moved to the back of the house toward the kitchen, passing Joshua's home office. An unnatural stillness draped the room, drawing her gaze.

At first, she wondered why he was napping on the floor. Blinking, she took in his posture where he lay prone next to his desk. The scent of death hung in the air. "Joshua?" She stepped into the room and knelt by him. She watched his ribcage and counted in her head, but after a minute, with no sign of movement, she reached a hand to touch him and had to accept the truth. The love of her life lay dead on the floor.

In that instant, she knew this was not a burglary. Everything was broken, but nothing obvious was missing. The smart thing to do would be to leave and call the police. But she didn't know if the authorities in Germany would have alerted anyone here. She couldn't risk calling the police, not knowing who would show up.

Gwen was not a woman to believe in coincidences. The likelihood of a connection to her recent experiences seemed doubtful, but anything was possible. She leaned closer to the empty shell who was once her husband. His body lay among shattered glass in a chaotic scene, his ruined face turned to one side. He was barely recognizable, covered in his own blood, now turned brown where it had dried around his head. He took a hard beating. *What could you have done that would have angered someone so much?* she thought. He was just an engineer, a nerd; he worked with schematic drawings on a computer screen. Who would want to kill him and why? Was more than one person involved?

Combat reporting experience served her well. She knelt in the middle of a crime scene next to her murdered husband, yet she hovered outside herself, focused on the facts. Fact one: he was dead, and nothing she could do would change that. Fact two: someone did this to him—and if they hadn't found what they were after, they might come back. In a moment of clarity, she pulled her phone from her pocket and photographed the scene, not because she wanted to preserve the horror, but because she had to. She had to show Joe. She needed help on this one, something she rarely asked for.

Without touching too much, she went upstairs—where nothing looked disturbed—and dug a backpack out of her closet. *Maybe they found what they wanted.* Grabbing what she could, the immediate essentials, she stuffed the backpack full, including her purse and both passports. She would not be back for a long, long while. She changed into athletic clothes and put on her best sneakers. As she left the house, she called Joe.

"Hello?" Joe answered in his normal gruff tone.

"Joe, it's me," Gwen said, out of breath.

"My God, girl, where are you?"

"I'm in New York. I need to see you." Gwen glanced around, hyperaware all her belongings were in a backpack hanging off one shoulder.

"Where?" Joe asked.

"The coffee shop."

"When?"

"Now!"

ACROSS TOWN, ALEX was on the line, listening as usual. Gwen's number changed from time to time, but Joe's hard line was dependable.

"Did you get that?" Alex asked the agent sitting next to him.

"Yes, but do we know which coffee shop?"

"I know it."

"Go there and make sure it's really her. See what you can find out."

This woman made things too difficult for them. Alex was crossing a danger-ous line, spying on American citizens on American soil, but they needed a break overseas. They needed to know what Gwen knew.

34

JOE STORMED OUT OF HIS OFFICE, grabbing his jacket on the way out. He hurried to the coffee shop a couple of blocks away where he and Gwen had spent countless hours talking over the years, working through story ideas and details away from the office. As far as they were concerned, stories were all talk until they had multiple sources of confirmation.

Joe hustled through the streets, narrowly missing people he passed. With sweat on his brow and a heavy breath, he composed himself before going inside; he didn't want to attract attention for Gwen's sake.

The café was crowded but not full. Joe bought a basic cup of black coffee and was glad to get an open seat in the rear, back against the wall, eyes on the doors. The glass street front allowed him to observe the outside crowds and see who was coming and going, and who might be interested in something other than coffee.

Gwen thought, ironically, she was getting good at covert maneuvers. She had arrived first and hid in the bathroom, keeping a lookout for Joe. Once he sat, and it appeared he was alone, she slid in next to him where she could watch the exits while having a private conversation with him.

Joe startled. "Where did you come from?"

"Back there." She tilted her head toward the narrow hall. "I was hiding in the bathroom, waiting for you, making sure you weren't followed."

The café wasn't exactly a secret and probably was not the most out-of-the-way place they could have chosen. But she was on a clock and needed familiar ground. She felt like she was trying to run uphill on sand.

"Followed?" Joe chuckled. "Who the hell would follow me, kid?"

She scoffed. "The CIA, the State Department—for all I know, the FBI is involved somehow. I'm pretty good at predicting people, you know?"

"What?"

"Joshua is dead!" Exhausted, frightened, and grieving, Gwen sobbed, unable to hold back the tears any longer.

Joe grabbed her in a hug, and she cried against his chest. He murmured low encouragement and patted her back with one hand. The loss of control freed the anxiety twisting in her stomach since she'd walked into her house. She was thankful for the close relationship she had with Joe as her mentor; these weren't the first of her tears he had soothed, but they felt like the worst. After a minute, she sat up straighter and leaned away and brushed loose hair out of her face.

Joe gave her a handful of napkins. "Joshua is dead? When? How?"

She managed to keep her voice low, to keep from screaming her anguish to the whole café. "Someone broke into our house, ripped it all apart, and they killed him, Joe. They killed my Josh." She stifled further sobs and shook open a napkin for her running eyes and nose. She had too much to convey to Joe to fall apart now. "I just came from the house, just now. I came straight here. This was everything I could grab." Gwen lifted her backpack. "I went straight home from the airport. I didn't see anything until I went inside. The place is trashed, and Josh is in his office, lying dead on the floor. I don't know for how long."

"Did you call the police?"

"No, I was afraid to. I didn't know if the police here were alerted about the chancellor's murder back in Germany. I don't even know if I'm wanted here, too."

"What?" Joe looked around then lowered his voice. "What the hell are you talking about?"

"At this point, it's anyone's guess. You have no idea what's been going on over there! I've got CIA agents up my ass, political activists tearing the cities apart, and German police agents first chasing me, then helping me. This story is getting completely out of hand." Gwen blew her nose. "And, the murder of Chancellor Jakob was not something I saw coming either. Having the chancellor murdered in broad daylight in the middle of a taping is a first, even for me, Joe." She took a breath to suppress the sobs and calm herself. "So, after I realized what happened,

I grabbed stuff and called you as I ran from the house. I can't go back there, not now, not for a while. I can't go to the office. The police may come looking for me there. I need to find somewhere to hide and work."

"Well, you can stay at my apartment." Joe dug into his pocket, pulling out his keys.

"Thanks, I appreciate it." Gwen reached for the keys he slid along the table. "Why would someone do this to Josh? The place was so trashed I couldn't even tell if they stole anything. All his drawers were turned out, all his papers were on the floor." She shook her head, remembering the scene. "His face was barely recognizable. He took such a beating." Tears threatened again.

"You know from your earlier reporting days, beatings are personal. They're always personal, no matter what any police report reads." Joe tapped his fingers on the coffee cup. "So, who did Josh piss off? If you can answer that question, you can probably solve his murder, too."

"I can't imagine Josh doing anything that could make anyone angry enough to beat off his whole face, for heaven's sake. I just can't."

"You can't predict human behavior." Joe rubbed her shoulder, his touch reassuring her. "You can't predict this kind of sick, human behavior, so stop trying. That's a no-win proposition. I'm sorry you walked in on that. It's going to take time to deal with it. I'm here for you." He took his hand away and leaned on the table. "But what we need to do is focus, because we have too many irons in the fire. Don't worry about Joshua's body. I'll call the police. You won't have to say you saw anything. It's your house, your fingerprints should be there, and as far as the cops are concerned, you're still in Germany anyway, remember?"

"At least until they check TSA records. I came through customs with my real passport."

"Were you on the passenger manifest under that name?"

"No … my new friend in the CIA—or not, I was unclear on that—gave me a fake passport to travel under. Nice plant, by the way. Rocco has interesting friends." Gwen smirked.

"What do you mean, plant?"

"He's a great cameraman, but he's not just a cameraman. I figured that one out by the way he handled the car bomb in the news van."

"Sorry, kid, I was just looking out for you. But he comes in real handy, and he does get great shots, doesn't he?"

"He does." She laughed, feeling hysterical. "I didn't know what to do, so I grabbed what I needed and took off to come here. I'm miles away from Germany, but I don't know if the authorities there have alerted anyone here. I couldn't risk calling the police." Her face crumpled. "I—I had to leave him just lying there."

"Let me call the police. It's the best way. It'll look like the murder it is, and that will begin an investigation. Too many murders are being swept under the rug this week labeled as accidents. But I swear, not Joshua—he's not going to be swept under the rug."

It would be hard to smash in your face that way accidentally, Gwen thought, but she understood what Joe meant. "Thank you. You don't know how much I appreciate that." She wanted to cry more, but she couldn't allow it right now. Joshua would get his grief from her later. The urgency and fear dogging her wouldn't let her feel safe.

"There's more going on in Germany, too," Gwen said. "Since Chancellor Jakob's death, his second in command Nikolaus is in office, and we have no idea what side he's on or if he's involved at all." Gwen rattled off more details of what had transpired in the last week. "Just a week ago, I was a happily married, world-renowned journalist; now I'm a fugitive from the German authorities, a widow, and the clock is ticking. Ticktock."

"Well, I have news of my own," Joe said. "It isn't good, either."

"What?" Gwen drooped, not surprised.

"Frank Solas didn't have a car accident. He was murdered." Joe let out a deep sigh. "Anyway, regular accidents don't end with those kinds of fireworks."

Gwen took a breath to speak but the front door swung open, slamming into the trash receptacles behind them. She and Joe both jumped, startled at the sound, and they weren't the only ones. A group of young friends raced through the door, horsing around, cutting each other off, trying to be first in line. They were laughing loudly and enjoying the ease of a beautiful afternoon.

A week ago, Gwen would have appreciated the obliviousness associated with their youth. Ignorance was bliss. But she was no longer blind; in fact, she learned in one week more than most people would consider safe. Very ugly people in this world wanted a lot more than good friends and good times.

"Anyway, as I was saying, Solas' accident was no accident. Someone planted explosives in his trunk, possibly while he was at a meeting here in New York City. Cameras caught several large SUVs surrounding him on the highway. The SUV occupants at one point dropped their windows and fired at Solas. They shot his tires out until he lost control of his car. He veered off the highway still going well over the speed limit, I'm sure, if I knew my friend. The combination of speed and the loss of control put him in the direct path of those sand-filled Fitch barriers, which aren't enough protection when your trunk is filled with explosives."

"I guess the barriers don't help when you're the last one to find out you've been sent on a suicide mission," Gwen said meekly. "Do they have any leads? Could your contacts at the state police tell you anything?"

"Yeah, a bit." Joe slanted his head. He and Solas went back decades, not an easy thing to say about many people in Washington D.C. or New York City. "They could tell me some things, but not enough. Never enough, kid. Solas passed through tollbooths coming south on the Garden State Parkway, which proved crucial enough to help time the events leading up to his death."

"How so?"

"Despite what they tell the public, those cameras are always recording, and they allowed me see the video. It captured his license plate and a photograph of the driver. It was him, alright. The picture of his face was clear, too. Undeniable, in fact. However, where the investigation gets more interesting is when the state police ran the license plate though their computers."

"What did they find?" Gwen leaned forward, hanging on every word, glad for the distraction from her grief.

"The car Solas was driving was leased to a German man who has ties to the former General Secretary of East Germany." Joe shook his head. "At least that's what my contacts have told me."

"East Germany?" Gwen frowned. "Who held the lease?"

"That name isn't important anymore. After some checking, I learned he died a couple of days ago, before Solas was killed—on the same damn day, if you can believe that." Joe's voice rose. "The two met here at the New York Harbor for whatever reason, and after they went their separate ways, someone killed this guy who leased Solas' car, and then they packed it with explosives before Solas left the dock. Is that where all the cash came from? I don't know." Joe shrugged, looking at Gwen with concern. "Listen, kid, whoever is pulling all the strings here is using Cold War tactics and isn't leaving anyone alive."

"I know, I know." Gwen wanted to reassure Joe she was done with taking stupid chances. *Who would have thought walking inside my own house was a stupid chance?* Her plans would be more thought-out now, more strategic. "Who did this guy work for? Wasn't the last leader of East Germany a man named Erich Strauss? He was a Communist—die-hard, if I correctly remember my history. He was relatively young at that time, I thought. What happened to him when the Berlin Wall crumbled?"

"No one knows. He just disappeared." Joe shrugged. "Rumor has it he had two children by a woman he never married, and she also disappeared shortly after the wall fell. Thousands of East Germans defected at that time, so it's likely she left the country. So, information of his whereabouts or even his children's is not going to be easy to find."

Gwen considered the possibilities. "Could Solas have been working with this dead man on the dock? I know Solas was your friend, but we need to deal in facts here. Was he involved in something illegal?"

"I suppose so. No one seems to be who they say they are anymore. Everyone seems to be living two lives, especially in Washington."

"Well, not us. Thank God for that, Joe, not us!" She might truly be the only real friend he had left whom he could fully trust. Outside of Rocco. Her heart squeezed, wishing he was here to watch her back.

Joe flashed a smile then sobered. "I hate to bring it up, but we need to talk about Lyle for a minute. The police have not identified his killer. They have no real leads, nothing concrete." Joe lowered his voice. "You need to be extra careful."

"They've made no connection to the Asian man?"

"No, nothing so far."

Gwen deflated in her seat, her resolve not to cry threatening to crumble. "Killing Lyle was so unnecessary. He was just a kid."

"Murder never makes sense, sweetheart." Joe twisted his coffee mug on the table. "But it does beg the question of why. Just one more puzzling fact in a cascade of puzzling facts."

Gwen nodded, not knowing what to say. Death was everywhere around this case, but no one was claiming responsibility. Everyone was lying low, as though in preparation for something.

"I have never seen as many murders as I have seen in the better part of the last two weeks," Joe said. "In all my years, I have never seen anything like this. People who seem to be benign or inconsequential are being murdered, and all these deaths are somehow linked to you, kid." Joe placed his hand over Gwen's.

"They're all linked to me?"

"Well, if you think about it, you either know the person, are related to the person, interviewed the person, or something," Joe said. "It's not your fault. Of course it's not your fault, but for some reason all these facts, and they are facts, swirls around you."

Gwen churned the events through her head, everyone in the body count of the past week. Joe was right: she knew them all, one way or another. But how she could be at the center of a story about German tax fraud? She could lie to Joe if she chose to, but she could not lie to herself. She was involved, deeply involved, even if she didn't know how or what would happen next. She was methodical by nature; she always knew what came next. The abyss of the unknown that drove her investigative reporting threatened now with terrifying shadows.

"That's not the end of it, kid. There's more."

Gwen rested her forehead in one of her hands, preparing for more news that should be shocking, but that emotion was past affecting her.

"Sources tell me a grand jury has been convened to hear allegations about possible money laundering by Congressman Becker and General William Jones. They're talking about overseas accounts and tax evasion, the whole nine yards. Keep that under your hat—it isn't out yet."

"Funny you should mention that." Gwen looked up at him.

"Why?"

"After dropping me off, Rocco and Karl checked out a bank in Andorra.

Rocco got a lead on possibly some, if not all, of the missing German money. They suspect it may be getting laundered through a bank in Andorra. I'm waiting to hear from Rocco to see what they learned. If not Andorra, any idea where Becker and the general would be stashing the cash?"

"No. But I'm going to pass that information on to my source in the FBI. Investigators could probably use the lead. Let them use their legal muscle to shake the tree and see what falls out."

"I'm glad you told me all this. This conversation is clarifying a lot for me."

Joe put his hand on top of hers. "But, unfortunately, kid, there's more clarification to come."

"What more could there be?" Gwen asked, eyes wide open.

"While you were in Germany, did you hear about all those missing SWAT team members that disappeared up the Elbe River in Hamburg?"

"Yes. It was on the news. Very tragic. The news said they were surveilling a drug deal off the docks in Hamburg, at the port."

"That wasn't a drug deal gone bad. That was what officials fed the media. That was an arms deal gone very well."

"How do you figure that?" Gwen lowered her voice. "How does an arms deal go well?"

"Long story short, everyone, and I mean everyone, got what they came for." Joe shrugged. "A source I have in the German government knows someone on the inside of that deal. Unfortunately, I can't give you any more detail than that, I just don't have them."

Gwen sat still as anger washed over nerves raw with grief. She hated hearing about the media being fed lies when the truth was known. This happened time and again, and no sources were ever held accountable for the lies. Instead, the media got blasted for spreading "fake news." They had to issue retractions and lose subscribers with egg on their faces. The dishonesty that followed fueled her anger and disgusted her. As a serious journalist, she sought truth and justice. More and more, she had trouble locating sources with personal responsibility, accountability, and integrity. "So, if everyone got what they came for, what was it? Guns? A lot of guns? More bomb-making material? What?"

"The shipment was in crates, a lot of crates, so it's anyone's guess what those crates contained. It's probably big stuff too, since they needed a forklift to move them. Kid, let's face it, they were probably moving heavy-duty shit," Joe said in a tone of concession. "The shipment originated from right here in New York Harbor."

"New York Harbor? Isn't that the site Solas was last seen leaving?"

"Yes, it was," Joe said with his head hanging low.

"So, basically, Solas is seen leaving the harbor, case full of cash, he has the means to provide customs documents, and that shipment heads straight for Hamburg."

"That pretty much sums it up."

"So now we have money moving out of Germany and weapons into Germany, wonderful. What's next?" Gwen chewed on her lip, thinking. "If that doesn't sound like a coup in the making, then I don't know what does. It sounds like they're weakening the people so when the savior swoops in, the population will be too hungry and drained to care, to put up a fight. Everyone will fall into line. Gee, haven't we seen this before?"

Joe gave a small nod.

"I should call Rocco, give him an update, too. This will give him time to continue digging around before I get back."

"Get back? Back where? Germany? Are you crazy?" Joe frowned, irritated. "If you go back and get caught, you'll be tried for Chancellor Jakob's murder and most likely convicted, since the person behind this madness appears to have people imbedded all over the place."

"Well I can't go home! If I slipped out of the country, then I can slip back in the same way. But I'm not going to do a thing until I have something more concrete to bring back, evidence to support a possible coup theory, and to present it in my defense. As we both know, the truth is the best defense of the innocent." Gwen speared him with a fierce glance. "I am innocent."

"Before you call Rocco, find out what's on that thumb drive you liberated off the dead Asian man." Joe sipped the dregs of his coffee. "There could be more answers in there that can move the story forward."

"Yes, that's right. I need to go see his hacker friend. It's not that far, just off Times Square." She checked her pocket for the thumb drive and told Joe which building.

"I know it," Joe said. "That's on Forty-second Street and Seventh Avenue. Come on, I'll go with you. You don't have to do this alone. I'm here now. Let me support you."

35

WHY WAS THE DEAD ASIAN MAN holding that thumb drive? Why was it the only thing he was holding? The two had more questions than they did answers, and it unnerved them both. Joe and Gwen slid out of the same side of the booth and left the same way they came. Taking a quick look around, Gwen was sure no one was interested in them, and no one would be following them.

They walked a couple of blocks south on 42nd Street on their way to the hacker's building. Being on foot gave them more freedom to change direction in case someone did show too much interest in them. Gwen was a woman on the run and didn't want to end up like Lyle. Or Joshua. She didn't have time for interferences from people outside her team of six.

She caught the reflection of a man she'd seen at the coffee shop and in a few shop windows since. They looked at each other for a split second, but that was enough time for Gwen to see his reaction. It was obvious he was not just some pedestrian; he was following her and Joe.

"Joe, we have a tail," Gwen said looking straight ahead.

"A tail?" Joe turned to look back.

Gwen grabbed his arm and entwined hers with his as though they were a couple. "Don't look, don't look, just keep walking. There's a guy back there. I saw him at the coffee shop. He didn't stand out then, but now I've seen him in the reflection a few times and the only thing he ever seems to be looking at is us."

"Okay, so what do you want to do? Do you want to skip the hacker for now and go back to my place?"

"No. We aren't skipping anything. I want to know what's on that drive, and I want to know today," Gwen said, more determined than ever. "I need to know if there's something on that drive related to my story—to our story, sorry."

"No, no kid, that's fine, it's your story. So far, you've taken most, if not all, of the serious risks. I'm lucky enough to be able to feed you information, any information. At the least, no one has put a bomb under my car. Well, not yet."

"Yeah, as far as you know." Gwen shot her mentor a look. "Listen, keep moving until we hit Bryant Park on the left."

"Then what?"

"I want you to hail a taxi, go directly to the building, go inside and wait for me there. Don't speak to anyone, and when you get there try to stay out of sight but keep your eyes on the door and look for me. Okay?"

"You're not going to pop out of the hallway like you did at the coffee shop, are you?" Joe asked, inserting levity into a stressful situation.

"I'll get in any way I can without being followed, so keep a lookout for me. Keep your head on a swivel, okay?"

"Okay, just kidding," Joe said as they hurried down the block.

"I know. And I love you for it."

As the two approached the New York Public Library at 5th Avenue and 42nd Street, Gwen made a quick and dirty turn to look back; she wanted their tail to know she knew he was following her and that he was caught. The only problem was, she didn't recognize him. She didn't know who he worked for, or who else knew she was in town. That raised more questions. But nothing was going to keep her from opening that drive, not today.

Joe got into a cab and did as Gwen asked. As the cab pulled away, taking Joe to the hacker's building, Gwen took a few steps back, getting her footing, and getting ready to run.

When Gwen caught the man's attention, she made a run for it. She sprinted down 42nd Street past Joe's taxi, now stuck in traffic. On foot, Gwen was great. She darted left into Bryant Park, ten acres of green grass, trees, and paths confusing enough for someone who didn't normally walk through it.

Gwen had the advantage and ran as though her life depended on it. For all she knew, it did. The lives of many people might depend on what was on that drive. Through the park and into the scenery she ran, leaping bushes and shrubs like an Olympic gold medalist. She gave the guy a run for his money, and frankly, he wasn't much competition.

Gwen ran through the park onto 6th Avenue. She dodged through traffic, fortunately bumper to bumper this time of day and mostly not in motion. She continued south, down West 41st Street, staying off the main 42nd Street. She needed to make it to Times Square; it was all she could think as her breath became heavier and heavier and her paced slowed. She asked God for strength to get to Joe, get to the hacker, and get inside that thumb drive. Gwen, briefly looking over her shoulder, saw no one following her. No one looked like they were running as fast as her. Gwen made a right onto Broadway Avenue, trying to blend in until she ran into 42nd Street, when she had no choice but to go south with the traffic. She made a quick left to the building.

God, I hope there is something useful on there, Gwen thought as she bent over, one hand on each knee, trying to catch her breath. As she watched through the door, relief swept over her when she saw Joe. He made it. Gwen stood, taking the final few steps before she slipped in through the door and the two reconnected.

"Okay, where to, kid?" Joe asked.

Gwen felt her pocket, double checking its contents.

"You got the drive, right?"

"Absolutely."

They took the elevator to the right floor and found the suite Rocco had specified. Gwen boldly knocked on the door.

A middle-aged Hispanic man opened the door. "How may I help you, Ms. Patterson? I'm Jose, the manager of customer relations. You know I'm a big fan of yours," he said with a smile.

Gwen looked over at Joe in disbelief. *I thought all hackers were unemployed college students,* she thought. Joe looked back at her, raising an eyebrow.

Gwen extended her hand, flattered by and grateful for Jose's recognition of her and her work. To her credit, and despite the day's misery, she smiled and gave him what every man wanted: the attention of a beautiful woman.

"Well, thank you, Jose, that is very nice of you to say." Gwen gave him a wide, bright TV smile.

"Excuse me, I'm her boss, Joe Bess." Joe extended his hand as well.

Barely glancing at Joe, José said, "It's nice to meet you, too."

Joe brought his hand back to his side.

"So how may I help you today?" José stepped aside and motioned them inside a basic white-collar office reception area.

Gwen smiled. "I have this." She pulled the thumb drive from her pocket. "I'd like to open the files on it, but I'm having trouble. Can you help me?"

"Absolutely!" José extending his arm toward the back of the office. "I will use our master key and we can open it together."

"That's wonderful, thank you so much. That is so kind of you." Gwen tilted her head.

Returning the warm smile, José led the way. The three proceeded to the back, where José took Joe and Gwen into a secure area locked with a keycode.

Behind the door was a large, chilly, windowless room filled with racks of servers. Gwen imagined they contained some of the secrets of New York society and those who had something to hide. In Gwen's case, it would be the latter.

José escorted Joe and Gwen to a normal-looking desktop computer. She hoped he could uncover what was worth killing over.

José took Gwen's thumb drive and inserted it into a USB port. The same small window popped up as it had on Rocco's laptop, asking for a password. José worked the keyboard, opening and closing mysterious coded windows in the background that Gwen didn't understand. Briefly, she wondered if Joshua would have known what José was doing.

Gwen didn't realize she had held her breath, as the anticipation was too much. This was the moment she had been waiting for. *Will we move forward, or does this story remain stagnant?* Gwen looked at Joe, but his eyes were fixed on the screen.

"Ah—here we are." José moved the mouse and clicked a short list of files on the topmost window. "Let me open the program this file type needs ... okay. You may open any of the files now. Just double-click like normal." José excused himself from the room after offering Gwen the rolling desk chair. "Call if I can be of any further help."

"Thank you, I will," Gwen replied.

She waited for José to leave the room and breathed a sigh of relief.

"Well, are you going to open the files or what?" Joe asked, throwing a hand in the air.

"Yes!" Gwen said in a hushed tone. "Hold your horses."

Gwen picked the topmost file of two first. It wasn't what either one of them was expecting.

Blueprints. But whose blueprints were they, and what were they blueprints of?

"What is that?" Joe asked Gwen, sounding unsure. "Drawings? Designs of some sort?"

"Yes, that's exactly what they are, blueprints." Gwen scrolled around the schematic drawing, looking for content clues. "They look like the ones Josh draws at home. If only he were alive, we could ask him."

Joe put his hand on Gwen's shoulder, offering support. Both Joe and Gwen again looked at each other, confused.

"This thumb drive was the only thing that man who assaulted me had on him, the only thing, so it had to have been very, very important to him. Wouldn't you think?" Gwen asked Joe.

"Well, I guess the next question is, what are these blueprints of? When we figure that out, then we'll know if they're important to anyone else." Joe said. "Another clue, I guess?"

Gwen opened the second file. This was a pulled-back view of a 3D-rendered machine no bigger than a lawnmower, according to the measurements listed.

"What are they drawings of?" Joe asked. "It looks like something that flies, like a flying kite?" Joe said.

Gwen looked at Joe, most serious.

"A motorized kite, like the ones I saw in Germany?" Gwen said. "Could it be?"

Gwen leaned in to take a closer look while Joe stood back, taking in the bigger picture.

"I'm not sure. It looks like it could be a couple of different things," Gwen said as she moved the mouse over the plans, trying to take in the overall concept. "It looks like a remote-control drone with four propellers, and another one with three," she said. "But they look modified. They appear less aggressive and more toy-like, but the legend reads they still have all the hardware of a military-quality drone but for commercial use."

"What do you mean, military quality but for commercial use?" Joe asked.

"I don't know much about this stuff, but this isn't what our American military uses. This style is for hobbyists, commercial use, not for weapons," Gwen explained. "This is something else, something new."

Gwen realized she was losing Joe, so she offered up more detail, what little she had.

"Look, hobbyists have racing drones that fly at about 2,800 rpm or roughly 100 miles per hour. But this drone is designed to fly faster. You can tell by the propeller span. That size will move this drone at double the normal commercial grade, like 200 miles per hour or 5,700 rpms." Gwen sat back. "Who could afford to make something this sophisticated?"

"That's damn fast, kid." Joe crossed his arms. "Why would anyone need a drone that flies that fast and then hide the blueprints for it? This makes no sense."

"Well, that's not all. There appears to be two different designs. One is a three-blade propeller and the other is a four-blade. It's a subtle difference, but still, the question is, why?"

Gwen studied the drawings closely looking for clues. She went to the door. "José?"

Their host stuck his head back through the door. "What do you need?"

"Would it be possible to print what we found? They're—"

He held up a hand to stop her. "I'd rather not know what's on the files, you understand. That program has a print function in the toolbar along the top. The printer is over there." He pointed across the room. "Feel free."

"Hang on." She turned to Joe, who was already hunting for the print icon.

The printer made noises, then began scrunching out a sheet of paper.

Gwen smiled at José. "Thank you."

"Uh-huh." He vanished again through the door and closed it.

She and Joe studied the printed page of each drawing. The biggest piece of the puzzle jumped out at Joe first.

"What's wrong? You suddenly got quiet," Gwen said without looking up. She turned the 3D design on the screen for another minute, then she looked up at Joe. "What's wrong?"

"Did you see this?" Joe pointed to the lower corner of the printed paper.

"See what?" Gwen asked.

Gwen looked to the spot where Joe was pointing, and she too was unable to look away.

"What the hell is this?" Gwen scowled at the printer, as though it was at fault. "What the hell is this?"

"I don't know, kid. I just don't know. I'm not sure what's going on here, but I do know that name."

Gwen rapidly became uncomfortable. Her pulse began to pound, a wave of warmth swept over her body, and her respiration accelerated even though she felt short of breath. Gwen's vision went blurry for a moment. She felt faint.

Joe grabbed her around her upper arm to give her much-needed support. "Are you okay?"

Gwen felt confused by what she saw. Was she seeing things? Was Joe seeing the same thing? "Yes, I think so. I'm fine."

But Gwen was anything but fine; she was in shock. She didn't have the luxury or time to faint or even to address the denial raging in her mind. She needed to process the evidence in front of her and accept the facts as they were. She now knew the horrible feeling she had inflicted on so many others so many times before when she presented those she interviewed with irrefutable evidence while the camera was rolling. The audience and the network loved the shock value of it. Even without a camera rolling, she now felt sick having done that.

"This is Josh's signature watermark. This is his work. Oh my God, this is my husband's work," Gwen said in a weak voice. "It all looked so familiar, and now I know why. This is definitely his signature." Gwen pointed at the top edge. "This is his company's logo. It's their header. Midtown Engineering. It must be embedded in all their design files so it prints automatically."

"What in the hell is going on around here? Now Josh is involved in this mess. How can that be? He knew you were going to Germany. Did he know why? And he didn't say anything?"

Gwen could not believe Josh knew about this and didn't say anything. It was incomprehensible. "Well, yes and no. I remember telling him it was a financial story, but I don't think he knew the story had any connection to whatever he was designing here or for whom. I never mentioned finding this thumb drive, so I don't think he knew the story would lead me here, to his work." Her face grew hot and her pulse increased. "This is crazy. Could this be why he was killed? I thought it was some random home invasion gone wrong. Nothing seemed to be missing, but everything downstairs was damaged. And now he's dead so I can't even ask him."

"Okay, okay." Joe held up his hands as if he could physically push away her panic. "I would like to give Josh the benefit of the doubt, too. He was a great guy, but if he is involved in this, then he's surely guilty of something. I'm sorry, Gwen, I liked him a lot, but the facts here state otherwise. This work is his, it's as plain as day."

"I know this looks bad, but there still has to be an explanation—there just has to be."

"Well, I would love to know what it is, kid. What's Josh's connection to the dead man?"

"He might have stolen this from Josh. For all we know, he's a red herring. The real question is, who was it intended to go to? You know what? I know just who to ask." She scowled, her desire rising to avenge her husband.

"Who?"

"His boss, Victor Travis. I bet that guy knows something. I'm going over there to find out what the hell is going on around here. It's not six yet; he might still be in his office."

"Do you want me to come with you?"

"No. You go back to the station and act normal. I'll catch up with you back at your place later."

"Call me, kid. I worry about you."

"I will." Gwen swallowed. "I worry for us all."

36

ALREADY IN MIDTOWN MANHATTAN, Gwen headed on foot several blocks over to Midtown Engineering, where Josh had worked for many years. Gwen knew he was a weapons designer, but she never considered what that meant until now. How many people had his designs killed? How many people were dead because of him? Why was he designing turbo-charged drones with additional compartments? This was way too much to absorb, but Gwen had several blocks to soak it up.

Gwen became angrier the closer she got to Travis' office. Entering the building from the front, she took the elevator straight to the top floor. Bypassing the reception desk, Gwen made a beeline for Travis' office. Without knocking, she threw open the door and found Travis sitting alone, staring out the window. He turned to see her, and his countenance shifted from haunted to relieved.

Gwen stood there, sweaty, breathing deeply, trying to catch her breath and regain her composure. She would need to muster all her capabilities right now for the most unforgiving off-camera interview of her career. She wanted the truth, damn it, and she wasn't going to leave with anything less.

"Gwen, what are you doing here?" Travis asked in a soft voice.

"Really, Travis? That's your first question? You have no idea why I might be here, infuriated, unannounced? You have no idea whatsoever?" Gwen seethed with anger.

"You seem angry," Travis said. "What do you have there, in your hand?"

"What do I have here?" Gwen loudly repeated. "What do I have in my hand? Are you freaking serious?"

Gwen stalked closer to Travis' desk. "What does it look like, Travis? What the hell does this look like?"

Travis looked at the printouts she tossed at his chest.

"They look like blueprints. They look like weapon designs drawn up by your husband, I'm assuming."

"Well, you got half of that statement right," Gwen said snidely.

"What do you mean, half of it?"

"Yes, these are blueprints with Josh's signature and your company's logo at the top, but he is no longer my husband."

Travis looked confused. He stared at Gwen for the longest moment.

"I'm a widow now! These blueprints made me a widow. Are you responsible for this?"

It took all the control Gwen had left inside her to not cry. She didn't know how her future would go forward without Josh, but she planned to expose his killers on international television. Clearly, they used him and murdered him. Gwen still held on to the hope that Josh may have been deceived in some way into creating this weapon and drafting these designs.

"What happened to Joshua?" Travis asked in a hushed tone.

"I found him in our house, beaten to death, Travis. He was beaten to death." Gwen leaned toward him, menacingly, slowly saying the words. "Josh's face was nearly unrecognizable." Her voice cracked.

Travis closed his eyes, looking pained but not surprised.

"Now I know you know something about this, based solely on your reaction. I know you know something, if not everything."

Travis sat speechless.

"Tell me now what the hell you know about these designs, or I'll call my boss, bring my camera crew in here, and get it all on tape. You can tell me privately, or you can tell a judge, jury, and the world publicly. At this point, I really don't care."

Gwen was not going to play nice if Travis was involved in Josh's death. She had nearly been killed herself several times this week and was reaching the end of her rope with the stress from a week on the run and her time in jail. She'd had enough.

"No, no, you don't need to call anyone," Travis said. "Please sit down. I'll try to fill you in, but you must understand, no one person knows everything. I only know a piece, and Joshua knew even less."

She blew air out through her nose and sat on one of the visitor chairs. "So, he didn't volunteer for whatever this was?"

"No, not exactly. But, not to speak ill of him, he did do it for the money."

"That's nonsense," Gwen shot back. "We didn't need any money."

"No, not your kind of money. Money not even the two of you could earn in a lifetime."

Gwen leaned back in her seat, surprised Josh would sell out to someone so dangerous. But, based on her interview experience and her ability to read people, she had no choice but to believe Travis. His facial muscles, eye position, his posture—it all said he was being truthful.

"Actually, he did it for you," Travis said, head hanging. "He loved you that much. He didn't want you going to all those dangerous places. More than that, he missed you when you were on the road. He worked too much and moped around without you home. His biggest complaint about being married to you, the great Gwen Patterson, was that you loved your career more than you loved him. He felt if he only had enough, he could keep you all to himself. He loved you, Gwen, more than you will ever know."

The ring of truth to that desperate thought sank in her stomach like a rock. Poor Joshua. They'd had that argument repeatedly over the years. He said he understood she wasn't a homebody.

"A year ago or so, I was approached by a young man who seemed nice enough at the time, but as it turns out, he's not a stand-up guy. You just missed him, in fact." Travis gave a small, ironic bark of a laugh. "He left here just before you arrived. He told me he killed Joshua, in great detail, but I didn't believe him until you came and confirmed it. I thought Joshua was too important to him, but I guess I was wrong. His name is Martin. He told me Joshua had a change of heart, which I guess was Joshua's first and last mistake." Travis teared up.

Gwen sat across from Travis, upright, stoic, wanting to know it all.

"Martin is the son of a former leader in East Germany, the guy who was the

General Secretary of the SED before the wall fell, Erich Strauss. He has plans to take his position back, and he recruited my firm in weapons designs."

Gwen glared at him, annoyed with the half-truths sliding out.

"Okay, he recruited me, but he was very persuasive, Gwen, you must understand. He was very persuasive, and so was his money."

"So, what will he do next, now that I have the plans and he doesn't?"

"I don't know." Travis shrugged. "I don't know, find another designer? I do know he has lots of cash—"

Gwen cut him off. "He has lots of the German people's cash, you mean. He has no cash of his own. The country is going bankrupt. That was the financial crisis I was sent to cover in the first place."

"Well, he's using that money to pay for his plans, but the only real part of the plan I know is my part, Joshua's part. Design multiple versions of a drone with several secret compartments."

"Secret compartments? What for? Why would you need secret compartments on a drone?" Gwen did not like the sound of that. She found it hard to imagine what they could be used for or used to carry. Clearly, her mind was not as creative or as sick as Strauss'.

"I don't know, but his request was quite specific."

"What else can you tell me about the drone? Why would he need multiple versions of a drone? What can one do that another can't?"

"I don't know, to tell you the truth. I just know some technical aspects about flying."

"Such as?"

Travis pulled a book off the shelf behind his desk and flipped to an illustration of propellers. He set the book in front of her. "A three-blade propeller normally provides top speed compared to a four-blade propeller, which can give a drone intense thrust and better or more level cruising. Four blades also have an additional lift at the stern of the aircraft, which helps accelerate the hull, especially if the stern is heavy. So, there is a difference, but why it would matter to this man is beyond me."

"So, what I am hearing is the three-blade propeller can zip around faster, and the four-blade propeller can carry heavier items but is slower and steadier at its cruising speed. Is this the sum of it?"

"Yes, that's the overall idea. Why he wants one with faster maneuverability and the other one sturdy enough to carry a heavier payload is beyond me, but that's what the man paid for."

"If Josh was designing the engineering schematics, where were they going to be built?"

"Good question." Travis sat back in his chair. "I assume somewhere in Germany. Strauss' son came for the blueprints to take back to his father. The original ones Joshua made were stolen, and Martin said the redone version was unworkable, according to their engineers. One thing I know is Joshua was anally precise and wouldn't have made the errors Strauss' folks found unless it was on purpose. My best guess is that between when they got stolen and … now, Joshua got cold feet. Tried to throw a monkey wrench into it. You see what happens when this man is disappointed."

"Yes, I saw firsthand what happens when he's disappointed." Gwen shivered. "These people are ruthless, and they mean business. But you know what, Travis? Me too. I mean business. There's no way in hell they're going to get away with all this. No way. Why this ex-secretary would siphon this money and build these drones is beyond me, but I swear I will find out. It isn't just me looking into this anymore—several well-connected colleagues of mine are teaming up with me to bring this all down."

"I believe you."

The two looked at each other. She had a feeling about what Travis was up to, but at this point, she felt justified to allow Travis the dignity to end his own story instead of going out like Josh. But she couldn't bring herself to feel bad about it. She just couldn't. She lost her love because this man brought him an offer he couldn't refuse. She knew it was true that Josh did it for her. She would have to live with that for the rest of her life; he was dead because he wanted it all for her, and she still would not have stayed home from her career. Not for any amount.

"I can't believe you were a part of this, Travis. I can't believe you lured my husband into this," she said. "And you're probably right, after the scene I saw at my house, they'll come back for you, most definitely."

"I know, but I can't reproduce Joshua's designs. It's not my specialty, and I don't know who else to ask. I don't want to drag anyone else into this, get anyone else killed. Strauss' son said he would be back soon, but I plan to … not be here." Travis said this like a man resigned to his fate.

"I suspect what you're planning to do, and I wish I could say I was sorry about it, but your contracts are to help people, help our government, not some ex-*Generalsekretär* who is trying to take over Germany and do God knows what else." Gwen stood. "Is there anything else you can tell me before I leave? I'm calling my contacts and moving this story forward, immediately."

"No. That's all I know. Like I said, no one person knows it all. This man is smart, cunning, and his son is dangerous. I'm sorry, you know. For what it's worth—not much to you, I'm sure—but I am sorry."

"I'm sorry your bad decisions cost you everything. Josh looked up to you. He thought the two of you were friends. Well, at least the two of you will die on the same day."

That was a cold-blooded thing to say. Her ruthless side was showing. She didn't know she could be so unfeeling, surprising even herself. Feeling awful for lashing out, she offered the only solution she could. "Call someone, Travis. Call the CIA and offer to give them information in exchange for protection. I know things are messed up, and it's hard to know whom to trust there, but maybe they can help you. Be a whistleblower and go out with some dignity."

He shook his head. "It wouldn't do any good. He's coming for me. You'd better go."

Gwen stormed out of the office, leaving Travis to lie in the bed he'd made. Travis pulled his Walther P38 from his desk and placed it gently in his lap. Ironically, the German-made firearm was a gift from the uncrowned king for his help in the recruitment of Joshua.

As soon as Gwen could get out of that building, she hailed a taxi and headed to Joe's apartment, where she could hole up for the night and rest.

37

AFTER TWO DAYS and multiple phone calls, Johann learned the whereabouts of his old friend and former East German Stasi member Herman Gottlieb. Herman reluctantly agreed to meet Johann, only after having learned of recent events. Even the former secret police watched the news, but Herman received a more detailed and accurate account from his old friend Johann. Johann briefly explained the intended nature of the meeting and asked Herman if he could contribute any additional information to Gwen's story.

The two men agreed to meet at a local Berlin pub, Dicke Wirtin on Carmerstrasse. As Johann arrived at the pub, he bypassed the popular outdoor seating added during the global pandemic. Johann moved inside in favor of the privacy the bar's interior offered. Sunny spring weather ensured the indoors were emptier than the sidewalks. For this gathering, privacy was paramount.

As Johann walked inside, he headed toward the back and the green lounge chairs his ex-Stasi officer friend described. Herman was sitting with his back against the wall, as many military men were trained to do, but he wasn't alone. Three men sat around his table, and they too saw Johann walk inside. These three men all looked professional, but they were a little too buff, though they showed their age. Their faces read like road maps from too much stress, too much politics, and way too much hard liquor. *Who are these tattered men?* Johann thought as he forged ahead to find out. Had Herman brought more fellow ex-Stasi to this meeting? It was too late to turn back. That wasn't even an option; Herman had already seen him enter and he was desperate for information. In moments of desperation, men made mistakes. Johann pressed his lips together in displeasure.

As Johann approached the table, Herman stood up to give his old friend a proper greeting. The other three men didn't move. Johann figured they were assessing him to determine if he was a man whom they could trust or if he too wasn't secretly working for the underground empire.

He reached for Herman's hand as his friend stood. "Thank you for meeting me here."

"It is not a problem, old friend, not at all." Herman shook his hand. "I didn't come alone, as you can see."

"I can see." Johann stood beside Herman. "I didn't say to come alone, but I didn't think you would bring others to our reunion."

"Well, to tell you the truth, I wasn't going to until after we hung up and I considered what you said. When you told me about the nature of this meeting, I knew you needed more information than I could provide. These men are on our side."

The other three stood to properly meet Johann, relieved by his quick acceptance of the changing situation and his steady composure, his openness to listen.

"This is Anthony, Brandon, and Stephen," Herman said pointing out each man with an open hand.

Each of the men nodded, as polite gentlemen did, shaking hands with Johann. As a group, they sat. Herman began the conversation since he was the only one familiar with all the parties involved. He told Johann that Anthony, Brandon, and Stephen were his *der Genosse*, his comrades, all of whom were ex-Stasi members but now good friends. This group had served its leadership honorably, but once the Communist tornado passed, it left a leadership vacuum in its wake. Thirty years later, they still waited for the right ruler to fill the void.

"So, Johann, what brings you here?" Herman asked.

The three other men looked at Johann, waiting to hear the words that would help bring down Europe's next disastrous wannabe dictator. A new insidious storm was emerging, the clouds and crowds of followers gathering for the rise of Europe's next king, or so these men feared. The kind of man who gained his power through deceit and wielded it using violence and intimidation as he took his people to the edge of calamity once again. Europe had seen enough of this cycle. It was time to carve a new path, a new future for Germany. These men had the information Johann and the team of six needed.

"The impending financial collapse of Germany brings me here," Johann bluntly said. "But somehow I don't think that surprises you, any of you."

The group remained composed as though they had heard this part before.

"So, your girl Gwen Patterson is peeling away at the onion, so to speak," Herman said with a half-smile.

"The onion has too many layers," Johann said.

"Yes, it does, old friend, it does," Herman said. "So what layer are you on, and how can we help peel away at the next?"

Anthony, Brandon, and Stephen all sat ready to share what they knew. No one ever had enough information, no one ever knew it all. That was the way Strauss liked it.

"You can begin by telling me what you know about the underground empire," Johann said.

Herman raised his eyebrows. "You have heard the term?"

"Yes, my team and I have heard it, but it doesn't mean anything to us. We have pieces to the overall story, but we're individually looking into how they all tie together."

"They do all tie together," Brandon said. "They tie together to make one scary story. So, I hope Gwen likes scary stories."

"What do you mean?"

The three men looked at one another with a look of quiet acknowledgement. With a simple glance and nod, they evidently agreed to trust him.

"One day, I get a call out of the blue. This man, Schmidt, asking me to attend a private meeting of like-minded people," Anthony said. "What in the hell does that mean? Like-minded about what? I did not ask."

"I received the same call," Brandon said.

"Me three," Stephen said.

Johann looked from one to the other of them. "So, all three of you get the same cryptic call asking you to participate in some meeting and without knowing what it was about—you just go?"

"It was from General Peter Schmidt. He was the military leader when East Germany was still under Soviet control. He is, even now, not a man you say no to," Stephen said.

Anthony and Brandon supported that statement with a raised eyebrow each and a nod.

"I know Schmidt, and these men speak the truth. Schmidt always seemed so unenthusiastic in the direction of the East German government at the time when they were in power, but he is first and foremost a soldier, and he follows his commander, setting aside his own personal agenda. I don't know how he is since the fall of the Iron Curtain, but that is how he was then," Herman said. "Even though he holds a leadership position in the new German government, his loyalties run deep. Schmidt's presence in both worlds commands power and respect. So, when Schmidt calls, you come."

The three men dipped their heads almost on cue.

"Okay, so what happened when the three of you found yourself at this meeting with Schmidt?"

"It wasn't just us. The room was filled with many former East German ex-Stasi members, among other military-type groups also invited," Brandon said. "That room was filled with scary people, even by our standards."

"*Ja*," Stephen said.

Anthony smiled. "Well, they were scary at a time when they needed to be, but now not so much."

"Not so much?" Stephen turned on him. "They were cheering for that crazy man."

"What crazy man?" Johann asked.

"The former General Secretary of the SED, Erich Strauss," Brandon said. "Who else could galvanize a crowd like that with his ideology and propaganda?"

"You saw him there? He is behind all this?" Johann leaned forward.

"Yes! Schmidt brought us there, but the ringleader of the event was Strauss himself," Anthony said. "The entire gathering was a recruitment effort."

"Recruitment? Recruitment for what?"

"Strauss and Schmidt were recruiting for support of the underground empire. Isn't that why you are here asking? You wanted to know about the underground empire?" Anthony asked. "Truthfully, I like our people on top, but I wasn't buying the violence he was selling to get us there."

"You are still such a supremacist!" Brandon ridiculed him.

Anthony rolled his eyes. "Yes, I like my people better, whatever, but I don't like all the death and violence required to move his underground empire along. I spent enough years of my life fighting. I am done with that."

"We are all done with the violence," Stephen said. "I just want to hear the truth. I want to know what the hell is going on in my country and why everything is such a mess. Things were more plentiful when the Communists ran the show, what a terrible thing it is to say that? Huh?"

"This is not the way, this is not the answer," Brandon said. "We as God's people deserve peace. Everyone deserves some measure of peace. No one man is better than the next."

Anthony snickered, teasing Brandon for his religious discoveries since the end of the Eastern isolation, but all three ex-Stasi agreed: they all wanted an end to extremist leaders, fighting, war, isolation, and death. They wanted to see their children grow up in peace. Enough was enough.

"We met at this castle, more like a fortress," Anthony said. "We were brought inside, and it was decorated in medieval times. Ornate, tacky, and strange in places, but elaborate in the decorations. After we entered, we were shown downstairs to the basement. I thought the basement location was an odd setting for the meeting, but there were many of us, so I went. I couldn't believe this was his home. It was a big castle with a complete 360-degree view. The basement was mostly empty, but he had weapons down there. Strauss promised to fill the room with armaments so vast we could take on the world, that it would be glorious."

Brandon and Stephen nodded in agreement.

"Take on the world?" Johann asked, confused and concerned.

"Yes, the whole world. We all heard it," Brandon said.

"Scary, huh?" Stephen asked.

The three men described the immense underground room, partially filled with various weapons intended for an offensive movement, for an assault, not for the innocent to defend themselves.

"But truly, all I heard was more aggression, more fighting, more war." Anthony shook his head. "And, as I said, I am done fighting, no matter how I feel about others. I am done fighting."

"More weapons?" Johann asked. "I am going to bet this has something to do with that shipment that arrived at the Port of Hamburg the other night."

Herman said, "I heard something about an encounter a few nights ago between two groups at the port, but my source wasn't sure of the contents of the crates, only that after the firefight ended, the forklifts moved in and worked for hours placing crates on truck beds and in train cars. My friend works with the police, and he said they heard of an arms deal gone bad. The news reported a drug deal gone bad, so it was unclear what happened the other night other than shots were fired and lives were lost. Based on that simple fact, the cargo must be valuable." He shrugged. "No?"

Anthony smirked. "It's probably all in Strauss' basement."

"My God, what is this man planning to do?" Stephen said.

"Nothing good, clearly," Brandon said.

"Then before something really bad does happen, we should do something," Anthony said.

"Do what?" Herman asked.

"We need to find out exactly what is in that basement." Johann tapped the table with antsy fingers. "I'm calling Rocco and Gwen, and we're breaking into that castle. We're going to expose that basement of weapons and expose whatever else we can find."

He looked around the table at the ex-Stasi officers. "Do you remember where this castle was located? I mean its precise location?" Johann pointed his finger to the table.

The three looked at one another, all nodding.

"His massive compound is located in Startseite Barockschloss Moritzburg," Anthony said. "It is a large castle on a mountaintop. Are you familiar with it?"

"A little bit," Johann said. "Southwest of Berlin, about a two-hour drive, *ja*?"

"*Ja*," Anthony said. "Moritzburg is old, going back centuries, and I believe a tourist attraction for that Baroque castle."

"*Gut, gut,*" Johann said. "Thank you all for your help."

"We are happy to help, and if you need anything else, please let us know," Herman said. "The one thing the four of us have in common, if nothing else, is that we are done with dictators and war. We will help you prevent this coup or whatever this Strauss is planning."

The four others agreed, each quietly saying, "*Ja.*"

"I'm glad you said that," Johann said.

"Which part?" Herman asked.

"That you men are willing to do anything."

The four looked at one another.

Anthony said, "In for a penny, in for a pound."

"What do you need, old friend?" Herman asked.

"You were all asked to join the underground empire, *ja?*" Johann asked.

The four men nodded in the affirmative.

"I think it is time you joined," Johann firmly said. "As a group, we can get better information from the inside than from the outside looking in."

"You want us to spy?" Stephen asked nervously. "Like, spy?"

Anthony, Brandon, and Stephen looked concerned. Johann heard their account of having been in that crowded basement with all those weapons and the very serious and scary people capable of unspeakable violence. If they got caught, they would die. He knew what he was asking of them.

"What would you have us do?" Anthony asked.

"Just listen, observe, and report," Johann said. "There is no need to wear a wire or carry anything else to make you look suspicious. I just want you to listen carefully for plans, names of people who are involved, locations of weapons, possible attacks or whatever, and remember as much as you can, then call me or someone else on our team to keep us all up to speed on what Strauss and his people are doing."

"Well, if that is all, then yes, I will do it," Brandon said.

Having heard Brandon's rapid confirmation to do good and not wanting to seem cowardly, Anthony and Stephen joined Gwen's Team B and became spies for the American reporter. Gwen's team of six was expanding as the movement grew to stop the advancement of the underground empire.

Johann pulled out the phone given to him by Carter and dialed a pre-programmed party line.

"I'm in the area. I will be right there," Rocco said.

Johann hung up the phone and told the men to wait, for another would be coming.

"Who is this man?" Herman asked. "Can he be trusted?"

"As much, if not, more than all of you," Johann said. "He is an American, but an American what, I have no idea."

"What do you mean, an America what?" Herman asked.

The four men looked on intently, wondering the allegiance of this new addition.

"He's Gwen's cameraman and an apparent bodyguard, but he appears to be more. He is too skilled in other areas to be just those two things. That is why I say an American what, because I don't know what he is, but I am certain of who he is. He is a man to be trusted. He is a member of Gwen's team, and you are all to speak freely with him," Johann said. "This man has earned my trust."

"As you say, it shall be done," Stephen said. "I want to know the truth about this man's plans."

As the group continued talking, Rocco came through the door. The American man stood out, towering and fit. The men immediately knew he was more than just Gwen's right-hand man. He carried himself like someone a man didn't want to cross. Johann took a moment to extend pleasantries among the group members, introducing everyone individually to put them at ease with one another, though he had just met three of them. All these men were ex-spies with military specialties, all were armed and suspicious, a dangerous combination.

Rocco sat down and asked for an update.

Johann filled in the blanks for Rocco, explaining how these four men were willing to risk their lives by joining Strauss' underground empire to help close the gap in the information loop and spy for Gwen. Rocco was stunned by their selflessness and their willingness to help. It gave him hope for the future. Pleased with Team B and their intentions to work as Gwen's moles and assist the team of six, Rocco returned the favor.

"So, what now can you tell us about Gwen's trip to New York City?" Johann asked. "What did she learn, if anything?"

"First of all, Gwen always learns something," Rocco said.

The group chuckled.

"I already spoke to Gwen, and her time in New York has been fruitful," Rocco said.

The group looked intrigued, but the four who knew how scary Strauss was took pause at the possibilities.

"So, what has Gwen found in New York?" Stephen asked.

"Well, to give you background first, about a week ago, an Asian man tried to mug Gwen in the back of a cab, or so she thought. We now believe him to somehow be involved with all this." Rocco twirled his finger in the air. "Anyway, in the struggle, the man fell from the cab and was killed. Gwen ran to his body to see who he was. The only thing on him was a thumb drive. Gwen took it, and she's been carrying it around ever since. I knew a guy in Midtown Manhattan who could unencrypt the information on it."

"What was on the drive?" Johann asked.

"Nothing good, we think," Rocco said. "The only files on it were blueprints, drawings, she said, that sketched out a drone with added compartments, not like the military drones we see today."

"A drone with added space for what?" Brandon asked, becoming visibly pale.

"That's the forty-thousand-dollar question," Rocco said. "We need to find out what he's hiding in those bunkers you described and his fortress, as well as try to figure out what the hell these extra compartments would be used for."

Rocco showed the men pictures of the drawings Gwen had texted to him off the thumb drive. None of the men had seen anything like this before, and none could offer any useful ideas, only scary possibilities.

"That's why I'm so glad you're all willing to help. Gwen's Team B." Rocco smiled. "We'll need you inside Strauss' circle to help find out what he's up to."

Rocco looked with concern at the five other men sitting at the table. The four ex-East German Stasi members had only that in common: ex-Stasi; they couldn't be any more different in lifestyles and personal motivations except for the one they shared. None of them wanted to follow Strauss back into an East German hell of Communism and lack, a lifestyle of struggle. They would help Gwen, and they vocalized their unity as a team. They all knew what was at stake. They all knew what they had under former Communist rule, and they didn't want that anymore. They all wanted more for their children and families.

"It looks like you four have a movement to join," Johann said. "As for us, we need to regroup with the rest of the team and figure out a way into that castle."

38

GWEN LEFT NEW YORK again after a night of sleeping like the dead and returned to Berlin the same way she left. She arrived in Germany the day of Jakob's funeral.

Rocco and Karl met her at Tegel Airport. Though she was exhausted from the complicated international travel on top of what she'd experienced in New York, the three had much to discuss on their way back to the safehouse. Gwen told Rocco and Karl about Joshua.

"I'm so sorry." Rocco's voice cracked. "I'm really very sorry."

Karl said nothing, going pale as she described the brutality of Joshua's murder.

"You're sure Joshua's death is connected to all this?" Rocco asked.

"It has to be. Nothing else makes sense, and Travis all but confirmed it." She told them about the company logo on the plans and Josh's watermark, and what Travis said about the redone plans not meeting the engineers' standards. The copy she had on the thumb drive must be the original plans.

Rocco asked whether she didn't want time to sit this one out and grieve.

"I'll properly mourn my husband after we bring down this fanatic. I'm doing this for Joshua too, now," Gwen said. "Even if he was involved in the beginning, he tried to make it right in the end, and that's why they killed him."

Johann was waiting at the safehouse for Carter and Heinrich to return from the funeral. In the meantime, Karl, Rocco, and Gwen came through the door tired but eager to plan their next move. They were all happy to see one another alive again. Hugs were exchanged, but the pleasantries were quickly curbed in favor of discussing all the new information.

When Johann learned of Gwen's husband's involvement, he looked grim. "Yes, we all make mistakes, and by the time we realize what is happening, we are too deeply involved to simply walk away. That is probably what happened to your husband, and when he made the mistake of trying to leave, they killed him for it."

When Carter and Heinrich returned from Saarland late that night, she had to repeat the tale again. The more she repeated it, the more distanced she felt from it, as though it happened to someone else. At some point she would have to reconcile her anger at Joshua for getting involved in this, but for now it helped keep the tears at bay.

"So, what of the plans you found on the drive, Gwen?" Carter asked.

"I have copies with me," Gwen said.

"You do?" Rocco asked.

"Do you have scissors or a knife?" Gwen asked.

Rocco came to the rescue, whipping out a butterfly knife from his shoe. Johann and Carter teased him, jealous at his readiness.

Rocco handed Gwen the knife without asking what she wanted it for. Gwen removed her blazer and laid it open on the table. She used the tip of the knife to separate the seam of the jacket from the lining as the men watched. Johann, Carter, and Rocco all smiled as the knife sliced the thread. Karl and Heinrich were not so schooled in spying and moving materials, so they had not yet caught on.

"I hid print copies of the blueprints in the lining of my jacket to get them through customs and also to keep them out of sight in case anyone else decided to follow me," Gwen said.

Karl and Heinrich looked at one another, now up to speed.

"You are so smart," Karl said, sounding like a man in love.

"Yes, she is," Heinrich said.

But Rocco scolded her. "We have the images on my cell and yours. You didn't need to risk bringing a physical copy."

"They're easier for everyone to see this way." Gwen carefully removed the pages of blueprints from the inside of her jacket, laying them on the table.

The team looked at Joshua's designs, his hard work for blood money, and none of them could believe their eyes. Drones of different sizes, shapes, capable of different speed, with added compartments. But why? The added holding containers caught the eyes of Rocco, Carter, and Johann. Those three talked about how scary the imagination of extremists could be, and they theorized various uses for the compartments.

"Okay, we're not going to figure this out right now, so let's plan our next move," Johann said.

"What will that be?" Karl asked.

"We need a peek inside Strauss' fortress before anything more escalates."

"Agreed," Rocco said.

"Whatever you guys think," Carter said. "But let's wait until the morning."

THE NEXT MORNING, Carter reached into his bag and pulled out another set of drawings, old-fashioned paper architectural blueprints they could use to move Gwen's investigation along. They were created on Strauss' orders to update the castle to meet the needs of his gaudy taste. Had Strauss' need for flash not overtaken him, there would probably be no floorplan on record, but Strauss had to have his own way, the Achilles heel of many would-be kings and leaders later turned dead dictators. Strauss could not have predicted those designs would fall into the wrong hands, meaning Carter's hands and now Gwen's. The six returned to the table to discuss the best way to enter Strauss' fortress.

"Okay, the castle is here," Johann said, pointing to the map.

"We need to identify the best way in," Gwen said.

Carter, Rocco, and Johann all looked at one another.

"I'm going in," Gwen said firmly. "This ultimately is my story, and there is no way I am missing any of it."

The men knew not to challenge her. With one look between them, they knew what they had to do, they knew what their job was—to protect her.

"We need to get her in and get her out," Rocco said.

"What about us?" Heinrich asked. "These people murdered my father. There is no way I am not going."

Gwen looked at Rocco. Heinrich had a point.

"I suppose you want to come along too for shits and giggles?" Rocco asked Karl.

"For a lot more than that," Karl said with a smile. "I am against this with my whole being. In for a penny, in for a pound."

"Okay, I guess this is going to be a family affair," Johann said. "We will figure it all out."

Carter, Johann, and Rocco studied the blueprints, looking for spacious rooms that could hold the kinds of weapons Herman and his men described. A clear depiction of the castle grounds showed open areas and other more covert ways of entry.

"What's this, over there?" Rocco asked.

"That is a long alley, if you like, that runs the length of the property," Johann said. "There is a statue there called the Well of Venus."

"That is an excellent point of entry for us," Rocco said. "Carter, what do you think?"

"Based on what I'm seeing on the other sides of the castle, this may be in fact the best ingress for us," Carter said. "We can split up into smaller groups of two and cover one another up to the castle, which is about one-point-two miles."

"Yes, we should slowly move in small groups, meet at the Well of Venus, and then we can follow the alley that runs straight up to the castle, just here." Johann pointed to a map. "The foliage is a safe area. It will provide full coverage until we get close to the castle. We want to avoid passing through the open garden until we have no choice."

"I think each of us should carry one of them to ensure safety, since they're untrained," Carter said to Johann and Rocco.

"Yes, you're right," both men agreed.

"I can walk. I don't need to be carried," Gwen snapped.

"The three of you have no field experience, and I wouldn't trust you with a weapon as far as I could throw you," Rocco retorted.

Karl, Heinrich, and Gwen looked at each other, none of them saying a word. Johann laughed.

"What's so funny?" Rocco asked.

"I don't think anyone has ever been able to shut Gwen up quite like that," Johann said.

Everyone smirked.

Gwen smirked, too. "Okay, okay, I know. So, what does that mean? Me, Karl, and Heinrich will each be assigned to one of you who's armed?"

"Yes, exactly," Johann said. "So, who wants Gwen?"

Every male hand shot into the air, and they all laughed again.

"Okay, let's figure the rest of this out," Rocco said. "I think camouflage is in order."

"Agreed," Johann said.

"I suppose you can hook us up?" Gwen asked Rocco with a smile.

"Of course," Rocco said.

Carter and Johann rolled their eyes.

"If Rocco can't, I can." Johann folded his arms across his chest. "It is my country."

Without looking up, Rocco took out his phone and dialed.

Carter prepared Heinrich and Karl for the upcoming operation, as it would be their first.

Heinrich showed his courage. "For my father, I will risk it all. I will not allow this madman to murder my father and impose his will on my people."

"None of us will. We're in this together," Carter said.

Heinrich silently nodded at Carter.

As the team regrouped and prepared to leave, Rocco wanted to pack a special bag, as a contingency plan, filled with items the regular, untrained civilian would never think of.

"Where's your makeup bag?" he asked Gwen.

"What? Why? It's in my purse," Gwen replied.

No TV reporter was ever without her makeup. Rocco grabbed her bag and removed her makeup kit, checking its contents before throwing it in his contingency bag. Gwen was confused, but she knew better than to question a professional, and clearly, he was proving to be one hell of a professional. Rocco took her aerosol hairspray, and a lighter from one of the guys, and packed other random tools—just in case.

BEFORE SUNRISE, Rocco was again behind the wheel as the team drove up the dirt road slowly, carefully. He didn't want to attract any attention. Carter sat in the front passenger's seat while Gwen, Johann, Karl, and Heinrich ducked down in the back. The police were not actively seeking Rocco and Carter, at least not yet.

The team made the short drive to Strauss' castle following their earlier made plans. As the six emerged on the castle grounds, they found it as Team B had described, except it seemed deserted. There was no one in sight.

"Is there anyone even here?" Gwen asked.

The property was eerily quiet; no cars, no movement at all.

"I don't know, but I want everyone on their toes," Rocco said. "We have no idea if anyone is here or where they're hiding."

"Agreed," Johann said. "I don't see any surveillance cameras either."

"Maybe nothing to hide," Karl said, looking at his buddy Heinrich.

The six moved in closer. The map had given an accurate scale of the grounds, and now the team would see if the architectural blueprints were as good.

"The plans my friends provided were perfect," Carter said as they crept closer to the structure.

"Of course, they were perfect," Gwen snapped. "You work for the CIA. They're probably watching us right now with one of those satellites swirling above our heads."

The team laughed while Rocco and Carter looked at one another. She was right. They probably were watching, especially since they had two of their own on the ground.

The team continued quietly and stayed low as they approached the castle. Surprisingly, they met with no resistance.

The guys laughed as they looked up one of Strauss' personal modifications to the rear of the castle. Apparently, he liked the open air and had a large sliding patio door installed, not something earlier kings would have done. The door opened to a beautiful stone courtyard that offered a relaxing atmosphere for the occupants.

Rocco smirked. "Well, let's see if that door opens from the outside."

Johann handed Rocco his crowbar.

It took only one twist of the tool to pop the door from the tracks. Carter and Johann quietly caught it and set it down.

"That was a little too easy," Rocco said.

"I agree," Johann said.

"I want everyone to stay here for a few minutes while I go in and check around," Rocco said.

No one argued. Rocco turned, slipped in the open door, and quickly surveilled the room. On his heels were Gwen, Johann, Carter, Heinrich, and Karl.

Rocco glared at the disobedience. "I told you guys to wait."

"We thought not," Gwen said.

"We should check the basement," Carter said. "That was the single largest room in the house capable of storing that many weapons."

The team agreed. Having already memorized the layout, Rocco led the way to the basement door. Gwen worried constantly they'd run into someone, even a servant, but the place was deserted. With a slight creak, the heavy wooden door opened, revealing a sturdy staircase descending counterclockwise.

"That's weird," Rocco said. "The stairs are backwards."

"This man knows his history," Karl said.

"What do you mean?" Gwen asked.

"In medieval times, as a defense measure, architects built the castle staircases anti-clockwise going up, clockwise down, to block the sword arm of advancing enemies. However, it didn't help if those enemies were left-handed. Then it probably helped them."

Five of them turned blank stares on Karl like he was a walking encyclopedia.

He shrugged. "Hey, I like history, what can I say?"

Heinrich smiled.

Single file, they carefully grabbed the railing and made the long, dark descent to the basement. Once on solid ground, Gwen thought, *Paydirt*. The room was filled with crates.

"Weapons!" Rocco said. "Weapons for his movement!"

He pried the nails from the container until the side fell open. The contents spilled around his feet. He jumped out of the way.

"What the hell are those?" Carter asked.

Gwen bent over, slowly recognizing the small, oblong shapes. The smell was familiar. But of course, it would be to a person with a healthy diet. She snicked one out of the pile, waved it under her nose, and then placed it in her mouth.

The team stood still and stared at her.

Gwen grinned at them, crunching it in her teeth. "They're almonds."

"Almonds?" the others echoed.

"Open another crate," Heinrich said as he and Karl tackled another.

"Almonds," Karl said.

The team checked all the crates, dozens of them, all filled with almonds.

"Where are these crates from?" Heinrich asked.

"Some are stamped from California, and these over here are from Asia somewhere," Carter said.

"What the hell is going on here?" a confused Heinrich asked.

Gwen looked at the wall-to-wall crates, now all assumed to be filled with almonds.

"This whole basement is filled with almonds," Rocco said, slightly out of breath and still holding the crowbar. "What could a crazy guy like this be doing with all these almonds?"

Karl took footage of the room.

"Let's get out of here," Gwen said.

WITHOUT SEEING or hearing a single person, the team of six left the castle. With the sun still rising, they walked right out the front door and drove back to the safehouse. Each came through the door with an audible exhalation, dropping their gear to the floor. Rocco immediately returned to the table and centered the blueprints one more time.

"What are you looking for?" Heinrich asked.

"There's got to be something here in one of these plans," Rocco said. "We've got plans for bunkers, the castle we were just in, and for the drones Josh designed with these strange added compartments. There's got to be something here we're not seeing."

Johann asked, "I don't understand where Strauss could have hidden all those weapons. There must be more. And what the hell is he going to do with all those damn almonds?" Johann threw his arms in the air.

"That's the question, isn't it?" Gwen asked softly. "That's the exact question. What in the world would he want with all those almonds?"

"More pieces to the bigger puzzle," Karl said.

Everyone stopped and looked at the young activist.

"The almonds are one more piece to a thousand-piece puzzle, but it seems none of the pieces fit. Do they?" Karl said. "We've got drones, almonds, weapon shipments, secret meetings, and none if it seems to line up, but we all know it eventually will, don't we?"

The team nodded at him.

"I do know one thing about almonds," Karl said. "I'm not sure if it is relevant, though."

"If not to eat, then what are they used for?" Gwen asked. "Tell us what you think."

"Well, you can make many things with almonds, but if turned into oil, almonds are among one of the most absorbable oils through human skin and tissue. If you mix something in it, like a chemical or a poison, boom—it will be absorbed right through the skin and into the bloodstream."

A dozen possibilities flew through Gwen's mind, landing on one clue. "The formula from Decker's mystery emails?"

Her conjecture broke the tension filling the room.

"Out of the mouth of a babe comes the truth," Johann said.

Carter looked dubious. "Poison? I suppose it's possible. But poison, really? Poison is usually up a woman's alley. I can talk to some of my friendlier contacts at Langley and see what they think about this theory."

"It would also explain those extra compartments on the drones, wouldn't it?" Johann asked.

"We're getting ahead of ourselves here," Rocco said, dragging the team back into reality. "It's a damn good theory, I'll admit that, but a theory only. Gwen can't run with theories, not tonight."

"Tonight?" Gwen swiveled her gaze at Rocco.

"Yes, tonight. Don't you think it's about time you put some of this on the air?"

Carter shrugged. "It may shake the tree a bit. We may learn of others' involvement. We'll see who gets rattled by your report."

The entire group agreed, but Gwen wasn't sure. "I need to talk to Joe. I'm not sure if I have enough information for him."

"I already did," Rocco said. "He wants our B-roll and a report by the end of the day, Berlin time."

Gwen scowled. "When did you call him?"

"I needed to talk to him about something else, okay? I didn't go behind your back." Rocco held up his hands. "There are other things we discuss besides you, you know?"

Gwen gave Rocco a snarky look. "Okay, what does he want?"

"He wants a live satellite feed, an update on the riots, and what you learned to date about the financials here."

"Yes, I can do that," Gwen said. "But there's so much more. I just need confirmation."

Carter said, "Well, confirmation eventually comes, as you know. It just usually comes in the form of some guilty party who wants absolution."

"How about it?" Gwen asked.

The group remained gathered around the table with the blueprints at the center, studying them to see if they missed something. There had to be more.

The loud ringing of a telephone filled the room, but it was not an electronic sound from a cell phone. Old-fashioned physical bells clattered instead, slightly muffled.

"Where is that ringing coming from?" Johann swung his head around.

Rocco also looked around, but Gwen zeroed in on the cabinet on the wall.

"I think it's coming from inside the cabinet," she said.

"Inside the cabinet? That's odd," Heinrich said.

"No, not really," Carter said with a half-smile.

Rocco randomly opened cabinet doors until he found the right one. Inside the cabinet was an old-style phone from the 1970s, which made Karl and Heinrich smile. Rocco removed the entire phone, and with it still in his hands, ringing, he gazed across the group, all of whom nodded he should answer it.

"*Ja?*" Rocco listened for a moment then turned to Gwen. "It's for you."

"Who is it?" Gwen asked in a hushed tone.

Rocco shook his head, eyebrows raised. "I don't know, but his voice sounds familiar."

Gwen stood from the table and took the receiver. "Who is this?" she curtly asked.

"I am a man close to Strauss now and when he was *Generalsekretär* of East Germany," the caller said with a thick German accent. "I have things I want to say to you."

The old-style telephone did not give Gwen the option of a speaker so everyone could listen. *That was probably the point of him calling on this number,* Gwen thought. Even if this conversation only gave her confirmation for her story, she was the one who needed to hear it; it was her story.

"What things?" Gwen asked the anonymous caller.

"There are things going on in this country as I am sure you are aware, bad things. Very bad things."

"Yes, I know, sir. That's why I'm here."

"Strauss is behind it all, his plans are vast, and his followers are many, with arms reaching beyond your contacts, even your sizeable contacts."

"Who is this?" Gwen asked again. "I can't use anything you're saying without knowing who you are. I promise to keep your confidence; you have my word."

"I know you to be a woman of your word. So, I will tell you, I am Peter Schmidt."

Gwen's mouth fell open as she heard the name of Strauss' most trusted confidant.

The group watched Gwen, clearly wanting to know who was on the other end.

"But I must never be known to be your source. They will kill me for sure," Schmidt said.

"Understood, and agreed," she said.

"That event at the Port of Hamburg was not drugs but weapons, a very large import of weapons."

"Yes, we already know that, but where are they now?"

"In bunkers spread throughout Germany. Strauss has many bunkers to hide his weapons and other imports items needed to achieve his goals. The imports just keep coming."

"Where are these bunkers?"

"The hour is growing late, *liebchen*, and you are way behind. So, you just listen."

Gwen didn't appreciate the condescending tone, but she did as she was told. She needed to hear whatever Schmidt had to say.

"The weapons are secondary only to Strauss' bigger plan and the main weapon he intends to use to carry out that plan," Schmidt said. "This weapon is still in development in the bunkers. He has aligned himself with many smart people, all of whom share in his warped view of how Germany should look a hundred years from now. This weapon is something no man or woman will ever see coming. This weapon does not kill the living but interferes with the future."

"Interferes with the future?" Gwen frowned. "How could a weapon interfere with the future? What does that mean? Does it have anything to do with all the almonds we found in the castle's basement?"

"Ah, yes the almonds, yes it does," Schmidt said.

Suddenly, Gwen heard Schmidt arguing with someone in his native language, but she didn't recognize the voice of the other man.

She screamed into the phone, "Mr. Schmidt, Mr. Schmidt, are you there? Are you okay?"

She blocked her other ear as the team gasped in surprise, each team member exposing their own personal shock. She heard nothing from Schmidt except a physical struggle for the phone. Schmidt dropped his end of the line, and the receiver hit the floor.

Gwen jumped. Then, by no surprise, came a loud, familiar sound. The blast of the gunshot was so deafening Gwen recoiled from the phone. Johann and Rocco who were standing next to her clearly heard it too. Someone got shot, and the struggle had ended. Was Schmidt dead? The body count steadily rose in this evolving and seemingly never-ending story.

Gwen replaced the receiver to her ear, and she heard someone breathing heavily into the phone.

"Mr. Schmidt, is that you?" Gwen asked. "Is that you?"

"No," a man said before hanging up the phone.

Gwen replaced the receiver and turned to Rocco, most serious. "You're right, we need to put together a piece for tonight," Gwen said. "Too much is going on here. Too many people have died, and now I think someone just killed Schmidt."

"What did he say?" Heinrich asked. "Did he mention my father's murder?"

"No, he didn't mention your father at all. I'm sorry," Gwen said.

Gwen recounted the conversation for the team.

"He wants to change the demographics of the country?" Carter asked. "Like that hasn't been tried before."

"Schmidt said Strauss has some kind of weapon in the works, something so startling the world has never seen before, something that doesn't kill the living but interferes with the future," Gwen said, shaking her head.

No one spoke for many heartbeats.

"Tell me the highlights you want for tonight's report and give me a couple of hours to screen the B-roll and edit the footage you need," Rocco said.

"I want it all," Gwen said. "But first, I need to find out how much airtime Joe can give me."

"I think Joe will give you all the time you need," Rocco said.

"I want footage from the earlier rioting and anything we have on the shootout at the Port of Hamburg. I also want to talk about the growing tension in the country, the riots, and the violence that has shocked the nation. I want to include the suspicious timing of Chancellor Jakob's assassination, my false imprisonment right after that, as well as the possible impact Jakob's death could have on the financial crisis and the revelation of the hidden bank accounts in Andorra."

Rocco grinned. "That should rattle a few cages."

"I'll say," Carter said. "I'll give my contacts in Langley a heads-up so they're on alert, just in case."

"I just want the people to know my father was not involved in any of this," Heinrich said. "My father was an innocent man who loved his country and his people."

"I know, Heinrich, and I assure you the truth will come out. What's done in the dark always finds the light," Gwen said.

"Well, it looks like you guys have work to do," Johann said. "I will scope out a safe location for your live shot, somewhere out of the way."

The group disbanded for the afternoon so each member could get their tasks accomplished with the clear understanding to regroup at the safe house before they traveled together to watch Gwen go live and listen to her report. She planned to be ready in time for the late-night news hour in Europe, which would hit at midday on the East Coast and mid-morning on the West Coast. Her hope and Joe's was to garner the largest possible audience. NIN would repeat it, catching even more attention as the day wore on in the U.S. and reaching Asia and Australia.

Gwen wrote the words and Rocco matched the video with Joe on conference, preparing for what was to come. The three understood the explosive nature of the material, but they concluded it was the only way to unnerve the significant players and cause them to slip.

Joe told the control room Gwen would be on air later this afternoon local time with a breaking story out of Germany, specific location withheld for security reasons. The team working in the control room didn't even blink, as it was widely known that Gwen always poked the sleeping bear and she loved to stir the pot. This tendency made her an effective reporter.

But this time, it was different. As the red light popped on and she recited her prepared narrative, her report started a domino effect. It caused a calamity; more people died as she asserted herself and did not back down from the story even in the face of more violence.

Viewers in Europe and America, specifically Washington D.C., carefully listened as Gwen's report blasted across the viewscreens of everyone who tuned in. The major players took pause, familiar with the facts Gwen presented and how accurate they were. She was on the right track, and all those who took heightened interest in her story saw her track led right to their front doors. Something needed to be done, and it needed to be done now.

Gwen laid out most of the pieces of Strauss' puzzle, and the concerned parties feared she would soon have it all. They each listened from their individual locations, hearing more and more about the riots that swept the streets of Germany as the government reached its financial breaking point, no longer able to help the citizens they were elected to represent.

Hearing this only reignited the anger of the youth, who felt their future was bleak, without hope. Faced with their country's destitution, they once again took to the streets. Gwen stated her investigation was ongoing and incomplete, but the young Germans didn't care; they had heard enough once she announced the hidden bank accounts in Andorra most likely filled with German money—their money. The accounts holders were all in alliance with Strauss, or they had close connections to Germany and the United States.

Martin Strauss sat in a New York City bar having his father's favorite drink over a lunch of greasy American food. The news was playing on the TV above the bar. When Gwen Patterson appeared with a live report from Germany, he asked the bartender to turn it up. His anger grew as he watched this woman's report. He called Becker.

Congressman David A. Becker was no stranger to controversy, but this scathing report was an exposé the likes of no other. Heads would roll, Martin told him. With his blood boiling, Becker called the head of the NIN Network.

"Henderson," he answered.

"What the hell is going on?" Becker shouted into the phone. "Get her off the air now!"

"I can't. I already tried. Too many people already know anyway," Henderson said. "I've been called by my contacts across the agencies. There's no way to stop this now. There's no way to bury it."

"You bury this story, or I'll bury you," Becker said. "We had a deal, and you took the money. There's no backing out now. Pull her fucking plug!"

Becker hung up on Henderson, who now began to feel sick. He was on the take, but he lost control of Gwen and Joe. Despite this, he called Joe down in the newsroom.

"Yeah," Joe answered.

"Henderson here. Pull the plug, Gwen has no sources for the story." Henderson hoped Joe would take the bait.

"No sources? Are you crazy? She's got all the sources and the video to match," Joe barked into the phone. "Just sit in your ivory tower and watch the report. This is going to be great!"

Great? Henderson thought. *Great for whom? Not for me.*

Gwen drew connections between Strauss, the late Congressman Solas from Chicago, Congressman Becker still in Washington, General William Jones, and a close college friend of the general's, Victor Travis, a weapons designer who recently committed suicide, thereby avoiding prosecution.

Wayne Robertson, head of the Joint Chiefs, managed to not have his name included in her scathing report. He was tight with several of those identified in Gwen's report, but she was not sloppy. She was not likely to include his name until she had a direct connection stronger than friendship.

A frightened and disillusioned Henderson left his office before Gwen's report concluded. He couldn't listen to it anymore. He was in trouble.

BECKER HANDLED THINGS differently.

He picked up the phone one more time and called a trusted associate, a "cleaner" who would send a message so loud and so clear that any others who thought they could take the king's money and not live up to their agreement would comprehend the severity of punishment. The cleaner would reduce the king's allies but also kill off the dead weight.

"Hello?" the man said.

"It's me," Becker said. "Henderson lost control of the woman. He needs to go, tonight."

"Wire the money to my bank account. I will handle him immediately."

"Done."

A blue van with a plumbing logo on the side pulled up in front of the Henderson home late in the afternoon, clearly his last stop of the day. A man in navy coveralls knocked on the door and told Mrs. Henderson he just received a work order to provide maintenance on the hot water heater in the basement.

"I didn't call for any routine maintenance," Mrs. Henderson said.

The man, appearing professional, looked down at a clipboard. "I believe your husband called. Are you Mrs. Charles Henderson?"

"Well, yes I am."

He showed her his clipboard. Mrs. Henderson could clearly see her husband's name and signature on the work order.

"Oh, my husband must have done this and forgot to tell me," she said with a smile. "That's fine. Come right in. Our water heater is in the basement."

The man entered, following Mrs. Henderson to the basement door. Once at the door, the man said, "I'll take it from here. I'm sure I can find the unit."

"Thank you. I hate those stairs," she said. "Please be careful."

With a smile and a nod, the repairman left Mrs. Henderson at the basement entrance, quietly closing the door behind him.

Later that evening, the Hendersons sat down for a peaceful dinner alone. Charles fully intended to take this opportunity to confess to his beloved what he had done and how they were able to afford the nicest things in life. His job as network head paid well, but not well enough to pay for all the shiny rocks the little missus wanted.

The two sat at the table, engaging in meaningless banter until he finally put his fork down. "Honey, there's something I need to tell you."

The blast rocked the entire neighborhood, shattering car windows up and down the block. Car alarms blared until drowned out by the ever-increasing wail of sirens as police cars and fire trucks approached what was once the Henderson home.

STRAUSS LOUNGED behind his ostentatious desk, drinking Stolichnaya vodka from Russia's oldest distilleries, watching the evening news. Like most German leaders, Strauss watched Allgemeiner Rundfunk Deutschland, more commonly known by the locals as ARD. Founded in 1950, it was Germany's first post-war television news station for a free society, paid for by the German people.

Like the rest of the country, Strauss sat in awe, watching Gwen's report. The pretty brunette mesmerized him; she resembled a woman he once knew, a woman he once loved. But he didn't let his affection for that woman override his interest in the inflammatory words dropping from her mouth. He felt an overwhelming ruthless determination to remove Gwen Patterson from the equation.

Gwen described the insidious way an underground movement in Germany, his underground movement, was surreptitiously transferring taxpayer money to secret bank accounts in Andorra, bankrupting the government and bleeding the German citizens dry.

Strauss' hiding place was no longer a secret. It wouldn't take long before the authorities investigated these allegations and froze all the accounts. Strauss could not allow that; he needed that money. The newscast was still on air when he put down his glass and picked up his private line to call his true second-in-command, his son Martin.

Martin answered on the first ring.

"Are you seeing this?" Strauss asked.

"*Ja*, I'm watching here. This bitch is on every television screen in the city."

"Get her off the air," Strauss demanded.

"I already spoke to Becker, and he was unable to get her off the air."

"He is a damn congressman. How could he be unable to pull a reporter off the air?" Strauss screamed into the phone.

Martin gulped his drink. "Government officials do not have the authority here as we do at home, they just don't."

"So, what did Becker do when Henderson told him no?"

"I told Becker to send the cleaner to Henderson's house. If he cannot control her, then we cannot control him. So, he goes," Martin said. "I'm sorry, Father, I should have called you first to ask your permission."

"No apologies needed, my son. A true leader makes unilateral deadly decisions. Excellent."

Martin preened at the pride in his father's voice.

"This woman also needs to go before she causes us any more exposure. I want you to get back here right away, find her, and kill her."

"Ja, of course, Father, I am on my way."

Martin made one more phone call to one of his associates to inform his men of his father's orders. "My father wants this intrusive reporter dead. I want you to find her and keep an eye on her. I am on my way back to Berlin."

"I understand. I will get the men together and we will find this woman," the man said.

"Good. Find her and don't let her out of your sight. I am coming home to kill her myself."

"Understood."

The bartender saw Martin's empty shot glass and without asking poured him one more drink. "This is on the house, pal."

Martin gave the man an agreeable nod as he returned his phone to his pocket. With much distain, he looked at Gwen on the bar's television screen and knew what needed to be done. He picked up his glass and threw back the last shot, enjoying the heated sensation as it rolled down his throat and into his chest. He threw cash onto the bar and gave the bartender one more nod before he turned and walked out the door.

Gwen's report swept over the ARD's four American member stations in Germany, the Bayerischer Rundfunk, Süddeutscher Rundfunk, Hessischer Rundfunk, and Radio Bremen. They carried Gwen's picture and voice up to the Netherlands, south to Italy, east into Poland, and beyond even into the Kremlin. Citizens in those countries listened in disbelief to the frightening narrative they had all heard before.

The airwaves carried details about a secret underground movement, financial misappropriation, and the murder of a well-liked German chancellor. Smaller news outlets jumped on the story as reporters took Gwen's lead. Countless members of the media jumped on the German money trail and onto the involvement of high-ranking American officials, accomplices of the underground empire of Germany.

WHILE GWEN REPORTED LIVE, Carter consulted with his CIA associates. They helped him identify more underground bunkers in locations where Strauss might be hiding that cache of weapons. To Carter's surprise, they found more than he anticipated. Countless bunkers and multiple possibilities were peppered throughout Eastern Europe, but one stood out. Carter identified one bunker with a large possibility, and it was nearby. Carter calculated this bunker was about two hours southwest of Berlin, an easy trip giving easy intelligence gathering.

"Everyone, please come sit for a moment," Carter said. "My CIA counterparts have helped us identify several bunkers all south and east of where we are now. But, luckily, one bunker is drivable, and I think we should check it out in the morning."

"Where is it?" Johann asked.

"The nearest underground bunker that might give us any information is in Bad Düben, 160 kilometers southwest of here. About a two-hour drive."

Johann looked at Rocco. "What do you think? Should we go?"

"Let's do it," Rocco said.

Gwen smiled. For a reporter with her tenacity, this story grew better by the day.

"We're going, too," Heinrich said.

Karl nodded.

"Yes, yes, we'll go together," Rocco said. "As with the castle, we seem to work well as a team—trained eyes, and untrained eyes alike."

Heinrich and Karl smiled at each other.

The team of six once again surrounded the table and studied a map of the area, roads in and roads out, and places to take cover if need be. They identified a point for a meet-up if anyone got separated from the group, and Rocco recommended what they needed to pack.

"Okay, let's get some sleep. We're getting up before sunrise," Rocco said.

No one argued. The team was tired but also excited about the morning that was to come.

Before sunrise, the group set off. Gwen wondered what they would find this time. Not knowing what they would be walking into and expecting the worst with their limited surveillance, Rocco, Johann, and Carter said they expected a show of force or even a heightened level of security. So, the team once again pulled off to the side of the road and parked the van. They covered it with foliage to conceal it on the side of the road.

Each weighed down with a backpack, the team continued on foot the rest of the way, expecting to encounter armed guards or even guard dogs. *Germans love their guard dogs*, Gwen thought. But there were none. To her surprise, there was nothing at all—no armed guards, no watchdogs, no security whatsoever. The entrance to the bunker was half-heartedly covered with a camouflage tarp and heavy rocks. This indifference, this inept attempt to hide the facility, made the covert-trained members of the party more suspicious.

"Something's wrong here," Carter said.

"I agree. This is not the greeting I was expecting," Johann said.

"Me neither," Rocco said. "Stay on alert. Something isn't right."

"I'm sure this is the bunker my people told me about," Carter said. "The longitude and latitude line up. This is the correct location."

"They must think they're so well-hidden no one would ever find them," Johann said.

"Maybe there are no guards here because there is nothing to hide," Karl said, sounding disappointed.

Rocco looked at Karl. "The kid might be right, or not. But we should check it out anyway."

Rocco, Johann, Carter, and the boys cleared away the rocks and the tarp, then lifted the heavy steel door. The door was starting to rust shut; it clearly hadn't been opened in a long while. Inside the opening, a long and narrow steel ladder disappeared into the dark of a vertical shaft, most definitely a safety concern. Rocco dropped LED light sticks down the shaft and shined a laser measurement tool to determine the length of the drop.

"Oh man." Rocco looked at Johann and Carter. "This single-man fixed ladder goes down about one hundred feet."

"Wow, no wonder there's no security. Who'd be crazy enough to take that risk?" Carter asked.

"We are." Johann tilted his head in Gwen's direction. "We're going to take it because you-know-who would never let us walk away."

"I packed a harness for everyone," Rocco said. "Everybody use the carabiner to secure yourself one step at a time. There's no rush. Safety first. Is anyone bothered by heights or tight spaces?"

No one indicated the affirmative. Rocco assisted everyone to strap on the climbing harnesses correctly and showed how to clip the carabiner to the side rail of the ladder for safety. Johann entered the narrow hole first, Carter next, then the boys, then Rocco. Gwen went last. Rung by rung, they clipped and unclipped and stepped down. Gwen was glad to be tall; the rungs had been spaced for someone with long arms and legs. She counted each rung to know when to expect an end to the tedious descent.

She found it odd to touch down in a fairly modern room, a security check-point with several desks, each with multiple monitors for guards to observe movement inside and outside of the bunker. This was clearly an area to welcome newcomers but also to search these new arrivals before they were permitted to roam free in the vast complex. As suspected, it was unoccupied.

The team, led by Rocco, made their way to the first opening and proceeded with caution. What Gwen saw sent a chill up her spine. She felt like they had stepped back in time, into a Cold War relic. They were surrounded by antiquated equipment and out-of-style amenities. Long cafeteria-style tables held countless black rotary-dial telephones, all precisely arranged four feet apart with a folding chair for every telephone. Most definitely workstations, but for whom? On a separate desk across the room, another table was home to three more telephones, two gray and one red. Who were the occupants of this underground bunker to communicate with?

Gwen asked, "Can they use these old telephones? I thought analogue phones no longer worked in newer digital networks."

Rocco said, "Yeah, they still work. The old wires are still in existence all over the world, so as long as the phone company allows service to the line, it'll work. Hard-wired PTOS lines were always more reliable than any satellite or wireless telephone, and harder for the enemy to eavesdrop on. The only thing they can't do is respond to digital network functions like 'press one for English' or other phone tree stuff."

"Rotary phone adapters exist that can connect to digital," Carter corrected. "It's not ideal, but it can be done."

Heinrich and Karl poked at one of the phones and asked something in German, sounding puzzled. Johann laughed and showed them how to pick up the receiver and dial. The American three also laughed at the boys' generational ignorance.

This bunker was clearly built in the 1950s. Rocco ran his hand along the interior wall and said it was warm to the touch, lined with material offering its occupants great protection. Carter, schooled by the CIA, said he had heard about this type of bunker but actually standing in one gave him pause. Oddly, there were random upgrades, as though someone was making improvements to possibly house thousands of occupants, but more work was needed.

Karl looked excited. "Whoever built this bunker clearly took a lesson from the ancient Turks. This reminds me of a vast underground labyrinthine complex in Turkey's Cappadocia region built more than one thousand years ago. They were literally underground cities, where thousands of people could hide during invasions and later during wars. I wonder if this is the only level or if there are more?"

"Similar to missile silos then?" Carter said. "Okay."

Karl nodded. "One such underground city in the Nevsehir Province is a multi-level city of similar construction called Derinkuyu. The curvature of the walls reminds me of that place."

"Well, anything is possible," Carter said. "My associates didn't say that, but we won't know until we take a look around."

Rocco continued to feel the walls and smell the materials. "I smell almonds, almond oil."

"Well, that's not surprising," Karl said. "I'm sure we'll find almonds if they're down here, and maybe even almond oil. Who knows?"

"That would give us proof of something," Heinrich said.

Carter flashed his light at the structure around them. "Look at the reinforcements of the walls, the ceiling. This bunker is bomb-, radiation-, and poisonous gas-proof. Nothing is getting down here."

"Could it withstand a nuclear strike?" Johann asked.

"Yes, I think it could," Carter said.

"Gwen? You're oddly quiet," Rocco asked.

"I'm not sure what to say or what to think," she said. "I need to look around, but I may have questions for you guys later."

"Whatever you need."

The group fell silent as they walked from area to area, room to room. The bunker was more than a mile long and contained every possible living amenity to sustain thousands of people. In every room, the walls were lined with gun racks, ammunition, and various other types of weapons. Enough to supply an army and mount a serious offensive strike.

Gwen shone her flashlight along the wall. "I guess we found the guns."

"It would seem so," Rocco said.

The team explored supply rooms, laundry rooms, recreational rooms, an indoor gym, cafeterias with attached kitchens, and a large old-fashioned telephone exchange which was clearly upgraded with new large-diameter cables running along the floor. Gwen ran her fingers along the dials of the colorful exchange moving from one workstation to the next. With so many points of connection, these switchboards could field thousands of calls. The largest cable ran under a closed door. When Gwen opened the door, she stood in amazement, looking at the detail in the room.

"Rocco, come over here," she said.

Rocco, with camera in hand, followed her. He whistled at the sight of the newly built television studio and the cutting-edge equipment it contained. "Somebody's been here recently."

"This is incredible. This is all new, never been used." Gwen ran her hands over the anchor's desk. "Who in the world does this guy think he's going to broadcast to?"

They strolled around the room, looking at the state-of-the-art equipment.

"This is incredible. We couldn't afford this equipment in New York," Gwen said. "This is top-of-the-line stuff."

Gwen sat in the reporter's chair and Rocco took pictures of her as proof of the room's existence. The backdrop read *Das Beste der Menschheit*; The Best of Humanity.

Gwen snorted. "I hope he's not including himself."

"This is like a city," Karl said. "A whole city could fit down here."

"I think that's the idea," Heinrich said. "But who are the city's residents? Not us, that is for sure."

As the team moved through the facility, they were amazed by the complexity of the design and the thoughtfulness of the details. The architects included an internal rail system, not like the modern subway, but still a series of transport cars to quickly move people from what was clearly residential areas and sleeping quarters to the command areas. A built-in pedway ran the perimeter of the bunker.

"I'll bet people could live down here for months," Karl said.

"Probably years. It would depend on the storage capability," Carter pointed down a long corridor. "In the area behind, there are multiple rooms all housing generators and backup generators. Whoever built this facility intends to stay down here for a long, long time."

Having seen the television studio, Gwen took a special interest in the tremendous number of telephone wires and the diameter of the lines and cables themselves. *They must be buried deep and go a great distance*, Gwen thought.

As she became more interested in the communication system, she traced the lines throughout the vast rooms. They converged on one area, where they disappeared into the ground in a protected tube. Rocco followed Gwen closely and took video. The large communication room contained thousands of lines.

Gwen walked past a switchboard a hundred feet long color-coded with dials in green, blue, white, yellow, and purple. None of them knew what the colors referenced. The room attached to the communication room appeared to be a command office. *Whoever is in charge, this must be where they work,* Gwen thought. She stood in the doorway of the large room and looked around. *Could this be Strauss' office?*

A long table off to one side of the room held scrolls of papers and maps lying open on top. Maps of different parts of Europe and Western Asia lined the walls, all of which had Germany in the center. There also sat a large, grand desk as fancy as the one she saw in the castle. *This must be Strauss' office,* she said to herself. *What is this man up to?*

Despite Rocco's warnings not to touch anything, Gwen couldn't help herself. She sat in the would-be king's chair behind his grand desk and picked up the telephone, curious if there was a dial tone. To her surprise, she heard someone breathing.

On impulse, she asked in German, *"Hallo, ist jemand da?"*

A man replied, *"Da tovarishch my zdes."*

Gwen went cold. He was speaking Russian, not German. A flash of light next to the phone caught her gaze. It was an automatic translator device, like those used for the deaf. The screen lit up, translating what the man said into German. She poked a few buttons and managed to switch it to English. "Yes, comrade, we are here," the machine said.

She bit her lip, saying nothing.

"U vas yest' progress, chtoby soobshchit'?" the man asked. "Have you progress to report?" the machine displayed.

Gwen said, *"Nein."*

"My videli novosti. Vash reporter slishkom blizko."

Gwen nearly dropped the phone when she read the translation: "We've seen the news. Your reporter is too close."

She returned the telephone to its cradle.

Rocco walked in. "I told you not to pick that up."

"I know," Gwen said, "but I needed to hear if it was connected to anything."

"Is it?"

"Yes, the man spoke in Russian."

"Whoa. Are you sure?"

"Yes, I'm sure. This doohickie translated it all, too; pretty cool, actually. He asked, 'Are you there? Do you have any progress to report?'"

"So, what rattled you?"

"He said they've seen the news and 'your reporter is too close.' That reporter is me, I just know it." Gwen stood and took a deep breath, bending over with one hand on each knee. "How are the Russians involved in all this? They left East Germany nearly thirty years ago."

"At least, that's what we all thought. But maybe not."

Johann joined them. "The Russians? Oh my God, what are we into here? The Russians?"

"We need to get the hell out of here." Rocco snapped his fingers to get the attention of the group. As they looked over at him, he circled his hand as a signal to wrap this up.

"No, we're not leaving empty-handed." Gwen crossed her arms. "We're here now and we're going to look around until we find real proof," Gwen said.

Even Heinrich and Karl nodded in agreement.

"I'm still looking for my father's killer," Heinrich said. "I will do whatever it takes."

The team looked at each other. No words were spoken; they were all in agreement.

The group fanned out, each taking an area and searching the premises. Johann, Rocco, and Carter looked over the maps on the table in Strauss' office while Gwen went through his desk.

The maps showed more underground bunkers clustered in and around East Germany. More were peppered throughout the east in Poland, Belarus, Ukraine, and Lithuania, clearly all leading to Moscow.

"Maybe the Russians are involved somehow," Rocco said. "Maybe it isn't all Strauss?"

"Well, if that's the case, the CIA is in the dark," Carter said. "But when we get back, I'll certainly tell them about Gwen's encounter."

"I remember when the Russians were here. I was young but my parents told me everything was terrible," Johann said. "Then, when they left, everything got worse, as if that were even possible."

"Well, the one thing I've learned is never rule anything out without proof," Rocco said. "People will always surprise you."

While the men continued to comb over the maps, Gwen methodically went through the king's desk, looking for anything she could find. In one of the side drawers, she found a short stack of photographs, pictures of Strauss from many years earlier with a young boy, and photos of the boy alone at various ages. Clearly, Strauss was proud of this boy. She guessed he was the son Travis told her about, Martin. As Gwen thumbed through Strauss' private life, one of the pictures caught her eye. Strauss and the boy stood next to a pregnant woman, arranged like a family.

Gwen's heart dropped and the air left her lungs. Her chest became a vacuum she couldn't fill. She felt dizzy, unable to breathe, but unwilling to lean into the fear of what she just found. She quickly looked around to make sure all the guys were still around the table before she pulled the photo from the drawer.

She let the other pictures leave her hand, but she held on to this one. The woman was younger than Gwen was now, but she knew that face. No mistaking it: it was her mother standing there with a monster, and worse, she was pregnant. But why was she with Strauss? She slipped the photo into her pocket. As soon as possible, she would ask the one person whom she knew could answer her questions.

As the four wrapped up their inspection of Strauss' office, Rocco remarked none of them had seen Karl or Heinrich in a while. As they left the office, taking maps and other items, Karl and Heinrich, with flashlights on, emerged from the darkness toward the rest of the team.

"Where have you two been?" Gwen asked.

"Looking for a way out," Heinrich said.

"We're going out the same way we came in," Rocco said.

"No, we're not," Karl said with a smile.

"What? Why not?" Rocco asked.

"If Russians are anything, they are thorough," Karl said. "For ventilation purposes, they would have dug an exit as soon as they dug an entryway. Plus, do you really think they hauled all this stuff in through that tiny hole we climbed through?"

The men looked at each other, eyebrows raised.

"Well, the kid's got us there," Johann said with a grin.

"You weren't thinking of that, were you?" Heinrich asked.

"Nope," Rocco admitted, his face flushing.

"Okay, stop bragging, where's the exit?" Gwen asked.

"There's an elevator over this way," Karl said.

"An elevator?" Gwen asked.

"Yes, an elevator," Heinrich said. "And there's more."

As the team climbed into the elevator, Karl hit the down button instead of up.

"What are you doing?" Gwen asked.

"Wait," Karl said. "It gets better. This is just like Turkey."

The team stood silent as the elevator took them down the shaft, floor by floor. Each floor had a similar setup with guns, ammunition, command centers, and guard posts. Karl estimated the facility went twenty floors deep, deeper than anything the Turks built.

"What the hell?" Rocco asked.

The team stopped on random floors so Carter could take pictures for his associates back home.

"They're not going to believe this," Carter said. "My God!"

"Well, I have a good idea where the German funds are going now," Gwen said.

Rocco continued to film the underground bunker as proof to the world what this man and his people were plotting. The elevator came to rest on what finally appeared to be the bottom floor. Karl was correct—there was more.

Large black drums stood in rows; each one was twelve feet tall. The team walked off the elevator and, shining their flashlights, they looked down the enormous, dark room filled with countless drums.

"I bet I can guess what's in these," Karl said.

"We're not doing any guessing," Rocco said. "We need to open one up on camera and take a sample."

"I can't be on camera, I'm in the CIA," Carter said. "But I can shoot you on film if you want."

"I'll do it," Johann said. "I'm German, and I have no reason to lie about my own people. I will collect the sample on camera."

"That does make sense," Rocco agreed.

Carter gave Johann an official U.S. government sample collection kit to retrieve some of the liquid and a pair of latex gloves. With the collection kit in his mouth, Johann climbed up the side of the nearest container to the top. Rocco tossed him a crowbar to pry open the lid. As soon as Johann cracked the lid, the overwhelming odor of almonds wafted throughout the room. Johann steadied himself and used the sample kit to scoop up oil, then sealed the sample with an official U.S. government label. Rocco zoomed in to show the reliability of the sample collected and the sealing of the container as proof of where it came from. Identification of the liquid would be determined later by the authorities.

"Gwen, why don't you take the microphone and tell everyone what we found down here today?" Rocco said. "As we're leaving, we can record something room by room, because I've taken plenty of B-roll from most areas of the bunker."

"Yes, that's a good idea, let's do it." Gwen took the microphone and positioned herself in front of the drums containing the almond oil.

"We're rolling, three, two," Rocco pointed at Gwen in place of saying "one."

Gwen began with the most passion she could muster given the unbelievable distraction in her pocket and the secret she held in her heart. Unable to tell the team this newest wrinkle, she carried on until she could speak to her mother.

"This is Gwen Patterson, coming to you from a hundred feet below the surface of the earth. I'm with colleagues in Bad Düben, a small town formally under East German control and Soviet occupation. This small town is situated about 159 kilometers southwest of Berlin, and it's under siege, but the residents of this town don't know it yet.

"While investigating Germany's greatest financial crisis since World War Two, my team and I have discovered an underground bunker built more than seven decades ago by the former East German government. At the end of the Cold War, this facility was decommissioned, and it remained so, at least until recently. This facility has been undergoing upgrades and technological advancements, allegedly under the direction of the former East German Socialist Party leader, Erich Strauss.

"Strauss' goal is to repurpose this bunker to suit his objectives, and allegedly to do the same with many other underground bunkers scattered across Eastern Europe. At this time, Strauss' true and complete intent for this facility remains unknown; however, we're going to tell you what we've discovered so far, and we'll try to connect the financial dots as our investigative team continues to shed light on this story."

Karl and Heinrich looked at each other and smiled.

"Did you hear that?" Karl asked. "She said team."

Heinrich smiled.

Gwen was not normally one to share credit, but she couldn't do this story alone. Something inside her was changing. As a new widow, she should feel more alone than ever, but instead, gratitude suffused her. She no longer felt like a woman on her own but part of something larger, something that should be acknowledged. She had lost so much in her personal life in such a short amount of time, but she couldn't deny the contributions her new friends made. They felt more like family with each passing day. Plus, she couldn't overlook all the times Rocco had saved her life so far.

Gwen stood quietly in the elevator as she and the guys rode it to the surface. Still clutching that picture in her jacket pocket, she didn't say a word to the team, not even to Rocco. As soon as she could get alone with a telephone, she had an important call to make.

With more footage than they could ever use, the team escaped the underground bunker. In haste, Rocco took the driver's seat and peeled out of Bad Düben without so much as a peek in the rearview mirror.

After returning to the safehouse, Gwen told the others she was tired and needed to lie down. She took the burner phone Carter had given her into a back bedroom. Ordinarily, she would never take such a risk with her life or the lives of those who trusted her, but she needed an immediate answer from her mother.

The phone rang three times before Gwen's mother answered.

"Hello?"

"Mom, it's Gwen."

"Oh, hello, dear, how are you?"

"Not good. I need some help from you."

"Of course, what do you need?"

"I found a photograph. I need you to tell me the truth about something."

"Okay." Her mother's voice cracked.

"Do you know Erich Strauss, the former General Secretary of the Socialist Unity Party of East Germany?" Gwen blurted. "Don't lie to me."

Her mother took a few deep breaths, and then no more sound came through.

"Mom?" Gwen looked at the phone.

The display read, "call ended," and listed the brief length of the connection.

Gwen's mother hung up without answering her questions and without saying so much as a word.

THE NEXT MORNING, Carter's phone rang, and it wasn't a call he was expecting. His CIA counterpart Alex called from the American Embassy in Berlin.

"Hey, what's up?" Carter walked out of the room, taking the call outside.

"Gwen's mother Margaret Stratton called the American Embassy. She wants to talk to her daughter, but she doesn't have a return number to reach her. Mrs. Stratton said she heard from Gwen last night, but they were disconnected."

"Return number? Last night? That's impossible," Carter said. "She was here last night."

"So was the cell phone you gave her. She used that. We dumped her calls. She made the call, Carter. She called her mother."

"Damn." Carter rubbed his forehead. "I never thought she'd be that reckless."

"You're supposed to be watching her."

"I am, but I can't take away her phone," Carter snapped. "She's not a child."

"Just give her the message. Tell her to call her mother. And this time, tell her to use the landline."

GWEN STAYED IN bed, lying on her back, staring at the ceiling, still confused by the photograph she found the day before. She'd slept horribly and felt guilty about not sharing the information in the picture. *Rocco and Carter don't share everything either,* Gwen thought. "Need-to-know basis," they said. Gwen made herself angry for a moment, but her thoughts betrayed her. The men downstairs were her friends. They cared about her, they cared about the story, but they, too, had a job to do. Sometimes that job required confidentiality, even from each other, even from her.

She sat up, feeling hungover but without the party the night before. Her mind raced and her heart pounded. It was anxiety, but she gave herself grace for it; she had a lot to be anxious about.

What would people think if they found out her mother knew this horrible man? What would Joe think about her? Joe meant everything to her. Countless possibilities rushed through her mind, none of them good. She wanted to go back to bed, roll over and block them out, but she had to get up and deal with the photo she found.

Her mother wasn't going to tell her anything. How else could she find out why her mother was in the company of that man? Who was that young boy—was it Martin Strauss? What happened to the child her mother was pregnant with, the one in the photo? Was that baby even alive now? Did she have a brother or sister somewhere? Gwen always knew her mother came from this area of the world, but never did she imagine her mother was among the Communist East German elite. *How could my mother have lied to me? How could my mother have kept so many secrets?*

A knock came on her door. "Are you up?" Carter called through the door.

"I'm up. Come on in."

Gwen swung her feet over the edge of the bed. Carter sat down next to her.

"Listen, my counterpart just called from the embassy. Your mom called this morning trying to reach you," he said. "She left word for you to call her at home."

Gwen listened but didn't confirm or deny anything. "Oh, okay. What's the safest way for me to call her, if it's even possible?"

"You can use the landline in the kitchen," Carter said. "But just so you know, someone is probably listening."

"Someone, who?" Gwen asked.

"Well, I don't know exactly. But probably someone back at Langley."

"Okay, that's fine."

It was anything but fine, but she had no other way to reach her mother, at least not this time. She needed answers, so she had to make that call. However, she still needed to keep her mother's secret for the immediate future. She would tell the team, her friends, but not until she could get answers first. She needed confirmation.

"If that's the only way, then it's the only way," Gwen said. "I can't hide the truth forever."

Even if Langley is listening, so what? The truth always comes out, one way or another—or at least that's what I tell all the people I interview, Gwen thought.

"Truth? What truth?" Carter leered at her.

"Don't worry about it right now, you'll know soon enough." Gwen gave him a deadpan look. "You'll all know."

Carter left, giving her privacy to get dressed. She stood, but her feet were like two cinder blocks. She could barely walk. She was afraid of what her mother would say, and she wondered if she was ready to hear it.

As Gwen entered the kitchen, she asked for the room. The men left, promising not to eavesdrop.

Gwen took the phone from the cupboard and dialed her mother.

"Hello," Margaret said.

"You left a message for me at the embassy?" Gwen said curtly.

"Yes, honey. I'm sorry about last night, but you took me by surprise, and you know how I am. When I don't know what to do, I run. I always run, or in this case, I hung up."

"Are you ready to tell me the truth now?"

"You were always tough as nails, dear Gwen. I guess that was something you got from your father."

"My father? You've never spoken of my father! Why are you doing this now? What's going on?"

"No, I haven't spoken of him, especially not to you, and I think now you know why." Margaret sighed. "You need to sit down wherever you are, dear."

Gwen's hand shook as she sat on the kitchen stool. Beads of sweat formed on her forehead. Her teammates were in the next room. They were curious, but they promised not to pry. She kept an eye on the door and her voice low to ensure privacy. If this conversation was going where she thought it was going—where she feared it might go—she needed to keep it to herself, at least until she had enough time to process it.

"You said you found a photograph?" Margaret asked. "May I ask where you found it?"

"I found it in an underground bunker, in the desk drawer of a man named Strauss. He's the former—"

"Yes, yes, he was the General Secretary of the SED many, many years ago, when we were all too young for that kind of responsibility. And, yes, Erich may have been the *Generalsekretär* at that time, but he was also a lot of other things, too."

"What do you mean?"

"Later, later. Now, you think it's me in the picture?"

Gwen sat stone-faced, her anxiety growing. *Is she going to deny what I saw?* Gwen thought. She had an idea of the direction this conversation was going, but she remained hopeful that her gut instinct was wrong, at least this time.

"Yes, Mom it's you, I'm sure of it," Gwen said. "Strauss is in it too, with a little boy, and you look pregnant."

"Was I wearing a blue dress with white flowers, and weren't we all standing on a grassy hill with a castle in the background?"

Gwen took the picture from her pocket. It was old and slightly faded, but she could see the white flowers on her mother's dress.

"Yes, you were," Gwen said. "That's it. That's the dress."

"Yes, honey, it's me. I knew Erich Strauss," Margaret said. "I was his girlfriend. We lived together, but we never married. He asked, and I said yes, but I left before the wedding."

"Mom?" Gwen gasped. "Oh my God, Mom!"

"He and I were young at the time, and it looked like he was going places. At that time, things were different for women, especially in East Germany. But when it came down to it, I knew what he was, and I couldn't marry him. I couldn't go through with it."

Margaret began to sob into the phone.

"Say it!" Gwen hardened her heart. "Say it!"

"Gwen, it isn't like that."

"Say it!"

"Okay, okay, sweetie, I'll tell you." Margaret took a deep breath. "Gwen, honey, Erich Strauss is your father, and the boy in the picture is your brother. His name is Martin."

The phone went silent, on both ends.

Gwen shook, feeling ill. *My brother killed my husband.*

"Please, let me explain," Margaret said.

"Explain? Explain what? Explain how you've been lying to me for more than thirty years?" Gwen's voice rose an octave. "What explanation could possibly make this okay? Are you kidding me? You knew why I came to Germany! You knew the story I was investigating! You knew! I almost died. Members of my team almost died, Josh—and you didn't think I needed an explanation then? Jesus, Mom!"

"I never thought you would get this far. I didn't, I swear it! I know you do excellent work. I know you do, but your father is good, too, maybe even better. He's so manipulative, you can't understand. I never thought we'd ever have this conversation. But know this: I always wanted to tell you, I swear I did, but I knew you would react this way."

Gwen sat silent, unable to find any words to respond. Her brain was without a single, active thought. She was in shock, but she didn't have the luxury to stay there. She would have to compartmentalize, like she had with Joshua's death.

"Please let me tell you some things now," Margaret said.

Gwen sat back down on the chair and hung her head, not wanting to hear what more her mother would say, but knowing she had to listen.

"I was with your father for many years, and then there came a time when I realized I was in big trouble. All of Germany was in big trouble, so I ran. I knew if I took Martin, Erich would search for me to the ends of the earth. Martin was his son, his protégé, a dictator in training. Truthfully, he was so much like his father, I couldn't stand him. I know he was just a small boy, and he was my child, but he had that mean streak in him he inherited from your father."

Gwen sat quiet, listening.

"I was pregnant in that photo with you, my darling Gwen."

Gwen's eyes rolled up to the ceiling, and she let out a large sigh, wondering what more her mother could possibly reveal.

"I want you to know I understand how shocked you must be, and I want you to know none of this is your fault," Margaret said. "I left my family and my country, and I left my son for you, not because of you."

Gwen silently nodded, knowing her mother was telling the truth. Margaret always looked out for her, always.

"After I already got it into my head that I was leaving, I told your father the baby was a boy, which made him ecstatic. So, this way if he did come searching, it might make finding me and you more difficult. But they, or at least Martin, now know where I am."

"What? How? How do you know Martin knows where you are?"

"He came here the other day, looking for his brother."

"Oh my God! What happened?"

"Well, like I said, he has your father's mean streak, but he's not very imaginative," she added with a small laugh.

"What do you mean?" Gwen frowned.

"Well, Martin just showed up here one day out of the blue, right here in Whiting, New Jersey. How he found me, I'll never know, but I couldn't believe it. He forced his way into my house and searched for his baby brother or of some evidence of him," Margaret said. "I was shocked he didn't recognize me. He didn't even recognize your photo."

"Really?"

"No, he threw some stuff around, demanding to know where his brother was," Margaret said. "He also had a photo of me and his father, which I denied, but he didn't believe me. I told him I had one child, a girl, and I didn't know what he was talking about."

"Did he believe you?"

"Truthfully, I don't know, I'm not sure. But I thought he'd kill me. He was so angry. But he just made a mess, like his father always did. He made lots of threats like his father, too, but at the end of it all he did nothing. He ran away like me and his father. At least that's one thing we have in common." Margaret took a breath. "But for me, the question is why all of a sudden is he so interested in finding his brother?"

"You don't know if it's all of a sudden. He may have been looking for you for years. It might be related to my story."

"Your story? How?"

"I don't know, but every lead we follow takes us right back to dear old Dad." Gwen sat straighter. "He's behind all of this, the financial turmoil in Germany, countless murders, probably Josh's murder—"

"Someone murdered Josh?"

"Yes. Martin did it, according to Victor Travis, who is also dead."

"When?"

Gwen counted on her fingers, trying to remember. "That monster you spawned bashed in my husband's face five days ago."

"Oh, Gwen." Margaret gasped. "Oh, honey, I'm so, so sorry."

Gwen waved a hand in resignation. "I'm in the center of all this, and now I know why.

"Strauss has inside people siphoning taxpayers' money and putting it in foreign bank accounts in other parts of Europe to finance his plans, whatever they are. He's modernizing underground bunkers, buying truckloads of almonds, importing weapons, you name it—and he's doing it! But the question is, what's his endgame? We're having trouble connecting all the dots."

"I wish I could help, dear," Margaret said. "But all I can tell you is, he loved the Russians more than the Germans. He admired their sheer will and their ability to gain power. That's probably why they put him in power at such a young age. He would have done anything for them."

"Gwen!" Rocco shouted from the next room. "Gwen! We need to get going."

"The guys are calling me. I have to see what they want."

"I'm so sorry about Josh, dear," Margaret said. "I'll be here if you want to talk later. I know this is a lot for you to take in, and again, I'm sorry for having kept if from you. But now you see why. You see what kind of man your father is. There would've been no point in telling you about him. It is a past I wanted to forget."

"Yes, I understand," Gwen said. "We'll talk later. I'll call you when I can."

"I love you, sweetheart."

"Thanks." Gwen hung up, reeling from the bombshell her mother had dropped on her. She and her team had been chasing her own father around Germany all week. Her own father. Gwen hung her head, still holding the phone, feeling dizzy and sick.

Rocco slammed through the kitchen door. "Gwen, let's get going."

"Where?" she asked without looking up.

"I got us access to some television equipment and additional staff to help us sift through the footage we took at the underground bunker. Let's not keep them waiting. Let's go."

"I need to talk to you about something." Gwen looked up at him.

"Later, let's go." Rocco left the room.

Would later come too late?

Rocco told Karl and Heinrich to find their friends at the university and start making calls. They should tell everyone to watch the NIN newscast tonight. Rocco intended to blow this story out of the dungeon and onto every television set across Europe and America.

KARL AND HEINRICH returned to their university campus to tell everyone to watch this evening's NIN news. They told their families, friends, and fellow protestors about their experiences during the past few weeks and the team effort that went into uncovering the information presented in Gwen's report. They regaled their friends with stories of secret phone conversations, covert operations, trips to Andorra, sneaking into Strauss' castle, and their explorations throughout a multifloor underground bunker. Their friends were impressed but remained skeptical of the twosome's heroic tales; however, they didn't dismiss the story out of respect to Heinrich and what he and his father had sacrificed for the good of their country.

"It sounds too incredible, like a movie," one classmate said.

"*Ja*, but this is not a movie, it is reality," Karl said.

"*Ja*, it is all true, and hopefully tonight Gwen will present as much of it as she can," Heinrich said. "But I want everyone to know my father is innocent, no matter what Nikolaus says."

"Well, hopefully, after tonight we won't have to do this anymore," another woman said.

"Do what?" Karl asked.

"Protest, of course," she said, exasperated. "I would like to just return to school and finish my degree and move on from this place. I feel my life has been on hold all this year."

Karl and Heinrich listened to their friends and classmates as they voiced agreement with that statement. Everyone was ready for this to be over, but would it be over tonight? The two men looked at one another with thumbs pressed and fingers crossed that Gwen, Rocco, Johann, and Carter would come through and expose Strauss' conspiracy to overthrow Germany. Strauss and his men had been plotting and planning for years, positioning their people in all levels of government, military, and the banks, like a chess match. But tonight, Gwen would declare checkmate.

Gwen and Rocco took the news van while Carter and Johann took their own vehicles to the Berlin television studio. Rocco said it would be safer if everyone traveled separately, to have a better chance of evading capture, since they had a better idea of who they were dealing with. Strauss' people were covert and slick, always blending in with the crowd, hard to identify.

The four met with Rocco's contact out in the parking lot.

"Is it clear? Can we use the editing bay and control room for a bit?" Rocco asked.

"Yes, it is clear," the editor said. "Let me show you in."

Carter and Johann would stand guard in the studio while Gwen and Rocco put together the news package.

Gwen looked around the television studio, initially unimpressed with the décor. It was nothing like her New York facility with sophisticated equipment and high-end décor, and nowhere near the tech level they'd found underground in Strauss' bunker. Ordinarily, she might have turned her nose up to such a humble facility, but this week snapped her high-class attitude back into the real world, the working world. Having already lost so much this week—her husband, then almost her life, her freedom, and her friends—all for a story that originally felt so small, so cookie-cutter, she would take their help and appreciate it, making new friends and contacts all over the world.

The five of them walked past the receptionist without so much as a glance. The receptionist, a reporter wannabe with multiple failed attempts at securing an on-air job, was reduced to working the front desk until something in the video department or audio section opened. She recognized Gwen immediately but didn't acknowledge her; she had other plans. Once the group walked by, the receptionist picked up the telephone and dialed her friend, a man who had been looking for Gwen for a long time.

"*Ja*," Martin said.

"*Das ist Neringa*," she said.

"*Was ist los?*"

Neringa told him exactly what was up. "Gwen is here!" she said in a hushed voice.

"Who?"

"*Sie ist hier! am Fernsehsender.*"

"At the television station?"

"*Ja, sie ist hier beim Fernsehsender?*"

"Keep her there. We're on our way!"

Martin abruptly hung up the telephone, determined that Gwen would not elude him this time. Quickly, he called his associates. Within minutes, several armed men in utility trucks pulled up to take Martin anywhere he wanted to go.

"Others are on their way," one man said to Martin.

"*Gut*," Martin said. "The more the better."

"What are you going to do with her once you have her?" another man asked.

"We are taking her to the castle Startseite Barockschloss Moritzburg, my father's home. He is waiting there."

Martin got on his radio and made an announcement. "Gwen Patterson is to be captured and captured only. Do not harm her. Grab anyone with her. Neringa said there are three men with her. So be prepared."

"After all she has put you and your father through? She has possibly set our movement back years with her nosy reports," a man radioed back. "I'm surprised you don't want a bullet to go straight through her head."

"You forget, comrade, that is for the king to decide," Martin said. "We serve at his pleasure, including me. *Verstehst du?*"

"*Ja*, Martin," the man said. "I understand."

The caravan sped through the Berlin streets with revved engines and tempered drivers swerving in and out of traffic, racing toward their destination. The men projected calm and a sense of unity in purpose. Strauss' supporters were warned Gwen was in the company of skilled men, all of whom were weapons-trained and could hold their own in hand-to-hand combat. But they would do as ordered, grab them all and take them to their future king. Strauss would make the decision.

Trailing the other vehicles was one windowless van with a neatly disguised driver who looked official, not someone who would attract the wrong kind of attention, such as from the police. The van kept a more moderate speed but stayed on their six. Once the men did their job and grabbed the four reporters, he and his passenger would quietly transport them to the castle.

Strauss danced in place after talking to his son. *What good news,* he thought. He would finally have an opportunity to put this woman in her place and a bullet in her head, putting this so-called "story" to rest once and for all.

Strauss went to his office and opened his one locked drawer where he kept his prized possession, a gift from a Russian he had admired so long ago. The man was Konstantin Chernenko, the last strong leader of the Soviet Union, whose reign was short-lived but long enough to place Strauss at the helm of East Germany.

I was so young back then, too young to lead a nation, Strauss thought. *But now, I can lead the world.*

"General Chernenko, I will get it all back, I promise. I will get back all of what Gorbachev lost in 1989," Straus said to Chernenko, who he saw standing in the corner of his office.

GWEN AND HER team edited their footage, creating a timeline including financial loss, bank account gain, maps of bunker locations, almonds, weapons—they included everything. Rocco called Joe on speaker. Gwen relaxed upon hearing his voice.

"Hi, Joe," Gwen shouted.

"Hey, kid," Joe said. "You've been gone a long time, you know. It'll be good to have you home soon."

"Home? I don't know when I'm coming back. This story seems never-ending."

"Things are unraveling over here, Joe," Rocco said.

"That's what worries me," Joe said.

Leaving the line open to Joe, Rocco continued editing video clips while Gwen laid an audio track, both diligently closing on a final package, when something loud occurred outside the editing room door. Rocco rolled back in his chair and quietly locked the door.

"What's that yelling?" Joe shouted through the speakerphone.

Gunshots rattled the editing room door.

Gwen and Rocco fell silent. Muffled voices on the other side spoke in German. One man yelled, "*Finde diese Frau!*"

Gwen knew they were coming for her.

Rocco picked up his phone and called Johann. He hit the speed dial again and called Carter. No answer from either.

"What was that? Gwen, are you okay?" Joe asked.

"Yes, shh, yes, I'm here, but don't speak. I'm going to send you something through the satellite feed, but it's not finished yet. Just in case, you know?"

"Understood," Joe said.

"The guys aren't picking up," Rocco said into the speaker, looking at Gwen.

"What should we do?" Gwen asked. "Call the front desk?"

"No, I'll go out and check," Rocco said firmly. "When I leave, lock the door behind me."

Gwen nodded. "Be careful."

"I will. Don't open this door for anyone but me."

Rocco pulled his sidearm from its holster and cracked the door. Her peered out at station workers on the floor; they appeared unconscious. Johann and Carter were not in view.

"Do you see them?" Gwen asked.

"No. Now get up and lock the door."

Gwen quietly did as Rocco said. As soon as the lock clicked into place, she put her ear to the door. Hearing nothing, she backed up and sat, hitting the send button on the satellite feed.

"Joe," Gwen whispered, "here it comes."

"I see the feed," he said. "It's downloading now. We'll fix it up on this end, don't worry about that. But I want you to get out of there. The guys can take care of themselves. Get out of there now."

The fighting down the hall grew louder. They were coming for her. She had to run, though she hated the idea of running from anyone.

"Remember what I told you. Get in the ceiling," Joe said.

While Rocco was trained to fight, Gwen was not. She wouldn't stand a chance against one motivated attacker, let alone a team of armed men.

"I am!" Her heart pounded in panic, but she had the presence of mind to recall the drills. "Stay on the line but stay quiet."

"Yep," Joe said.

Gwen climbed up on the desk. Using both hands, she lifted the ceiling tile out of its square, exposing the plenum space. She sidled upward, relying on her plantar flexion from her ballet days. Popping her head up above the tile, she saw a pipe within reach. Fortunately, the pipe wasn't hot, and it was narrow enough she could wrap her hands around. As she struggled to lift her own body weight, she heard more shots and then the worst sound ever—rattling at her door.

"*Öffne diese Tür,*" one man shouted to another.

Oh shit, Gwen thought, *they're coming in.*

Gwen continued to struggle as the adrenaline surged through her body, giving her the much-needed boost to lift herself to safety. A blast knocked the door off its hinges, leaving no barrier between her and the would-be king's men. Smoke filled the editing room as she pulled her legs up through the ceiling.

"*Was denkst du, wo du hingehst?*" one man shouted as he grabbed her ankle.

"I'm getting out of here, that's where I'm going," Gwen yelled back at him as she struggled with the soldier. "Let me go."

"*Lass sie nicht gehen,*" another man yelled.

"*Töte sie nicht,*" shouted the man who appeared to be in charge.

"I am not going to kill her," said the man who grabbed Gwen. "I would never do that."

Smoke filled the room and hallway, making it difficult to see what was happening below. Gwen held on to the pipe as tightly as she could. Her grip was slipping from sweaty palms, and it became harder and harder to hold her position with the man's hands around her ankle. She struggled violently, swinging her legs to free her foot. She kicked the man in the face. Blood sprayed from his nose and mouth as he fell back. But her luck didn't last. Another man immediately stepped forward and grabbed her by both legs. With unmatchable power and strength, Martin's comrade pulled her from the ceiling plenum. Gwen lost her grip, giving the man full control. She came down hard, hitting her head on the desk of editing equipment with a loud smack.

Her limp body hit the floor.

"*Du hast sie getötet,*" the man in charge said.

"I did not kill her," the other man said, as he leaned down to check her pulse. With a sigh of relief, he said, "I did not kill her. She is unconscious."

"Even better. Put her in the van with her friends," the first man said.

The soldier flipped the reporter over and she lay on the floor just as the men liked—eyes closed and mouth shut. The man picked up Gwen and threw her over his shoulder, taking care not to cause any more damage. The king said he wanted her alive, and that was how he should have her, unspoiled.

Joe, in his office thousands of miles away, listened helplessly, horrified by what he was hearing. He kept his mouth shut for as long as he could. He was not there, but it was clear what was happening. They were going to get her. One way or another, she was not coming home.

Joe hung up and called all his German contacts, the good and the bad. He didn't care if former terrorists saved Gwen, he just wanted her back. In between his overseas calls, he made one in-house call to the control room. He told the director they had breaking news and he should run whatever Gwen sent in its entirety without any additional edits, along with the audio he recorded on his phone of her abduction.

The soldiers, having gotten what they came for, left the television station the same way they arrived except for the man carrying Gwen. He left through the service entrance, where the white windowless van waited. With the engine already running, the driver got out and went to the back of the van. He opened the outermost door, exposing the interior security door to a cage. The van resembled an official prisoner transport. Already lying in the van, hands tied, were Gwen's three teammates, Carter, Johann, and Rocco. The soldiers placed Gwen on top of the pile and locked the interior and exterior doors. As the engine roared, the foursome began to regain consciousness. Two men rode in the back with the four conspirators, one on each side. Johann, in German, asked his fellow countrymen where they were being taken, but neither answered, nor did they even look at what they considered a disloyal German who now lay at their feet.

With a hard double-pound of his fist on the van's rear door, the driver, his armed passenger, and the two guards in the back began the two-hour drive southwest to Strauss' home, Startseite Barockschloss Moritzburg Castle. They would present Gwen and her team to the future king. Gwen looked at her teammates, unsure of what was to come, but she knew this would not be the end of their story.

The man irrational enough to want that crown was sitting behind his desk polishing his pistol, waiting for this meddlesome reporter. He anticipated what he would do to her and her friends when she got there, and he knew right where he would bury her body.

"Today, we are victorious," Strauss said to Chernenko, who was sitting on the other side of his desk.

"You were always thorough. That is why I chose you," Chernenko said. "You were a party loyalist, and you have the ruthlessness of a Russian. You have a lot to be proud of, my son."

"You were always like a father to me, Chernenko," Strauss said. "Russia was the best thing to happen to the East German people."

"You will help the emperor when he reveals himself to the world, *da?*" Chernenko asked.

"*Da, moy otets,*" Strauss said most respectfully to his Soviet father figure. "For you, I will do whatever I can to support the true, rightful emperor when he reveals himself to his subjects."

Martin walked into Strauss' office as the van came up the long drive leading to the castle's back doors. Both men looked out over Strauss' empire with cold-blooded determination mixed with excitement. Strauss would be the one who killed Gwen and put her in a deep, dark grave.

When Strauss turned back to tell Chernenko of Gwen's arrival, Chernenko was gone. Strauss didn't hear him leave. Snapped back into reality by the wet work to be done, Strauss remained behind his desk, watching the door with his gun at the ready.

Martin's men came through the door carrying sheets of plastic large enough to wrap up a human body like a sausage. The men laid out the plastic sheets on the floor across the room, away from Strauss' desk. It was important to Strauss not to make a mess. As the men covered the walls with plastic, the others came up the stairs. At gunpoint, the four conspirators walked through the door, first Rocco, then Johann, Carter, and finally Gwen.

The men had their tied hands up. Not Gwen. She followed with a determination that wasn't understood. No one in that room knew what she knew. But if she was going to die, she was determined to let Strauss know whom he was killing. The foursome was surrounded and outnumbered. For the last week, they lived and worked as a team, and now they would die as one, too, or at least that's what Gwen thought. From across the room, Strauss looked Gwen straight in the eye. She didn't look away.

Gwen had no plan to go quietly. Now was the time to reveal that photograph she had found. She would tell this madman what she had learned about him, his son, and herself, his daughter. Her mother's tale made her sick, but she could not keep this secret. She had to swallow her pride and reveal their connection to save her life. The photograph in her pocket was their one possible ticket out. How could a man, even a man as sick as him, murder his own daughter? If he saw children as an investment in the future, he would not kill her, not without first trying to turn her.

The captives were forced into Strauss' office and lined up on the plastic sheets, each on a separate one. They were ordered to kneel.

"I'd rather die on my feet," Rocco said.

"Get on your knees!" Martin kicked Rocco in the back of his knees, making them buckle.

Rocco was roughly put in his place next to Johann, Carter, and Gwen, all on their knees at the mercy of a madman who clearly was fresh out of caring, if he ever had any to begin with.

"*Du machst einen großen Fehler!*" Johann said.

"My father is making no mistake," Martin said.

Strauss, a gun in his hand, stood from the desk and walked across the room.

"I don't know who you think we are," Rocco said.

Strauss crossed to Gwen and stood in front of her. He racked the slide of his pistol, preparing to kill. "So, you are the one making all this trouble for me?"

"I think you're confused with yourself," Gwen said.

"I am not confused about anything, woman," Strauss said in a raised voice. "I want what he wants, and that is what is best for Germany, all of Eastern Europe and beyond."

He? Gwen thought. *Who is he?* Aloud, she asked. "This is what's best, stealing money and murdering people? Please, explain that to me."

"You will see—you will all see this is what's best for our people."

"Our people?" Gwen asked. "Who in the hell are 'our people'?"

"People like us, woman. Do not be so naïve!" Strauss shouted. "Do not be so stupid."

Martin stood next to his father, looking down on Gwen.

Strauss said, "His plan will free up land, resources, money—all of it will be for us, as it should be, as it was meant to be."

"Yes, Father," Martin said, like an obedient dog.

The rest of the men quietly listened to Strauss as if they were listening to words of a king. Strauss gazed into the distance, performing for some ghostly audience. Gwen looked around to see what Strauss was looking at, but she saw nothing.

"And, young Gwen, this is where your story ends for you and for your friends. I am just sorry you could not see the right way, our way," Strauss said. "So, now it is time. You must die."

"I don't think so." Gwen smirked.

Strauss laughed. "You do not think I would kill you?"

"No, I don't."

"Why is that?" Strauss narrowed his eyes, clearly curious.

"Because I'm your daughter! Would you kill your own daughter?" Gwen looked her father in the eye over the barrel of his gun. "I think you're too arrogant for that."

Still on their knees also, Rocco, Carter, and Johann whipped surprised faces toward Gwen.

"What daughter?" Martin shouted. "There is no daughter, woman. I have no sister. I have a brother."

"I'm your sister," Gwen said.

Martin sneered in disgust and slapped her across the face.

Gwen turned her stinging face to look Martin in the eye. "That isn't going to change a thing, brother dear."

Martin removed his sidearm and forcefully pointed the barrel to her temple. "You shut up, woman! I have no sister."

Strauss took a step back, slightly lowering his weapon. "Stop, my son. I want to hear what she has to say."

"We will not entertain her lies, Father." Martin spat, looking at his father and still holding the gun to Gwen's head.

"Wait, my son, just wait a minute. This could be entertaining. I want to hear." Strauss gently placed his hand on his son's gun, easing it away from Gwen.

Gwen exhaled. From the corner of her eye, she saw her teammates looking at her.

Martin huffed. "All right, woman, you heard my father. Let's hear it."

Strauss took a good, long, hard look at Gwen. His expression shifted from curious to hardened. She was about to speak and state her case when Strauss interrupted her.

"Pick her up off the floor." Strauss gestured to two of his soldiers. "Do it nicely."

Obeying, the men eased Gwen to her feet while Rocco, Johann, and Carter watched with the same curiosity as Strauss' men and Martin.

Gwen said, "I'm going to reach in my pocket and show you a picture."

Martin took a defensive posture, tightening the grip on his gun.

"Show me, child," Strauss said.

Gwen removed the picture from her pocket, the one she had taken from his desk. It was bent now, but she unfolded it and held it in both her hands. She trembled. This moment would change everyone's life forever; she would be known as the daughter of a wannabe dictator, a thief, and a murdering monster. Strauss would know her mother, Margaret, was still alive, and Martin would have to face his biological sister. Martin would know with complete certainty there could be no brother.

"Let me see, child," Strauss held out his hand gently.

Strauss' sudden shift in attitude chilled her. She went from "that woman" to "child" so quickly.

She turned and showed Strauss the picture. pointing to him in it. "This is you. You were a lot younger then, but this is you, right?"

"This woman is your mother?" Strauss asked.

"That is my mother, Margaret Stratton. She was your fiancée?"

"Yes, she is the love of my life." Strauss teared up but quickly regained control of his expression.

"You mean she *was* the love of your life. She left you because you scared her."

"She did not understand the bigger vision I had for all of us, and for our lives," Strauss said. "I would have done anything for her, and I still would."

"So, this is you with my mother, and this boy is Martin here?" Gwen asked.

"Yes, and she was pregnant, as you can see," Strauss said. "This photo was taken before she left for a holiday in Austria. She never returned. I searched for her, fearing the worst. The babe was due that summer; she had told me it was to be a boy."

Gwen told them all her birthdate. It aligned with the photo and when Margaret went missing. "Surprise. I was a girl."

Strauss laughed thoughtfully. "Clever Margaret."

Martin forcefully stepped forward and ripped the picture from Gwen's hands.

"I know this woman, Father. I was in her home more than a week ago. She lives in America in some old people's community. That is how she is living, Father, in shit."

"You met with her? You met my love, your mother?" Strauss rounded on his son, face red with anger. "You know where she is? Where is she?"

"Yes, I know exactly where she is." Martin stepped back, arrogance on his features. "I didn't know who she was at the time, so I got rough with her trying to get information."

"Did you hit her?" Strauss grabbed his son by the shirt.

"No, no. I didn't strike her, I promise." Martin widened his eyes. "I swear I didn't strike her. I may have messed her house up and forced her into a chair, but I never hit her in the face. I wouldn't do that."

Strauss slowly let his son go but looked fearsome. "I better never find out you struck her, ever!"

Gwen was taken aback by the protectiveness this man felt for her mother. On a visceral level, it was beautiful yet scary at the same time.

"This woman is my mother?" Martin asked his father.

"Yes, Martin, she is your mother, and she is also Gwen's mother."

Martin looked at Gwen. She could see the wheels turning as he realized they were siblings, and he had a living mother. For the first time, Martin's eyes were not cold and empty but showed an ounce of feeling. He had more in this world than just his father; he had a family, however reluctant they were to be together.

Rocco, Johann, and Carter remained on their knees and listened as Gwen's family skeletons ran out of the closet and paraded around the room.

"*Ich möchte privat mit dir und Gwen sprechen,*" Strauss said to Martin.

Strauss took Gwen by the back of her arm, gently, and led her through the door.

"Where are we going?" she asked.

"I want to speak with you and your brother in private," Strauss said.

Strauss gave his son a nod. As Martin walked through the door with his father and sister, Martin turned to his men and said, "*Töte den Rest!*"

"Martin just gave the order to kill the three of us," Johann said.

"Get ready," Rocco said.

Rocco and Carter had pretended to be wimpy news people, so the soldiers weren't at their highest state of readiness. In fact, they took a lax stance. Clearly, they thought killing those two would be easy; a bullet a piece, one and done. Johann they were familiar with. They knew his previous job and the training that came with it. They would need to keep a closer eye on him, at least until he was dead. But the soldiers waited until the king and his children had left the room.

As Gwen disappeared through the door, Martin's men moved in toward the three on their knees and raised their weapons, taking aim. With a glance, Rocco and Carter were on the same page, but Johann had a different way of doing business. These men angered Johann; they gave Germans a bad name.

Rocco looked at Carter and said, "Krav?"

Carter nodded. "Maga."

The gunmen looked at one another, giving Rocco and Carter the split second they needed to leap to their feet, drop their ropes, and test their martial arts training. Johann had been trained by the German military, which favored jujitsu.

As Rocco and Carter sprang into action, Johann brought down two men to the floor with one sweep of his leg. *No mercy* was Johann's motto, and Rocco and Carter were onboard with that. The guards, stunned by the collaborative effort, found themselves no longer armed. They took a defensive position as Rocco and Carter took higher ground, standing above their captors. They beat the guards with their bare hands until the guards were no longer a threat. Johann was less forgiving. He picked up one of the men's weapons and struck him with the butt of the gun repeatedly. The head bled like no other body part; blood spattered the ceiling, the walls, and the plastic the soldiers had laid out for Gwen and her team. Now it would be used for their graves.

"Well, at least the plastic didn't go to waste," Rocco said coldly.

Carter pinned his captor to the floor with a knee on either shoulder, leaving him unable to move his arms or mount any type of defense. He punched at the man's face until he was unrecognizable and unconscious. Carter, who appeared to Johann and Rocco as a bookworm, was nothing of the kind. He was a fighter, and he was hardcore.

"Damn, Carter, I didn't know you had it in you," Rocco said.

"There's a lot you don't know about me." Carter climbed off the unconscious soldier covered in blood.

Rocco threw a gun to Carter. "Let's go get our girl."

Carter gave an affirmative nod as he used his sleeve to wipe his face of the man's blood. "What a mess."

Johann wiped the blood from the shotgun handle, lowered the barrel, fired it once into his adversary to finish the job, and then gave it a pump before looking up to answer Rocco. "*Ja*, let's get her."

Rocco this whole time thought he was alone in his protective detail of Gwen, but Carter's combat skills and Johann's ability to pull the trigger without hesitation impressed him. Rocco was glad they were on his side.

The three men, clothes stained with blood, went through the same door as Gwen. They could hear her screaming as her father and brother dragged her off. Rocco was unable to hear what the men were telling her, but, clearly, they wanted her alive. As they ran for Gwen, who was being dragged to a waiting car, Johann let off a round into the air.

Stunned by the shot, Martin and his father turned around and saw them coming.

"They will not stop their pursuit until they get her back," Martin said.

"Let me go." Gwen struggled to free her arms and wrists.

"Please, child," Strauss said. "You are my daughter, and we are your family. Together, we can rule the world."

"You're crazy! Let me go!"

"Come with us and listen to me! This all can be explained."

"Father, she will not come," Martin said, loosening his grip.

Gwen broke free from Martin and the old man. She turned and ran.

Strauss cried out for her to understand and to come back. "It's not over!" he yelled. "I will begin again! It's all for you, my children! I will find you, my child. I love you!"

Those words stopped Gwen. She glared at the man who claimed to be her blood relation, whom before today she had never met nor heard from, and now he declared his love for her in front of his son Martin, in front of her peers. This monster was ultimately responsible for Joshua's death. Part of her wondered if Strauss would have had her husband killed if he knew then who she was to him and who Joshua was to her.

Strauss and Gwen made eye contact. She felt an undeniable connection, even if he was a dangerous and delusional individual. Gwen's mind was clear; she didn't agree with anything he was doing, but she wanted to know everything about him, to understand what made a man hold such disdain for his fellow humans. As the two continued to share a visual lock, Rocco grabbed her by the waist and lifted her from the ground, carrying her away from them.

A car pulled up for Strauss and Martin and the back door flew open as the car came to a stop. Martin and Strauss jumped in and the car sped away.

45

GERMAN CITIZENS again marched in the streets from Berlin in the north to Hamburg in the west to Munich in the south. Higher taxes, lower wages, and government programs were always considered a poor-man's problem—ironically often pinching the middle classes the most—but now even the wealthy emerged from their slumber, knowing if the country continued this path, they would be next. It was as though all hope had died, life had stopped, and people were congregating in death marches looking for the next hangman. Someone was going to be held accountable, but who? Germans came out en masse, filling the streets, blocking the roadways; for miles, drivers were unable to navigate the city streets and even abandoned their cars to join the crowds. People were mad; taxpayers were incensed. Protestors held up homemade signs of *"Diebe,"* calling their elected officials thieves. Others called for the same officials to resign; they shouted, *"Zurücktreten! zurücktreten!"*

People wanted answers; they wanted to know where their money was going. They would soon find out. Strauss could do nothing now to stop the wheels already in motion. When Gwen hit the send button before her capture, she exposed her father and his conspiracy to the world.

However, her report was only a small part of a much larger story; they had just scratched the surface. To get below the surface, they would need to dig. Gwen would need a shovel, many shovels, to unearth the most gruesome part of her father's plot. Eventually, Gwen and her team would have more work to do and greater risks to take as more and more humans were sacrificed in the name of one man's greatness.

Out of New York, Gwen's report zoomed over the airwaves across Germany, Europe, and around the world. In America, the newly exposed corruption in Washington surprised no one, yet heads would roll; in America, it was all about appearances. As the report went live, cell phones simultaneously chimed with different alerts, making all people aware of Gwen's report and her progress; before the story could even be local, it went viral. Those rallying in the streets stopped in all cities as people watched and listened to her broadcast.

Gwen read her account of what transpired over the last week and more. She even included statements from her sources inside Washington and New York. Their contribution was beneficial, as it supported what Gwen and her team had seen overseas. She started this broadcast as she always did all her taped and live shots.

"This is Gwen Patterson. Unnamed Washington sources have confirmed the involvement of Americans, our elected officials who have participated in an overseas attempted coup.

"Among those being charged in this financial scandal are American political figures bought and paid for with German taxpayer money to help fund and facilitate the movement of weapons, currency, and other materials all needed for a coup. This coup is being led by Erich Strauss, the former General Secretary of the Socialist Unity Party, or SED, in East Germany. Several influential people are dead as a direct result of their participation in this campaign to steal from the German people and return them to a time of oppression.

"It has been reported that the death of U.S. Congressman Frank Solas is directly linked to the Port of Hamburg arms sale, and that he was murdered because he became a liability.

"Congressman David A. Becker is being charged in the deaths of NIN network president Charles Henderson and his family after refusing to squash this investigation. Henderson was accepting bribes from Becker for his own personal gain. As chairperson for the Federal Communications Commission, Becker wielded a great deal of power over Henderson and every other media outlet. Investigations into other media outlets and their possible participation will be ongoing.

"Many Washington insiders and those with other government agencies are under investigation for having knowledge of this coup attempt but looking the other way. Those names are too numerous to mention, and with no charges filed at this time, I am unable to name possible conspirators in this report."

Gwen hated to write and read that disclaimer, but she had no choice. Becker had quickly rolled on General William Jones for his assistance to Strauss, but without any direct evidence, an indictment was unlikely. And, of course, Jones denied everything. Yet Jones might be pushed out as a political scapegoat, which remained to be seen.

She braced herself for the more difficult portion of her report, but she could not keep the emotion out of her voice.

"Among the dead are two men I knew personally. Victor Travis, head of Midtown Engineering, my husband's boss, is dead allegedly by his own hand. Midtown Engineering often contracts with the U.S. government in the design of weapons systems. I confronted Mr. Travis about the facts my team and I uncovered regarding his under-the-table work for a foreign power, an act that would be treason should those weapons be turned on America. After I left his office, he died from what investigators have determined was a self-inflicted gunshot wound."

Gwen stood naked before the world. She swallowed hard, fighting the tears welling in her eyes. "And my husband, Joshua Patterson. He was a talented engineer and draftsman, and he was also a weapons designer. At the direction of Victor Travis, he helped Erich Strauss design a horrifying drone capable of possibly distributing biochemical weapons." She drew a bracing breath through her nose. "I, too, was in the dark and unaware of his participation. I am as confused by his involvement as the rest of the world. His death is still under investigation."

46

BEFORE HEADING OFF to the airport, Gwen said a proper goodbye to Carter and Johann.

"Thank you for what you said about me in the report," Johann said. "It will allow me to return to the *Bundeskriminalamt*, and my boss has already called me. I am free. I am exonerated. My fellow BKA agents stood and clapped when you said that."

"You're a hero." Gwen gave the handsome German agent a quick hug.

"I am not a hero," he said. "I am just a man who took a chance on a reporter with a reputation of having great integrity."

"Thank you for that," Gwen said. "But you are my heroes, all of you."

Carter gave her the biggest hug. "I'm going to miss you, but I'm glad this is over for now, at least."

"For now," Gwen echoed. "But I'll be in touch. We still have to find my father and Martin. They're still dangerous. Who knows what else they might have planned. A man like that always has a contingency."

"Agreed," Carter said. "I'll speak to the people in my office, and we'll be in touch."

Gwen left Germany on a private chartered plane, seen off by Rocco.

"This is fancy, even for me," Gwen laughed, waving at the sleek jet.

"Nothing but the best for Joe's girl," Rocco said with a sad chuckle. "I'll come to visit as soon as I can."

"You're not coming with me?"

"No, I can't, but you'll see me again. I'm sure there are more stories to cover, but I have to do something here first."

Rocco gave Gwen a soft embrace and an easy kiss on the forehead. She smiled. She allowed him to hold her for a moment, the wall of his arms shielding her from the world, the reality of her new life situation she would have to face upon returning home. Gwen climbed the stairs into the jet, turning back to give Rocco one last wave.

She collapsed on the plane, exhausted but unable to sleep. She became lost in deep thought and reflection, analyzing all the details and the facts of the story. More so than the story itself, she was overwhelmed by the identity and reputation of the father and brother she never knew about. Both were amoral monsters. She still didn't know where to put this information or what she would do when her familial connection to them was made public. The only thing she could do was speak with her mother to find out how all this came to pass.

She could not dwell on family ties and dysfunction now. She had more important priorities. She needed to know where her father and her brother were going and with whom they were meeting. She racked her brain trying to think of who would provide her father and brother sanctuary when the whole world knew of their coup and their crimes. More people than the two of them were involved, obviously. What level of the Russian government was tied to Strauss' hoped-for revival of Eastern rule? The possibilities swirled through Gwen's mind.

As long as her father and Martin were alive, they would be a threat, but they would need time to reestablish the underground empire and contact those following his lead. *Plus,* Gwen thought, *we still have team B undercover within Strauss' organization.* Possibly through Carter or Johann, she could stay in contact and learn of any news from the inside.

After the plane landed, Gwen stood at the top of the stairs, happy to see Joe waiting for her. She lumbered down the stairs step by step. The wind mussed her hair, her clothes were disheveled, she was without makeup, but she didn't care. She was home on U.S. soil, her team was safe, and she was with her boss and mentor who personally came to welcome her back.

In the car, Joe showed her copies of several renowned newspapers, all of which had jumped on her bandwagon. They not only reported her facts, but they had also delved deeper into the Andorran bank account scandal where the involved Washington elite held their cash.

Gwen sighed as Joe pulled up in front of her home. The outside looked the same, but she dreaded going inside. She could only picture that the inside was still a mess, her memories lying in pieces on the floor.

But other than the books on the shelf being out of order from how she always arranged them, her home looked untouched and perfectly clean. Joe had contacted a crime scene cleaning service and paid them extra to tidy the whole place after the coroner took Joshua's body away. Joe left, with a promise to call her tomorrow and plan their next story.

Alone at last, Gwen sank to the floor in Joshua's office where she had found him, crying when all that stared back at her were steam-cleaner tracks in the rug. *How can I do this without you, you big fool?*

Despite always being on the road, Gwen hadn't slept alone at home in years, but tonight she had no choice. She took a quick shower—using Joshua's shampoo and soap—then fell into bed. Beyond exhausted, she fell asleep, divorced for a time from the void left by her husband's death.

WEEK THREE

STRAUSS' PRIORITIES had shifted, his distraction understandable. Instead of a second son, he had a daughter—a beautiful, famous daughter with powerful connections—and he wanted her and her mother by his side. But now was not the time for aggression. Now was a time for reflection, recruitment, and a time to make plans for improvement. Strauss would see Gwen again. He would see Margaret, too, but where and when he did not know.

AFTER A RESTFUL but lonely night, Gwen pondered her life. Her mother had lied: her father was alive, she had a brother who murdered her husband and menaced her—their—mother. The only positive out of her whole trip to Germany on a personal level was gaining a handful of new friends.

She made coffee and sat down at her computer to check her personal emails and catch up on all she had missed over the last couple of weeks. She read gushing emails from friends expecting a baby and others getting married in the upcoming year. They only served to remind her what she'd lost.

Among the endless list of emails was a new email from Joshua sent a week ago. After he died. She shook, heart in her stomach as she read it. With tears rolling down her face, she at last understood her husband's full involvement.

Dear Gwen,

My love, I did this for us. I want you to know that. Travis sold me an idea that sounded good at the time. I wanted you to be able to stay home, to not have to fly all over the world to earn enough for us. You work so hard, and I miss you when you're gone. But now I realize I made a big mistake. Travis was helping Congressmen Becker and Solas and an old friend from school, General William Jones. I had nothing to do with Solas' death, and I am not sure who did.

I will not make excuses. I did it for us, but I don't want you to feel bad. It was my decision, and I take full responsibility no matter what happens. I am so sorry.

Please see the attachment.

I love you,
Joshua

Gwen thought, *Josh, I didn't need those things, only you.*

Before she could open the attachment, she heard a knock at the front door. Glancing up through the doorway, she smiled. On the other side of the door was a silhouette she recognized. She rushed to the front door and opened it. They stood across the threshold for a moment, staring at one another.

"I'm so glad it's you," she said.

He gently brushed her hair to the side like a father would comfort his daughter.

"Hi kid."

Joe lifted his arm and wiggled his wrist, waving a bottle of bourbon he had taken from his desk.

Gwen smiled, took a step back and extended her arm, inviting Joe in. Once inside, Gwen closed the front door, and Joe began to open the bottle. Gwen reached in the cabinet for a couple of glasses that were still intact after Martin had trashed her home. Joe and Gwen took their glasses to the living room and without saying a word, began to share a drink. They both sank into the sofa and then Gwen broke the silence.

"What am I going to do now?" Gwen asked her mentor in almost a desperate tone.

"Kid, I think you need a vacation."

"Do I?" Gwen said as she took another sip.

"And, you're not the only one."

Joe handed Gwen an envelope.

"What's in here?"

"That's a ticket to paradise—trust me."

BEHIND THE LARGEST desk concealed by a great shadow sat a very tall man, the puppet master himself. He was the true mastermind and instigator of all the recent turmoil and suffering felt by millions. Those unfortunate or lesser individuals were mere pawns on his East European and Russian chessboard. He played Strauss, Martin, countless troops and supporters, the police, and now even Gwen Patterson like marionettes. They danced to his tune.

Strauss and Martin were on the run, but not for long. They would make contact. Strauss must come calling if he wanted the crown of Germany, and the only person who could crown a king was an emperor. So, the emperor waited for his would-be king to return, and waited patiently. People are so predictable.

ABOUT THE AUTHOR

TANYA WAS BORN AND RAISED in New Jersey and moved to Chicago in 1990. She holds a master's degree in Journalism. Tanya has published countless print articles from Chicago and its suburbs and later worked on-air in Pennsylvania and Kansas. Eventually, she retired from a reporter's transient lifestyle and returned to Chicago to attend Loyola University Chicago, where she graduated in 2008 with a bachelor's and later a master's degree in nursing.

With the closures of 2020 caused by the COVID pandemic, Tanya resurrected her writing pursuits and finished producing her first novel. Currently working full-time as a nurse, in her spare time she likes to grab dinner with friends and binge-watch mind-bending shows on streaming platforms. In books, she favors thrillers, but she also maintains a comedy collection, seeing humor as the way through the most serious situations. In constant learning mode, she values education and writing and believes everybody has a story.

tanyakornelsen@gmail.com

Twitter – @TMKornelsen

https://www.facebook.com/TMKornelsen

www.ingramcontent.com/pod-product-compliance
Lightning Source LLC
Chambersburg PA
CBHW070911260626
47162CB00007B/2631